10/10

P9-CEK-262

The Sleepwalkers

The Sleepwalkers

Paul Grossman

ST. MARTIN'S PRESS ⚏ NEW YORK

THE SLEEPWALKERS. Copyright © 2010 by Paul Grossman. All rights reserved. Printed in the United States of America. For information, address St. Martin's Press, 175 Fifth Avenue, New York, N.Y. 10010.

www.stmartins.com

ISBN 978-0-312-60190-4

First Edition: October 2010

10 9 8 7 6 5 4 3 2 1

I go the way that Providence dictates
with the assurance of a sleepwalker.
—A. Hitler

Book One

CITY OF NO TOMORROWS

One

**BERLIN
NOVEMBER 1932**

Dietrich's legs were magic wands, slim, hypnotic instruments of sorcery that mesmerized millions. Willi could unfortunately only imagine their charms beneath the mannish pantsuit she wore that afternoon to Fritz's. Bored to tears by the political sooth-saying that muscled into every conversation these days, Willi had to fight to keep his eyes open. Lucky for him the tubular Bauhaus chair he was sitting on was killing his ass.

"And for you, Herr Inspektor-Detektiv?"

He reached for another glass of champagne. Even though his brain was flying, this celebration was depressing. Where else would Marlene Dietrich have shown up but Fritz's house-warming? Half of Berlin were best friends with his old war pal. And all of them seemed to have turned out to see his new palace in suburban Grunewald. Sleek, long panes of glass wrapped around a curvilinear living room filled with paintings by Klee and Modigliani. The house was another masterwork by Erich Mendelsohn, architect par excellence of the Weimar Republic, who bowed at the effusion of compliments.

"So light. So free." Dietrich fingered a shimmering Brancusi statue. "So moderne!" As for the rest of the city, her face collapsed into a mask of tragedy—it stank. In the two years since she'd last been here, the great star declared, Berlin's famously invigorating *Luft* had got truly rotten.

"How you breathe here, I cannot understand." She flicked a gold cigarette case open, joining the others on the raw-silk couch. "Everywhere, the stench of Brownshirts. Hulking like baboons in front of the department stores. Shaking those goddamn cans at you."

"Because they're hopelessly in debt." The general across from her placed a silver monocle in his eye. Dressed even for a casual afternoon in full uniform and a chestful of bronze medals, he had, if not the wisdom, certainly the position to ascertain his facts. Kurt von Schleicher was minister of war, commander of the army, and Berlin's most infamous backstage schemer. "The Nazis," he proclaimed, "are on the verge of ruin, my dear. Financial and otherwise."

Willi's eyes glazed over.

"Just look at this month's elections," von Schleicher chuckled. "'Hitler Over Germany,' indeed! The man flew to ten cities and lost twenty percent of his Reichstag seats."

"And still the strongest party," Fritz's ex-wife, Sylvie, dolefully reminded.

"They have reached their zenith." The general pulled off his monocle. "A year from now I assure you—you won't remember Hitler's name."

What a relief when Fritz's butler leaned over and whispered there was a call for Herr Inspektor-Detektiv.

"You may take it in the library if you would please, sir."

"Pardon me," Willi excused himself, shaking his half-dead legs.

Limping down the long, white hallway, he arrived at a glass-enclosed room that looked more like a fish tank than a library. It was Gunther calling from the Alex.

"Is she as beautiful as on screen? Sexy as Naughty Lola?"

"What are you calling about, Gunther?"

"Sorry to interrupt, Chief. But another floater's turned up. A girl this time. Out in Spandau, under the citadel."

Willi's throat constricted as he toyed with the black receiver. "All right then, I'm on my way."

"Yes, sir. I'll let them know."

"Oh, and, Gunther?"

"Yes, sir?"

"She is. Every goddamn inch of her. Even in men's trousers."

"I knew it! Thanks a million, Chief."

Returning the earpiece to the hook, Willi stood there. Bodies in rivers were hardly news in the chaos passing for Berlin these days. But he'd never heard of one surfacing in Old Spandau, that picture-postcard village far on the outskirts of town. A girl no less.

Back in the living room, they made a big fuss about his having to depart so abruptly. "Off to catch another fiend?" Sylvie leapt to escort him, slipping an arm through his own.

"Quite a star you've become, eh, Kraus?" Dietrich scrutinized him as she might a fine racehorse. "Even in America they know of the great Detektiv who nabbed the monster Child Eater of Berlin. You ought to come to Hollywood. I bet they'd make a picture about you."

"I don't think they could find anyone quite boring enough to play me." He forced a little smile.

At this Fritz laughed much too loudly, the long, jagged dueling scar across his cheek turning bright red.

Willi took the new speedway out to Spandau. A racecourse in summer, the Avus was otherwise open to vehicular traffic and usually empty, one of the best-kept secrets in Berlin. The forest pines cast a baleful darkness as he picked up velocity. How Germans loved their forests, he thought, shifting into fourth. The deeper and darker the better. Personally he preferred the beach. Hard, bright sunshine. Open space. This road though was truly superb. A white streak through the wilderness. He was driving far faster than he should, he knew, after so much champagne. Yet the adrenaline rush was too exhilarating to forgo. This silver BMW sports coupe was the only luxury he allowed himself. He didn't collect art. Didn't travel. Didn't keep women. He was boring. The 320's six cylinders soared to 100 kph. Just boring enough to have become the most famous police inspector in Germany. The machine took the road as if it were barely moving at 110, leaving the forest pines a dim blur. What an ass Fritz could be when he was drunk. Willi floored it and rocketed past 120, seeming to hover over the highway.

Willi'd trust him with his life though.

In half an hour he was slowing to a crawl through the medieval streets of Old Spandau, one of the few parts of Berlin with real provenance. Narrow roads lined with half-timbered houses led toward the fifteenth-century citadel whose stalwart walls still rose where the River Spree joined the Havel. As he parked, he could see the sun beginning to set over the gray water. Down by the riverbank he spotted several uniformed officers in their leather-strapped greatcoats and shiny black-visored helmets.

"Inspektor," they said, parting, instantly recognizing him.

Even in the street these days people recognized him, asking for his autograph. Taking their photo with him. The Great *Kinderfresser* Catcher. A mixture of awe and envy enveloped him as the cops grouped around. A lot of guys in the department didn't care for his fame. He didn't care for it either, frankly. What he cared for was being a Detektiv. Enforcing the law. Without the law, the weak were defenseless.

"Be prepared for a mess," an officer named Schmidt addressed him.

Willi'd seen more than his share of corpses in the Homicide Commission of Kripo, Berlin's Kriminal Polizei. Mutilated corpses. Decapitated corpses. Cooked-and-stuffed-into-sausages corpses. But this time his heart froze. Even in a city such as Weimar Berlin, maddened by years of war, defeat, revolution, hyperinflation, and now the Great Depression, nearly a million unemployed, its government paralyzed, the whole place topsy-turvy with depravity . . . sex maniacs, serial killers, red- and brown-shirted thugs battling for control of the streets . . . a city that had reached the end, of no tomorrows, teetering on the brink . . . of insanity . . . civil war . . . dictatorship . . . something . . . this was a portrait of horror.

Faceup on the water's edge, a girl was cradled like Hamlet's Ophelia in the mud and weeds. Girl. She was a beautiful young woman, maybe twenty-five. Her alabaster skin was bloated but not so much as to obliterate her features. Young. Fresh. Alive. Even in death. Her glassy eyes were wide open, warm, dark, Adriatic pools, reflecting the cold German sunset. A smile of tranquillity, triumph even, twisted across her lips. As he bent nearer, Willi sensed some long-encrusted lever in his heart shift, and he was seized by an urge to reach out and take the poor thing in his arms. Around her shoulder, like a toga, a thin, gray cotton smock half-torn away revealed her large, round breasts, the nipples already blackening. He noticed at once the dark hair was far too short . . . as if her head had been clean-shaven not long ago.

What really got him though, like a hammer blow, were the legs. Stretched out before her as if she were napping, they seemed almost supernaturally misshapen. He crouched toward the orange glare of the water, holding his breath against her stench. The feet were normal, but from the knees down all the way to the ankles, the bone structure appeared . . . backward. As if someone had taken giant pliers and turned the fibula around.

"Like a mermaid, eh?" Schmidt smirked.

"That's what we've been calling her, sir." Another cop made it clear the joke was not Schmidt's. *Fräulein Wassernixe.*

"Never mind that. Has the pathologist been sent for?"

"*Jawohl,* Herr Inspektor-Detektiv." Schmidt saluted. "He should be here momentarily."

"I've never seen anything like it," Dr. Ernst Hoffnung declared minutes later, after Schmidt and the others had lifted the poor girl onto the back of the ambulance.

Willi watched the senior pathologist give the body a quick going over.

"Suture marks," Hoffnung said with certainty. "Somebody's tampered with these legs. It's extraordinary. From the feel of it . . . well, I don't even want to say. I'll have to open them up and look." Hoffnung's gloved fingers pressed and poked the entire length of the corpse, ending with a quick tour inside the mouth. "I'm not sure yet what the cause of death is, but I can tell you this. She's almost certainly not German."

Willi had worked with Hoffnung enough times not to underestimate his talents, but this was magic. "What tips you off?"

"Wisdom teeth all removed. Not one in a thousand German girls could afford it."

"Any guesses where she's from?"

"The only place they routinely work on teeth like that is America."

Willi looked across the wide, gray expanse of water where the two rivers converged. Rain was coming in from the west, making a silvery sheet as it moved across the dense network of islands and inlets on the opposite shore. Somewhere out there, he ruminated, feeling a dozen eyes upon him, this girl had breathed her last.

"Who did you say called this in?" He turned to Schmidt.

"A Frau Geschlecht. Lives in that house, over there. Kroneburg Strasse seventeen."

He handed Willi a report. The handwriting was blurry. Or was it Willi's eyes?

Unable to look at it, he glanced across the street.

The house was more like a compound, several old buildings behind a high, white wall. Squinting he could just make out a sign above the doorway: INSTITUTE FOR MODERN LIVING. A sudden pounding filled his skull. Thunder. The first drops of rain. Checking his watch, he saw it was after six. At seven he had a dinner appointment he couldn't miss. He'd have to come back in the morning.

The rain caught up with him, and by the time he reached Kurfürstendamm, the Ku-damm as natives called it—Berlin's Great White Way—his speedy little BMW was hopelessly stuck in traffic. When he was a kid, motor vehicles were a rarity even on the Ku-damm. Now, despite the traffic signals, between the autos, trucks, streetcars, motorbikes, and double-decker buses, it was faster to walk than drive the grand boulevard. On the buildings all the plaster decorations, the scrolls and shells and roses of the past, had been stripped away for streamlined glass and steel. A thousand neon advertisements flashed from the sleek façades, their blues and reds blurring in the rain, bleeding across puddles, mesmerizing him as he inched past sidewalks thronged with people pouring from movie palaces, overflowing cafés, eddying around blazing department-store windows. Crowds. Neon. Noise. Berlin carried on. Despite all reason.

His throat never failed to tighten up when he passed Joachimstaler Platz, where Vicki had been killed. A truck jumped the curb one morning and crashed into the café window where she'd been sitting. Glass slashed her carotid artery. Two years and the pain had just slightly eased. Only the thought of Stefan and Erich a few blocks farther cheered him on.

He was a good half an hour late when he entered Café Strauss, a colossal affair on Tauentzien Strasse with seemingly hundreds of white-gloved waiters. Even across the crowded dining hall, though, the boys spotted him and began shouting, "*Vati! Vati!*

Over here!" Willi could see their maternal grandmother, Frau Gottman, in her black hat and fur-trimmed suit, frowning at them for such a display, drawing attention to themselves like pygmies. And then at him . . . for being late. Stefan, eight, and Erich, ten, however, never ones to be stifled by etiquette, jumped from their chairs, napkins still tucked to their collars, and flung themselves into his arms.

After Vicki had died, he and the Gottmans had agreed it was probably healthier if the boys came to Dahlem to stay with them. They had a big villa with a large garden, and Vicki's younger sister, Ava, could care for them while completing university. Miraculously, the arrangement had worked. The boys were thriving. And the miracle worker was Ava. How she gleamed at the boys' happiness, Willi saw as he hugged them. He had always thought she looked like Vicki, if a slightly more down-to-earth version. But her love of the children made her appear even more similar.

As Willi sat between the boys, their little arms hooked through his own, Frau Gottman adjusted her black feathered hat. A great beauty, once an actress on the Viennese stage, she possessed a skilled repertoire of subtle emotive abilities. "You knew of course dinner was for seven." Guilt being one of her best.

Generally Sunday dinner was at their house, and every once in a while he was late. Okay. It was a far drive from town. They forgave him. But today the Gottmans had taken the boys *into* town, to see the Ishtar Gate. Ergo, no reasonable reason to Frau Gottman for Willi's tardiness, since he lived a few minutes' walk from the restaurant.

"If you must know," he said with greater terseness than he intended, "it was police work. A young lady's body in the Havel."

His mother-in-law's eyes widened. That he could say such a thing in front of the children! But his children weren't the ones disturbed by his work, Willi knew. When she started fiddling with her pearls, he reached across the table and squeezed her hand, earning a slight smile. They'd both lost Vicki, after all.

And they both lived in a Germany growing worse by the week for people like them.

To the Gottmans, to most German Jews—his own parents had they lived long enough—it was incomprehensible that he'd become a Detektiv. Centuries of oppression made careers in law enforcement anathema. Police were the enemy. The tools of tyrants. If he really was so interested in the law, why hadn't he become a lawyer? But a cop he'd become. A famous one at that. And to a man rooted in practicalities like Max Gottman, founder of Gottman Lingerie, achievement was what mattered, not bourgeois sensitivities.

"Goodness knows, Bettie"—he shot his wife the severest of looks—"it is the police alone keeping any stability in this country. The man is serving the republic, not the czar." He turned to Willi with a look of concern. "How are you, my son? How was that terrible cold you had?"

After the boys had recited a roster of school achievements— Erich the highest grade on a geography exam, Stefan a part in his elementary school's winter festival, Willi asked Ava how things were at the university.

"Willi. Don't tell me you forgot. I graduated. A year and a half ago."

His face turned red. "Yes, of course. How dumb of me." He examined his plate as if something were written on it. "What are you doing now then? Besides raising the boys so superbly, I mean."

Sometimes he really found it hard to look at Ava, so similar was she to his lost wife. Same velvet skin. Same chestnut eyes. That long, sleek curve to her neck.

"I've told you a dozen times. I have a part-time job."

"Yes. Sorry. Doing what, again?"

"I'm a stringer, Willi. I send in reports about what's going on at the university to one of the big Ullstein papers."

"That's fascinating. You know my old war pal Fritz—"

"Yes, I know, you goose. It's Fritz I work for."

He noticed Ava's bemused smirk. *How you live in your own little world,* it seemed to say.

Vicki'd had such a natural air of glamour about her. Ten times a day Willi had looked at her and thought they ought to put that pose on a billboard in Potsdamer Platz. It was so perfect, so full of unconscious grace. Ava, he'd always thought, belonged more behind the camera than in front of it. Not that she was any less lovely, just endowed with a different elegance: that of keen intellect and artistry. It pleased him to know she was pursuing her writing. What she was doing with Fritz was another matter.

"So then . . . how *are* things at the university?"

The chestnut in her eyes quickly darkened. "Positively awful. A year ago I'd never have believed it. The whole student body's stampeded to the Nazis. Anti-Nazi faculty are being boycotted. Jewish teachers and students get hate mail telling them to get out. It's no different in the high schools. Erich hasn't complained about it yet, but I'm the one who picks him up at *Volksschule.* Every week more students show up in Hitler Youth gear. I don't know how much longer things will stay tolerable for him there."

Willi felt like a man on an ocean liner who suddenly finds water around his feet. "But . . . what are you suggesting, Ava?"

"I don't know." She lifted one eyebrow just the way Vicki used to. "Maybe we'll have to send him back to Young Judea, with Stefan."

"Erich." Willi looked at his oldest son. "Are you having trouble at the *Volksschule* because you're Jewish?"

Erich turned white. He seemed about to say something, then stopped. He was not a child reticent with words.

To Willi this said more than enough. "Can you finish the semester out?" he asked, alarmed. "It's only, what . . . another two weeks?"

Erich shook his head. "It's not so bad, *Vati*. Really."

"Then over recess we'll assess the situation and take appropriate action. How does that sound?"

Erich nodded.

Willi noticed him quickly rub away tears.

After the main course Grandpa ordered the boys to go have a look at the dessert counters. "Take your time. Examine each one carefully before you choose," Max instructed, knowing that dozens of creamy tarts and intricately layered cakes were on display.

As soon as they were gone, the jovial smile dropped from his face. "Willi, listen to me." His voice descended to a tremulous whisper. "I know you're not involved in politics, that you are merely an Inspektor-Detektiv with the police. But you do serve the government, and I know you have friends. So I'm asking you, begging you really, if you have or ever get even the least hint of information as to what is going to happen . . . you will promise to let me know, won't you? It's just that all our money is tied up in the business. If something were to happen, well . . . I'm thinking of the boys. Their future. If the time has come to pull out, I want to know, before it's too late."

"Pull out? What do you mean?"

"Sell the firm. Liquidate my assets. Transfer them abroad."

"Why on earth would you do that?" Willi's throat constricted. "Everyone's in the same boat. England, France, even America, have all got just as many unemployed."

"But they haven't got Nazis." Max's eyes widened. "What if, God forbid, those maniacs manage to take over? The things they promise! How can one make rational choices in an atmosphere like this, never knowing what tomorrow will bring?"

Willi respected his father-in-law greatly, but inside him an anger exploded that made him feel like grabbing the man's lapels and shaking sense into him. Pull out? What was he talking about? Had fear overcome all logic? They still had a constitution, yes?

An army. Laws. Had Max so little faith in Germany, in his fellow Germans, that he thought they'd sell themselves out to a gang of criminals? Had men like Willi fought and bled and died in the Great War, won an Iron Cross for bravery behind French lines, so that men like Max had to pack up and run?

Two

Alexanderplatz—or the Alex—was the great traffic hub of central Berlin, a sprawling plaza crisscrossed by streetcar lines, swarming with motor vehicles, bicycles, and pedestrians, and framed by two of the city's largest temples of mass consumption: the Wertheim and Tietz department stores. Beneath all this was the new U-Bahn station, a juncture of several of Berlin's busiest subway lines, and overhead the S-Bahn station, which sent elevated trains hurtling to every far corner of the metropolis. The Alex was also home to the vast, old Police Presidium building, occupying one full corner on the southeastern side of the square, a soot-covered behemoth built in the 1880s, half a dozen stories tall with several churchlike cupolas. Coat and hat already in hand, Willi entered Entrance Six at precisely 8 a.m.

As an Inspektor-Detektiv he was head of one of numerous units in the Homicide Commission, with three Detektivs and a staff of fifteen working under him. As the only Jew in the commission, in the entire building practically, he felt it imperative to maintain an air of authoritarian distance with them all, except, that is, for his secretary, Ruta, and his junior apprentice, Gunther—both of whom he treated more like family than underlings.

"What news, Ruta?" he asked the sexy grandma of six, who despite the new longer skirts managed to show most of her leg. Years ago, she claimed, she'd been a Tiller Girl at the Wintergarten.

"All quiet on the western front, boss," she replied, grinding away at her little wooden coffee mill. Every morning she made the most delicious fresh brew on the small gas stove Inspektor-Detektivs received. When she was in a good mood, they got hot *Brötchen,* too, from the Café Rippa downstairs. "No casualties since Miss Mermaid."

Somehow, she always knew about things practically before they happened.

"Oh, and Pathology called. Dr. Hoffnung wants you to drop by as soon as you can."

"Excellent. Gunther in?"

"Not yet."

"Send him down to Hoffnung's when he comes."

The pathologist, smoking a pipe in his white smock, was staring out a window when Willi arrived. The moment Hoffnung turned around, Willi was struck by the dark disquiet in his eyes.

"It's an extraordinary thing I've seen." He motioned Willi to sit. "Had you told me about it the day before, I wouldn't have believed it possible. But there it is." Hoffnung relit his pipe.

Willi saw the pathologist's hand was trembling. Really trembling.

"Let's begin with the externals." The smoke seemed to relax Hoffnung. "That gray smock the girl was wearing is standard issue at Prussian state mental asylums. Numerous scratches on the scalp indicate her head had indeed been clean-shaven, a practice at several of those institutions. Other than that, there were neither major internal nor external injuries. She was very much alive when she went into that water. And didn't drown. Managed to keep herself afloat fifteen or twenty minutes before she succumbed to hypothermia. Six, maybe seven hours before we pulled her out. I'd say she was one very determined young lady. Sure as hell wanted to live."

"Those legs, Doctor—"

"Well, as I said. I'd never have believed such a thing possible. In both cases the fibula, the bone that runs from knee to ankle, had been surgically removed and replanted in the opposite direction, grafted in place with some highly advanced techniques I am wholly unfamiliar with. For years doctors have been hypothesizing about the possibility of bone transplants, but as far as I know, none has ever been successfully performed. Until now."

"Bone transplant?" Willi, who thought he'd heard it all, was dumbfounded. "But—why?"

"I don't know. To see if it could be done, I suppose. I only report what I saw."

"How long ago might this transplant have occurred?"

"Six months, at most. The grafts were completely healed. The legs completely healthy—except of course that she never could have walked on them. Hobbled, perhaps. With crutches."

"Hobbled." Willi was trying to grasp this. "You mean the surgery crippled her?"

"Yes." The doctor lowered his eyes. "That's precisely what I mean."

Willi felt his throat tighten. "The girl had been healthy? Her legs were healthy? And she was . . . experimented on? Deliberately disabled?"

Hoffnung stared out the window. "Almost beyond belief, I know. We all assume doctors are guardians of life. Implicitly trustworthy. Even ancient civilizations revered their medicine men. But here, today, in Berlin in 1932, we have a surgeon who appears to have had no qualms about using a human as a guinea pig."

He turned to Willi with pained dismay. "Inspektor, whoever

did this was a genius. A madman. But with exceptional talent. Surely one of the top orthopedic surgeons alive."

Closing the door to Pathology, Willi ran straight into Gunther. At least a foot taller, though probably half Willi's weight, this towering beanpole with a long Prussian nose and virulently infectious smile had come to Willi straight from the top tiers of the Police Academy in Charlottenburg. A country bumpkin from up north, all Berlin to him seemed a fairy tale. Oh, he stuck his foot in his mouth on occasion, no easy task considering he wore a 14 shoe. But he was smart. Efficient. Tenacious as a battering ram. And totally in awe of Willi. They got along supremely. Willi'd been planning to take the boy out to Spandau. But the autopsy report changed that.

"Gunther—"

"Yes! Good morning, sir!"

"Regarding the case from yesterday . . . I need some information."

"*Jawohl.*" Gunther smiled, instantly ready with a notebook.

"I want the name of every top orthopedic surgeon in Germany, in the Berlin area especially."

"Orthopedic surgeons. Got it."

"The name of every American and Canadian female missing in Berlin over the past year."

"Okay."

"I want you to check with every Prussian state mental asylum if any female patients between the ages of twenty-three to twenty-six have gone missing in the past year. And find out which of those institutions shave their patients' heads."

"Shave heads. Okay. What else, sir?"

"I need you to dig up whatever you can about bone transplants. See which doctors have written about it, lectured on it, whatever."

"Bone transplants. Yes, sir. What else, sir?"

"That's all. No. Wait. Better go to Hoffnung's office. Tell him I want you to see the girl."

"Go to Hoffnung. See girl." Gunther kept writing.

"Look at her closely, lad. Listen to what the doctor tells you. And ask yourself, Gunther, ask yourself, what kind of world is this we live in?"

Willi drove alone in an unmarked police car back to where the Mermaid had surfaced. First stop: Kroneberg Strasse 17. The Institute for Modern Living. Stepping through a medieval-looking iron gate, he approached the large, white stucco house and pressed the front bell. Eventually slow, heavy footsteps approached. When the dark oak door finally opened, he was relieved not to have brought along Gunther.

Before him stood a naked woman, at least seventy, suntanned head to toe like burned toast, breasts sagging.

"*Guten Morgen,*" she said with an inquisitive glow in her eyes. "How might I be of service?"

"I'd . . . I'd like to speak with Frau Geschlecht if I may."

"Frau Geschlecht's in gymnastics now. She won't be finished until half ten. Might I help you? I'm Fräulein Meyer."

"Yes. How do you do, Fräulein."

"You may come in of course. Everyone's welcome here, regardless of race, income, age, or physical condition."

"How nice."

"But you'll have to take off all your clothes. Gawkers who refuse to disrobe are not permitted." She smiled.

Willi heard some kind of strange drumming coming from inside.

"I'm not here to gawk, Fräulein, I assure you."

He showed her his Kripo badge.

Her face, if not her body, registered appropriate alarm. "Oh, dear. My. Yes. Then you must come in. Frau Geschl-e-e-echt," she yodeled into an open doorway.

Willi followed her uninvited, then froze at the sight.

In a large room with a wooden floor and not a stick of furniture, a dozen mostly elderly women, hair pulled tightly into "Gretchen" braids, danced completely naked, thrusting arms and legs about like nymphs in a magic spring, while a naked man who had to be ninety kept rhythm on a tom-tom.

"Beauty! Health! Movement!" they chanted.

"Frau Geschlecht!" Fräulein Meyer shrieked above it all. "There is a Kripo man to see you for goodness' sake. An Inspektor-Detektiv!"

The tom-tom halted. The dancers turned in unison. One of the women stepped forward with a sagging chin held proudly, graciously high as she walked.

From magazines such as *Berliner Illustrierte,* Willi was familiar with the nudist movement sweeping Germany. Everyone from good middle-of-the-road burghers to socialist health-food fanatics seemed to have joined the cult of the naked body. Curative gymnastics, hydrotherapy, colonic cleansing, sun worship, sour-milk diets, electrical-wave treatments, were thought to bring about an exalted state of tranquillity, health, and beauty. A new awareness that the naked body radiated perfection. It was as if the whole German nation, Willi thought, desperate to rid itself of the past, were trying to start all over again—from scratch. And Germans, whatever else they were or weren't, did what they did to the ultimate.

Dramatic though her entry may have been, Frau Geschlecht had little information to offer that wasn't already in the police report. She had been on the third-floor solarium holding a yoga position, she reiterated, as unconcerned with her lack of clothing as Adam or Eve, when through the window she spotted what looked like another naked body. At first she thought it might be someone from the institute gone for a morning dip. But the longer she held the position, the clearer it became that the body wasn't moving. After she'd phoned the Spandau police, Schmidt and the others arrived. She'd pointed out the spot on the shoreline and that was that.

"You've been a great service." Willi smiled and put away his notebook.

"Please do come again." She offered to let him kiss her hand. "We have introductory lectures every Wednesday and Sunday at seven."

He retreated from the naked paradise with little more than unsightly images to shake from his head.

Outside, sunshine had broken through the morning clouds. The tall, round Citadel tower rose against the medieval town. Far to the right he could see the S-Bahn station, and across from it a large café with an outdoor beer garden. Perhaps I should snoop around in there, he thought. But over the inn's front door he noticed the red flag and white circle branded with its fierce black swastika. Hitler was said to have designed the banner himself. And Spandau, Willi remembered, was a Nazi bastion.

He turned to the river. A long, white pleasure boat was working hard to cruise against the strong, gray currents. It hit him. Of course. The boat was traveling the same route the Mermaid had, in the opposite direction. He jogged the steps down to the pier and inquired when the next one was.

"But where would you wish to go, *mein Herr*? We have *two* boats," he was none too pleasantly advised. "As it says right on this sign: the northern route or the southern. To Wannsee, or Palace Oranienburg. Each ten marks."

He looked at his watch. It would have to be Oranienburg at noon. But before investing three hours on a boat ride, he knew, he ought to check in at work.

Next to a news kiosk stood a yellow phone booth.

"Kommissar Horthstaler says you're to call him at once, urgent." The very constraint in Ruta's voice conveyed her excitment.

"Urgent. Ah, well, yes. Then be so good as to connect me with the Kommissar, would you, my dear."

Through the open phone-booth door Willi noticed the late-morning headlines: **Government Crumbles! Von Papen Forced to Resign!**

"Kommissar Horthstaler—Kraus here."

"Kraus, you are to go directly and at once to the Presidential Palace."

"*Jawohl,* Herr Kommissar." Willi was stunned. "May I ask why?"

"The Old Man wants to see you."

"See me?"

"Von Hindenburg's office was adamant. You are to get there immediately."

"*Jawohl.* But . . . why would the president wish to see me?"

"How the hell should I know? Maybe he wants to appoint you chancellor."

Had he not just read the headlines, Willi might have found this funny.

Three

Almost universally referred to as the Old Man, General Paul von Hindenburg was not merely president but the symbolic father of Germany. At six feet five, 250 pounds, with a great barrel chest and huge walrus mustache, this veritable giant of a personage, eighty-five now, had led imperial Germany to her greatest victories in the World War. He had stood as a stalwart figure of national unity through the dark postwar years of the Red Revolution, the Counter-Revolution, the Kapp Putsch, the Beer Hall Putsch, the Great Inflation, and the murderous struggle between extreme left and right. There was no reason on earth Willi could imagine the fellow would wish to see him.

Waiting to be called into the Old Man's office on the Wilhelm Strasse, Willi felt a confused whirlwind in his chest. On one hand, you had to respect a guy who could hold Germany together. On the other, Willi knew, Hindenburg had propagated the entirely false idea of the November 1918 "stab in the back," which had nurtured such intense bitterness. According to this myth, the German army had never been defeated in the Great War but was forced to withdraw in 1918 because of Communist revolution at home. Indeed, the German people, subject to the strictest censorship, hadn't a clue they'd lost the war. They simply thought an armistice, an agreement, had finally been reached with the Allies. Not until the terms of that armistice were revealed did they discover they'd not only lost, but were guilty of starting the war—and responsible for paying their enemies for the damage they'd caused.

The Stab in the Back made sense to them.

But Willi had been there, among the advance shock troops in the great spring offensive of 1918, when a million German soldiers had left the trenches and stormed in for a coup de grâce. He had been there deep in France, farther than they'd ever got, only miles outside Paris, when it became clear the army had overextended itself. That they had far outpaced their supply lines. That the attack had sputtered out. And that now they'd made themselves vulnerable to counterattack. Which is exactly what happened. Three-quarters of a million fresh Americans moved in to join the British and the French, and the exhausted Germans could not withstand them. To say the German army had never lost a battle in the Great War was a lie. The German army had been completely defeated in France that autumn of 1918. Willi had been there.

He jumped like a marionette when his name was called. The president would see him now. Von Hindenburg was seated behind an ornate gilt desk the size of a billiard table, his head bowed low. Willi was reluctant to announce his presence, especially once he realized that the Reich president was not at prayer but sound asleep, snoring. Not knowing what else to do, he clicked his heels as loudly as possible, cleared his throat, and said, "Herr President!"

Thankfully the Old Man's eyes fluttered open.

"Kripo Inspektor Kraus here."

"*Ja, ja,* Kraus." The president stroked his enormous mustache, glancing over his shoulder as if for a word of advice. "Now, what did I want you for? *Ach, ja!* King Boris. What a *Schweinerei.*" The Old Man embraced his massive stomach. "The king of Bulgaria's daughter has gone missing, Kraus. From the Adlon of all places. You are to find her at once."

"But, Your Excellency, may I remind you I serve the Homicide Kommission. We have a most excellent Missing Persons Department full of experts on—"

"*Kvatch!*" The Old Man's blue eyes narrowed. "Those *Idioten* couldn't find an elephant in the Pariser Platz. No, we need you, Kraus. You! Our most famous Inspektor. King Boris is a friend of mine. A friend of Germany. Germany values its relationship with Bulgaria, from whom she purchases many raw materials she sorely needs. Am I making myself understood? I wish to assure King Boris that our best man is working to find his daughter. And you are our very best. So they tell me."

"*Jawohl, mein* President."

"My adjutant will give you all the relevant information. You will find the missing Bulgarian princess, and you will make certain she is safely returned to the arms of her waiting papa."

Willi clicked his heels and retired to the adjutant's office.

"Princess Magdelena Eugenia." He found himself in an antechamber with a rheumatic, pink-eyed man every bit as old as his boss. "Her photo."

Willi was not happy about this. Not happy at all. Why now of all times was he being asked to play Emil and the Detectives, with the most heinous of murderers loose? The doctor in the Mermaid case seemed to him more evil even than the Child Eater, who was a psychopath. A disease of the sort infecting a doctor who would intentionally cripple a healthy girl was something of an entirely new order. Something Willi could barely even conceive, much less be sure how to subdue.

The missing Bulgarian princess, however, caught his eye. The photo was taken at a beach, and Magdelena Eugenia, a slim, athletic young woman of twenty-three or -four was showing off her legs in a bathing suit. She was not a great beauty but vivacious with dark eyes and a broad, gleaming smile. The legs were worthy of the reverence feigned by the young man in the photo pretending to bow before them.

"That is her husband, Konstantin Kaparov," the adjutant said through the phlegm in his chest. "It was he who reported the princess missing, yesterday morning."

"And this Herr Kaparov I might find where? At the Adlon still?"

"*Nein,* I believe you will find him today at the Six-Day Bicycle Race."

Willi looked at him. "His wife is missing and he's at the bike race?"

"*Nein,*" the old man gurgled as if drowning. "He is not *at* the race. He's *in* it."

Since it was practically around the corner, Willi decided to drop by the Adlon first, the city's most illustrious hotel on its most regal boulevard, Unter den Linden. Everyone from Charlie Chaplin to the Rothschilds were regulars. And Hans, the head concierge, was an old pal.

The red-carpeted lobby sparkled under the chandeliers.

"Yes, yes, a great misfortune." Hans shook his head over the missing princess. "The entire staff is most upset. But you know of course she did not disappear from her room, Willi. She walked out herself. Just after midnight."

"Anyone speak to her?"

"Yes, I believe so. Rudy. The night doorman. Unfortunately he's off duty. I could get him here, maybe in two hours. He lives all the way in Berlin-North."

"Make it three hours." Willi slapped Hans's shoulder. "I'm off to the Six-Day Race."

"Ach so." Hans instantly understood.

The fastest way to the Sportpalast was by streetcar. Willi took the crowded No. 12. Over the swaying sea of padded shoulders and big felt hats, he could hardly avoid the afternoon headlines: **Who Will Lead?**

Hanging on to a leather strap, he gazed at *Berlin am Mittag* over someone's shoulder. Bad enough half of what the papers printed was pure garbage, he knew from experience. But the press had positively addicted Germans to living in perpetual crisis. In Berlin, which had more daily papers than any other city on earth, half the population lived off the adrenaline fix provided by the morning, late-morning, early-afternoon, late-afternoon, early-evening, and late-evening horror headlines.

"What the hell do you think you're doing, Jew?" Every head in the streetcar turned. He looked to see whom the sharp-faced man in a black derby in front of him was accusing, then got it. "Get your dirty Jew nose out of my newspaper!"

Willi was stunned. He barely even thought of his Jewishness, except on High Holidays. But his dark eyes and curly, dark hair advertised it as clearly as any flashing sign on the Ku-damm. Germans were becoming more brazen by the hour in their anti-Semitic outbursts. The next thing you know they'd want to put Jews back into yellow dunce caps, like in the Dark Ages. All this nut had to do was accuse him of trying to pick his pocket and there'd be real trouble. If he wasn't who he was. He pulled out his Kripo badge. The change on the guy's face was almost worth the insult.

"Oh, pardon me, Herr Inspektor-Detektiv." The man removed his derby and held it trembling. "I had no idea to whom I was speaking. I meant nothing by it. Forgive my stupidity. We've all heard of the great Inspektor Kraus, the *Kinderfresser* catcher!"

How German was it to torment the weaker and grovel before the more powerful.

Willi stared until the man got so uncomfortable he pulled on his derby and fled the tram.

The Berlin Sportpalast, a templelike stadium built 1910, was the city's largest indoor arena, home of professional boxing matches, major political rallies, and the wildly popular Six-Day Bicycle Race. Begun in 1920, this grueling marathon pit teams of cyclists in a round-the-clock run for high-stakes prizes. Only one rider from each team had to be out on the track, so the second could eat, sleep, or bathe while his partner racked up points by gaining laps on the competition or in ball-busting sprints every third hour.

Willi was admitted through the front doors with the flash of his Kripo badge and hit by a wave of humidity. Inside, cones of brilliant white floodlights transported him into the arena. The whole place shook as if in an earthquake, the air exploding with the roar of thousands, the bleachers thundering with stamping feet. A dozen cyclists bent parallel to the ground insanely pedaled the track of wood that circled the arena floor, trying to pull ahead, an inch, a foot, flying past in a blur of color. "Around and around and around they go!" the loudspeakers were blasting. "How long can they last, *meine Damen und Herren*? How long?"

Willi soon enough learned that Konstantin Kaparov, No. 8, was out there right now. Fortunately though, in just a few minutes, the section would end and Kaparov would retire to let his teammate take over. Willi'd shown up just in time.

Lucky day, he thought.

Until he saw Kaparov stumble off the track after six hours of racing.

Poor guy's eyes were rolling into the back of his head. A crew wrapped his heaving body into a towel and led him to a rest area. The man looked on the verge of death. Willi gave him a few minutes to at least regain some consciousness before showing him his Kripo badge. Kaparov nodded, taking another glass of juice, then summoned what seemed his last ounce of strength. "Thank God you're here."

In between dizzy spells and spasmodic convulsions he told Willi his story.

They'd arrived in the afternoon two days ago by train direct from Sofia, Bulgaria. They'd never been to Berlin before. "Vee came for zee bike races." His German was heavily accented. "For two years I have trained."

After settling in at the Adlon, they hadn't done anything. Only dinner at a nightclub. Where? He couldn't remember the name; he was too tired to think straight. On the Friedrich Strasse somewhere. How had they found it? No idea. Magdelena must have known about it. No, of course, no one knew she was a princess. They always used his name when making reservations. Dancing? No. Magdelena couldn't dance that night. She'd twisted her ankle earlier on the train and it was still bothering her. Unusual? No. Nothing. Nothing unusual at all, that he could recall. After dinner? She was totally normal. They went straight back to the hotel. By taxi. He had to race the next morning. He needed his sleep.

"An hour later in bed, I notice Magdelena putting on coat. 'Where you going?' I ask her. 'I vant cigarettes,' she tell me. 'Cigarettes? So why going out? Call room service.' 'I vant fresh air,' she say. 'To stretch a little my legs.' I think to myself, before ankle killing her, now she wants walk. But half the time Magdelena's a little how you say, cuckoo? So I am thinking nothing strange. Only all the time about race next day. I'm closing eyes. Maybe I sleep a little, maybe not exactly. Then I see clock. It say three a.m. Magdelena still gone. Now, I say to myself, Konstantin, something not right."

Willi had a sixth sense about when he was being lied to. Whatever had happened to the missing princess, her husband, he felt certain, had nothing to do with it.

"Find her for me, *bitte*, Herr Inspektor." Kaparov's eyes had begun rolling back into his head again. "I don't care about zees fuckink race. I only want Magdelena back."

When Willi returned to the Adlon, since Rudy the doorman

had still not arrived, he was treated to a six-course dinner at the lavish Grill Room. "Eat!" Hans insisted, joining him midway through. "God only knows where this town would be without men like you. Hey, you'll never guess who's staying with us."

Willi pondered over a most delicious stuffed grouse. "I don't know . . . Hitler's dog?"

"*Nein.*" Hans laughed. "But just as big a bitch, I tell you! The great Marlene Dietrich. What a pain in the ass. The trouble with these international stars is, just because they're special, they think they ought to be treated that way. Complain, complain. Everything's a hundred times better in America. Well, if you feel like that, why not move to America, is what I say."

"She may just yet, Hans." Willi dug into a tureen of asparagus au gratin. "She may just yet."

He was finishing up a Sacher torte and coffee, more satisfied than he'd been all day, when Hans announced the doorman's arrival. Willi met him at the entrance to the hotel under the long, striped awning.

"Herr Inspektor-Detektiv." Rudy was already in uniform. "How was I to know I'd be the last to speak to her?" His servile eyes had a look of real fear, as even the most innocent often had when being interviewed by Kripo. "She was acting strange, it's true. But is it my place to question our guests?"

"Relax, Rudy. Nobody said you did anything wrong. Now tell me exactly what happened. What do you mean, she was acting strange?"

"It was right after midnight. Our busiest time. The lady came up to me, very exotic looking. Big dark hair. Dark eyes. Wearing a leopard coat, but no hat! Very quietly she inquires about the nearest S-Bahn station. Strange, I think, for an honored guest of ours to take public transportation—much less a lady alone so late at night. But truly odd was her voice . . . and the look in her eyes. I have a boy, you see, ten years old. Quite frequently he gets up in the middle of the night and starts walking around and talking . . . but he's asleep. Sleepwalking. You're never supposed to wake sleepwalkers, just lead them back to bed, which is what I do with Tommy. This lady had the same look . . . like she wasn't awake. The eyes were open but she wasn't really there. I had the strongest feeling I ought to lead her back inside. But like I said, is it my place to question our guests? And at just this moment the Italian foreign minister and his wife arrived. I had to attend to them. So I told the lady, the nearest S-Bahn station is at Friedrich Strasse. I asked if she wished me to hail her a taxi. 'No, no,' she said. 'I want to walk.' And that was the last of it. As I opened the minister's door, I saw her going down Unter den Linden, alone, in that leopard coat and no hat!"

"Did she tell you where on the S-Bahn she wanted to go?" Willi was astonished by the story. "Think, Rudy. This is important."

"Why, yes." His eyes widened as he recalled. "Yes, she did. She said, 'Where is the nearest S-Bahn that can take me to Spandau?'"

"Spandau!" A shiver ran through Willi's veins. "You're sure?"

"Yes, quite. I remember asking myself, does the S-Bahn even go to Spandau?"

Willi pictured the station he'd seen there this morning.

For a second he was speechless. Could it possibly be mere coincidence? He looked at his watch. It was nearly nine o'clock. Despite his exhaustion there was only one thing to do, he knew. Back to Spandau, again. By S-Bahn this time.

Four

Even though he was almost thirty-six and had lived here all his life, hurtling across the capital on the elevated train still held the feel of a magic-carpet ride for Willi. The landscape ever mesmerizing. A vast city of brick and limestone, new by continental standards, most of it less than a century old, Berlin was Europe's Chicago, ambitious, arrogant, driving itself ever onward. Toward what, he and 4 million other Berliners had no idea.

From Friedrich Strasse they flew along the Spree River, passed the great glass dome of the Reichstag. After skirting the edge of the Tiergarten, the city's great rustic park, the train shuttled into the fashionable West End, running parallel to block after block of handsome apartment buildings, allowing passengers unrivaled access into the lives of all whose shades were not tightly drawn. Scenes of domestic composure flew past Willi's eyes. Families listening to radios. Gathered around pianos. Trimming Christmas trees.

The farther north and west they shuttled, the shabbier the buildings grew, and the sadder the pictures they presented. Bony housewives bent over ironing boards. Fathers in undershirts spanking their children. As the train slowed to round a bend beside an enormous warehouse, through its big, cracked windows he saw it had been turned into a dormitory for homeless men, packed with countless hundreds of souls, the stench of hopelessness all but reeking into the train car.

Reaching the new housing estates built by Siemens Electronics, the carriage virtually emptied of passengers. On a Saturday night perhaps more people might be on it, Willi considered. But all in all it must have been a lonely ride for the princess. Why had she done it? What could have possessed her? Where had she gone when she reached the station? Forty-five minutes after leaving Friedrich Strasse they ground to a halt in Old Spandau, the end of the line.

Down the steps to the street, darkness engulfed him. After the lights of central Berlin it always took a while to adjust to the dimness of the rest of the world. A single source of illumination caught his attention . . . directly across the street. The inn he'd noticed this morning, with the outdoor beer garden and swastika above the door. The Black Stag, he saw it was called. Unless someone at the station was waiting to pick her up, the princess would almost certainly have gone there. There was simply nowhere else. He headed toward it.

Taking a deep breath, he passed beneath the Nazi flag and entered. Inside, a large, wood-paneled room with twenty or so wooden tables was maybe a third full. A bosomy proprietress, forty-five or fifty, was at the register going through checks, a slightly cross-eyed bleached blonde. She asked Willi what she could get him. Experience had taught when and how his Kripo badge worked to his advantage. Sometimes, such as now, he sensed it better just to hold it in reserve.

"I'm looking for a friend of mine. A woman. I was wondering if she might have come in here the other night."

The crossed eyes gave him a skewed once-over.

"What are you, an actor from Babelsberg Studios—rehearsing a spy scene? How should I know who is your friend and who isn't?"

"She's about twenty-four. Dark hair. Dark eyes. Wearing a leopard coat."

Now the woman laughed. "A leopard coat, you say. Does this look like the kind of establishment where women wear leopard coats?"

"She might have wandered in here from the S-Bahn station. It's likely the only place she would have come."

"Listen, mister"—her voice grew a little sharper as two men in long wool coats entered—"I don't know what you're thinking, but this is a family restaurant. Single women don't just wander in here, with or without leopard coats. Even from the S-Bahn station."

"What's going on here, Gretel?" one of the men asked. "A troublemaker?"

"Not exactly." She made a sour face. "Just bothering me with stupid questions."

"What sort of questions?"

Willi turned to them. Both were in their thirties, very proper looking in ties and hats. Both with silver Party pins stuck on their lapels.

"I'm looking for a friend. She might have wandered in here Saturday night."

"Like the lady said." One stepped forward with an aggressive smirk, removing his hat. He was an Aryan of the nonblond variety, dark, oiled hair brushed straight back off his forehead, with a mocking smile that revealed an exceptionally large gap between his two front teeth. "This is not the sort of place women come in unescorted. It's a decent place. For decent Germans."

Willi thought he saw a doctor's smock beneath the man's coat.

"Where do you think you are, *mein Herr*?" the fairer-skinned one with black eyes offered with a real sneer. "Perhaps you got out at the wrong S-Bahn stop. The Jew-damm is the other direction."

At this, the men and the waitress all burst out laughing.

"Jew-damm. Ha, ha, ha! Good one. I must remember that, Schumann," the first man said, delighted, then returned his gaze to Willi, losing the smile. "Go back to your Jew-damm. Enjoy it while you're able."

Willi felt now was the time to call in his reserves.

He broke out his Kripo badge.

It did not produce the desired effect.

The three seemed unsusceptible to the power of the state.

"You think you can scare us with that?" The dark-haired one laughed, showing his teeth. "Your Jew republic with your Jew constitution. We shit on it!"

"*Alles in Ordnung*, Josef?" A man emerged from a back door in black boots and full SA uniform, smacking a wood truncheon against a hand.

Willi calculated he had about thirty seconds to save his skull.

"I was merely looking for a friend," he said with the friendliest of smiles. "But since nobody seems to have seen her . . . I'll be on my way."

It broke the tension long enough for him to beat a tactical retreat. No use getting killed for this princess, logic affirmed. A minute later he was boarding the S-Bahn back for Berlin-Center.

Schumann, one had been called. His friend with the bunny teeth—Josef.

One way or another he'd have to get back into that friendly little tavern.

Half an hour later, Berlin-West whirring past his eyes, he wondered, what could have possessed Princess Magdelena Eugenia to have taken this train alone at midnight? To meet a lover? To purchase narcotics? It all seemed so improbable. And what about this sleepwalking business? Could she have really not been awake?

It seemed even more absurd. Perhaps she hadn't come to Spandau at all. Perhaps she only took this line and got off at any of a dozen stops along the way. He was just too tired to think.

Like a sleepwalker himself.

Even before dawn his eyes popped open. He'd been dreaming. At the Gloria Palast, Berlin's most famous movie theater, he'd been watching Marlene Dietrich's newest Hollywood hit. She was magical as ever, only the audience was horrified. People began running out of the theater, screaming. Willi looked closer and saw the great star's legs were monstrous. Inside out! Instead of strutting across the screen, she hobbled, her body growing more hideously mutilated every frame.

He was still in a strange state of wide-awake exhaustion when he arrived at the Police Presidium, surprised to find Gunther already in his office. Ruta, whistling, brought in fresh coffee and *Brötchen*.

"You look funny, Gunther," Willi said, the moment he saw the kid's expression.

Gunther shot him a troubled glance. "Here." He slid over a sheet of paper. "The top orthopedic surgeons in Germany."

Willi didn't recognize any of the names, but was glad to see all but a few had Berlin addresses. He folded the paper and slipped it in his jacket pocket.

"I haven't found anything yet on bone transplants. It's a pretty obscure topic."

"Try the university medical library. Or Charité Hospital. There's got to be something."

"Yes, sir." Gunther wrote these down. "Now, as far as missing Americans go, there were three in 1932, but only one was female. Her name, Gina Mancuso, from the State of New York, a little town called Schenectady."

Mancuso. Willi recalled those dark, warm eyes.

"Let's see her file."

"It wasn't there."

"Come now."

"Her name and country of origin were on the Central Missing Persons Manifesto, but her file was missing from Archives."

"Not only she, but her file missing? That's very odd."

"You know the pretty one down there, Elfrieda?" Gunther added. "She swore she saw it a week ago realphabetizing the *m*'s. But she searched and searched and it sure wasn't there now."

"No one checked it out?"

"Not officially."

"Well, I'm going to have to put you on this, Gunther, while I go chasing after the Bulgarian princess. You've got to find out everything you can about Gina Mancuso, and let's see if we can't at least make a positive ID."

"There's more, sir. Remember, the Prussian state asylums?"

"Yes, of course. What did you find? Had this Mancuso been institutionalized?"

"No record of that. But regarding the shaving of hair—all state institutions abandoned the practice more than four years ago."

"I see." Willi thought about it. On one hand this was good news. On the other, a puzzling bit of information.

"And would you like to take a guess at the number of inmates who've gone missing from only one of those institutions, the Berlin-Charlottenburg Asylum, in the past year?"

"I imagine there's always a fair number."

"Try two hundred and fifty-five."

"Seems high."

Gunther slid Willi a typed list several pages long.

"All these people escaped?"

"Not a single one. They were removed. Eighty-five at a time. In three evacuations. Months apart."

Willi read the top of each page. "What is this, 'Special Handling'?"

"No one seems to have any idea."

"Well, who removed them?"

"No one seems to have any idea."

"That's preposterous." Willi was getting annoyed. Why was Gunther bothering him with this? "Somebody must know who took them. Why do you even say they're missing?"

"Because that's exactly it, sir. They are. There's no record any-where of where they went."

"Gunther—" Willi exerted the utmost effort to control him-self. "I can't be worried about this now."

"But don't you think I should at least—"

Back in the war, Willi recalled, when they'd penetrated en-emy minefields, there was only one way to make it. One foot in front of the other, eyes locked straight ahead, exactly on the spot the next foot had to step. Anything to your left or right was su-perfluous, a potentially fatal distraction. Even your best friend blowing up.

"You are to drop this matter immediately, Gunther, do you hear me!"

The boy looked at him, astonished. It was the first time since they'd been working together Willi had raised his voice.

"You are to find where Gina Mancuso lived, and where she worked, and whom she knew in Berlin. And nothing else."

Willi found Konstantin Kaparov a distraught and broken man, weeping in his hotel suite at the Adlon. He had dropped out of the Six-Day Bicycle Race, his team having hopelessly fallen be-hind. "I no could concentrate. I think only my Magdelena." Willi wished he could offer some encouraging news, but all he had were questions. This time, at least, Kaparov was in a better state to answer.

"Last time I forget to tell . . . before we go dinner, Magdelena went to doctor . . . for ankle. Very swollen."

"You went with her?"

"Yes. Doctor say only sprain. No broke. Wrap in bandage. Give pills. We leave."

"This doctor's name?"

"This I am not remembering. But hotel recommend."

"What about the name of the club you say you dined in? Do you remember that now?"

"I find matchbox. Was call Klub Hell."

Hell. Willi was familiar with it. An expensive tourist trap in the guise of one of Berlin's great halls of decadence. Naughty floor show. Cabaret acts.

"Also I forget last time to say. Was hypnotist performing at Klub. During act he wants volunteers for stage. Magdelena go up. Always she like silly things. And attention. Love attention."

"Was he able to hypnotize her?" Willi couldn't help remembering what Rudy the doorman had said.

"Oh, yes. Yes. Very funny. I laughing so hard. Magdelena, he has her speaking Chinese!"

Willi knew a bit about hypnosis from his cousin Kurt, a doctor at the prestigious Berlin Center for Psychoanalysis. Kurt had been a student of Sigmund Freud himself down in Vienna and employed hypnosis in his work. He loathed shysters who used it for crude entertainment.

"Do you recall this hypnotist's name?"

"The Great . . . something."

"The Great Gustave?"

"Yes!"

Most of all Kurt hated the Great Gustave, Berlin's most famous psychic, the "King of Mystics," who had recently made headlines—and himself preposterous in many people's eyes—by predicting a complete Nazi takeover in 1933.

"How was the princess after this hypnotic act?"

"Absolutely normal," the husband insisted. "Until, like I say, several hours later, when she puts on coat to get cigarettes."

Willi felt a ray of hope. So, the Bulgarian princess had been hypnotized by this Great Gustave the night she disappeared.

Downstairs, Willi obtained the name of the doctor the princess had been referred to: one Hermann Meckel, orthopedic specialist, with an office several blocks down the Unter den Linden. A chill of astonishment flashed through him when he saw Meckel's name on Gunther's list of top orthopedic surgeons. Another coincidence? Was it possible? Twice now something had tied the missing princess to the Mermaid.

The doctor's office was extremely swank: crystal chandeliers, Persian rugs. Mahogany furnishings. Unfortunately, according to his young, attractive receptionist, he was not in this afternoon. Tuesdays he devoted to volunteer work down at the *Klinik*.

"I see. And what *Klinik* would that be?"

"The SA Klinik. Down by Spittlemarkt."

"I see," Willi said.

So the fancy physician was a Nazi, too.

Over lunch in the police cafeteria, trying hard to redeem himself, Gunther proudly delivered the last known address of missing American Gina Mancuso, which he'd uncovered in the 1931 Housing Registry.

"And," he added, the enormous Adam's apple jumping around his giraffelike throat, "she had a roommate, Paula Hoffmeyer—still lives there."

Willi read the address. One of the poorest districts in Berlin-North.

"Excellent. I'll go myself, at the first opportune moment." He slipped it in his notebook. "Gunther, tell me something . . . have you ever been to Hell?"

"Excuse me, sir?"

"Hell. The club. Have you ever been there?"

"No." The lad's long face broke into a corny grin. "But I sure as heck'd like to."

"Buy yourself a dinner jacket. We're going tonight. In the meantime, dig up whatever you can on this Dr. Hermann Meckel."

The Nazi medical center at Spittlemarkt was more like a small hospital than a clinic, with X-ray equipment, operating rooms, and large wards filled with storm troopers who'd been busted up in street brawls with the Reds. Willi had served in the military long enough to recognize the stripes on the uniform sleeve of the man someone pointed out as Meckel. The good doctor was an SA general.

The *Sturmabteilung,* Storm Division, was not a real military of course. It was only one of several private paramilitary armies the Weimar Republic had allowed to thrive in the name of tolerance, despite that it was committed to that republic's destruction. In Berlin, the Communist Red Front had been every bit as powerful as the SA. But since the trauma of the Great Depression, under the charismatic leadership of Ernst Roehm, the SA's expansion had been explosive. Its membership recently eclipsed the half million mark—five times the size of the German army—with their characteristic knee-high boots, wide brown breeches with matching tunics, tall-peaked caps, and bloodred swastika armbands. The original function of the SA had been to guard Nazi political meetings. The Führer however soon discovered the expedience of using it to break the skulls of his opponents, mainly though by no means exclusively Communists. Eventually, under Roehm, the SA developed an extensive social-services system: soup kitchens, skills-training programs, free medical clinics. Not a town or city in Germany today lacked a Brownshirt division.

"Doktor Meckel." Willi held up his ID.

The physician was middle-aged with not much hair, but had a ruddy physique and the strong, nimble hands of a pianist. He examined Willi's Kripo badge, and for an instant his sharp blue eyes tightened. Then they all but exploded with charming light.

"Why Inspektor Kraus, what an honor! Of course I'm familiar with you. Who in Berlin isn't? The way you used psychological insight to stalk the Child Eater—positively exemplary. How may I be of service to you today? Sit down. Have some coffee."

"That's all right. I'm here in reference to a recent patient at your office." Willi pulled out the photograph of the princess.

The doctor looked it over as if with the fondest memories. "Ah, yes. Marilyn something, wasn't it?"

"Magdelena."

"Yes, yes, of course. Came to me with a sprained ankle. Made a big fuss about it as some women will, you know. I bandaged her up and gave her some codeine tablets. Told her to try to keep off the ankle as much as possible."

Codeine? Willi wondered. Might that have caused the wide-eyed state Rudy took for sleepwalking?

"How strong were these tablets, Doctor?"

"Five milligrams. For placebo effect mainly. Why? Did something happen? You're with the Homicide Commission. She isn't—?"

"We hope not, Doctor. But the princess has gone missing."

"Princess!" He looked genuinely shocked.

Willi's sixth sense was doing somersaults. Meckel was lying through his teeth.

"Yes. Daughter of the king of Bulgaria. Her father is most anxious to have her returned. So is President von Hindenburg. The Berlin police are leaving no stone unturned. Since you were one of the last to see her, Doktor Meckel, it's likely we shall wish to speak with you more."

"Yes, of course. But I've told you everything I know."

An orderly appeared. "Doktor Meckel, major street fighting in Wedding. The injured are starting to arrive."

"Herr Inspektor, you must excuse me."

"Yes, of course, Herr Doktor. Until we meet again."

Five

"Welcome to Hell." The hatcheck girl winked at Gunther, handing him a ticket for his coat.

"Simmer down, boy," Willi cautioned. "Remember, this is work."

For more than a decade the very name *Berlin* had been a byword among the in-the-know sets for decadence and depravity, and Klub Hell on raunchy Friedrich Strasse dished up a particularly stagy version. Topless barmaids in devil's horns. Surrealistic murals of Dante's inferno. And boiling cauldrons of dry ice that kept the place in a perpetual fog.

Gunther was in heaven.

They were given a table on the mezzanine with an excellent view of the stage. Willi could see how a provincial princess might be entranced by the theatrical glamour of the lighting and décor. But who had sent her here? Doktor Meckel?

When the lights dimmed, Gunther wiggled in his chair like a kid at the circus. Before a backdrop of lurid red gauze, the floor show began: a series of tableaux vivants composed by squads of scantily clad vixens, each scene depicting a moment of particularly prurient history—Joan of Arc being burned at the stake, topless; Jack the Ripper tearing apart a naked London lady of the night. These were followed by silhouette compositions, *avec* vixens behind the red gauze: eroticized torture mainly, forced gratification, bondage, humiliation. There was endless cracking of whips, spanking of fannies, and exaggerated cries for pity. Gunther, Willi noticed, was not merely enthralled, but embarrassed to the core, his long, bony face turning continuous shades of red and purple.

"For goodness' sakes," Willi whispered. "Don't act like you never left a farm."

"I never did, until Police Academy."

"Well, you must have had cows and bulls and whatnot."

"Sure. But they never spanked each other!"

A buxom acrobat named Helga was soon twisting herself into a Bavarian pretzel. Three topless Negresses demonstrated the latest dance craze from New York—the shimmy-shake. And a satanic ventriloquist tried to seduce a sexy schoolgirl dummy.

Finally all the lights went dark, except for a single spotlight onstage. The room fell into silent expectation. From the rafters a small choir of half-naked angels in silver sequins descended by wires, bearing with them a large cage. Inside, as if being cast from heaven into hell, was the Great Gustave in top hat and tails, hands held dramatically overhead, seeming to writhe in pain.

The audience applauded wildly.

Onstage, the angels released him and Gustave stepped from captivity, silently surveying his new environment. Then slowly, deliberately, tugging on each finger of his white gloves, he prepared to master whatever came his way.

"*Meine Damen und Herren,*" his deep baritone boomed through the room. "So this is Hell!"

The whole nightclub shook with laughter.

Gustave was a veteran showman, Willi knew from his cousin Kurt's tirades. A born carny who'd mastered everything from lion taming to mind reading. After thirty years in the business, he was pure stagecraft, from his whitened face and dark eyes to the exaggerated silent-screen expressions.

"Hell"—his voice trembled like a stage villain's—"is a state of mind as much as a physical place. Which is why Klub Hell has dragged me down here tonight to journey with you into realms of the mind normally experienced only during sleep. The realm of the deep subconscious.

"For our journey this evening I am going to require several volunteers, which I will choose from among the females. No offense, gentlemen. I just happen to like girls.

"Now, ladies, as I walk through the audience, I'm going to ask you all to raise your skirts—nothing indecent, only to the knees. My job, I confess, was easier a few years ago when we had short skirts. But these days I must ask you all to lift your skirts, ladies, back to where they were in 1929, lift them so that I may note their shape and character. That's right. Thank you. Thank you all so very much."

Willi found it astonishing that not a single woman failed to obey this command, but almost in unison they hiked their skirts to the delight of their male companions.

"It's not merely that I like looking at women's legs, which I do. But it's a little known fact, *meine Damen und Herren,* that there are nine basic types of women's legs, and that they can say as much about a woman's character as her face or her palm. Now, for example, this lovely lady here has what are called Champagne Bottle legs, not merely because they are expensive and delicious, which I'm sure they are, but because of their shape, with thin, delicate ankles and firm, fulsome calves. The knee is never bony but rounded, spherical. This tells me she is soft and affectionate, motherly. That she has many friends and a warm, loving home. Am I right?"

"Yes, yes, you are!"

"Do you agree?" he asked the man next to her.

"Yes, quite."

"Then you're a lucky man. Unfortunately women with Champagne Bottle legs do not make the best subjects for our experiments. No, I am looking for what are called Baby Doll legs, where the ankle tapers imperceptibly to the calf, delicately complementing the knee, because a woman with Baby Doll legs possesses an acute sense of trust and curiosity. Or I am looking for the Classic legs, which indicate a woman who is both intuitive and imaginative. Or best of all, Ideal legs. You may wish you had these, ladies. But only one in a thousand women does. The Ideal leg, like anything wonderful and perfect, indicates a strong, vital life force. Passion!"

Willi couldn't help but picture the Mermaid's monstrously mangled legs. Or that photo of the Bulgarian princess, with her husband bowing to her. Could she have had Baby Doll legs? Or Classic? Something about this Gustave seemed more hellish than just his nightclub act. He was assessing not merely the legs, but the faces of these women, their postures, their clothing. Selecting the exact subject he wanted. Or am I just being paranoid? Willi wondered. Feeling natural resistance to a force of obvious power? Because this Gustave had his game perfected all right. He was choosing only the sexiest ladies to participate in his hypnotic high jinks.

When the six loveliest women in the room were seated on stage in a semicircle, the lights went back down on the rest of the crowd.

"Ladies . . . ," the voice boomed. "I want you to keep your eyes fixed directly on mine. As I talk, they will begin to feel tired. Very tired. You will find yourself wanting to relax. A feeling of pleasant tiredness and drowsiness overcoming you . . . you feel fine . . . you feel relaxed . . . close your eyes and in a few minutes you will fall into a pleasant, gentle sleep."

His voice was so deliberately low and monotonous, even some

people not onstage could be seen with their heads nodding over.

"*Meine Damen und Herren,* the ladies now are in a light hypnotic trance. There is nothing magical about it. They are aware of everything that's going on. Right, girls?"

All the women nodded. Gustave tapped a pretty brunette on the shoulder. "Sweetheart, what is your name?"

"Hannah Lore," she said with her eyes still closed.

"Hannah Lore, how do you feel?"

"Lovely. Just lovely."

"I shall now take them into a deep trance.

"You are comfortable now. Completely comfortable. Your whole body is relaxed. You have no feeling of tension. You are drifting asleep. A deep, deep, delightful sleep. I'm going to count backwards from ten, and when I finish, you will be asleep, deep, deep asleep. . . . Ten . . . nine . . ."

At the end of his countdown the Great Gustave tested each subject for signs of a trance. "The arms should be as limp as rope," he tells the audience. As he lifts them, several arms indeed fall back corpselike. "The eyeballs should be turned up." He demonstrates by yanking several of the ladies' eyelids.

"Hannah Lore." He returns to her. "Can you hear me?"

"Yes."

"How do you feel now?"

"Lovely."

"Ladies and gentlemen, I will now demonstrate to you the power hypnotic trance exerts over the human mind.

"Hannah Lore . . . can you speak Chinese?"

"Of course not." She giggles. "I'm from Düsseldorf."

"When I snap my fingers, you will awaken and you will no longer be Hannah Lore from Düsseldorf, but the dowager empress of ancient China. You are very angry because one of your servants has stolen your favorite teacup. You're not sure who it is, but you vow to catch the thief and cut off his head. Here we go now. One. Two. Three." He snapped his fingers.

Hannah Lore jumped from her seat and with a furious scowl started screaming at the top of her lungs. *"Ching how ni gon! He how gon ni how? Chow kow ling chew! Ling chew! Ling chew!"*

She kept making slitting motions with her finger across her throat.

The audience was in hysterics.

"When I clap my hands, you will fall back to sleep!"

Gustave clapped, and the empress collapsed as if poisoned, dead into her throne.

"Hannah Lore," he said. "Do you speak Chinese?"

"No, of course not." She giggled again. "I'm from Düsseldorf."

In this manner the Great Gustave entertained for an hour.

Willi was astonished at the patent aura of seduction to it all. How the man stood above these limp women's bodies, commanding them with his deep, demanding masculine voice, his every wish instantly obeyed. Turning women into bumblebees. Ballerinas. French maids.

Gunther clearly was not oblivious to the implications either. "What I couldn't do with six girls under my control like that," he muttered, forgetting himself in Willi's presence.

Every man in the audience, Willi was sure, was thinking exactly the same.

But not every man in the audience had the Great Gustave's gifts.

After the show the King of Mystics returned his subjects to the world of ordinary consciousness, and the adoring arms of their men. They recalled nothing of their adventures. All felt marvelous, they reported, as if they'd just spent a week at Baden-Baden's finest spa. The clients of Hell were left well satisfied with their evening's peek into the bizarre, expensive netherworld of Weimar Berlin.

As soon as the lights came up, Willi led Gunther backstage and sought out the dressing room of the Great Gustave. They found the performer at his makeup table already half-transformed. Gone was the jet-black hair, sitting now on a wig stand, the deathly looking black eyes crumpled on a dozen paper napkins. The white skin. The strange red lips, all washing away under cold cream.

"Kripo? My word!" He rose to his feet showing more natural emotion than he had all night. "What on earth have I done now? Come, come in."

"Herr Gustave," Willi addressed him. "Saturday night you hypnotized a young woman who later went missing."

"What, missing?"

Willi handed him the picture of the princess.

"I don't remember her. Honestly, I'd tell you if I did. I've nothing to hide. But you know how many shows a week I do? All these women's faces blur together in my mind. My work requires so much concentration. Perhaps nearly as much as yours, Herr Inspektor-Detektiv."

"What about the legs?" Willi asked. "Would you say she had Champagne Bottle? Baby Doll? Or the Ideal?"

"Oh, that!" Gustave laughed, wiping the rest of the cold cream from his face and turning into a perfectly unremarkable man in his late forties, with thin brown hair, calm, gentle eyes, and a rather amiable expression. "You don't really take that leg stuff seriously? It's all part of the act. I just use it to rile up the women. Women are my calling card. I must live up to my reputation, to prove I can get even the most attractive completely in my power. There's no such thing as the nine kinds of legs. I just made that up to sound as if I possess all sorts of esoteric knowledge. People want to believe in magic. They want to give themselves up to a higher power. It's all part of my job, gentlemen. You do yours. I do mine. I'm sorry this poor girl has gone missing. Truly I am. I hold no malice toward any living being. But I certainly had nothing to do with it. Once I wake these women up, they are completely back to normal. You saw that with your own eyes."

"Yes, of course I did. But surely you'd be the first to admit"— Willi's voice was not as harsh as he'd have liked—"that what one *sees* and what really *is* are not always the same." Despite himself he liked this man. Something about his off-stage persona was downright sympathetic. "Sorry to have disturbed you, Herr Gustave," he concluded. "Your show was most enlightening. Most enlightening indeed."

He'd seek a warrant at once, he decided, to search the King of Mystics' home.

Six

It was all meetings the next morning. Meetings with the unit heads.
The division heads. Those above him. Those below. And then a
most enlightening meeting with Gunther in the early afternoon,
who'd just returned from Charité Hospital's medical archives.

"I finally got something on bone transplants." Gunther's face
had lost the wolfish lust Willi'd seen creep through it last night.
He was simply good old Gunther again. The wolf in him asleep.
"A major address in 1930 at the Medical College of Leipzig.
It focused specifically on the possibility of implanting human
bones, and utilizing grafting techniques to allow their regenera-
tion in a host body. Take one guess who made it."

Willi just loved when the kid got playful at moments like these.

Gunther leaned forward, his blue eyes sparkling. "Dr. Hermann Meckel."

Then it *was* all related! A thunderclap shook Willi. Meckel was involved both with the Mermaid and the Bulgarian princess. Something big was in the works here.

Terribly big.

"And not only that," Gunther added, "but Meckel's file's also missing from the Charité archives. He's on their board, but there's not a single record of it. The clerk assured me the file had been there, but now again for some reason, it's gone."

"There could only be one reason," Willi said, feeling a sudden darkness looming. "Because someone's taking them before we get there, Gunther. Someone, or something, is keeping one step ahead of us."

Gunther swallowed, his enormous Adam's apple dropping down his throat. "Maybe that gold pin they found on the Mermaid's clothing will give us a lead."

"What gold pin?" Willi looked at him.

"You didn't know? I saw Dr. Shurze from Pathology. He told me they'd discovered a gold Nazi Party pin in the fabric of that gray smock the Mermaid was wearing."

An alarm went off in Willi's head. "Dr. Hoffnung never mentioned any gold pin. And who is this Shurze?"

"The new head of Pathology. Hoffnung's retired."

"Retired? But that's—" Willi spotted one of his Detektivs, little, black-mustached Herbert Thurmann, lingering near the door. "Very interesting."

Alone finally, Willi leaned back in his office chair and stared out the window. He was sane enough to realize that it was delusional to imagine a Jewish inspector could take on an SA general single-handedly. But it didn't mean the guy was untouchable. Just that it was time to call for bigger guns. Fritz. One of Germany's most famous journalists. There wasn't a soul in Berlin he didn't know. Not so much because of his incisive political analyses but because his last name was Hohenzollern. Same as that of the deposed royal family, of which he was some kind of cousin. Deposed or not, the name opened any door in Germany.

Willi reached for the phone.

"For God's sakes where have you been?" Fritz was thrilled as always to hear from him. Willi had saved his life not once but several times in the war. Fritz would do anything for him. "I have the most marvelous woman I want you to meet. Smart as a whip—"

"Fritz, listen: I need an interview with von Schleicher. Urgent."

"Von Schleicher. Tall order. But if it's really urgent—"

The whole thing was set up by the time Willi had returned from the men's room.

"No one gets things done like you. *You* ought to be appointed chancellor, Fritz."

"Never mind that. We've got to meet up for coffee. I must tell you about this wonderful woman, Willi. Before some swine grabs her up."

At von Schleicher's chambers in the Ministry of War, the general's desk was an enormous gilded affair, perhaps two-thirds the size of Hindenburg's, Willi calculated. In Germany, everything was ranked according to status, from your desk to the entrance you walked through each morning. Unfortunately his own rank, he couldn't help but feel, was slipping the longer he went on.

The minister looked more incredulous by the moment. An SA general? Medical experiments? Willi felt sweat dripping down his back. The man was shrewd, he knew. Able to play both sides of a coin. Where would he come down?

At last the general tore off his monocle. "The army will support you!" His blue eyes crackled with what seemed a thousand hatching schemes. "If this Meckel proves guilty of the crimes you suspect, the entire nation would be scandalized. Exactly the excuse I've been looking for, Kraus. Very good. Very good."

Von Schleicher appeared to see it all before him. "These Nazi swine must be stopped with the only thing they understand:

force! Roehm and his henchmen have been dreaming for months of doing away with me and co-opting the army. This will enable me to move first. I'll crush them. Annihilate them. Grind them into horse fodder."

It seemed a bit extreme to Willi, except in the context of German political discourse, in which bloody solutions had become as commonly discussed these days as the weather. But he felt an enormous weight lift from his midsection. With von Schleicher and the army on his side he stood a chance at taking down this sick SA surgeon. Until he heard the minister say he would contact Ernst Roehm at once. And the weight returned.

"Herr General, I was hoping to keep this between the army and the police. Why bring in the SA führer?"

"Because Ernst Roehm happens to be a buddy of mine. A little queer, but a solid soldier. A man with whom I can do business."

"You just finished telling me you want to crush him. Annihilate him. Grind him up for horse fodder."

Von Schleicher looked at Willi as if he were a little boy. "Herr Inspektor, what does one thing have to do with the other?"

Thus went the forked-tongued, double-dealing, backstabbing, two-faced world of politics in the Wilhelm Strasse. Exactly the way the World War had begun, Willi grimly recalled.

Von Schleicher picked up the phone and vehemently clicked the receiver for the operator. The SA leader was unavailable. "Never mind." He hung up. "I'll take care of it. Roehm will work with us on this, I assure you."

"Superb." Willi barely made it sound as if he meant it.

Before he rose to leave, he did something entirely against his principles.

"Herr General—" He kept flashing onto his father-in-law's desperate face the other day at Café Strauss. And his sons. "Might I take a moment to inquire of you, quite confidentially of course, what you foresee in terms of the next leadership at the Reichs Chancellery?"

Von Schleicher was silent. Willi feared he'd overstepped his bounds. Undermined the foundation of the alliance he'd just forged. But the minister of war banged on the desk again, rising as if to address the nation.

"What Germany needs is a man of iron character and will. A man who will not flinch at taking the necessary action required to get this country onto her feet. A man of steel, like Russia's Stalin. Whom the people will tremble before and respect as a father."

Who? Willi kept thinking.

"Don't you worry." Von Schleicher put his monocle back in and stared directly at him. "I have a plan. Stick with me, Kraus. You won't regret it."

"I regret day I am stepping feet into this cursed city."

Konstantin Kaparov was furiously packing in his suite at the Adlon. Since he'd been so close by, Willi had dropped in for a few more questions. But Kaparov was having a Bulgarian fit. His face bruised. His eye blackened.

"Yesterday I walk in Tiergarten, get jumped by Nazi animals who think I am Jew. Imagine me Jew."

"Anyone with dark hair . . . ," Willi stammered apologetically.

"I leaving. No come back. You not find Magdelena after four days, you no find at all. This city—it killed her. This city—hell!"

"Speaking of which," Willi interjected, "the hypnotist at Klub Hell the night you were there, did he say anything about the kind of legs Magdelena had? Did he call them Classic? Or Ideal?"

"No. Nothing he call them. I tell you, Herr Inspektor, hypnotist not have nothing to do wit zees. After show Magdelena completely normal. Nothing strange. I know. Am husband. Or . . . was."

"I'm so sorry, Konstantin, that I haven't been able to find her."

"No one find her. She disappear in Berlin. Same as dead."

Back in the dingy lobby of the Police Presidium, waiting for the ancient elevator to descend, Willi found himself standing next to Wolfgang Mutze of all people, head of Missing Persons. "Well, well, Kraus. How's ghost hunting? That's what we call it in the biz, you know." Mutze's multiple chins rolled around his collar as he chuckled to himself. "What have you found out so far about this missing Romanian princess?"

"She's Bulgarian. And not much. Oddest thing though," he said as the rickety old cage finally arrived. "The last person to see her, the doorman at the Adlon, claims he thought she was sleepwalking."

"Another sleepwalker?" Mutze bellowed as they stepped in. "Could you press five for me please there, Kraus?"

"What do you mean another?" Willi closed the metal gate.

"Well, we must have had a dozen in as many months."

"A dozen sleepwalkers, disappearing?"

"Sure. It started early last year. Some strange cult, we think. Berlin's brimming with them."

"But I must see all their files. Immediately."

Mutze's face stiffened. "Feel free to speak to my secretary then. They're certainly not all neatly grouped together. We haven't compiled a Sleepwalker File. They're simply random cases."

"You never thought to put them together?"

"Listen, Kraus, they may have made you an Inspektor-Detektiv but you've no right to speak to me like that. Do you have any idea of how many people go missing in this city every day? Fifty to sixty. On a slow day. You have it cushy up in Homicide. I don't think you have one-twentieth the number of cases we handle. And when you solve one, they act like you're some kind of Hercules."

The elevator ground to a stop on five. Mutze stormed out.

"I'll have my boy come to your office at once," Willi called after him.

"Do that."

A dozen sleepwalkers. Willi could hardly believe his ears. He reached the sixth floor and was about to shout for Gunther to come immediately when he remembered something else he had to do and hit the button back down, to Pathology.

"Yes, of course." The new head of the department, Dr. Shurze, rose from the desk Dr. Hoffnung had occupied. Pulling open a wide, thin drawer from one of the medical cabinets, he handed Willi a glass container.

Inside was a sparkling gold men's lapel pin.

Willi took it out. "These gold pins, if I'm not mistaken, are only given to longtime Party members."

"Correct," Shurze replied.

Something about this new guy Willi didn't quite trust. Perhaps it was the eyeglasses, so thick it was hard to believe he could really perform autopsies.

"The gold pin," Shurze went on, apparently well versed in Nazi history, "is only bestowed upon those Party members who participated in the Beer Hall Putsch of November 1923. So whomever this belonged to was a high-ranking man."

"What is this insignia here?" Willi asked of the small staff with a snake wrapped around it embossed just below the swastika.

"This indicates the SA Medical Corps, Herr Inspektor-Detektiv."

"The SA."

"Yes. The SA Medical Corps was founded in 1923."

"And where exactly did you say you discovered this pin?"

"It was stuck—accidentally or on purpose, I couldn't say—on the inside of the gray garment the victim was wearing."

Willi found this hard to believe, impossible almost. Dr. Hoffnung would never have missed such a key piece of evidence.

Nor would he retire so suddenly without so much as a word. Might someone, even Shurze, have planted the pin and got rid of Hoffnung? But why?

"Gunther," Willi said, "we're going to switch jobs for a while, you and I."

"You mean, *I* have to order *you* about?" Gunther seemed none too pleased by the prospect.

"No. You are going to pursue the missing Bulgarian princess, and I am going to have a chat with Gina Mancuso's old roommate. There's an inn out in Spandau called the Black Stag. I want you to insinuate yourself into the crowd. It may take some time. Don't rush things. Drink. Be merry with them. And find out whether the Princess Magdelena ever stepped foot in there or not."

"*Jawohl.*" Gunther wrote it all down.

"Plus, there were two fellows there the other night. One named Schumann. The other's first name was Josef. I want anything and everything you can find about them. I have a hunch they may be doctors. Oh, and, Gunther, be careful. Very careful. It's a real nest of Nazis. None too friendly to me."

Gunther's eyes widened. "Which is why you're sending me." His pale cheeks quivered excitedly, exactly the dogged response Willi was counting on. "Don't you worry, Chief. I'll find out for you. Everything there is to!"

Seven

"Paula, you're looking for?" The charwoman glanced up in surprise. "You sure as heck won't find her lounging about at four in the afternoon." She dropped her brush in the bucket. "She's a workingwoman, Inspektor. Just like the rest of us." She stood up, wiping her hands on her apron. "What's she done now?"

"To whom do I have the honor of addressing?" Willi was well aware that in Germany a building's cleaning lady knew all there was to know about her tenants. But such information more often than not became ammunition in personal vendettas—and nothing, he'd learned the hard way, could derail an investigation faster.

"I am Frau Agnes Hoffmeyer." The woman held out her skirt and curtsied, as if being introduced at a ball. "Related to the lady in question by motherhood."

Like big-city dwellers everywhere Berliners often eased life's grind with the lubricant of sarcasm. Willi felt as if he'd known this saucy lady all his life.

"This is in regard to a former roommate of hers, an American named Gina Mancuso."

The sauce evaporated. "You didn't find her?"

She quickly offered up whatever she had on the subject, which wasn't much. Gina had lived upstairs with Paula for more than a year, a lovely girl. Nice. Neat. Stunned by her disappearance, they were. Paula loved her like a sister. Used to be in a chorus line together. Which club? She couldn't say. But she'd started hanging out with the wrong crowd, Paula used to tell her about that. Which crowd? She had no idea. He'd need to speak with Paula personally.

"Where might I find her, Frau Hoffmeyer?" Willi was writing everything down.

"I can tell you where she works. Where you'll find her, who the hell knows. Try Tauentzien, between Marburger and Ranke."

For a moment their eyes met.

Go on, hers seemed to say. *Make something of it. Shouldn't I be ashamed? Humiliated? No, Herr Inspektor-Detektiv. Humiliated am I only when I haven't food to put in an empty stomach.*

"Is there some way I could recognize your daughter, ma'am?" he asked, knowing that dozens of girls worked that block, just down from one of Berlin's main train stations. He walked past them every morning on his way to work.

"Yeah, sure. You can pick her out in a second." Frau Hoffmeyer dropped back to her knees with a grunt. "The one in the purple, lace-up boots."

The boots radiated even across the avenue.

In Berlin, a city whose main industry some said was sex, the Boot Girls of Tauentzien Strasse were a virtual brand name, elite among the many layered cultures of prostitution thriving here. Ten thousand women were registered with the Berlin city government, certifying them as disease-free professionals. Countless tens of thousands more competed on an amateur level, at lower cost/higher risk. Boot Girls were in a category all their own: professionals of the most highly specialized type, for a boot on Tauentzien Strasse was no mere footwear. It was carefully coordinated advertisement.

Of the kinkiest variety.

"Mud bath?" the girl in the brown anklets might whisper as you pass; her friend in hip-high yellow counters, "Better yet, how about a nice refreshing shower this morning, huh, *Bübchen*?"

Entire guidebooks were devoted to interpreting the color codes.

Before crossing the street Willi observed Miss Paula Hoffmeyer. Quite a creation. Waist up she was in full men's formal attire: black tails, bow tie, white carnation in the lapel. Every detail perfect down to the leather riding crop under her arm. Her brown hair, blunt at the neck, was oiled into tight marcel waves, her hands wrapped in fingerless black gloves. The eyes were covered in almost as much dark makeup as the Great Gustave's. Waist down she was femme fatale. Black silk short-shorts revealed the garters and straps holding up her stockings. And those boots. Extra-high-spike-heeled, pointy-toed, purple patent leather with flaming red laces up the front.

Without a guidebook Willi was helpless to decipher the meaning. Only that unlike the other girls, who walked almost exclusively in teams, Paula strut the sidewalk alone, holding her body erect, fiercely almost. He darted behind two passing streetcars across the busy avenue.

A truck honked.

A motorcyclist roared around him.

On the far corner a newspaper vendor shouted the early evening headlines: "Hitler—*Nein* to Vice Chancellorship! Hindenburg—*Nein* to Hitler!"

"Fräulein." Willi tapped Miss Hoffmeyer on the shoulder.

She turned around with a brash smile. "Craving discipline? Why, you must have been a very naughty—" The smile dropped as she saw the badge. "What? I'm up-to-date. So now I have to show my permit card?" She started fishing through her jacket. "*Mein Gott,* this place is turning into a real police state."

"I'm not interested in your card, miss. I'm with the Kriminal Polizei."

He could see the color flush from her face.

"Might I buy you a cup of coffee?"

"It's a joke, right? You want to buy *me* coffee. Well, this must be really bad. Just tell me, Inspektor. Come on. I can take it. Who got it this time?"

"Please. Let me buy you a coffee. Anywhere you'd like."

"Anywhere I'd like? Hmmm. Let me think . . ." She tapped her half-gloved hands on her chin. "How about the Romanische then."

Willi had to hand it to her. She could have said the Kaiserhof or Adlon. But this girl clearly knew how to dish out as well as she got. Of all the many hundreds of cafés in Berlin, the one he'd most *not* want to be seen with someone like her was the Romanische. Not that it was fashionable or even terribly expensive, but it was just the sort of place everyone was sure to know him. "Okay then," he said. "Come."

Luckily for them it was practically around the corner, because the moment they began walking, the sky opened up with an absolutely frigid rain. "You saved me from a miserable fate!" Paula cried, holding her hands over her head as they passed below the Kaiser Wilhelm Memorial Church. The enormous bells overhead began pealing five o'clock. Willi took her arm as they darted amid traffic across the Breitscheidplatz.

On one of the busiest corners of Berlin-West, with its multiple rooms of high-arched ceilings and countless comfortable wicker chairs, an intoxicating blend of coffees enriching its already rarefied air, the Romanisches Café was home to Berlin's many artistic and intellectual giants. Not that Willi belonged to this crowd certainly. But Fritz did. The journalist and distant relative of the ex-kaiser was best friends with positively everyone here. And positively everyone knew Fritz's oldest friend, his war pal/lifesaver, formerly the Detektiv, now the great *Kinderfresser* catcher, Willi.

Max Reinhardt, the illustrious theatrical impresario, and Bertolt Brecht, the brilliant young playwright, in his trademark black leather cap, both looked up from their table and waved hellos, noticing with curiosity the Boot Girl Willi'd brought along. Thomas Mann, Germany's most famous modern novelist, rose to shake Willi's hand and was introduced with fascination to his companion. And who else could that head of wildly orbiting hair have belonged to other than the most famous German of all, Albert Einstein, who put down his newspaper long enough to grab Willi's sleeve and whisper intensely, "I've decided to leave for America, Willi. Right after New Year. This climate's getting menacing. You ought to consider going, too, while the going's still good."

Willi squeezed the great scientist's hand and wished him all the luck in the world.

The moment he and Paula got a table, he felt a hard slap against his back.

"You old dog." Fritz grabbed his shoulder, shaking him with manly approval. Running a finger up and down his mustache, Fritz took in Paula from head to purple toes. "And here I thought you were languishing away in loneliness."

Willi was about to explain, but the girl cut him off.

"Paula." She held out her demi-gloved hands. "*Enchanté.* Sorry to have kept this such a state secret, but now that we're certain, we can tell the whole world. Inspektor . . . what's your name again, *Liebchen*? Willi. Willi and I are going to be wed!"

Fritz stared as if she were positively mad, the long dueling scar across his cheek flaming bright red as he burst out laughing. "You old dog," he reiterated, wagging a gleeful finger at Willi.

Backing away, Fritz pretended to dial and mouthed vociferously, "Call me, bloody hound, you!"

Paula and Willi looked at each other.

"Sorry." She shrugged, barely bothering to suppress her delight. "You must admit it was funny though."

It was hard to tell exactly how pretty she was under all her makeup, although Willi suspected it was more than she let on. Her figure however made her face almost irrelevant. At least for business purposes. The fulsome breasts beneath her men's shirt pushed up hard against the white cotton, straining the buttons almost to the breaking point. Where the shirt ended, the curves of her thighs made the black silk shorts sparkle, the inch of rosy white flesh peeking out before the garter almost irresistible. And those legs—Willi noticed her slowly crossing them under the table—surely the Great Gustave's Ideal.

When their orders arrived, she dug into her Black Forest cake as if she hadn't eaten in days. But when she sipped her coffee, she extended her pinkie delicately, as she'd no doubt seen in the cinema. Despite himself Willi was enchanted. He felt as if something terribly real and poignant was trying to break through the aura of a dream she wore as resolutely as her costume.

She swallowed, putting down her coffee cup. "Okay. So let's have it, Willi. What's the deal?"

"Gina Mancuso."

The last crumbs of cake fell off her fork. *"Mein Gott."*

"We're not certain it's her we found. But we think so. We want you to help us make certain."

"I don't suppose she's . . . alive?"

"No."

Paula sat motionless except for the tears that burst down both cheeks, carrying away the mask of mascara in thick black swaths.

"I really didn't think she could be. After all these months. Oh, her parents will just be devastated. They came all the way from Schenectady, New York, looking for her." She buried her head in her napkin and wept. "I loved that girl. The only real friend I ever had. Poor kid. Came here because she heard it was the only place to be. Everybody's gotta see Berlin! God, she loved life. Lived it like there was no tomorrow. Which there wasn't for her, was there?"

"Where did you two meet?"

"A nightclub on Kleist Strasse. Could that child ever dance. You think I have legs? Don't be stupid, Willi: I saw you staring before. Gina's would have knocked you out."

Willi's throat tightened at the thought of how those legs looked now.

"Fräulein, when I spoke to your mother earlier, she said you'd mentioned to her that Gina had gotten into the wrong crowd. What did you mean?"

Paula's eyes, so green and sparkling but strangely distant all this time, now clouded completely over. "Ever hear of Gustave Spanknoebel?"

"The Great Gustave?"

"Yeah, Great."

Willi had to strain to keep from shouting, *Eureka!* Gina Mancuso, the Mermaid, and Princess Magdelena Eugenia had *both* fallen into the same hands. Not only Dr. Meckel but the Great Gustave, *both* were involved. What kind of sick, sinister circle was this? But then again, hold on a second. Logic took him back a step or two. How is it possible that I should so conveniently stumble on this, as if some higher power had so nicely set it all up?

"I saw the Great Gustave's stage show recently. It seemed perfectly harmless."

"The show, sure. It's what goes on behind the curtains, Willi. Behind. Gustave has this yacht, see. Takes it out on the Wannsee and Havel, weather permitting. Has parties. If you want to call them parties."

"How do you know? You ever go?"

"Gina told me plenty enough. Gustave's a big Nazi. Well, maybe not really, but hangs around with all the Party big shots. Predicted Hitler would come to power next year."

"So I heard."

"They all come to his yacht for these . . . getaways. He always has the most beautiful girls in Berlin on hand. And hypnotizes them. Lets the men do whatever they want with them. It was all fun and games, until Gina." The green in Paula's eyes almost faded away. "She was the first who never came back."

"There have been others?"

"I don't know. I hear things."

"Fräulein Hoffmeyer, when Gina went missing, did you report what you knew about the Great Gustave to the police?"

"Did I. To anyone who'd listen. Ask me if they cared. I told you, this guy has friends. Big friends."

"Fräulein—"

"For Christ's sakes, stop calling me that. Only my customers call me Fräulein, and only once I order them to. Please. It's Paula."

"Okay, Paula. Let me ask you this. Do you think there's any way to arrange it so I might get invited to one of Gustave's 'getaway' outings?"

She looked at him and burst into laughter. "Forgive me, Herr Inspektor-Detektiv. Willi. Really. But you don't exactly look like a Nazi."

"There are ways to disguise yourself, Paula. I believe you know that."

She stopped laughing. "I suppose there are."

A new respect suddenly gleamed in her eyes. She smiled, with some trepidation. "I do know people. I could try to arrange something."

"I'd really appreciate that. I want to put a stop to this nightmare. Before any more Ginas go missing."

"You know, I honestly believe you do."

Outside, the freezing rain had turned to sleet. A thick layer of slush already covered the ground.

Willi couldn't just dump her on the sidewalk. "Come on. I'll hail you a cab home."

"But I haven't made any money."

He reached in a pocket and yanked out a fifty, for her a half month's salary. "I used enough of your time."

A long, black cab pulled up. Willi opened the door, and as she got in, her green eyes lit with a gratitude that penetrated right through the armor he'd carefully riveted around his heart.

He tried to close the door.

"Please." She blocked him, sounding more like a lonely young woman than a boot hooker. "Not for you. For me," she whispered. "I promise."

Despite every logical impulse still at work in his brain, he slid in.

And they drove off together.

Detektiv and whore.

Eight

The attic room, two flights up from her mother's apartment, was not much bigger than a prison cell and pretty much as drafty. A small coal stove in the corner served as both heat and kitchen. The single bed had an eiderdown cover of faded red roses. A window with a box of dead geraniums looked deep into a courtyard crisscrossed by laundry lines.

That was about as far as he saw before she pulled him into bed.

His own need shocked him.

In an irresistible explosion, the libidinous animal in him leapt awake from its hibernation, and with a primitive ferocity he'd forgotten he even possessed, he ravished her, heedless of all but his own overwhelming hunger. When he released, it seemed to never end.

Afterward he tried not to but couldn't help weeping softly in her arms. It had been such a long time.

A long, empty, painful time.

She stroked his hair and kissed his forehead and whispered, "It's okay, Willi. People need each other."

He felt guilty and ashamed.

And thrilled beyond belief.

He couldn't get close enough to her.

"Your turn next." He ran his nose along her velvety shoulders.

"You'd better believe it, lover."

She was naked except for the little, black demi-gloves, which he found unbelievably erotic.

"Give me a sec. I'll be right back." She kissed him.

For a few minutes she was gone in the bathroom, and when she climbed into bed again, it was in the most wistful, dreamy mood.

"What choice was there for a girl like me?" She told him about her life as they lay in each other's arms. "A factory. A go at show business. I tried both. Believe me. Can you picture me at sixteen standing ten hours a day twisting yarn into mop heads? For two years I did it. Until the Depression. Then I was out on my ass like everyone else. I figured I'd better use it. What did I know about dancing? Well, it wasn't my skills in tap or ballet that got me in the chorus line, *Liebchen*."

"Now, now, I've no doubt you were the most stunning girl in the show."

He took her breasts and kissed each one.

"I was pretty darn fantastic, actually."

"You don't have to convince me."

She seemed to ponder, then sat up, apparently deciding to prove her point. "Want to see?"

He had no chance to answer before she'd leaped from bed, pulling the cover with her, leaving him there stark naked. Cranking up a phonograph with great determination, she wrapped the coverlet around her waist and began raising and lowering her hip in time to the syncopated music launched into the popular hit, "Naughty Lola," the wisest girl on earth, whose pianola got "worked for all its worth." Holding out her arms as if embracing girls on either side she kicked first one leg than the other, Can-Can style. Up, down. Round and round. Her big white breasts bouncing in rhythm. He watched as if in a dream, thinking: My God, she's magnificent.

When she bowed, breathless, he applauded joyfully. She really was terribly good, he thought. Perhaps, had fate dealt her a different hand, it might have been her on the silver screen. And her demanding people about at the Hotel Adlon. But it wasn't. And inside something tugged at his heart. If only she'd sung about something a tad less . . . autobiographical.

"What is it, Willi?" She climbed back into bed and wrapped them both under the faded roses. "Don't you like my singing?"

"I love it." He kissed her.

The moment her tongue penetrated his mouth, the animal leapt back awake, ravenous again. How had he lived all this time neglecting its demands? But even as his body burned with delight, he couldn't help hearing her song playing over and over like a broken record: *The boys all love my music. I can't keep them away. So my little pianola . . . keeps working night and—*

Oh!

He felt himself nearing climax, but she pushed him away, hard.

"Don't you dare, buster."

He laughed, glad she wasn't a woman to hide her needs and make a man pay for it later. Kissing his way lovingly down her stomach, he gently lifted her legs.

"No. Not that. Do as I tell you."

A cold panic shot through him, threatening to send even the hungry beast into retreat. He saw those purple spike-heeled boots.

Heard her asking if he'd been a naughty boy. Felt himself bound tightly to the bed, his back and butt mercilessly whipped by her leather riding crop. But she surprised him, flipping onto her stomach, slowly, enticingly raising her buttocks.

"Spank me, Willi," she commanded. "And don't be gentle about it."

Now he really recoiled. Even more terrible than the thought of being bound and whipped was the idea of having to do it to someone else.

"You don't understand, *Liebchen*." She turned and looked back at him, her green eyes flaming with desire. "It's how I get my pleasure. Please, Willi. For me."

Arching, she raised her full white backside to him again.

And still he could not bring himself to hit her.

"Do it!" she commanded.

But it only made him shrink.

"For God's sakes, Willi." She was begging now. "You know how little pleasure I get in li—"

He smacked her hard with his open palm, then stared at the bright red fingers emerging on her flesh.

"Yes," she whimpered. "More please, Willi. Until I beg you to stop."

He awoke in the morning as if in a dream. No idea where he was. When he realized the weight on his arm was Paula, he pulled her to him and began making love to her the way he felt she should be made love to: gently, worshipfully. But again, at the height of their passion, she wanted him to spank her. He couldn't this time. He climbed from bed and looked around in a daze, stunned to realize it was seven o'clock, and that he was going to have to go to work in the same clothes he wore yesterday.

"You'll call again, I know." Paula pulled him by the tie as he tried to get out the door.

He kissed her quickly on the lips.

"Yes," he said. "But only because you're getting me onto the Great Gustave's yacht, my dear. Not because you want some schoolmaster to whip you into shape."

As he fled the dingy building, he made a note to call his cousin Kurt the moment he got to the office.

On the S-Bahn, even he got a jolt by the morning headlines: **Hindenburg Appoints New Chancellor—von Schleicher Vows Iron Fist!**

Von Schleicher, chancellor now. The third in as many years. "Stick with me, Kraus," the words reverberated. "You won't regret it."

Willi sure prayed not.

Down the long flight of steps from the station he emerged onto Alexanderplatz, the smell of grilled sausages from an open cart reminding him he hadn't had breakfast. It had got cold out. Cold enough to snow, he thought, although the sky was bright blue. As he stood on the corner devouring a leberwurst, he could still feel Paula's warm body in his arms. He comprehended why an impoverished young woman could turn to prostitution. But the pleasure she took from pain distressed him. He hadn't liked hitting her. Not any of the times she made him do it. The gratification it gave her though was undeniable. Why? Why did people get pleasure from pain? Wasn't life painful enough without confusing that which hurt and that which felt good?

Despite the sunshine and upbeat holiday windows at Tietz, featuring lingerie-clad mannequins flying reindeer toward 1933, as he trudged toward the Police Presidium, Willi felt miserable. He didn't understand life. Didn't want to. If only Paula could be different. How happy he could be with her. It was the first time since Vicki he felt this way. Alive.

Pausing for a double-decked bus with its bright blue ad for toothpaste, he thought . . . perhaps I can help her. Perhaps we could help each other.

Traffic swirled around Alexanderplatz, oblivious to the concentric worlds of life along the sidewalks. Up against the buildings, rows of beggars in little more than rags held out hats to passersby, many veterans of the Great War, legless, eyeless, noseless. Nearer the curbside, hundreds of the *Arbeitslos,* the out-of-work, milled about smoking listlessly, chatting pointlessly. Some spread blankets on the pavement, selling matches, pencils, shoelaces. Others stood with handwritten signs begging for a job. Most just hung about waiting for the weekly dole or the soup kitchen down the block to open. Hands in pockets, collars over ears, hats between their sunken shoulders. The Great Depression had left three-quarters of a million Berliners unemployed. One man with all his worldly possessions packed in filthy cardboard boxes on his shoulders shuffled past with wide dead eyes. Another sleep-walker, Willi thought.

A streetcar rolled by with a clattering screech, pulling several cars behind, each urging a visit to Wertheim's giant holiday sale just across the square. Leaning up against an advertising column with competing Nazi and Communist slogans—*Work, Freedom, and Bread!* versus *Work, Bread, and Freedom!*—Willi noticed an old pal of his, if that's what you could call him.

"Kai." He stopped and held out his hand.

The boy looked up startled, then broke into a huge grin, his thick, dangling gold earring glistening in the sun.

"Inspektor Kraus!" He took Willi's hand, shaking it gladly. "Always a pleasure. Particularly today, seeing as it's such a great morning for me."

Even among the myriad souls milling about the Alexander-platz, Kai stood out. He was one of Berlin's most famous Wild Boys, gangs of homeless teens who roamed together, surviving in basements and abandoned buildings, supporting themselves by everything from sidewalk performances to prostitution. Kai had his own gang, the Red Apaches, who worked the Tietz Department Store side of the square. They were easily identifiable by their red kerchiefs and black makeup around the eyes. Kai, their chieftain, a genuine blue-eyed Aryan, was always the most flamboyantly dressed, in a striped wool Mexican poncho, feathered bush cap, and of course his trademark gold earring. As tall as Gunther but far more chiseled and muscular, Kai was defiantly proud of his preference for boys. While he and his ilk were abhorrent to people like the Nazis, the Red Apaches had been instrumental in helping find the Child Eater. The SA for all its drumbeating had been useless.

"And what is so special about today?" Willi noticed a particular gleam in the boy's eyes.

"Why, it's my eighteenth birthday, and I've decided to settle down. So I've given up the gang. Handed it over to Huegler. At four this afternoon I report to my new position."

Knowing Kai hadn't attended a day of school since he was seven, Willi couldn't imagine a terribly upstanding career in store for him, despite the many fine characteristics he possessed. So he simply wished him the best of luck and added, "Remember, if there's anything I can ever do for you—"

"It's *I* who soon may be in a position to do things for *you*, Herr Inspektor." Kai winked mysteriously.

"She was there!" Gunther's cobalt gaze sizzled as if with X-ray vision.

Thank goodness he looked right through Willi's being in the same clothes as yesterday, although Ruta certainly hadn't.

"I sat there all night drinking beer. God, I love this assignment, Chief. Anyway, I kept steering the conversations to women's legs like you suggested. You'd be amazed how many leg-men there are. I always thought breasts were the thing. But not at that place. Finally, third or fourth guy I spoke with, I get into one of these greatest-legs-I-ever-saw conversations and he brings up this exotic-looking minx that showed up at the Black Stag last weekend wearing, check this out—a leopard coat!"

Well, there it was, Willi thought.

The princess, having first seen Dr. Meckel and then having

been hypnotized by the Great Gustave, went back to the Adlon, got ready for bed, then at midnight put on her leopard coat and took the train to Spandau, where she went into the Black Stag Inn and was never seen again. It still did not explain why, if she was absolutely normal after the hypnosis as her husband insisted, she would willingly deliver herself several hours later directly into her kidnappers' hands.

"What about Schumann and pal?" Willi asked.

Gunther shook his head. "*Nichts.* But I did hear something about an institute where several of the doctors worked. Couldn't get a name."

"Keep drinking with the swine," Willi said. "We're getting somewhere here. Although, where that is I'm not certain I really want to go."

Nine

Arriving at the Berlin Center for Psychoanalysis, Willi was amazed to discover Kurt hard at work packing all his books away into crates.

"*Mensch,*" he said, "what gives here?"

His tall, bald, bespectacled cousin smiled somberly.

"You look good, Willi. Better than you've any right to. What does it seem like's going on? I'm closing shop. Getting out. If you had any sense, you'd do the same."

Just what Einstein said to him yesterday. Funny. He'd always viewed Kurt, two years younger, as the Einstein of his family. A genius who'd soared to the top of his profession, published papers, and gave university lectures. So superrational. Why this sudden hysteria?

"You know what we had here last week? Storm troopers. A whole gang of them. Must have been thirty. Burst right in during the middle of the day, marching up and down the hallways shouting, 'Down with Jewish science! Germany for Germans!'"

"So you're running?"

Was it because Willi'd fought in the war, he wondered, faced the greatest dangers a man could, that he didn't feel this wave of panic gripping so many others?

Kurt stopped packing. "Yes, Willi. I am. I am taking Kathe and the kids and never looking back."

Willi felt a pit open in his stomach. "Where to?"

"Palestine. January second we leave for Bremerhaven. From there we sail to Haifa. My sister's rented a place for us to live. In Tel Aviv."

Willi had a sister in Tel Aviv, too. Greta had emigrated with her husband in 1925 because they felt there was no future in Europe for Jews. Willi got letters from her telling him about the first Hebrew city since ancient times, how free one felt there, how beautiful and white and fresh it was, built right along the sea. He liked the sea all right but—

"At least get the boys out." Kurt's eyes burned behind his glasses. "Do you have any idea what's going on in the schools? They're turning the Jewish kids into outcasts."

"We're sending Erich back to Jewish school," Willi conceded. "Right after the New Year."

"Willi, things are not going to get any better, don't you see that? They've unleashed the genie. There's no putting it back. You want to know about hypnosis? Listen to Hitler and Goebbels. You'll learn all you have to. They're hypnotizing Germany. Turning it into a nation of sleepwalkers."

"Von Schleicher's in control now. And he despises the Nazis."

"*Ach.* You don't want to face it."

"What I want from you, Kurt, is to explain how it's possible for a person who's been awakened from a hypnotic trance and is seemingly completely normal, to suddenly, inexplicably, revert back into it hours later."

Kurt put down a stack of books. "Easy." He pulled off his

glasses and started cleaning them with a handkerchief. "It's called posthypnotic suggestion. A person's given a cue under hypnosis. A word, a sound, a time of day. When that cue is triggered, no matter how many hours later"—he put the glasses back on and stared at Willi—"they feel an irresistible compulsion to carry out whatever they'd been commanded."

Astonishing. The ugly pieces of this puzzle were filling in. The Bulgarian princess with her sprained ankle had gone to Dr. Meckel. He probably sent her to Klub Hell for dinner. Gustave had chosen her as a "volunteer" and given her a posthypnotic command, so that when it reached midnight, she put on her coat, took the S-Bahn out to Spandau, and went to the Black Stag Inn. Willi was dealing with a level of conspiracy here he would never have believed possible. More than ever he was glad he had enlisted von Schleicher, who now wielded the entire power of the German state.

Before saying good-bye to the last of his extended family here, he needed to ask one more thing. It was hard.

"Kurt, can you explain to me why a person would get sexual pleasure from . . . pain."

"Oh-ho. Now there's a topic we could spend several weeks discussing, and not come up with any conclusive answers. But just now, I'm afraid there isn't time, Willi. There just isn't—"

As if to punctuate his point, the bells of the Kaiser Wilhelm Church began pealing the hour.

Dr. Shurze was kind enough to give Willi the gold Nazi Party pin allegedly found on the Mermaid's gray garment in order to try to trace its origin. He was even kind enough to give Willi the name of the goldsmith that manufactured all Nazi Party pins, H. Bieberman on the Dorotheen Strasse. Willi got there before the jeweler shut and had the kind assistance of H. Bieberman himself, who examined the item under a magnifying glass and identified its manufacture number and was able to say with certainty that the twenty-four-karat solid-gold pin had been given to Hermann Meckel on the seventh anniversary of the November 9 Beer Hall Putsch, for his longtime service to the SA medical staff.

Adding flesh to the unmistakable finger of guilt pointing directly at the doctor was that the surgeon, according to his jeweler, came into the store only Wednesday morning, extremely upset, and told Bieberman he'd inexplicably lost this pin at a dinner party the night before. He wished a replacement made at once, for which he would personally pay. Only he must have an exact replica. Imagine, losing such a thing! And he demanded Bieberman make every effort to finish the replacement with all haste. What doubt then could there be that Meckel, top orthopedist and longtime Nazi, was the surgeon Willi was after?

Except that if the pin went missing Tuesday night—and why would Meckel lie to his jeweler about that?—it could certainly not have got on the Mermaid's garment while she was still alive because she'd already been dead for three days. It had to have been nipped off his lapel at some point, most likely at that dinner party, then planted in the morgue. Meckel may or may not have sent the Bulgarian princess to Klub Hell, but he definitely was not the surgeon who'd mangled Gina Mancuso's legs.

Someone was trying to frame him.

"Herr Bieberman, thank you. You've been of tremendous service."

Willi decided to pay a visit to the "retired" Dr. Hoffnung, out in Wilmersdorf.

To his great chagrin, however, he learned from the building concierge that the Hoffnungs no longer resided there.

"But where have they gone?"

"This, I can not say. Only that they have gone and left no forwarding address."

For the first time real fear shivered through Willi's body.

Hoffnung and his wife both disappeared, with no forwarding address?

He suddenly felt as if dark hands were weaving a web around him.

And he was a stupid fly.

Book Two

ISLAND OF THE DEAD

Ten

DECEMBER 1932

"There is a young lady waiting in your office, Herr Inspektor-Detektiv." Ruta smiled through curls of cigarette smoke. "Very sexy. Indeed, one of the sexiest young ladies I've ever met." She was laying it on thick, staring at Willi with motherly scrutiny. "Normally I would not approve of such a woman. I wouldn't think her wholesome. But this one, well, don't ask me why—I find agreeable. Perhaps because she's a chorus girl. Like I was. Yes, we had a nice long chat, Fräulein Hoffmeyer and I."

Willi closed the door behind him.

Paula sat cross-legged on the chair opposite his desk. Gone were the short-shorts. The garters. The purple boots. Instead, a suit: coordinated shoes, matching jacket, sweater blouse. It was as if a magic wand had transformed her into a respectable young woman. The black lace demi-gloves were replaced with suede kid. The hat, in the latest fashion, high peaked, short brimmed, dipped in a curve over one eye. She even had the latest 1933 skirt, he noticed, tragically several inches longer than last year's. But she looked fantastic in it.

Perfect.

How dignified her composure. How resolute her self-assurance. She must have spent most of the fifty marks he'd given her on the outfit. And it thrilled him. It was far more than just the clothes. She was showing respect. To herself. To him. Without the garish makeup her face was so lovely. He was ashamed of the sudden swelling of his eyes. It *was* possible then. She *could* change. He *had* helped her. And now she'd come to help him.

"Don't look so shocked, Herr Inspektor-Detektiv," she said with a half smile. "A little assistance and most any girl can look nice."

"No. You have to be nice to look nice. And you look just . . ." He lowered his voice. "Wonderful."

"I'm sorry to barge in like this unannounced. But I thought you'd like to know right away. The Great Gustave is holding a holiday party on his yacht this Saturday. I wrangled us invites."

"Us?"

"Well, you can't go to these things unescorted. It just isn't done."

Willi laughed.

"Besides, you need someone to look out for you in that crowd."

"Do I?"

"Who knows . . . maybe you're not so smart as you think. And even if you are, brains sometimes aren't enough. You need street smarts with these characters. They may be dressed in top hats and tails, but they're gutter rats, all of them."

"Well, it just so happens some of my best friends are gutter rats."

"Oh, you." She play-slapped him.

"Had breakfast yet? There's a wonderful place around the corner."

"I'd be honored." She daintily clasped her purse.

When he pulled the door open, Ruta pretended not to be listening.

"Fräulein Hoffmeyer and I will be out for a short time, Frau Garber. I'll check in for my messages."

"*Jawohl,* Herr Inspektor-Detektiv," she said drily. "*Bon appétit.*"

They wound up going directly to his place.

After Vicki died and the boys went to Dahlem, he'd moved into a small but comfortable one-bedroom in Nuremberger Strasse, just a block from Tauentzien where Paula worked. "Familiar neighborhood," she said as he held the door for her, the deep tolling of the Kaiser Wilhelm Church bells following them inside.

The living room was filled with sunlight, overlooking the busy street below with its screeching streetcars and traffic. Two of the four walls were completely filled with bookshelves. She looked around with genuine amazement.

"What's this, a library?"

Opposite the windows she stopped to examine a dozen or so old family photos, transfixed by the long-bearded men with funny hats, the wedding ceremonies under elaborate canopies, the young boys wrapped in Hebrew prayer shawls. Entrancing to her was the picture of little Willi on his first day of school in 1903, in a sailor suit with short knickers, carrying a decorated paper cone filled with fruit and candies.

"Look how precious."

Next to it hung a group portrait of twenty or so young men in the imperial uniform of the Great War. Willi had been a captain, she saw. And had won the Iron Cross, First Class. It didn't seem to surprise her. More visceral was the wedding portrait with Vicki. Her chest heaved as she looked at it.

"Wow," she said, wiping a tear with her suede-gloved finger. "She really was beautiful. So ... refined. How you must have loved her. And look here, the boys." Paula moved on to Erich and Stefan. "How they take after you."

Willi felt like a schoolboy himself, playing hooky. He couldn't believe he'd actually brought a girl home at ten in the morning. On a workday. Not since he'd sneaked off to a French whore-house before the battle of Passchendaele had he felt such a buzz of illicit excitement. Paula here with him, transformed into a wholesome young woman, it was just . . . a fantasy come true. He'd mourned for Vicki so long he didn't even realize how strong his passion for life remained. Not mere existence. But life itself: thrilling, satisfying, full of promise. He didn't want to be alone anymore, living only for his work. He wanted to really live. To love and be loved. To screw Paula every day!

He took her in his arms and kissed her as he had once kissed Vicki, with all his heart and soul. She trembled and sighed, succumbing tenderly. They fell to the couch, their breaths in-creasing. He pulled up her sweater and went for her breasts. But she wouldn't take off her gloves.

"Willi, give me a minute." She wiggled away. "Unmake the bed, sweetheart. Put on some music." Taking her purse, she dis-appeared behind the bathroom door.

Willi prepared the bed as commanded, stiff as a cannon. He stayed that way for endless minutes. When she emerged, she was completely naked except for those black lace demi-gloves. The sight of them felt like a bucket of ice water. Why had she gone and done that—reminded him of what she did for a living?

As she approached though, holding her large, white breasts toward him, their long pink nipples erect, her eyes glazed with such watery desire he had to admit his prick got stiffer than ever. When she climbed atop him, the connection was so warm, so wonderful, he felt as if she'd been sent like an angel from above, to ease him out of his years of grief.

Then he began to fear the moment she would beg to get hit. The thought sent his mind reeling. Since their last time together he'd read up on the subject. Psychiatrists theorized sexual masochism was a neurotic "eroticizing" of early childhood trauma. Whether or not that was true in Paula's case, or at all, he decided the relevant point was that *he* did not get pleasure from it. That in fact he found it genuinely *un*pleasurable. What he was going to do if she wanted it again, he didn't know.

He wanted to give the woman her share of happiness.

Fortunately, she remained as conventional in her lovemaking that day as in her dress. They stayed in bed all morning, and well into the afternoon. Only the sunlight fading from his bedroom and the tolling bells of the Kaiser Wilhelm Church roused him from her charms.

"My God," he said, feeling like a teenage truant. "I've got to get back."

After his shower she was still lying in bed, stroking her hair with her demi-gloved fingers. "You can stay, you know," he said. "All day if you'd like."

"Can I really?" she replied dreamily.

"Yes. Yes." He kissed her up and down the neck. As he stepped into his trousers though, she sat up, pulling the blanket over her breasts.

"Willi, you know you never told me. How did Gina die?"

He paused before pulling up his zipper. "She drowned," he said, grabbing his shirt. "In the Havel. Her body washed up just beneath the citadel in Spandau."

"*Mein Gott,*" Paula stammered, clutching the blanket to her throat. "You mean . . . they threw her off that yacht?"

"No," he replied without thinking.

Her green eyes flashed on his, demanding the truth. "How do you know?"

He pictured Gina Mancuso's deformed legs lying there in the icy water. "You'll just have to trust me."

When he got back to the office, it was nearly three o'clock. He expected Ruta to be all over him like a ruffled mother hen, but found her instead in a state more akin to apoplexy. "Willi," she stammered, not even realizing she'd addressed him informally, something she only did at parties when they'd been drinking. "You cannot imagine who just left this office ten minutes ago."

"Pancho Villa," he said, making a stab at humor.

"Nein, nein." She looked at him, positively white with fear, unable even to get her cigarette to light. "A captain of the Brownshirts, Willi . . . with a message from the SA führer! Ernst Roehm invites you to dinner tonight at the Kaiserhof. Nine p.m.!"

Willi felt his throat dry out. So, von Schleicher hadn't been bluffing.

"Well, Ruta, nothing to fret over a little dinner invitation."

One by one he'd been examining the dossiers of the top orthopedic surgeons in Germany, but so far nothing seemed to link anyone else to this case. Meckel may have been just a fall guy, but what choice was there except to go after him and try to figure out who'd laid the frame?

"Willi. You mustn't. You absolutely mustn't. These people aren't human."

"Yes, they are, Ruta. All too human."

The massive Hotel Kaiserhof on Wilhelm Platz was just down the block from the Reichs Chancellery, much older and far gloomier than the glittering Adlon, but unquestionably among the most formidable Berlin hostelries. The moment Willi entered the brass revolving doors he recalled that the upper floors had recently been rented to the Nazi Party—as their headquarters. Was it any wonder he felt cast back to his army days, penetrating enemy lines? The lobby was positively swarming with Nazis, SA Brownshirts mainly, but a whole horde of Blackshirts, too. Black being the uniform of the *Schutzstaffel*—the SS—originally Hitler's bodyguard but more recently evolved into the Party's intelligence-gathering unit. In its near civil war with the Communist Red Front, the Blackshirts provided the who, what, and where the Brownshirts went to battle with.

Icy prongs stabbed his neck as he made his way into this crowd. He felt as if his nose had grown several inches and he were wearing a tall yellow dunce cap. After several steps across the red carpet though, he began to notice brown and black shirts alike stepping aside for him. Why? He couldn't understand— until finally he got it. To face Ernst Roehm, a real soldier's soldier, he'd pinned his Iron Cross to the upper right of chest of his jacket, a transparent tactic no doubt. But he figured he could use all the help he could get. Now the ornate medal was working the miracle of Moses, parting the sea, earning him nods, salutes even. Why not? He deserved it.

A week before the great spring offensive of 1918 he'd led a squad of five men, including Fritz Hohenzollern, deep behind French lines to survey enemy artillery and troop positions. After more than a week sending reports back via carrier pigeon, they were discovered and found themselves trapped in a farmhouse, battling it out with a whole French company. Willi had stayed behind to cover his men while they made it back to no-man's-land. Three days later the entire German army was astonished to hear that he'd turned up alive, too, on the German side of the lines. In the Great War, many won medals for bravery. Many even won the Iron Cross. But few earned the highest of all honors: an Iron Cross, First Class.

All at once the crowd in the Kaiserhof stiffened.

Out of the elevator came a small gang of men, everyone quickly parting to let them through. Willi's blood got cold. Unmistakable among them was the blimpish figure of Hermann Göring, the number two Nazi in Germany. Despite his reputation as a fearless World War flying ace, he looked absurd in wide-thighed uniform trousers, belly hanging like the *Graf Zeppelin* over his belt. On the far side, furiously limping with one short leg, was Josef Goebbels, the brilliant propagandist. To his left, the handsome Nazi Party secretary Gregor Strasser. And in the center, pushing aside his famous lock of hair, twisting his square mustache every conceivable direction, Adolf Hitler himself, screaming at the top of his famous lungs. "It is betrayal of the highest order, Strasser! You cannot talk your way out of it!"

"On the contrary, *mein Führer*," Strasser defended himself. "I think only of the Party. And how to save it from bankruptcy and ruin."

"You dare! You dare!" Hitler stopped short and raised his fist as if about to strike him. "Von Schleicher offers you vice chancellorship and you tell him you'll consider it? Any idiot can see he's trying to undermine our unity. Destroy everything I have worked a decade for: One people. One party. *One* Führer!"

Flamboyantly turning his back, the enraged Führer resumed his rapid stride across the lobby, his short tie flying behind him. As he neared, the jagged bolts of hysteria grew in his eyes. The man's soul, Willi thought, as Germany's savior raced past like a runaway horse, is as twisted as his swastika.

"If the Party falls apart"—Hitler turned to yell to Göring and Goebbels, both racing to keep up with him—"I'll put an end to it all in one second." He aimed a finger at his head. "You'll see. But before I do"—he glared back at Strasser—"I'll crush him like a cockroach!"

As ostentatiously as they entered, the top Nazis vanished through the revolving doors.

This little drama was quickly followed up by the surprise Willi got when entering the Apollo Room, smallest of the Kaiserhof's many banquet halls, where it seemed as though he'd walked straight into a Roman orgy.

Or Greek.

Beneath a scaled replica of the Fountain of Apollo, backed by a roaring fireplace, thirty or so mostly young, strapping, blond Aryan exemplars, many naked from the waist up, caroused around a long banquet table decked with pine boughs and glowing red candles. Each held a hefty arm around the shoulder of the man to his right, the other clasping a giant beer stein as they swayed back and forth and sang along with an accordion:

Bier hier! Bier hier!
Oder ich fall um!

Willi had never seen such a collection of hypermasculine beefcake, as if a whole herd of stud bulls had been corralled at one table: giant square torsos, arms the size of tree trunks, rippled, rock-hard, brainless creatures, lacking only rings in their noses. Yet some of them, he noticed, were cozily snuggling on a neighbor's lap, or running fingers through the blond hair of the stud bull beside him.

Bier hier! Bier hier!
Oder ich fall um!

Seated as if on a throne in the center was the short, dumpy figure of Ernst Roehm, absolute master of the SA. He looked like a neighborhood butcher, Willi thought—cropped hair parted razor-sharp down the middle, a block face with a squashed-up pug nose. His relationship to the Nazis went back to a time when he was more powerful than Hitler, the only Party leader, it was said, who addressed the Führer with the familiar *du* instead of *Sie*. Hitler depended on him, an absolute genius at organization, like a third arm. But a year ago a Communist paper, whose editor had since disappeared, published a most explicit packet of his personal correspondence, and Roehm's homosexuality became front-page news. Not that he'd ever tried to hide it, but it left the SA commander with a distinct lack of friends in the Nazi brass, according to Fritz's sources. And now Roehm was as dependent on the Führer as the Führer was on him.

The man may have given up the army to become a political soldier, but he remained a soldier to the bone, and the moment he spotted the Iron Cross, First Class, on Willi's chest, he rose. "Herr Inspektor-Detektiv. How excellent you could make it. I hope you're hungry."

"*Nein.* I can only stay a moment."

Willi's attention had by now been drawn to perhaps the most ironic surprise of the evening. Directly next to the SA leader, Roehm's brutal hand stroking his blond head, sat the chief of the Red Apaches—Kai, sans makeup and gold earring, transformed into a rather sinister-looking Nazi, his normally merry blue eyes sharp and distant now as a wolf's. So this was his new "position." Why be surprised? He'd simply graduated from the world of childhood gangs into the big league. Yet there was a real sting of betrayal. Kai liked him. They'd helped each other. More than once. For a second, the eighteen-year-old's sharp Prussian gaze took him in and, with a secret glow, seemed to say, *Isn't this ridiculous? Me, a Nazi!* Then he looked away as if he'd never seen Willi in his life.

Roehm had meanwhile taken Willi's refusal to sit as well as could be expected. *"Ach so."* Roehm assumed an amused tolerance. "Let us speak over there then, in the corner.

"I know of course what this is in reference to, Herr Inspektor-Detektiv," the SA leader added as they stood face-to-face. He was truly ugly, a good foot shorter than Willi, his face badly scarred from bullet wounds and burns. "And you will have my one hundred percent cooperation."

Willi also recalled von Schleicher saying the brute was a man one could do business with. He certainly spoke more like a company executive than the usual shrieking Nazi.

"When I assumed command of the *Sturmabteilung*"—Roehm folded his arms thoughtfully—"in 1930 . . . we had roughly seventy-seven thousand members. One single year and we tripled our strength. This year we doubled it again. The problems for any organization with such rapid growth are numerous, I assure you. The task of absorbing so many tens of thousands each month, keeping them in line. We've had outbreaks of poor discipline; I'll admit it. We've suffered a lack of capable leaders. But I have never tolerated disobedience of any sort, and certainly not criminal activity. Cohesion and discipline are of paramount importance to me. If there is even one rotten apple, it must be purged."

Roehm stopped to catch his breath, casting a fierce glance at Willi. "All levels of our Party agree that power in Germany can only be attained legally and with the support of the army. General von . . . that is *Chancellor* von Schleicher has made an urgent request that I offer you my assistance." Roehm paused. "Of course, I am not fond of Jews."

"No less than I am of Nazis, I'm sure."

Roehm lifted his battle-scarred chin. "Then I must ask you, Herr Inspektor-Detektiv, what exactly do you need from me in regards to your investigation of General Meckel?"

"First off, that you ensure the safety of my officers and I as we conduct it."

"*Natürlich.*"

"We will want to search Meckel's residence. The SA guards posted there will have to stand down."

"Very well. Let me know in advance, and it will be done."

"I want every scrap of information you have on Dr. Meckel, including his file from the Charité Hospital archives that went missing."

"You shall have it."

"And I want Meckel completely in the dark about this."

"In the dark he shall be, Herr Inspektor-Detektiv. Completely in the dark."

Eleven

Soft candlelight filled the dining room when Willi entered his apartment. Paula had dinner waiting. She took his coat and hung it up like a perfect bride.

"It's nearly ten, you know. But don't tell me: an Inspektor's job is never done."

It had been two years since he'd come home to a meal. To a woman. He could hardly control his excitement.

"Don't," she said, pushing his face off her neck. "I'm starving, Willi. Let's eat, please."

She was wearing those damned black gloves again, he noticed. What was with those things? Another of her fetishes? Seeing the dreamy-eyed look though as she placed the food on the table, he opted not to make an issue of it. He'd had enough posturing for one night.

Paula was a most decent cook. Not like Vicki, of course.

Vicki had gone to Paris for cooking classes. But Paula had taken the few things he'd had around, added some fresh fish, and made a fine bouillabaisse. He was proud of her. More than that. He was falling in love with her.

"Paula, don't go back to work. I'll take care of you."

She turned her head, looking at her plate, her tight-waved hair glistening in the candlelight. "For God's sake, Willi. Don't rush. There's no need to."

"Don't go back to work."

He lifted her chin.

Their eyes met.

"You think I'm crying because I'll miss those purple boots? Now eat the damn soup before it gets cold."

Over dessert she brought up Gina Mancuso again. "I can't stop thinking about her. When I'm sleeping. When I'm awake. It's like a ghost haunting me. Telling me to go after Gustave." She dropped her fork. "This girl was really something, Willi. A tower of strength. I don't mean physically, but inside. A real fighter. Maybe it was her American spirit; I don't know. I remember once when she argued for a raise. She wasn't afraid to confront the big shots, like we were. But where did it land her, huh? In the river."

Willi had been thinking about what had landed Gina Mancuso in the river, too. All this time he'd been assuming it was somebody else. That she had been murdered. But now he found himself pondering, if whoever had operated on those legs wanted her dead—why not just bury her? Or make her steak tartare? Why throw her in a river and take even the slightest chance she might be discovered?

Paula's words rang through his brain: *a real fighter. Tower of strength.* If that was true . . . perhaps she *hadn't* been thrown in. He recalled the strange smile of tranquillity, triumph even, on her dead, blue lips. Perhaps she'd gone into that water of her own free will. Perhaps . . . she'd escaped. If so, then after she'd been found, the surgeon who disfigured her would have no choice but to try to pin the deed on some other qualified candidate . . . a comrade, no doubt.

It was snowing the next morning, big, fluffy flakes that melted as soon as they hit the sidewalk. The streetcar tracks glistened against the gray cobblestones. All the little dachshunds had on winter sweaters. At the Zoo Station, Willi found himself staring once again at the headlines. This time they felt like a sword between his shoulders: **Doctor Suicide! Meckel, Famed Orthopedist, Shoots Self in Head!**

For a moment he just stood there with the morning crowds rushing by, his eyes shut tight. So this was how Ernst Roehm did business. He'd kept Meckel in the dark all right. All Willi could see was that hideous battle-scarred face. With a shiver that seemed to penetrate his very marrow, he realized that now every step he took was behind enemy lines. By the time he'd made it to the office a quiet determination had seized him. He closed the door and picked up the phone. "Ava," he said when he reached his sister-in-law. "I'm going to ask you to do something terribly important. I can't explain it now, but it's essential that you do exactly as I— Ava, what is it? You're crying?"

There was a long painful moment before she was able to speak.

God forbid . . . not one of the boys.

"I lost my job, Willi."

"What? Fritz fired you?"

"No, not Fritz. Ullstein Press. They're letting go of half the Jews on their staff."

"But that's absurd. The Ullsteins are Jewish."

"They think the Nazis are growing too powerful. They're tripping over themselves trying to keep low and stay out of their crosshairs."

Willi couldn't conceive of how to respond.

"Listen. This only makes what I have to ask of you simpler. I want you to get the boys out of the country, Ava. At once."

"You can't be serious."

"Take them to Paris. By car. By train. I don't care how. But go. Stay with your Aunt Hedda. Or book a hotel if you must."

"Willi, school is still in session."

"Never mind. You are to take them immediately. Your parents ought to go, too."

"But . . . for how long?"

"Not long. A few weeks at most, I hope. I'll come out and speak with you tonight."

"You haven't forgotten? Tonight's Stefan's winter festival. You promised to be there."

"I will be. But, Ava . . . in the meantime . . . make the necessary arrangements. Please. By tomorrow afternoon—I want those boys out of Germany."

"They're positive dummkopfs down in Missing Persons," Gunther complained as he arrived in Willi's office carrying a stack of files practically as tall as he. "They can't even put two and two together." He dumped the small mountain on Willi's desk. "If that's the way the department is run, it's no wonder people like the Nazis think the police are inept."

Willi appreciated the frustration, if not the point of view. "What is all this, Gunther?" he mumbled, distracted. He couldn't stop thinking of Hoffnung suddenly, and his wife. Where could they have vanished? Those SA thugs would stop at nothing. He was right to get the children out.

"The sleepwalkers! It took me a day and a half working with that nincompoop in Mutze's office, but I finally dug up all these. Can you believe it? People have been roaming the streets of Berlin like zombies for a year now, vanishing into thin air, and these fools never think to put it all together."

Willi and Gunther worked the rest of the day to sort through the files. By late afternoon the picture had grown not only clearer but far more frightening. In the past nine months, three different showgirls, one Greek, one Russian, and one Serbian, had all been seen "sleepwalking" the night they'd disappeared. Mila Markovitch, the Serb, had been working in nightclubs where the Great Gustave was appearing. She was seen boarding an S-Bahn train in the direction of Spandau. In addition, two female members of a Czechoslovakian track team had vanished under similar circumstances after a "Mystery Night" hosted by the Great Gustave. Although they found no connection between Gustave and two sets of female twins—one Polish, one Italian—nor an entire family of Hungarian dwarfs, all these, too, disappeared after witnesses claimed they appeared to be "going somewhere in their sleep." Not a blond-haired, blue-eyed German was among them. And not a bit of evidence other than circumstantial that linked Gustave to their disappearances. Where the hell was he sending these people?

And why?

Sometime after four, Ruta danced in with a large envelope just arrived by messenger. "Somebody got an unmarked package," she teased. But handing it to Willi, she noticed it was not unmarked. On the back, the return address was clearly stamped with a large black swastika.

"Don't open it," she stammered. "It could be a stink bomb."

It was in a sense. The files of the late Dr. Hermann Meckel.

Ernst Roehm had followed through on one promise, at least.

Willi and Gunther pushed aside all the other stacks. Meckel's dossier was thick, but deadly boring. An excruciatingly detailed family biography went back centuries, with a minor novel about his medical training, a synopsis of the papers he'd given, including the one Gunther had already found on bone transplantation, and even more numerous pages on the various professional associations he'd belonged to. The committees he sat on. The clinics he served. One particularly odious-sounding involvement with something called the Institute for Racial Hygiene had been terminated six months ago, no explanation why. Willi made a note to check the dossiers of the other top orthopedists for any reference to this place. He was about to turn the page when Gunther grabbed his hand.

"Wait a second. Hold that page up to the light, Chief. Look."

In the column following the Institute for Racial Hygiene, under "Associates," the bright light revealed what appeared to have been a list of names blotted over in white so as to make them illegible. Willi grabbed a blank sheet of paper and tried to trace the names, but nothing came through.

"Yoskowitz," they said simultaneously.

Willi slipped the page in an envelope. "All right. I'm off to my son's school tonight. I'll take this to her first. You keep working on these."

"Right, sir. And then it's back out to the Black Stag for me."

"*Ach so.* Poor Gunther."

"Not at all. I happen to be bringing along a most attractive date tonight."

Willi raised an eyebrow. "Well, don't get her into any trouble, Gunther. And I don't mean the usual type."

"Yes, sir. I know, sir. No, you don't have to worry. She's like me, sir. A solid republican."

Bessie Yoskowitz had a small studio down the street in a handsome new office block called Alexander Haus, right across from Wertheim's. As he entered, Willi could hardly ignore a noisy detachment of SA Brownshirts in front of the famous department store, holding signs with grotesque caricatures and chanting, *"Every time you buy from Jews, you harm your fellow Germans! Every time you buy from—"*

Yoskowitz, a tiny-framed woman in her early sixties, gray hair meticulously pulled in a bun atop her head, with a distinct Polish/Yiddish accent left over from youth, was among Berlin's most accomplished paper conservators. Her skilled fingers worked on everything from Egyptian papyrus for the Pergamon to numerous police-related documents, such as what Willi now brought her.

"I see." She looked over the page with a thick magnifying glass of the sort the jeweler had used. "Yes, of course it's possible. I've got chemicals that can lift the white ink right off the black. But it'll take time. You see the work I got piled up here?"

"Bessie—"

"I know. I know. For Kripo it's top priority. It's Friday already, so give me till Monday. That's Christmas Eve. We'll close early. Let's say noon then, huh?"

"You're the best."

"Listen, Willi." Her tiny hand stopped him from leaving. "Before you go. I hope you don't find this impertinent. But with things as they are . . . I was wondering. By any chance . . . might you have a hint of what is really going to happen, politically I mean?"

Even on the sixth floor they could hear the echoes from the street: *"Every time you buy from Jews—"*

Despite their electoral losses—or precisely because of them—the Nazis had ratcheted up their anti-Semitic campaigns, calling for boycotts against Jewish businesses, harrassing Jews in public places. One old, bearded man had been pushed to his death from a moving train. Such atrocities inevitably made front-page news and terrorized at least 1 percent of the population, which is all Germany's Jews comprised. A mere six hundred thousand people, according to Hitler, destroying the German nation.

"You see, after all these years I'm still not a citizen. And the Hitlerites—may their name be cursed—if they ever really came to power, it's people like me they'd go after, no?"

"I really doubt that, Bessie." Willi patted her little hand. "I think they have more important prey." Like me, he thought morosely.

"But if you should ever get some idea which way the wind will blow . . ."

"You'll be the first to know. Promise."

At the Young Judea School, tucked behind a high wall on a side street in Schoneburg, every second person that night seemed to have the same request. Greenburg the accountant. Steiner the plumber. Rosenbloom the insurance man. Stefan's teacher. Stefan's principal. Even Stefan's rabbi. All approached Willi at one point or another wanting the same advice. What should we do? What? What? "Take precautions if it makes you feel more secure," he began to answer each the same. "But I can tell you von Schleicher will do everything in his power to destroy the Nazis." But don't you think . . . and isn't it possible . . . and couldn't it be . . . and what if God forbid . . . At last he felt like crying aloud, *What do you think I am, the Great Gustave? How should I know what tomorrow will bring?*

The winter festival celebrated the story of Hanukkah. The Hebrew revolt against the ancient Greeks. The miracle of the temple lamp lasting eight days instead of one. The songs. The dancing. All seemed especially warm and hopeful to the uneasy crowd of Jewish parents filling the auditorium that night, Willi included. During the performance he turned to Ava, seated next to him. The quiet expression on her face belied the nervous shifting in her chair.

Yes, she said wordlessly, with just one glance. *It's all arranged.*

"How about your parents—do they know yet?" he whispered.

Her head shook rapidly back and forth.

The big confrontation happened later, at the Gottmans' house in Dahlem.

"It's not because I'm afraid the Nazis are about to seize power," he made sure to emphasize. "I've become involved in a murder investigation which has taken a rather sinister turn. The people I'm after may well attempt to intimidate me by threatening my family."

"These people, they're Nazis?" Max Gottman seemed to have no doubt.

Willi didn't answer.

"You really think *Mutti* and I should go, too?"

"I can arrange a police guard for the house. The business I don't think you need to worry about."

"And what about you?" Willi was surprised to see his mother-in-law looking at him with real fear.

"Me? I'm the last one you need to worry about, *Mutti*."

Stefan took the news well enough. "Oh, boy, Paris for a holiday!"

But his older brother looked about with grave, sad eyes. "Why do I feel like we'll never see this place again?"

"Nonsense." Willi squeezed Erich's shoulder. "I told you, it's only until I catch these bad guys."

He made sure though to slip Ava a small valise to take along, full of documents and family heirlooms.

The apartment was dark when he got home. He didn't like the feeling. Paula had left a note on the table: *Went to my place for the night. Needed to take care of some things. All's set for tomorrow— yacht sails at noon. Pick me up eleven. And don't forget . . . look like a Nazi! Your Paula-wutzi.*

He hung up his coat and went to the bedroom. As soon as he turned on the light, he knew something was wrong. His desk. The books. They weren't in order. Instinctively he spun around. No one was in the apartment. He checked everywhere. But at last, when he came back and sat at his desk, he knew he wasn't being paranoid. Someone had gone through his drawers, all right. The white envelope in which he always kept a couple hundred spare marks was missing. He banged the drawer and stared at the wall as if a bullet had entered his gut. Why would she take his money when she knew he would gladly give it to her?

Twelve

Down several dark hallways in the Police Presidium a set of double doors led to the mysterious Department K, where Kripo agents could procure not only identity papers but whole new wardrobes and whatever else necessary for an investigative alias. At eight a.m. Willi arrived to be transformed not into a Nazi but a wealthy factory owner from the industrial city of Essen. His dark, curly hair was fitted with a light brown wig, and his eyes shaded with a pair of tinted tortoiseshell glasses. Genuinely impressive, he thought, was the two-piece wool dinner suit with silk lapels and a silk stripe down the trouser legs. The latest from Savile Row. By the time he left at ten thirty-five, even his car had been fitted with new license plates that confirmed his identity as Siegfried Grieber, chief stockholder of Ruhr Coal and Coke.

At eleven he was waiting for Paula outside her apartment

building. People on the street were staring at him. It was not every day a BMW 320 sports coupe driven by a man in eveningwear parked on this block.

When Paula emerged, a small crowd gathered.

"Look—Paula's become a movie star!"

She certainly was all dolled up like one. But like some swank sister from a bad B movie, Willi thought, in a tight pink evening gown with great puffed sleeves festooned with bows and a neckline that plunged God knew where. Over her shoulders she had a full-length black cape outlined in marabou.

"Getting married?" an old woman asked.

"Yes, that's it." Paula held out her hands like a chanteuse to her adoring fans. Willi saw she was wearing those damned black lace gloves still. "I'm off to the chapel now. Wish me luck!"

Mein Gott," she exclaimed, climbing into the front seat next to him. "I hardly recognize you." Her glassy eyes took him in, and she broke into a fit of laughter. "It's astonishing, really. I can't even tell you're . . ."

"Jewish?"

"Yes."

"Well, isn't that the point?"

"Of course it is, *Liebling.* I'm not criticizing you."

"The nose by the way is all mine."

"You have a perfectly darling nose. Did I ever say otherwise? How do I look?"

He started up the engine. "Like a real Nazi beauty."

"What's that supposed to mean? Hey, what—not even a kiss?"

He landed his lips against hers, then shifted into gear and drove down the block, not wanting to start up with her now. But they hadn't made it around the first corner before she realized something was wrong.

"What is it, Willi? You found out about the money, is that it?"

He didn't say anything.

"You think I stole it, huh? Is that it? Well, you're wrong. I tried to call you at the office, but you'd already left. I had to buy an outfit. I couldn't go today looking like some cheap secretary or a telephone operator. There's going to be earls and baronesses on that yacht. You think I wasn't going to tell you?"

Willi felt his throat tighten. "That outfit cost you three hundred marks?"

"Not exactly. A little less than a hundred. I still have the rest at home. I'll give it to you later."

Clenching his jaw, he shifted angrily into third, not knowing what to believe.

The Berlin Yacht Club was on Wannsee, the most fashionable of the many large lakes surrounding the city. Among the flotilla of polished vessels, the Great Gustave's cabin cruiser, *The Third Eye*, stood out like a Taj Mahal, twice as long, twice as high, twice as full of flags and colorful bunting as the others. Armed SA guards checked the invitations of the well-dressed throng waiting to board.

"Don't be upset, Willi, please." Paula took his hand as they clambered up the gangplank. "Remember, we're in this together."

"Keep your nose out of it," he said, angrier than he realized. "The last thing I need is for you to disappear, too."

"My nose"—she coldly dropped his hand—"is already in it."

At noon the yacht set sail. There had to be sixty people aboard, although with two enormous galley decks below, it hardly felt it. Paula hadn't been kidding about the sort in attendance. In the first few minutes Willi recognized more aristocrats than at a diplomatic ball: the prince of Pomerania, the count of Koblenz, the baron and baroness of Brandenburg Saxony. Among the crowd also were representatives of some of Germany's most powerful industrial families: Thyssen, Krupp, Porsche, plus a bevy of stage and screen actresses in gowns with décolleté that made Paula's look modest. Dozens of waiters in tasseled turbans passed tall champagne flutes from silver platters or manned buffet tables piled high with delicacies. The whole boat was decked out with boughs of holly and pine.

By now Willi had done enough research on Gustave Spanknoebel to know that the fortune amassed for such a lifestyle was not from his public nightclub appearances or even the many private clients who depended on his every word. No, the real money came from his publishing empire, which in addition to one of the most popular weekly newspapers in the nation, the *Clairvoyant,* produced countless books on the occult that outsold many of the titles by the country's great novelists. His biggest money-maker though was a topical ointment he'd invented called Viril Kreme, which millions of Germans, men and women, swore enflamed sexual passion. Some saw Spanknoebel as the greatest Svengali in German history. Even Adolf Hitler, it was said, took lessons in public speaking and mass psychology from him. Perhaps it wasn't surprising the man had remained immune from the law all this time.

Also clear, as Paula had forewarned, was that this event was strictly couples only. A good thing he'd brought her. Not a man or woman appeared unescorted. He wound up having to tug her about as if she were handcuffed to him.

"Tell me the truth," he whispered at one point, still furious with her, though for what he wasn't even certain anymore. "Why is it you wear those black lace gloves all the time, Paula?"

She tried to pull her hand away. "Because I like them."

Now he wouldn't let go. Nor would he allow her to take any alcohol.

"You want to get involved? Keep your eyes and ears open then."

"Yes, sir." She frowned angrily. "Are you going to accompany me to the bathroom, too?"

He ignored her, yanking her through the star-studded crowd. Spotting two powerful scions of Germany's steel industry, he kept her from speaking. "Shhh!"

"Unfortunately everyone's losing faith Hitler can even gain

the chancellorship." He concentrated on listening in on young Helmut Krupp, whose grandfather was probably the richest man in Germany.

"But we must make sure he does," young Georg von Thyssen, whose grandfather came in second, replied through a mouthful of caviar. "God forbid the Reds take over—we'd all be shot the next day. Once the Nazis tear apart the Commies, we can lock the big baboons up."

"Exactly," Krupp snickered.

Pity Fritz wasn't here, Willi thought, dragging Paula along again. These two were just the idiots he ranted about in his newspaper column, completely unwilling to see that the big apes they thought could do their dirty work would by nature turn from tearing apart "Commies" to tearing apart them.

After the yacht was far out in the Wannsee and most of the guests were good and soused, Gustave made his grand entrance, floating through the crowd in a full swami outfit: long white robes and red turban.

"Pardon me for such a late arrival," he begged of them all.

Everyone gathered around to hear him speak from a small altar-like podium.

"I have been delayed by a most momentous task." His voice trembled with import, his eyes widening with knowledge and mystery. "All morning I have been hard at work plotting an astrological chart of the greatest consequence to our nation . . . the chart of Adolf Hitler. And you, my most honored guests, will be the first to hear its astonishing revelations. Yes . . . yes . . . I have seen it all!" He held out an arm far in front of him.

The man, Willi thought, took theatricality to new dimensions of absurdity.

"We all know that in the past few months the Führer and his Party have faced exceedingly adverse conditions. This was because of the Uranus-Moon alignments settled in the First and

Twelfth Houses. But in the fourth week of the next year, this alignment will pass into Hitler's Sixth and Seventh Houses. It will not come easily . . . not without subterfuge and perhaps even bloodshed . . . but all the planets will have reached the proper positions for him to achieve a great and lasting victory over his enemies!"

The crowd cheered.

"And won't life be grand," Paula muttered.

Willi felt a little better holding her hand.

"But there is more. Yes. Just a few brief weeks after this historic victory, in February 1933, I see a great conflagration burning through the House of Germany. A terrible fire that will shock the nation. But this is not something to fear, *meine Damen und Herren. Nein. Nein.* It is all as it must be. This will be the mystic cleansing from which the phoenix of a Great New Germany will arise!"

The audience erupted into applause. As if on cue a small brass band broke into a happy fox-trot. Couples began dancing. Top-hatted men with monocles and diamond cuff links. Elegant women with long cigarette holders. Laughing and dancing madly. What was this fever gripping Germany? Willi watched, aghast. Had things got so rotten that reality itself was now the enemy? Did the future seem so terrifying that even among the most privileged few, nonsense like this could pass for truth?

"The real action's going to be on the lower deck," he heard a baroness whisper to a friend. "Special invite only."

Or was it all just a fad with these elite?

Only too happy to escape this spectacle Willi yanked Paula's arm, determined to gain entrance to whatever was happening downstairs. But his name was not on the list, a burly guard advised. Sorry.

Willi had to think fast.

Among the VIPs on line to enter he noticed the same young von Thyssen he'd eavesdropped on earlier and gave the dice a toss.

"Why, Georg!" he exclaimed, holding out a hand to the bewildered twenty-five-year-old. "Don't tell me you don't remember me? I dated your sister several years ago, quite seriously as a matter of fact. Siegfried Greiber, Ruhr Coal and Coke."

Willi staked all on the rich kid needing to feel in command of the situation, and not wishing to show he hadn't the foggiest recollection of any Greiber dating his sister.

"*Ach*, yes. Of course. How are you, *Mensch*?"

The gamble paid off. Any friend of von Thyssen's was a friend of the Great Gustave's—and thus Willi and Paula gained access to the inner sanctum.

The small space for maybe twenty was dimly lit with flickering torches and draped in red damask. Thick Persian rugs covered the floor. The only furniture was a scattering of satin pillows and one thronelike chair up front, floodlit from below. The starlets, tycoons, and assorted nobility selected for this elite assemblage were busy pulling off shoes and propping themselves on the floor, readying for what was sure to be an experience to tell one's friends about.

Willi looked them over.

Might one turn out to be Gustave's next victim? His gaze fixed on a stunning brunette with a neck full of glittering diamonds. Without a doubt the King of Mystics was involved in the disappearance of dozens of foreign women. But Willi didn't have enough evidence to win a search warrant on him. Of course, the son of a bitch was only a pimp, he knew—a procurer. But so far, Gustave was the only conduit to where the sleepwalkers wound up. All Willi knew for sure was that it was within floating distance of Spandau.

After what seemed an eternity, Gustave arrived, no doubt delayed by some momentous project for the future of mankind. In his flowing robes and absurd red turban he escorted the Duchess Augustina von Breitenback-Dustenburg on his arm, a true old Prussian aristocrat. The thronelike armchair at the front of the room everyone had assumed was his he gave to her. Not that she was all that old, fifty-five or sixty at most. But her sparkling black evening gown, worn with white gloves practically to the armpits, looked generations out of date. Her face expressed not a ray of emotion, other than a grave flicker now and then.

"Hello to you all, my special friends and firmest supporters," Gustave greeted in his stagiest voice. His whitened face, with its dark red lips, shifted from one Kabuki expression to another. "I'm sure you all know the duchess here. Well, she has a little confession to make. She wishes me to convey to you that she does not believe that I can hypnotize her, although she very much wishes I could. In her heart of hearts she told me she really would like to be commanded today to do something completely . . . how did she put it?"

"Outrageous," the duchess filled in with a deadpan look.

The room broke into laughter.

"So. You do not believe that I can hypnotize you. Are there any other women who feel this way, too? Who believe themselves impervious to my powers?"

Willi, with his arm around Paula's shoulders, could feel her muscles tense.

"Don't even think it," he whispered.

The dark-eyed brunette with the glittering diamonds stood from the floor.

"Madame." Gustave held a hand to her. "Tell me, what is your name?"

"Melina von Auerlicht. This is my husband, Count Wilhelm von Auerlicht."

"Countess, you are not German originally?"

"*Nein.* I am Greek."

"And you do not think that you are susceptible to hypnosis?"

"*Absolut nicht.* My willpower is far too strong. Ask my husband."

"Count Wilhelm, is that your opinion?"

"Is it ever!" the count, evidently quite drunk, replied loudly. "The woman is a total bitch. She won't deny it."

The crowd roared.

"And what's more, I'm proud of it," the woman returned. "Even you, King of Mystics, cannot exert your will over mine."

But she was wrong. Within minutes both she and the stodgy old duchess were slaves to the Great Gustave's commands.

"So there you have it, *meine Damen und Herren*." He pointed to the two of them, sprawled like corpses on a pile of pillows. "Most people, most females especially, have no understanding of the depth of their own suggestibility. They think they can resist, that they are stronger. But what they don't acknowledge is how very much they actually long to be mastered."

"Duchess," he said to the older one. "Sit up, darling. Open your eyes. Tell Papa . . . what is your wish. Now that I have you in my control, what 'outrageous' thing should I command you to do?"

The duchess sat up. Her eyes opened. But for what seemed the longest time, nothing came from her mouth. The whole audience leaned forward in tense anticipation. Had Gustave failed?

"I wish . . . ," the duchess finally said quietly, "I wish to do an American-style striptease."

She was greeted with absolutely stunned silence.

"Luigi!" Gustave motioned for his assistant. "Bring some musicians. The duchess wishes to dance the striptease."

In seconds, it seemed, a snare drum with cymbals and a few brass horns were ready to one side of the room.

"Duchess," Gustave cried. "Are you ready?"

"Yes," she replied from her hiding place behind one of the thick red curtains.

"And now . . . the great Scala Theater of Berlin is proud to present . . . straight from America . . . that international sensation . . . Duchess Augustina von Breitenback-Dustenburg!"

The musicians struck up a hard-grinding beat full of trombone whines and sexy trumpet calls. The duchess emerged leg-first from behind the curtain, swirling her hips. Slowly, tauntingly, she began pulling off the fingers from one of her long white gloves, until the whole thing was circling above her head. When it went flying to a gentleman in the front row, she leaned forward and wiggled her chest, growling in English, "Hey, big boy! Got dinner plans?" The audience shook with laughter and applause, and one of the assistants moved in to capture it all on a home-movie camera.

Gustave let the act proceed until the duchess was dancing in nothing but a long black slip, hoisting it to show off her flabby white legs and purple varicose veins. Then he stopped the music and told her that, at the snap of his fingers, she would emerge from her hypnotic trance feeling refreshed and in wonderful humor.

Snap.

The room was silent as the crusty old woman realized she was standing half-naked before them all. *"Gott in Himmel!"* she shrieked, breaking into a fit of laughter and throwing her arms around Gustave. "You did it! You wonderful, wonderful man, you!"

As for the feisty Greek, Gustave turned to the husband and said cheerfully, "Count Wilhelm, as long as we finally have her under control, is there something you'd like me to do with your wife?"

The count thought it over a moment, then raised a champagne glass. "Yes, master," he called. "Make her climax. The frigid bitch never did with me!"

There were shrieks of shock and hilarity.

Gustave gave a small salute, as if glad to be of service. "Melina my love." He propped the dark beauty up and sat her in the armchair. "Tell me something . . . are you hypnotized now, sweetheart?"

"No," she replied, her eyes firmly shut.

"May I ask you a personal question?"

"No."

"If you could make love with any man in this room . . . who would it be?"

"You."

There was generous applause.

Gustave bowed modestly. "All right then, Melina. You and I are going to make love. Right here. Right now. Is that okay?"

"No."

"When I count to three, Melina, you and I are going to make love. Mad. Passionate. Insane love. It will be like nothing you have ever experienced in your life. It will thrill you to the core. Every cell in your body will pulsate with pleasure. And you will have orgasms, Melina. Not one or two. But every time I command you to, you will have another orgasm. And you will love it, Melina. You will love it like you've never loved anything before. Are you ready?"

"No."

"One."

"No."

"Two."

"No."

"Three!"

The woman's arms sprang from her sides and she let out a deep, almost frightening shriek that sent shivers through the audience. Gustave stood back with his arms behind him, watching as she desperately clutched a completely imaginary lover to her breast.

"Oh, yes, Gustave. Yes, yes. You don't know how long I've waited for this." Her face went bright red and her breathing quickened as she lifted her legs and began squirming in the chair. "Oh, yes, Gustave. Yes!"

"Climax now, Melina," Gustave ordered. "Climax!"

"Yes. Oh, yes. Oh, yes, yes, yes!"

"And again, Melina. Climax again."

"Yes. Yes. Oh, God. Oh, God. Oh, God!"

Seventeen times, those who kept count swore afterward.

The armchair had to be thrown away.

But Melina von Auerlicht, poor thing, was commanded to recall nothing of her adventure—and the moment she came out of the trance she proudly denounced Gustave as a fraud, unable to hypnotize anyone with a willpower that could match his own!

Thirteen

"Get me out of here," Paula whispered.

Willi saw her face had turned green.

He hustled her upstairs, feeling how cold and clammy her skin had become, hoping to get her out to the deck before she fainted, or vomited, or both. Gradually, outside, the fresh air revived her.

"I've never seen anything so horrible." She clutched her demi-gloved hands to her throat. "It was like . . . he raped her."

Willi put his arms around her waist and felt, despite the unseasonably warm day, the calm lake all around them slapping against the hull, that Paula was really traumatized. Trembling to the core. As if something had touched a raw nerve and was squeezing it with metal pliers.

"Willi," she whispered. "Get me off this boat. Even if we have to swim."

Before setting off for the evening, *The Third Eye* was scheduled to pick up latecomers from a place called Peacock Island. Paula and Willi were the only two to disembark. Another twenty or so merrymakers pushed past them to join the fun. Among them Willi noticed five or six officers in full black uniform, each escorting a bejeweled blonde. As they brushed by in opposite directions, one knocked into Willi's shoulder.

"Pardon me," he said with a smile, tipping his SS officer's hat as he continued up the ramp. From his big-gapped bunny teeth Willi instantly recognized him.

It was Josef, his friend from the Black Stag Inn.

When the ship pulled away, Willi and Paula stood there, his arm around her cape as it fluttered in the breeze. It wasn't even four o'clock, and such a strange, warm afternoon. The air almost sultry. As the sound of the jazz band from the ship faded, he could feel Paula's breathing return to normal, the trembling ease from her bones. He yanked off his wig and ran his fingers through his dark, curly hair. That phrase went through his mind again from the psychology text on masochism: a *neurotic eroticizing* of childhood trauma.

Poor girl, he thought. God knows what you've been through.

But what a wonderful place to find themselves now. The breeze so fresh. The pine trees so green. Tiny Peacock Island, between Wannsee and Babelsberg, had been fashioned into a nature reserve at the end of the eighteenth century. A park now, it was widely regarded as an apotheosis of German romanticism. Walking its picturesque paths, Paula leaning on him in her tight pink gown, clasping him for support, they sauntered past emerald fields alive with strutting peacocks, sun-filled meadows, and little garden pavilions built to look like the ruins of medieval castles.

Everything was so calm. So rustically peaceful.

Paula began to cry. "Why can't the world be beautiful like this?"

Why? He handed her a handkerchief.

The world's oldest question.

At the end of the island a little ferry shuttled them back to the mainland. Paula still didn't feel well. She wanted to go home. They had to take the S-Bahn back to fetch Willi's car in Wannsee. Neither had much to say. Besides feeling bad for her, Willi simmered with frustration. It had been a fruitless afternoon. He certainly hadn't got any smoking gun on Gustave. He hadn't got anything. Only a depressing glimpse of the future. And another lesson on the wretchedness of humankind.

As if he needed it.

As he drove back into town, a dozen thoughts competed in his brain. Just about now, he knew, his sons should be arriving in Paris with Ava and the Gottmans. When would he see them again? How long would they have to stay away? He already missed them so much it hurt. But so far, all his efforts on the Mermaid and the Bulgarian-princess cases hadn't got him far, nor scored him any points with his boss. In fact, the Kommissar had made it clear that von Hindenburg was most disappointed in Willi's lack of results. The king of Bulgaria had personally hung up on the Reichs president. A great humiliation. In other words, Willi was causing an international incident. Horthstaler reminded von Hindenburg that it had taken Willi many months—and many children's lives—to catch the *Kinderfresser*. Was this a compliment or an insult?

It was getting hard to tell these days who or what was on your side.

He'd considered bringing more of his Detektivs onto the case, but two already had full workloads. And the third he didn't trust. Pasty-faced Herbert Thurmann had joined his unit under a most dubious promotional route, and Willi had more than once found him snooping in files he didn't belong in. Rife were rumors of how the Nazis were attempting to infiltrate the Berlin police. If true, his own little fascist mole had to be Thurmann. He had no intention of letting the man anywhere near this case.

And then there was Paula. Could he ever really trust her? What the hell was he doing with this child anyway, in her pink gown and black marabou? Last night he tried to imagine introducing her to his sons. To his parents-in-law. It was ridiculous. The whole thing. Completely irrational. Did he think he could reform her, for God's sakes?

A boot whore?

The literal fork-in-the-road came along Spandauer Damm, past the baroque gardens of the Charlottenburg Palace. To his left, the bridge across the Spree into Berlin-North where she lived. To the right, the Kaiser Friedrich Strasse into Berlin-West, and his place.

"Well, which is it going to be, *Liebchen*?" She spoke his thoughts. "I won't hold it against you if you take me home. Really. I never expected anything. I'll miss you of course. But what the hell. We can say hi when we pass on Tauentzien, huh?"

He made the right, unable to leave her. He didn't care if it was rational or not.

What was rational these days?

As he drove, he felt her hand slip through his arm and her head lean on his shoulder. "Oh, Willi, Willi, you're such a good boy."

"You know what I'd really like to do tonight?" she said, yawning, when they reached his apartment. He expected Paula to say go to sleep nice and early. But no. She wanted to go out. As ordinary people do on a Saturday night. "Yes, just like ordinary people." The idea seemed to entice her like a beautiful doll might a child. "We'll freshen up and put on casual clothes and go to a movie and out to dinner. Doesn't that sound divine? Just like an ordinary couple."

Freshen up, Willi noticed, inevitably meant a long time in the bathroom with her handbag. In the meantime, he phoned Paris. His family had just arrived in the Gare du Nord, Aunt Hedda informed him. They were on their way over by taxi now. Everything had gone smoothly. Everyone was fine.

"Send them my love," Willi told her. "I'll call again tomorrow, when they're settled in."

"Yowsah! Look at the Christmas lights," Paula exclaimed as they strolled arm in arm onto the Ku-damm. The whole boulevard seemed to glow. Neon flashing. Store windows sparkling. Towering rows of self-illuminating advertising columns, radiating countless promises. Around Breitscheidplatz, cinema after cinema competed for the crowds. Loudspeaker barkers screamed out the titles and the movie stars' names. The smell of fresh-roasted chestnuts filled the air. Not even the Brownshirts shaking their cans seemed to damper the holiday spirit. At the new Universum, a long, sleek, ultramodern building designed by the very same Mendelsohn who did Fritz's house, a soaring color marquee board displayed the great British actor Charles Laughton portraying Nero, fiddling madly while Rome burned. It was Cecil B. DeMille's latest spectacular, *The Sign of the Cross*.

"Oh, let's see this." Paula pulled his arm. "It's got Claudette Colbert."

Only Hollywood, only DeMille, could have made such a movie. The screen overflowed with images of wanton cruelty, vice, and degradation. Christians, old men, women and babies, thrown to the tigers. Crucified. Burned alive to the cheering of thousands. Men battling bulls. Women battling pygmies. Elephants treading on people's heads. Paula was absolutely entranced, standing along with the rest of the audience to applaud the final triumph of good.

"Wasn't Colbert magnificent?" She took Willi's arm as they left the theater. "That milk bath. I've never seen anything so sensual. Would you like me to take a bath in milk, Willi? Would you, huh? You can tell me—"

"All I want you to do in milk," he replied firmly, "is boil oatmeal. So. Where would you like to go for dinner?"

Paula grabbed his jacket lapel. "Promise you won't laugh?" She shook a fist at him menacingly.

"I won't. I promise I won't."

But when she told him, he couldn't help it.

The "Jolliest Place in Berlin!" The "Department Store of Restaurants!" An "Inexpensive Holiday Trip Around the World in Twelve Eating Environments!"

Kempinski's Haus Vaterland was unrivaled among Berlin's entertainment venues. Brilliantly lit, its great domed roof rising above the Potsdamer Platz, a pinwheel of spinning, flashing neon sparkling across the city, it offered twelve bands, fifty cabaret acts, and the famous Haus Vaterland Girls.

Willi had been to it numerous times. His father-in-law adored it. The Bavarian Beer Garden seating a thousand, including a man-made lake, barmaids in traditional dirndls and yodeling waiters. The Wine Terrace on the Rhine, with its paddleboats floating past miniature castles, and every hour on the hour a five-minute rainstorm. The Hungarian Pastry Restaurant. The Japanese Tea Garden. The Wild West Saloon. There was nothing else like it in Europe. Feeding six thousand customers simultaneously, the place was an absolute madhouse.

Paula chose the Viennese Café, a hundred crowded tables overlooking a diorama of Old Vienna and the river Danube. A massive trompe l'oeil of the central railway station with electric trains crossing bridges and mechanical boats sailing beneath. Scores of couples twirling madly to an orchestra playing Strauss waltzes.

"What the hell. You only live once, heh?" she cried as the waiter brought them menus. It was a splendid evening. They danced. They laughed.

Just like an ordinary couple.

Both were plenty tipsy when the taxi dropped them home. Paula made coffee and they sat up babbling about their childhoods. As the crow flies, they calculated, Willi having spread a big city map on the table, they'd grown up only a few kilometers apart. Yet it might as well have been on different planets. Neither landscape occupied by the other seemed the least familiar. Willi could not believe that she had never once been to Berlin's greatest park, the Tiergarten.

"It's an outrage," he said. "You're culturally deprived. Tomorrow," he commanded, folding the map back up. "We go."

As they readied for bed, she disappeared again into the bathroom, and when she came out, she was like a soft, clinging, needy kitten. She sat on his lap and put her arms around his neck, running the lace-gloved hands through his hair. Out of the blue she wanted to talk about Gina.

"Tell me the truth." She cuddled him purposefully. "I need to know, Willi. What happened to her, really? How did they kill her?"

His defenses were down. He felt so close to her. He made her sit opposite him.

"It's ugly, Paula. You sure you want to know?"

"I need to, Willi. Don't ask me why."

He told her everything.

"Experimented on? Oh, that can't be true! Willi, it just can't be! No one could be so cruel."

In dark, mournful tones she slowly confessed that she and Gina had been more than just roommates. Much more. And that all this time she'd burned with guilt because she hadn't kept Gina away from Gustave, who everyone knew was a swine and surrounded himself with worse. She looked at Willi full of fear, expecting him to strike her or toss her in the gutter. Or kick her face in. But instead he took her in his arms, embracing her like a lost child, a precious unearthed treasure.

They made love like newlyweds. At one with the universe. With each other.

"Willi, don't deny me," she panted desperately. "I need you so terribly. I need you *to*. Do you understand? Not just with your hand this time, but your belt. Hard!

"Don't be a coward. Oh, God, please don't. . . . Don't think you're hurting me. . . .

"Ahhh . . . yes.
"That's it, Willi, harder! Don't think you're—
"Ahhh. Yes. Yes.
"Harder, Willi.
"Harder!"

Fourteen

Monday morning was foggy. Gray. Paula stayed in bed. It was Christmas Eve. She was going to visit her mother. Did Willi want to join? The food wasn't going to be much. Not like Haus Vaterland. But . . .

"I'll take a rain check." He leaned and kissed her. "Like you said, there's no need to rush."

Outside, buttoning his coat against the damp, it didn't take long to realize something was wrong. There weren't any streetcars. Or buses. Crowds of agitated people clustered about, mumbling about a strike. No one knew whether the S-Bahn was running, so Willi continued up past the Kaiser Wilhelm Church, its mournful bells tolling the hour. At the Zoo Bahnhof, an extraordinary sight greeted his eyes.

The giant train station was empty. In front of it hundreds of Communists and Nazis, instead of tearing each other apart, were marching on a picket line—together. Archenemies who had for years now drenched the cobblestones of Berlin with blood, they had forged a devil's pact apparently, uniting for a six-hour shutdown of all public transport. Far left and far right joining forces to protest von Schleicher's demand that all paramilitary organizations be disbanded. Unprecedented. Their aim: to cripple the capital. And what a job they were making of it. Seeing traffic hopelessly snarled in every direction, Willi came to the same conclusion apparently everybody else did: the only way to work was to walk.

Half of Berlin trudged through the Tiergarten. Men in black derbies and fur-collared coats, briefcases tucked under arms or, in the European custom, hands clasped behind the back. Rouge-cheeked secretaries hanging on to their purses, knowing very well that no matter how much they hurried, their bosses would have to be patient today. Many looked fearful. Or stunned. Not since the revolution of 1919 had public transport shut down. How easily the city could unravel. Everything one took for granted, in the wink of an eye, gone. Some made merry of it, singing traditional hiking songs or breaking into Christmas carols. And still more rode bicycles. Bicycles, bicycles. Where had they all come from? Clearly a lot of people knew about this strike, Willi thought. At least before he had.

Yesterday, he'd hiked these same park grounds with Paula, exactly as he'd promised her. They'd strolled the old hunting trails of the kaisers, sat by the streams, tossed pennies in the goldfish pond. How wonderful it was showing her white Bellevue Palace and the towering Victory Column, Berlin landmarks she'd never laid eyes on. She was like a tourist from some faraway place. What was she doing now? he wondered. Lounging in bed still? In the bathroom, freshening up?

It took him an hour to reach the far side of the Tiergarten. People were by then collapsing on benches, removing their shoes despite the cold, rubbing their feet. Emerging from the trees, the great gray Reichstag building with its dedication, "To the German People," appeared half-shrouded in mist. Squads of mounted police were already deploying around it, preparing for mass demonstrations. Or another revolution. A military putsch. The return of the kaiser.

God only knew these days.

Directly ahead rose the grand Brandenburg Gate, crowned by its gold goddess and chariot, quintessential symbol of Berlin. Paula had probably never seen it, either. As he passed underneath its giant colonnades, time itself seemed to collapse. Suddenly he was back in 1915, marching off to war. His mother and sister in the crowd waving handkerchiefs. And again in 1923. Another uniform, another brass band. A full police Detektiv this time, his wife and infant son to cheer him on. Every strand, every fiber in his memory, he realized, was wound up in this city.

Beyond the gate, in Pariser Platz, he joined the masses of cars and pedestrians flooding Unter den Linden, its famous rows of lime trees bare now, strung with countless Christmas lights. He passed the French and British embassies, the Adlon Hotel, the busy corner of cafés at Friedrich Strasse—Schon, Bauer, Kranzler, Victoria. Elegant ladies on terraces sat bundled up in overcoats and white gloves, sipping coffee, eating *Brötchen*, watching the chaos caused by the strike. An outrage. A scandal. The new government was a joke. With all his promises von Schleicher was only making matters worse.

Past the Palace of the Crown Prince. The great Schinkel Opera House. The Berlin Cathedral. The center of the city was outsize. Garish. Not nearly as beautiful as Paris or Rome. Or distinguished like London. Or as exciting as New York. But teeming. Alive. Home.

Across the city's most elegant bridge, with its marble statues of Greek gods lining each side, loomed the baroque *Stadt Schloss* of the Hohenzollerns. For five hundred years the dynasty had ruled from this gargantuan brown palace, the absolute heart of imperial Berlin. Then practically overnight they were deposed and exiled. Now it stood empty. Nobody sure what to do with it. What to do with Germany.

Block by block as he trudged the city, thoughts began flitting through his brain of the long march home in 1918, the defeated German army retracing the invasion route of 1914, northern France, the plains of Belgium, back across the Rhine. Town after town, city after city, had been nothing but blackened rubble. Back then Germany was spared. But what if, God forbid, there was another war? Now, with advanced airplanes, tanks, and more lethal artillery than anyone imagined fifteen years ago? A grotesque image filled his mind—all Berlin, all the grand avenues and crowded streets he'd just walked, the palaces and parks, the opera, the Reichstag, all the way up to the Kürfurstendamm—an endless sea of ruin.

It was too terrible to contemplate.

When he reached Alexanderplatz, his feet were throbbing. The huge square seemed empty without its streetcars and buses. Fortunately the strike was only due to last until one o'clock. At least he'd get a ride home . . . if not a seat.

Before going up to his office he stopped by the Alexander Haus to see his paper conservator. The good woman, not surprisingly, hadn't made it in to work. He didn't expect her to walk from God knew where. But it meant he couldn't pick up his document until after Christmas. What could one do? He was famished. And chilled. The flashing red sign of the Café Rippa lured him inside.

Thoroughly enjoying a bowl of hot soup, he suddenly sensed a strange presence over his shoulder. He nearly dropped his spoon. Looming over him was Kai, the former Red Apache turned Nazi. For an instant Willi feared the worst. But seeing the kid clad again in a verdant wool poncho, his eyes darkened, the gold ring dangling from his ear, Willi breathed a sigh of relief. "Kai! Had any breakfast? Say, what happened to your new position?"

"Wasn't for me." The kid screwed up his chisled features as he joined Willi at the table, lighting a cigarette. "Uniform's too ugly. Besides"—he exhaled, his smirk turning virtuous—"Roehm's a pig. If I'm gonna put out for fat, old swine, I'd just as soon get paid."

"I see," Willi acknowledged the logic.

"Can you believe this strike?" Kai's bright blue eyes were full of insurrection again. "On Christmas Eve? Screw the Nazis. And the Communists."

Willi shared the sentiments.

"Kai, perhaps . . . we can be of help to each other again."

It made the whole morning worth it, watching the kid's face light up.

As he pulled off his hat as he stepped into the Police Presidium, the waxy smell of the vestibule automatically set Willi's mind in gear. He decided that over the holiday he would take the files of Germany's top orthopedic surgeons home and inspect them again with a fine-tooth comb. He'd read them a dozen times already. But other than for Meckel, there was nothing. Not one of the doctors had written about bone transplants. And not one was affiliated with the Nazis. But one, Rudolf Kreuzler, head of the orthopedic unit at Charité Hospital, had listed on his staff a junior surgeon named Oscar Schumann—same last name as his friend from the Black Stag Inn. But so what? Scores of Schumanns were in Berlin, and so far nothing he could find on this one linked him to Meckel or Spandau. In any case, just to play it safe, after the holiday he intended to visit the fellow. He also intended to pay a call to General von Schleicher and make certain the chancellor knew how his buddy Ernst Roehm had handled the Meckel case. Not that the man didn't have enough to worry about, with the Nazis and the Communists ganging up on him.

No surprise to find Ruta'd made it in. The woman would walk through artillery fire to get to work. "How's the hike, Inspektor?"

She was energetically grinding away at her coffee mill. For a second he thought she said *kike*.

"Oh, fine, fine. A good walk never hurt anyone."

"Certainly not. Look at your cheeks—all nice and ruddy. Makes you handsome. Which is excellent, because a pretty lady is waiting to see you. For more than an hour already."

He took off his coat. "Same one as last time?"

"No, Herr Inspektor-Detektiv." Ruta barely suppressed her mirth. "A different one. Not so sexy perhaps. But very pretty. Elegant."

"Well. It must be my new cologne."

"Nonsense. You're a handsome man. A most eligible bachelor."

He was surprised to find his old friend Sylvie, Fritz's ex-wife, sitting by his desk, looking elegant indeed in a shimmering black suit and red lace veil over half her face. Once upon a time she and Vicki had been close as sisters.

"Willi." She crushed out a cigarette. "Finally."

"Don't tell me you were just in the neighborhood."

She laughed, crossing her long, slim legs. "*Au contraire.* I had to battle priests and old ladies to get a taxi."

"What brings you by?"

Through the veil he saw a look of disappointment. For quite a few months now she'd been letting him know that as long as Vicki was gone and it was over with Fritz, well . . . Certainly she was more appropriate for him than Paula. Good family. Educated. Very pretty, as Ruta said. Gorgeous legs. But she wasn't his type. Had never been.

So what could he do?

She lifted the veil. From her alligator purse she pulled out a newspaper carefully folded inside and slid it across the desk. Willi immediately recognized it. *Der Stürmer.* The most obscenely anti-Semitic of all the Nazi publications. Typical was the drawing on the front page of the fiendish-looking, hook-nosed Jew. Only this time, he realized—the caricature was of him. Right above it, the headline screamed, **Jew Inspektor Kraus—Red Agent!!**

"You know in a million years I'd never show you something like this," Sylvie mumbled, redder than her veil. "But I think you need know. Go on. Read it."

As if there was any more need to convince the public of the corruption of the Berlin Police . . . according to inside sources the department's most celebrated Inspektor—Jew Willi Kraus—is being paid by the Soviet Union to bungle the case of missing Princess Magdelena, in order to disrupt harmonious relations between Germany and the Kingdom of Bulgaria. Reichs President Hindenburg is said to . . .

Willi pushed it aside. "What else do you expect them to print."

"That's not the point." Her lean figure straightened. "You're in their crosshairs now, Willi. Don't you see . . . once they start, they never let up."

"What would you have me do?"

Her cheeks paled. "If you had half a brain, you'd get out of this country. Until the mess blows over."

"And if I had less than half?"

She shrugged hopelessly. "Then I have no advice. Only, if you should ever need it . . ." She slipped him a card with her address. "I'll do whatever I can to help."

His throat clenched unexpectedly. "Thank you." He forced a smile. "That's really kind, Sylvie. Let's pray I never have to take you up on it. Now, how about a nice cup of coffee?"

Christmas Day was blessedly tranquil. Below Willi's window the streetcars sparked and rattled again reassuringly. Midday he phoned his family. They were having a delightful time. Been to the Louvre. On a boat ride down the Seine. Tomorrow it was off to Versailles. When he hung up, his throat ached from missing them so badly.

The whole day he lounged about in his pajamas, reading and rereading those damn dossiers. It was useless. He couldn't concentrate. He kept looking at the photographs on the wall, his ancestors staring down at him. Sylvie was the third person this week who'd told him to get out of Germany. It was getting annoying. His family had been here what, since the time of Charlemagne? Why would anyone think he'd just pack up and run? And yet . . . he couldn't keep himself from wondering if he ever really did have to leave . . . where would he go?

A hot bath, he told himself.

Stepping into the steamy tub, he tried to imagine poor Gina Mancuso entering the freezing water that day. The Havel was such a wide river, almost like a lake in parts. If she had been trying to escape, he considered, lying in suds up to his ears, there must have been something she was swimming toward, no? An island perhaps. Or another shore. Somewhere before the river widened. Within floating distance of Spandau.

He jumped from the tub.

Hoffnung said she'd died within twenty minutes of entering the water, just six or seven hours before they found her. Those currents were strong. But time itself limited the distance. Wrapping a towel around his middle, he went to find a map of Berlin.

Just as he'd got it spread on the table though, a furious knocking froze him.

"Kraus! *Aufmachen!*" a shout came from the hall.

It definitely wasn't Santa Claus.

A delegation of Ernst Roehm's "businessmen" maybe?

Leaping for his bathrobe, he grabbed a pistol and stood by the door, still dripping suds.

"*Machst auf,* fool! It's me. Fritz!"

"*Mensch.* You half scared me to death."

Willi unbolted the lock. Fritz was wearing a top hat and tux-edo with a long black cape over his shoulders, his arms full of champagne bottles.

"I knew you'd be holed up here." Fritz barged in, his glassy eyes advertising the head start he had on things. "And I just couldn't bear the thought of you spending the whole holiday—" He noticed the gun. "Willi—"

"It's nothing." Willi put it away.

Fritz dropped the bottles on the table and took off his hat. "Hell. Someone's after you."

"No one's after me."

"You're lying."

"Why would I lie to you, Fritz? I'm just on edge. Like every-body else."

"So you come to the door with a pistol?"

"I promise you it's nothing."

Fritz stared at him helplessly, throwing off his cape. "Okay. If that's the way you want it." Fritz shrugged. "Then let's cele-brate. I bear good tidings."

He popped open a bottle. "To *mein Kapitän*!" He raised a glass. "Without whom I would not be here. Or anywhere. Prosit."

They clinked.

"Prosit." Will felt compelled to keep up with him, downing it all without a breath, the bubbles rushing to his brain.

"Tell me, Fritz, what's your good news? I could use a little."

"Strictly confidential." Fritz put a finger over his lips.

Willi placed his hand on his heart.

"Strasser's broken with Hitler."

"*Nein.*" That furious scene between them at the Kaiserhof popped back into Willi's mind.

"Hasn't been made official yet," Fritz clarified. "But I naturally have my sources. And the Führer is *insane* with rage. Tearing apart drapes. Chewing the carpet. Literally. The man's certifiable."

"Does it mean the Nazi Party will split?"

Fritz poured them another round. "Too early to say. But von Schleicher's divide-and-conquer scheme has clearly torn open a real rift."

"Well. That is good news." Willi raised his glass. "Dare I say it? To 1933."

"Nineteen thirty-three!"

Wiping his mouth, Fritz looked down at the big, open map on the table. "Let me guess. You're planning a holiday along the Havel? No? It must be work then. What a surprise. All work, no play, friend . . ."

Willi felt the champagne rapidly undermining his discretion.

"Come on, Fritz. Crime doesn't take any holidays. Wait a second . . . you're a yachtsman. You know the Havel."

"Like the underside of my prick."

"Hypothetically and *completely* off the record, Fritz." Willi put down his glass. "If a body wound up on the riverbank here"—he pointed at Spandau—"and it had been in the water six or seven hours, given the currents, how far upstream might she have been when she started?"

"She?" The long dueling scar on Fritz's cheek, a souvenir of his college days, stretched with sarcasm. "Hypothetically?"

"Yes, Fritz. And strictly *off the record.*"

"Well, use your Jewish *Kopf,* Willi." The jagged scar contracted now with a teasing edge. "It would completely depend on how long she'd been lying on that hypothetical riverbank, wouldn't it?"

Fritz loved nothing more than a good mystery, Willi knew. Fritz was a congenital snoop, which was why he'd volunteered for intelligence ops behind enemy lines and why he made such a great reporter. The man was brilliant, but a two-edged sword. He had a big mouth. Especially when he drank. Which was all the time.

"I mean, it is possible she could have gone in the river just a short ways upstream, and most of the time she was lying right there, where you found her."

Willi visualized upstream from where they found her.

The Black Stag Inn.

But she couldn't have had her bones transplanted there.

"Maybe," he conceded. "Let's assume though she was floating for most of those hours."

"I'll tell you what." Fritz grinned. By the way he was rubbing his yachtsman's hands, Willi could tell he was about to propose one of his famous wagers. "I'll help you calculate the nautical mileage. I'll even help you find this mythical place *she* might have gone in the water . . . if you tell me one small thing about yourself."

"What on earth could be of interest about a boring man like me?"

Fritz put an arm around Willi's shoulder. "Why have you been avoiding me," he said as if weary to the bone, "when I've repeatedly told you I have the most *marvelous* woman I want to introduce you to? A woman so smart. So beautiful. So exactly what you need. But there's this absolute cad you see, just dying to—"

A determined knock at the door turned both their heads. "Willi—open up. I've got enough food here to feed an army and my arms are about to break."

Fritz looked at him, mortified. "*Ach nein,* Willi. The Boot Girl?"

Fifteen

"Why, Fritz!" Paula exclaimed as if they were dear old friends.

She was wearing a tight, red sweater dress with a matching ribbon in her hair.

And those goddamned black lace gloves.

"Merry Christmas, *Liebchen*. You, too, Willi."

She kissed them both on the lips.

"Can you believe what I lugged on the streetcar? Half a goose. My mother's apple tarts. You could smell it in Kreuzberg."

As they put away the food, Fritz couldn't stop looking at Paula. He was entranced by her, Willi could tell. Her bravura and her unstudied warmth. Her whole proletarian manner. Actually Fritz could be very liberal. For ex-royalty. It never seemed to matter to him, for instance, that Willi was a middle-class Jew, a mere civil servant. Fritz was devoted to him. And if an aristocrat can overlook such fundamental differences, Willi tried to convince himself as Paula snuggled between them on the couch, perhaps I can, too. Although Fritz of course was a total black sheep. His family had disowned him years ago. The man could take liberalism way beyond the pale. When he and Sylvie were still together and Vicki was alive, Fritz always wanted him to stop being so bourgeois and try swapping partners. He'd even wanted them all to go to bed together. "*Ach,* Willi, it's 1928, for crying out loud." Willi looked over at him now. From the gleam in his eye it seemed the son of a gun might have similar notions.

Indeed, after finishing several bottles the three had grown chummy on the couch, tapping each other's knees as they listened to Beethoven's Ninth from the Opera House. The music was heightening. The "Ode to Joy" approaching its fantastic climax. When out of the blue Paula jumped up and switched off the radio.

"Willi, don't you dare be pigheaded about this." She stared at him as if they'd been arguing. "I've given it a lot of thought. And the only way to find those sleepwalkers is to send in a decoy."

Willi's body stiffened. "You can't just go blabbing about this wherever you feel. It's police business, Paula. You make me sorry I ever told you."

"Who's blabbing?" Her emerald eyes glistened. "You told me Fritz was your oldest friend. You trust him with your life. With characters like these—you're going to need all the help you can get."

Fritz sat up. "So that's why the gun. You *are* in trouble."

"You're carrying a gun now?" Paula demanded.

Willi felt backed in a corner.

"Come on, *Freund.*" Fritz looked insulted. "I'd never forgive myself if anything happened to you. And you know very well I can hold my tongue when required. I didn't spill about the Child Eater, did I? Until you gave the word. So fess up: what's all this about sleepwalkers?"

Willi shot Paula a furious look.

She gave it right back. "Well, don't let your big fat head get in the way. Three brains are better than one."

Outside, the bells of the Kaiser Wilhelm Church tolled six o'clock. Willi looked at the four eyes seeming to burn through him. He tried to hold out, but couldn't. He did need help. And he trusted no one on the force anymore.

By the time he finished telling them, the three were cold sober.

"Sons of bitches." Fritz crushed a whole pack of cigarettes between his fingers. "Just when you think they can't be anywhere near as bad as they seem, they turn out a hundred times worse."

Paula paced. "Look, Willi. You gotta admit you can't go near Gustave incognito. He'd see right through you. But I never met the man. Have you, Fritz?"

"Me? No, never. Thank goodness."

"So there you have it. There's no choice but to let Fritz and me do it."

"Do what? What are you talking about?"

"I'll pretend to be Polish. My accent is perfect. If legs zis Gustave lookink for . . . vell . . . so . . . vat more he can be vanting?" She ran a hand up hers suggestively. "We'll go to Gustave's floor show. He'll hypnotize me. Give me his posthypnotic instructions. Fritz will accompany me home. And when I start walking, you and half the Berlin police follow me wherever the hell I go. It's the only way to find their lair."

Leave the rats bait, then watch them scurry back with it to their hole. Very good, Willi saw at once. If it worked, it could eliminate weeks of legwork and useless stakeouts. But even for a trained policewoman, it was too dangerous. These bastards didn't kidnap for ransom.

"Absolutely not."

"Maybe you don't want to admit what a fine plan the lady has, huh?" Fritz taunted. "Tell me: what have you come up with?"

"I'll take Gustave into custody. Search his house. With or without a warrant."

Paula shrugged. "You said it yourself, Willi: Gustave's just a pimp. What if you nab him and he doesn't talk?"

"Or worse," Fritz pointed out. "What if he really doesn't know. Maybe he just sends victims to some prearranged locale."

"He's still got to arrange it. Speak to someone."

"Maybe they keep him in the dark."

"But why?"

"Because," Paula guessed, "maybe he's not really doing this voluntarily. Maybe . . . they've got something on him."

Willi recalled the Great Gustave's yacht. His publishing empire. The millions he was worth. He certainly didn't need to abduct women for money, Willi had to admit. Maybe Paula was onto something. But even so. There was no way on earth he'd take a risk like that with her.

The church bells were tolling midnight when Fritz left. Willi was boiling mad. Paula had made a big show as if she were going to go with him as long as Willi was being such a stubborn mule. She gave Fritz a long kiss on the mouth, running her fingers through his hair, calling him *Liebchen* and making sure Willi heard her say how much she hoped to see him soon. Willi had no patience for games like that.

When she closed the door, he let her have a good firm crack across the face. He didn't enjoy it. But he meant it.

She stared at him, shocked. Then the green eyes filled with more love than ever. He turned away, too upset to look at her. "I'm going to freshen up," he heard her say, and she closed the bathroom door. He slumped against the kitchen counter.

Yesterday at Café Rippa, just as they were about to leave, his conversation with Kai had taken an extraordinary turn.

"Pardon me for butting in, Inspektor Kraus," the kid seemed

to say out of nowhere. "But as long as we're being honest here," he whispered from the side of his mouth, "I hear you've gotten chummy with a certain Tauentzien lady."

Willi was so shocked he didn't know what to say.

Despite its 4 million people, Berlin could be awfully small.

"Don't misunderstand me." Kai shrugged, pulling on his poncho and looking around for his hat. "Paula's the greatest. Everybody loves her. But I hope she hasn't given you the wrong impression."

"What do you mean?"

"Well, about her being she's something she isn't." He found the big slouch cap and put it on.

"I know who she is."

"Do you?" Kai adjusted the red feather on the side.

"What are you trying to tell me, Kai?" Willi asked as the boy got up to leave.

"Just this." Kai placed his huge hands on the table, his blue gaze piercing Willi, his gold earring dangling. "Have you ever looked between her fingers, Inspektor?"

And with a wink of a dark mascaraed eye, he left.

Paula emerged eventually from the bathroom, changed into a kimono. Her hair pinned up. Eyes as cloudy as waxed paper. There was a big red mark where he'd hit her.

"Ummm. I feel better." She stumbled toward him. "Give me a drink, Willi. Want to hit me some more?"

"Take off those goddamn gloves," he commanded. "Let me see your hands."

"No." She thrust them behind her back and pressed against a wall.

"I said take off those gloves."

He grabbed her arm.

She let out a shriek.

"Shut up, you fool." He clamped down on her mouth.

With his free hand he ripped one glove off, its thin lace tearing easily. Then he thrust her fingers up to the light. She fell passive and silent.

Between each finger was a dense black rash of needle marks.

She pulled away. "Don't tell me you didn't know." She glared at him bitterly.

He hung his head. He hadn't. He absolutely hadn't.

Unless . . . he just didn't want to admit it.

All those trips to the bathroom.

"So now you see how it is. Your beautiful Paula, a morphine addict. Since she was fifteen. You still want to take care of her? Still want to marry her?" She stopped, gasping for breath. "I didn't think so."

Then she grabbed him, turning him around, making him face her.

"Which is why you've got to let me do it, Willi. You could never be happy with somebody like me. Nobody could. I can't even. For God's sakes, don't deny me the one chance I'll have to do something useful with my—"

He turned away.

"We could finish off this whole sick operation." She was weeping bitterly now. "Think of how many lives might be—"

"No. No. No."

The phone startled them.

"Sorry for calling so late, Chief." It was Gunther. "I just wanted to let you know . . . there's been another sleepwalker. Greek this time."

Willi's stomach turned. "You got a name?"

"Yeah. Von Auerlicht. Melina. A countess of all things."

"Thanks, Gunther." Willi hung up, looking at Paula's cloudy eyes. She was begging for approval.

"Please, Willi. Please. Let me go."

"All right," he finally said, his throat clenching. "But only after I prepare every goddamn detail of this. I'm not offering you up as some sacrificial lamb."

"Oh, Willi, Willi." She hugged him fiercely. "You're such a wonderful boy."

First thing next morning he went to see Fritz.

Everybody knew the House of Ullstein. Eleven newspapers. Eight magazines. Ullstein Books. Ullstein Patterns. The uncontested publishing giant of Germany. As Willi entered their towering headquarters on Koch Strasse, he climbed a grand staircase lined with paintings of the famous Ullstein brothers—five in all, each heading up a different division of the company. Looking down from the top, a life-size portrait of their father, Leopold Ullstein, founder of the firm in 1877. And just below him, Fritz was waiting, his long dueling scar looking out of place, clashing with the furnishings, with his own pinstriped suit.

"Willi," he exclaimed, demanding a hug as if they hadn't seen each other in years. "After how many times I begged you to visit me here."

Excited as a twelve-year-old, he insisted on giving Willi a tour of Ullstein's nerve center. "This switchboard," he boasted, as if he were the sixth brother, "puts through forty-three thousand calls per day. And these pneumatic tubes blow editorial copy down to the composing rooms. On the roof, the largest radio receiver in Europe. And look at these new Teletype machines. They don't stop even for a moment."

"I heard Ullstein's fired half their Jewish employees," Willi muttered. "Including Ava."

Fritz hung his head. It seemed as if he had some important message to convey, but all his wires had crossed. "You have to understand," he stammered, pressing the elevator to the top floor, where both he and the Ullsteins had their offices. "We had a full-scale invasion here just before Christmas."

As they stepped out into the corridor, Willi saw workers whitewashing several enormous swastikas painted on the walls, and a giant slogan in what looked like dripping blood: "Down with Jewish Domination!"

"Ullstein represents everything these fascists hate. Democracy. Progress. Intellectual freedom. And of course . . . Jews. The company made a brutal sacrifice, trying to lower its profile. Those let go will be hired back of course, as soon as this blows over."

If men as powerful as the Ullsteins were trying to duck the Nazis, Willi wondered, who would stand up to them?

Maybe, he thought as they entered Fritz's office . . . me.

If he could uncover the beasts that mangled Gina Mancuso, perhaps he could undermine their whole lousy operation.

Samson and the Philistines.

Willi and Goliath.

Fritz already had a huge map of Berlin/Brandenburg/Havel River pinned up on his wall. He closed the door behind him and they got to work.

Based on the average river currents for the month of November, he told Willi, he'd calculated that the farthest Gina Mancuso could have entered the river was here: he pointed at the little village of Oranienburg. Some fifteen nautical miles north of Spandau. His finger traced the river south. Both shores were lined for miles with thick forests, dotted with countless inlets, channels, and tiny marsh islands.

Despite a great deal of boat traffic, barges mainly, and in summer recreational boating galore, tour ships, yachts, sailboats, etc., there was little human habitation. A small holiday village here, on the Tegel Peninsula—he pointed. A boathouse belonging to the university rowing team here, about three miles south. And an army installation, the Tegel Firing Range, way out here. Only one road ran the eastern shore, from Tegel to Spandau, and another on the western shore, from Potsdam as far as Pichelsdorf— but no farther. Through the dense Spandau Forest were only utility lanes and hiking trails. It was probably the closest thing to wilderness in metropolitan Berlin.

Willi's eyes scanned the lines and symbols spread before him, like a cabalist trying to decipher the universe. Somewhere out here Gina Mancuso had breathed her last. But where?

"Fritz"—Willi found himself mumbling without meaning to— "have you ever heard of a morphine addict kicking the habit?"

Fritz turned to him. "You mean . . . the black gloves?"

Willi nodded.

"I had a feeling." Fritz shook his head. "Girls like her, Boot Girls especially, always shoot between the fingers. With fetishists all over their feet. But no one kicks that stuff, Willi. I've seen plenty try. All those guys that got hooked in the war . . . withdrawal's worse than combat. It either kills them, or they go back— and the needle does. It's an ugly fate."

Yeah. Ugly, Willi thought. She could have been a Dietrich.

"What's this over here?" His finger landed on two small islands nestled in an inlet several kilometers south of Oranienburg.

Fritz stared at it. One of the islands had building symbols with capital *K*'s for *Krankenhaus*. Hospital. The other had several crosses, indicating a cemetery. Unlike the rest of the facilities featured on the map, however, these had no names.

"That's strange." Fritz's eyes darted around the room. From one of his crowded bookshelves he reached and pulled a giant atlas off the shelf: *Germany, 1900*. Leafing through it, he found a corresponding map of the Havel River. The islands were clearly named—Asylum Insel and Insel der Todt. Island of the Dead.

"A potter's field and an insane asylum. They must have been abandoned years ago," Fritz suggested. "I don't recall ever seeing them from the river."

"You wouldn't, unless you entered this channel. The peninsula obscures them."

"I don't know." Fritz shrugged. "It's just as possible as a dozen spots along our perimeter. The army range. The holiday village. Maybe even the tannery, here."

Willi put an arm on his shoulder. "Fritz, I'm sending in Paula. It's the only way. Gustave's playing at the White Mouse New Year's Eve. You in?"

From Koch Strasse, Willi took the U-Bahn back to Alexanderplatz. How cheerful it looked under a blue sky, with streams of
yellow streetcars and buses sweeping across, the early editions
crying out, **Strasser Walks! Nazis in Turmoil!** A surprising
confidence lifted him. Fritz's sources had been right. Perhaps
there was hope after all for '33. Perhaps he'd send in Paula and
she'd be fine. The whole operation would work like a glockenspiel.
They'd put these criminals on trial, and all Germany would see
the kind of creatures they were. The Nazi Party would crumble.
The republic would flourish. The world would be set in order.
He paused by the cake-filled windows of Café Rippa, remembering the Berlin of a few short years ago—thriving, dynamic. No
economic catastrophes. No battles in the streets. But out in front
of Wertheim's Department Store he saw the picket lines again, a
score of Brownshirts chanting in unison, *"Every time you buy
from Jews—"*

Upstairs in the Alexander Haus, he was shocked to discover
the damage inflicted by a plague of these troops just before dawn
this morning. All the Jewish offices had been broken into, desks
overturned, typewriters smashed, papers scattered through the
halls. Where had the police been? Outside. Guarding the doors.
Poor Bessie Yoskowitz hadn't been spared. Her entire workshop
had been ransacked, her chemicals strewn about, valuable documents trampled.

"Small fry like me." She looked at Willi bitterly. "You said they
wouldn't bother, heh? So now it's back to Poland. Anti-Semites
they got plenty of, but Nazis, thank God, not yet. Still, you don't
worry, Inspektor. Your work I got done." She shuffled through
the broken glass and came back with an envelope. "Here." She
handed it to him. "Safe and sound."

"Thank you, Bessie. I'm so . . . sorry about this."

"Yeah. Sorry. Me, too."

Willi handed her all the cash in his wallet, almost a hundred marks. "Take this," he insisted. "And *sei gesund,* Bess. Be in good health."

Back outside, the crowds of unemployed milled about in the sunshine, moving unconsciously to the rhythm of the Nazi chants. Willi leaned against an advertising column and opened the envelope.

Yoskowitz had done her job gorgeously, completely lifting the white ink off the black, leaving a legible list of Meckel's associates from the Institute for Racial Hygiene. There were six. Five he'd never heard of. But the third—well, well. Dr. Oscar Schumann. Associate surgeon of orthopedics at Charité Hospital. It didn't prove much, he told himself, slipping it back in the envelope and turning toward the Police Presidium. Only that Meckel and Schumann had worked together. But it definitely was a step forward. He reached Entrance Six and pulled open the doors. Now all I have to do is figure out what this Institute for Racial Hygiene is.

And where.

Gunther had more news.

"Remember those two hundred fifty-five inmates missing from the Charlottenburg Asylum?" The kid's blue eyes flamed. "I know you told me to drop the matter . . . but I just couldn't. I found out who took them. This wonderful girl I met, see." His Adam's apple quivered. "Christina. So pretty. And crazy for me. Anyway, she works in the accounting office out there and—"

"Damn it, Gunther, get to the point!"

The blood was pounding through Willi's skull. He couldn't stop picturing those ransacked offices and the pain-filled face of Bessie Yoskowitz. Where would all this end?

"The point, sir"—Gunther swallowed—"is that all those inmates were taken by the same people Meckel was associated with."

He handed Willi a sheet of paper.

It was a copy of a transport order. Eighty-five inmates of the

Berlin-Charlottenburg Asylum to be transferred for "Special Handling" to a place called Sachsenhausen. No address listed. A black stamp underneath read simply, IRH.

Institute for Racial Hygiene.

Sixteen

"Ernst Roehm had nothing to do with Meckel's death," von Schleicher insisted at the Reichs Chancellery the next afternoon. His new desk, Willi noted, was almost as big as Hindenburg's—but not quite. The Reichs president was still the most powerful man in Germany. He'd appointed von Schleicher with a nod and could just as easily dump him.

Willi was stunned by this assertion. "If not Roehm, who?"

The chancellor removed his monocle and leaned all the way back in his red leather armchair. He looked haggard. Years older than when Willi'd seen him a few weeks ago on Bendler Strasse, a mere minister of war. Now his voice was weak and hoarse. As if he did nothing all day but shout orders—to no avail.

"Whose exact finger pulled the trigger"—the chancellor grimaced as he pinched his nose—"I wouldn't care to speculate on."

He glanced dimly at Willi. "Only that in all likelihood the rest of the body was clad in a black uniform."

"Black?"

Willi was sure it had to have been brown. Since when did the portfolio of the Blackshirts, an intelligence-gathering unit, include assassination?

Von Schleicher gave a grim little grin. "Roehm thinks it was an attempt to discredit the SA."

"I don't understand. The SS is part of the SA."

"Yes. But its leadership would like nothing better than to foment a rupture—and become responsible directly to Hitler. Himmler and his new deputy, Heydrich—a cold-blooded reptile if ever I met one—have this dream, you see. They wish to build an elite Aryan militia." The general's gaze filled with contempt. "A Master Army of the Master Race. If that were to happen, of course, the SS and the SA, which as we all know consists largely of the dregs of society, would be, well, shall we say . . . snakes in a basket. Eventually one would have to perish. Perhaps this was a first bite."

An apt metaphor, Willi thought.

But it only made the knot in his stomach tighter.

This operation was starting to make the hunt for the *Kinderfresser* look like a junior league football match. Back then the whole crowd had been on his side. His quarry had to dart through the shadows alone. Now it was Willi who stood nearly alone. And what he was up against . . . God only knew. He still had no idea where any of these people had vanished to. How many there even were. If Gunther's asylum inmates had wound up with the Great Gustave's sleepwalkers . . . this mass kidnapping dwarfed any crime he ever heard of.

Where could they have taken so many people?

And why?

Not merely the logistics, but the motive, as he was starting to grasp it, was of mind-boggling dimension. The *Kinderfresser* had no motive, other than pathological compulsion. But a single afternoon at the Prussian State Library and Willi began to perceive that the insanity he was dealing with this time was nothing irrational. In fact, just the opposite: it was rationality taken to the extreme. A fanatical ideology masquerading as science.

The Institute for Racial Hygiene had been founded by something called the Fraternal Order of Blood Germans—no address listed—but a national organization, according to its newsletter, devoted to the science of "race advancement" through selective breeding. Eugenics. Its twelve-thousand-strong membership firmly believed the German nation was under attack from "inferior genes." In 1930, their anonymous steering committee had established an anonymous institute of biologists, geneticists, psychologists, and anthropologists charged with the task of formulating concrete proposals to "strengthen the national body through the eradication of degenerating genetic transmissions."

Among the recommendations put forth in a 1931 manifesto, before the institute seemed to disappear entirely, was something called a Law for the Prevention of the Genetic Disorders. Willi could not believe what he read. Every German who suffered from schizophrenia, manic depression, epilepsy, congenital blindness, deafness, physical deformity, alcoholism, hemophilia—an estimated 4.5 million people, according to the good doctors at this institute—needed to be sterilized, forcibly if necessary, to expunge their genes from the race pool. The most practical method for such a large-scale program, they wrote, was under investigation. Willi's bones had rattled. They were investigating how to sterilize 4.5 million people?

Also proposed was a "blood protection" law, to criminalize sexual relations between Germans and Jews. Only the "complete elimination of the Jewish race from Germany would lessen the Semitic threat to Germanic blood."

These purported scientists declared, "Human history is racially determined. Race is the decisive force. Every great nation rejects gene-mixing. This is as innate in people as in animals."

Now Willi remembered his bunny-toothed friend from Spandau, Josef, pushing his way up the gangplank that afternoon to the Great Gustave's yacht, dressed in an all-black officer's uniform. The first time he'd seen him at the Black Stag, under his wool coat he'd had on a doctor's smock. Willi was sure of it.

"Herr Reichs Chancellor." He put his hands on the desk and leaned toward the tired-looking general. "Does the SS have a medical staff?"

He left the Reichs Chancellery armed at least with some of what he needed—von Schleicher solidly behind him.

"I am this close"—the chancellor had actually shown him on a yardstick—"to destroying the Nazi Party. Thanks to the three election hurdles I forced them to leap this year, they are in debt to the tune of ninety million marks. Their electoral support is flagging. They no longer possess an aura of invincibility. And now"—he smacked the stick on his palm—"I've induced Party Secretary Strasser to walk, threatening to take a third of the membership with him. If we can expose this criminal ring, Willi, I am convinced it would be the final straw."

With so many top scientists, an anonymous fraternity, and the SS possibly involved, though, both men agreed a routine investigation was out of the question. A strike at the heart was the only plausible option. The swiftest way: send in their decoy. Find this base. Then spread out a dragnet for those left at large. Unfortunately, both also agreed that the loyalty of the Berlin police force had grown too risky to rely on. Willi was stunned to learn from von Schleicher that Willi's own boss, Kommissar Horthstaler, had joined the Nazis a month ago.

"These scum have been erecting an underground network to take over the police department the moment they seize power," the chancellor spelled out, angrily bending the yardstick. "But you and I," his voice rumbled ominously, "can stop them, Willi.

You and I, and men like us"—he clasped the ruler—"can be the ones who go down in history." He whacked the desktop. "Not them."

Willi wished he had the general's conviction. What he did have now, though, was an army unit of the Reichs garrison in Potsdam at his disposal. And their latest secret weapon—portable radio. Three transmitter/receiving units small enough to be mounted in the back of a truck or a boat. At least it would give them a leg up in communications. What they could have done with that in the last war.

The next morning . . . another step forward.

Gunther confirmed that Dr. Oscar Schumann, Meckel's associate at the Institute for Racial Hygiene, was the very same "Jewdamm" Schumann from the Black Stag Inn. *Unwarhscheinlich!* He'd actually seen him there last night and heard him addressed by his full name. That friendly little Spandau tavern, if not a base, was definitely a staging area for this whole dirty business.

"I recognized him right away from your description." The kid's white cheek quivered. "Wearing a white doctor's coat. With Mr. Bunny Teeth at his side. Josef. Whose last name unfortunately I didn't get. But also in a doctor's coat. And how do you suppose the two arrived, Chief? By boat! There's a small dock at the edge of the beer garden. I saw them tie up. They were complaining about how foul the air was at Sachsenhausen, how glad they were to be rid of it."

Sachsenhausen, again.

If only they could locate it before New Year's Eve.

Then Paula wouldn't have to go.

But neither he nor Fritz nor von Schleicher's spies, nor Ernst Roehm's Brownshirts, nor even Kai and his gang of Red Apaches, could pinpoint this mythical place.

So on the final evening of 1932, Paula zipped into her pink movie-star gown and "freshened up" for her mission.

The knock at the door came at eight.

Fritz arrived in top hat and tails and long black cape.

"*Szczęśliwego Nowego Roku!*" Paula hailed, giving him a great big hug. "Happy New Year, *Liebchen!*"

In her former profession, one had to know a little of every language, she explained in her Polish accent.

There was time at least for one final toast.

"To 1933." They all clinked glasses.

"You'll see." Her eyes flashed like green neon. "It's going to work, Willi." She planted a big kiss on his cheek. "And when I come back, I'll start all over again. Fresh as a newborn babe. You won't even recognize me. There are new clinics, you see, abroad mainly, that help people like me." She ran her gloved finger along his cheek. "Naturally they're expensive. But supposedly terribly effective. Isn't that right?" She clutched Fritz by the arm.

"Oh, yes, of course, quite." He patted her hand. "In fact Hermann Göring just got back from one in Sweden. Hooked on morphine for years. Now I hear he's sober as a Lutheran minister."

"It's all going to work this time. I can feel it in my bones." She clutched Willi by his lapels. "I'll come back to you. I promise."

"Damn right. As soon as Gustave's show is over. Just make sure he chooses you to volunteer."

"*Nie rozśmieszaj mnie.*" She kissed him, modeling her legs again. "Don't make me laugh."

After the door closed, Willi fell into an armchair. The wind was howling outside his window, the bells of the Kaiser Wilhelm Church slowly tolling. Picking up the phone, he got the long-distance operator and asked for Paris. Ava answered. Her voice was like a warm scarf around him. "Willi, you all right?"

"Fine. Fine. The investigation's moving along. If all goes well, we could wrap it up, I don't know . . . in a couple of days hopefully. How are the kids?"

"Having a ball. Mom and Dad have taken them out to see the

light festival on the Champs-Élysées. They're so excited to stay up until midnight. Are you there all alone?"

Willi's throat went dry. If only he were in Paris with them.

"Yes. But just as well. I could use a little time to unwind. Listen, send my love to them, Ava. And your parents. And to you . . . the happiest of all New Years."

At midnight the bells tolled. The streets filled with firecrackers and party horns. A drunken man kept shouting out the window, "Happy 1933! Happy 1933!" Willi was not religious at all, but he felt like praying . . . Lord, please make this one better than last.

Sometime around one thirty he heard drunken laughter in the hallway. There was no mistaking Paula's cackle. "Well, what happened?" He let them in. "Did he hypnotize you?"

"Did he ever," Fritz cried, his dueling scar aflame. "Do you realize that in addition to Polish, our brilliant little Paula here can speak Chinese? *Ling ni how chu. Ling tang! Ling tang!*" he imitated hysterically.

"Stop." She slapped him, gasping from laughter. "I did not."

"Tell me what happened." Willi sat them on the couch.

"Gustave died when he saw her legs."

Paula hoisted the pink gown. "He called them Ideal." She pretended to blush, then deepened her voice to imitate him. " 'You may wish you had these, ladies, but only one in a thousand women do."

" 'The Ideal leg, like anything wonderful and perfect,' " Fritz picked up, " 'indicates a strong, vital life force.' "

And together they both shouted, " 'Passion!' "

"But did he give you any posthypnotic suggestions?"

"How should I know? I don't remember a thing beyond him drooling over me."

"Well, did he, Fritz?"

"I sat as far up front as I could. But Gustave leaned so close to all the women, right on top of them practically . . . I just couldn't tell."

Willi inhaled. "Then there's nothing to do but wait."

"Good." Paula clapped. "More drinks!"

"No. From here on in—coffee only."

Willi was pouring them a second cup when the bells on the Kaiser Wilhelm Church struck two o'clock.

Paula's eyes fluttered a moment. *"Mein Gott."* She clasped her forehead. "I completely forgot. Cigarettes."

Fritz looked at Willi. "Cigarettes? I've got plenty here."

"No. I don't smoke those." She looked around for her cape. "I'll just run down to the corner. The kiosk'll have my brand, I'm sure."

In her black cape and pink evening gown she drifted up Nuremburger Strasse, Willi and Fritz keeping several yards behind. The sidewalks were more crowded than at two in the afternoon. Whole parties were out, singing, laughing, throwing firecrackers. Every pub and restaurant was full. But Paula moved as if in a dream. Her gait, slow and steady, gradually picked up pace as if she started feeling late for something.

On Tauentzien, one of the Boot Girls recognized her. "Paula! For goodness' sakes. What have you been up to, *Mädchen*?" But Paula ignored her and walked by like a blind deaf-mute. "Some nerve." The girl scowled. "Found yourself a gentleman, huh, tart!"

Past the Kaiser Wilhelm Church, the Gloria Palast, and the Romanisches Café, she floated ghostlike through the holiday mayhem. Once she slowly peeked over her shoulder and seemed to see Fritz and Willi, but didn't care. Arriving at the Zoo Station, she lifted her dress and hovered up the stairs. On the westbound platform she stood while trains came and went, clutching her cape and rocking gently back and forth, as if she'd fallen asleep. When one marked SPANDAU rattled in though, she quickly stepped on board.

It was packed. Teenagers were drinking and throwing strings of firecrackers among the passengers' feet. The staccato explosions made women scream as if they were being machine-gunned. One actually passed out. Paula stood like a zombie in a corner, as if she weren't there.

At the end of the line, a dozen or so people were still on board. Fritz and Willi let her off first, in case she was being followed. They stood on the platform and watched her pink figure descend the long flight of stairs. She seemed to know exactly what she was doing. On the street she slowly walked to the corner, looked both ways, then crossed.

Directly under the Nazi flag, she disappeared into the Black Stag.

Seventeen

An hour later Fritz jabbed him with an elbow. "Reminds me of Soissons, huh, Willi? Spring, 1918. Remember? Behind French lines."

Willi was hardly in the mood for reminiscing. But now that he thought about it . . . yeah. Kind of. The moonlight on the river. The heavy, dark air. A million stars.

Anxiety tearing up his gut.

At any moment Paula could come out that door with her captors—and the chase would be on. They had the Black Stag Inn surrounded. He'd parked the radio trucks a few blocks down the only side streets leading in and out, manned by Reichs Wehr officers handpicked by von Schleicher. He had more of Schleicher's men inside the S-Bahn station, posted up the Citadel tower with binoculars, and down in the alley behind the tavern. Inside, Gunther was ready to telephone him the minute Paula was about to leave. Willi and Fritz waited downstream at the Havel River Cruise pier, where Fritz's new cabin cruiser, *The Valentina,* was all tanked up, with the third mobile radio installed.

Because Willi had no idea what to expect wherever they were going, he'd no choice but to confine this stage of their operation to reconnaissance. Clearly this Sachsenhausen place was remarkably secluded. But was it armed? If so, by what force? How many people were they holding? He had to know before mounting any sort of assault. So he'd pulled a plan from one of the old war books. He and Fritz were going to launch an old-time scouting raid. By car or by boat they would follow Paula however and wherever these bastards took her. Then they'd reconnoiter the enemy dispositions. Once they knew what they were up against, then and only then would they call in reinforcements.

Waiting was the worst part. On the Western Front they'd learned that the hard way. As he fixed his binoculars at the Black Stag, just beneath the Nazi flag, Willi didn't stop Fritz from jabbering nonstop, knowing it eased the tension.

"Remember that day we saw Ludendorff lose his marbles?"

Not a favorite memory.

November 1918, the bitter end, they had witnessed Erich Ludendorff, supreme commander of the Imperial High Staff, sitting in his open limousine, stuck in traffic with the rest of the retreating army, having a nervous breakdown. Ranting, crying, punching the car, blaming the kaiser, the Reichstag, von Hindenburg, everyone but himself for the lost war.

"I swear to you, Willi, half of Berlin's gone just as crazy." There was no mistaking the angst in Fritz's voice. "I've never seen anything like it. Sheer hysteria. Scheming like there's no tomorrow. The whole thing's ready to blow."

Through the binoculars Willi watched the swastika flying in the wind.

"Von Papen's absolutely hell-bent on revenge against von Schleicher for having him sacked last November, determined to forge a new alliance—with Hitler. I interviewed him the other day. Totally lost all reason. He actually believes the Nazis have been weakened enough that if Hindenburg snaps the presidential whip and he wields the vice chancellor's chair, Hitler could be tamed as chancellor. Every idiotic rumor circulating in Berlin he repeated to me. The Communists ready to move with Soviet troops. The kaiser plotting a return with the help of the British crown.

"And as for our dear friend von Schleicher . . . well, far from carrying off a third of the Party, Strasser's fled the country—alone! The Socialists are ready to bolt from his coalition, and the Junkers are backing Papen. No, I'm afraid our future now lies either with the Communists or the—"

The phone in the yellow booth cried out. Willi grabbed it.

"Side door," Gunther whispered. "Through the beer garden."

Finally. In another hour the sun would start rising. Camouflaged pursuit, especially by boat, would be impossible. But now, through the binoculars, Willi just made out Paula's pink evening gown in the predawn darkness, two men in overcoats escorting her through the beer garden, down a dock, and onto an inboard motorboat.

Its engine suddenly roared to life. Willi passed the binoculars.

"She's a V-10." Fritz listened more than looked. "Maybe one hundred and eighty horsepower. I can dance a Charleston around her."

"Tango would be fine," Willi said. "Come then, *vorwärts!*"

They scrambled aboard *The Valentina*, twenty-five thousand marks' worth of "art," according to Fritz—custom-made with chromium hardware, mahogany deck, the finest leather upholstery. And 250 horsepower, he reminded himself now, furiously untying her. On board they ducked in the shadows, waiting as their quarry neared, then roared by them into the wide, dark Havel. A moment before they vanished, Fritz hit the ignition.

Wind was suddenly tearing through Willi's hair. Icy spray smacking his face. As he went to turn on the radio, he found himself clutching the seat to keep from getting chucked overboard.

Only with great determination did he manage finally to contact one of his communications trucks. "North by northwest, across the Havel," he practically had to scream to be heard.

"*Verstanden*, Herr Inspektor."

He wished he'd brought gloves. And a hat. Even as a kid he'd never liked boating. The faster they went and the harder they rocked, the more miserable his stomach felt. There was a definite reason he hadn't joined the navy.

"Are you sure they don't see us?" His mouth was filling with saliva.

"No guarantee," Fritz cried from the wheel. "I'm keeping far back as I—"

Willi grabbed the side rail and threw up.

Fritz laughed so hard he almost lost control of the boat.

In half an hour they were rounding the edge of the Tegel Peninsula, heading due north toward Oranienburg, where the river narrowed by half. They had passed the boathouse and the holiday village. Where was Sachsenhausen?

Willi'd just finished radioing in their latest position when he heard Fritz cry:

"Jesus Christ, they spotted us."

"No—"

Willi dropped the microphone, stumbling to his feet, praying it wasn't true. But even in the misty darkness there was no denying the boat ahead was making a sharp right turn, sending up a huge spray as it tipped practically on its stern and headed straight toward them.

Disaster.

The choices were appalling. They could shoot it out, Willi knew—he hadn't been foolish enough to come unarmed. But Paula might get hurt. They could turn and outrun them—but Paula would be lost. So would Sachsenhausen. They could let themselves be overtaken, pretend they happened to be out here fishing at five a.m. But the maniacs would just as likely believe that as turn a machine gun on them and dump them in the Havel. His face, his scalp, all the way down his neck and back, broke into a freezing sweat. Frantically he searched the horizon. There had to be some way out. A shoreline somewhere. Like . . . that one . . . draped with giant fir.

"Over there!" he shouted.

Fritz got it.

Directly among the thickest of green, the boat angled in to the riverbank. As they scraped bottom, Fritz cut the motor. The moon disappeared. They were shrouded in darkness. Great draping branches mercifully embraced *The Valentina*.

The roaring engine of their former quarry—now their hunter— grew louder. Fritz and he clung to the deck, Willi's head practically bursting with anxiety. If they were spotted, all was lost. Louder . . . Louder . . . The boat was upon them. It was tearing right past . . . oblivious to their whereabouts. They'd done it!

With any luck they could finish this mission still.

But his optimism proved premature.

A minute later, suspicious they'd been given the slip, the boat doubled back and began reapproaching, this time slower, nearer the shore.

Bang-bang! Bang-bang-bang! Like strings of firecrackers a machine gun opened fire—randomly into the trees. As it neared, the deck around Willi's face erupted into mahogany splinters. Chromium was tearing loose with shrill, pathetic shrieks. Sparks flew. Branches fell. *Bang-bang! Bang-bang-bang!* The enemy kept moving down the shore, gunfire cutting through the trees for what seemed minutes. Then it stopped. Their engine picked up. They were heading back into the Havel, upstream, on their original course.

Fritz groaned loudly. Willi pushed the branches from his face. Coughing from sulfur, he realized the boat was listing hard right. The radio receiver was a heap of smoking wire. And Fritz was sprawled on his leather upholstery, his shoulder red with blood. "What have they done to my beautiful *Valentina*?" he moaned.

Damn your *Valentina*, Willi thought, searching for the medical box.

What have they done to our mission?

Eighteen

Beneath the enshrouding green a hellish gloom prevailed. On the ground the carpet of needles echoed back every futile step. Great birds shrieked derisively. They were lost in the *Urwald*. The forest primeval.

It could have been worse. They could have been killed. Or captured. Taken to Sachsenhausen. Flayed alive. But it was bad enough. The boat and the radio were gone. So was Paula. A bullet had lodged in Fritz's shoulder. The bandage Willi had fixed didn't keep Fritz from losing blood. He was starting to get delirious.

"Did you know . . . ," he stammered, all but dragging his feet now. Willi had to hoist him along, every step, so heavily painful. "Did you know our Germanic forefathers believed the whole world was supported by a giant evergreen tree?"

"For God's sakes, *Mensch*, save your energy."

"That under its branches dwelled the forest gods, who sat in judgment of the dead beneath its roots."

"Fritz, I said shut up."

The last thing Willi needed was to be reminded of the pagan past.

They were stumbling in preternatural darkness. No idea where they were. No road. No trail. Just conifers. Mile after mile of them. Barely a ray of sunlight penetrated. With their compass destroyed, they were hopelessly adrift. Like Hansel and Gretel in the woods.

"Fear makes the wolf bigger than he is," Willi remembered his mother telling him as a child. But even a cub just now was more than he'd care to face.

Fritz stumbled, then collapsed, a branch on the ground snapping from his weight.

Willi's heart wrenched. He leaned down and lifted his old friend's torso. The bandage, he saw, was sopping with blood.

"Leave me, Willi," Fritz panted, deathly white. "Go on. Save yourself."

"I didn't in France. You think I'm going to abandon you twenty miles from Berlin-Center? There's got to be someone in this god-forsaken wilderness."

"*Hilfe!*" Willi shouted from the bottom of his lungs.

But all he got back was his own fearful voice.

As he stood there looking at the forest, filling with rage, he realized there was nothing else to do. He was going to have to carry Fritz.

He yanked and hoisted him piggyback style, feeling the weight in his knees. His shins. His ankles. Ignoring it, he started to walk. But in which direction? For all he knew, they'd been circling for hours now. Still, what choice was there but to pick a route and stick to it? He did. But it wasn't long before the burden became unbearable. His back began cramping. His thighs shook. Every step he took became impossible, beyond what he could endure. *Not bricht Eisen.* Another of his mother's sayings hammered through his skull. Necessity breaks iron.

"You know this forest used to be mixed conifer and deciduous," Fritz was mumbling in his ear. Willi could feel his shoulder getting wet from Fritz's blood. "During the war Berliners trekked out here for firewood. They cut down all the birch and poplar, the alder and the—"

A sickening feeling filled Willi's gut as his foot began to sink. He looked around trying to contain the rising panic. He'd stumbled into a bog. He couldn't see where it began. The ground had turned to thick, black peat, gluelike, grabbing his feet, refusing to let go. A shiver of terror went through him. He'd survived infantry assaults, artillery bombardments, gas attacks. Why did he feel this was the end?

"Leave me, Willi," Fritz kept saying.

Necessity breaks iron. Necessity breaks iron.

The ground seemed intentionally resisting his every effort to extricate himself, like the clasp of Satan. He pictured centuries from now . . . their skeletons unearthed . . . displayed in a museum next to a woolly mammoth. With no small irony he realized it was New Year's Day. Happy 1933. He wondered about Paula. Had she come out of her trance? Did she feel as helpless as he did right now? How could he die? He had to rescue her. All those people at Sachsenhausen. His heart was pounding faster than a machine gun. He cursed and swore, spewing fire. Managing a step. A half. Another.

Not bricht Eisen. Not bricht Eisen.

What choice was there but to believe?

To just keep—

His foot flung loose and the next step he took landed on something hard. It made him lose balance. Fritz and he went plummeting, tumbling headfirst into a blanket of pine needles. Pain. But the earth beneath them . . . solid. Terra firma! They were saved from the bog. Delirious though. Both of them.

Fritz kept yammering about the trees that had been cut down. "The poplar, the ash, the alder . . ."

Willi pressed his face into the dry earth, heaving with agony, so light-headed he actually thought he heard singing on the horizon. *Valderi, Valdera!* What a joke. The angels were coming for him—singing a hiking song. *Valderi!* He wasn't imagining it. They were coming. And they *were* singing a hiking song. *Valdera-ha-ha-ha-ha-ha!*

But they weren't angels. It was the *Wandervogel.*

The wandering children of the German forests.

Book Three

THE MEISTERSINGER

Nineteen

JANUARY 1933

Willi's vision filled with light.

A long, bony face looked down at him.

"Chief . . . it's me. Gunther."

Why am I home in bed? Willi wondered. Gunther in my chair? He sprang from the pillow, remembering. "What time is it?"

"Relax, sir. Take some hot broth." Gunther's eyes brimmed with doctorly concern. "It's not even two o'clock yet. Happy 1933."

Willi took the broth. There was reason for gratitude, he realized.

Just not quite enough of it.

The *Wandervogel*, some thirty in all, had made their appearance not a moment too soon. These student hiking groups had been a passion for decades now, embodying the ideals of romantic German youth: Comradeship. Nature. Wanderlust. Increasingly though they'd become politicized, more and more merging with the Hitler Youth. He had to thank his lucky stars these were the old-fashioned kind, rucksacks and hiking poles, singing away with buoyant spirits as they completed the first leg of their twenty-kilometer New Year's Day hike. In minutes they had a stretcher fashioned for Fritz from their hiking poles and branches. A delegation carried him back to the forest station where they'd begun their trek.

An hour later Fritz was in surgery at the Brandenburg Medical Center in Potsdam. As far as Willi knew, he was there still, recovering in stable condition. A sergeant from the Potsdam garrison drove him back to town. It wasn't even 9 a.m. Gunther was waiting in front of Willi's apartment building, half-crazed with fear.

"When we lost contact, we didn't know what to do, Chief—"

Now, Willi was the one who didn't know what to do.

Paula. Those goddamn animals had her.

"Gunther." He put down the broth, trying to swing his legs off the bed, realizing how weak he was. Exposure, the doctors had told him. A day or two in bed, at least.

"Help me get dressed. I'm going after that son of a bitch Gustave."

"But, sir—"

"Never mind."

Outside, it was cold and windy. Willi's head was throbbing. When they reached his little silver BMW, he handed Gunther the keys.

The kid's bony face reddened. "You're kidding, right?"

"Just don't get us killed. I've had enough aggravation for one day."

"Yes, sir!"

The Great Gustave's palatial apartment was on Kronprinz Strasse, just off the Tiergarten. Gunther pounded on the door. A petite French maid with big, wide eyes answered.

"*Oui, messieurs?*"

Unfortunately the King of Mystics wasn't home. He'd been

out already several hours. Where? She certainly had no idea. But she'd be terribly happy to tell him the *messieurs* had paid a visit if they wished to leave their—

Never mind.

Far down the road, the winged statue of Victory waved her golden laurel wreath from her column in the Plaza of the Republic.

It seemed to be Paula calling him:

"Willi—how could you do this to me? When I trusted you?"

He had to find Gustave.

Kai. At the Café Rippa the other day the SA dropout had promised his Red Apaches gang would keep an eye on the showman.

"Gunther, *mach schnell*. To the Alex."

The problem now was finding the Wild Boy.

Street by street the little BMW circled the enormous Alexanderplatz. Past the department stores and cafés, the beer halls and the S-Bahn station. People by the hundreds milled about on the sidewalks. Whole clans of working-class families out for a holiday stroll. Street hawkers. Cardsharps. Beggars and prostitutes. But no Kai. Where would a kid such as him hang around today?

The choices were substantial.

"Gunther, prepare yourself. I foresee an eye-opening New Year's Day in store for you."

"The farther open the better." Gunther laughed, shifting into third.

Their first stop was nearby Alexandrinen Strasse 108. La Petit Maison. The entrance in a garbage-filled alley. Behind a black door, a silver lamé curtain opened into a small room decorated like a French bordello: red velvet couches, fake chandeliers. A dozen or so overdressed girls, mid-to-late twenties, sat around courted by gangs of older men, who practically clawed each other over them.

"All these dames are hookers?" Gunther whispered, clearly believing himself finally wising up to ways of the world.

"The actual question, Gunther, would be whether these dames are dames at all."

The kid's eyes widened all right, to twice their size.

Willi went to the burly bartender to ask if he'd seen Kai around. The guy shook his head.

"If you do, tell him Kraus is looking for him."

"You're kidding, aren't you?" Gunther grabbed Willi's arm back out in the alley. "Come on, Inspektor, the truth. Jeez. Some of them were cute."

Next stop, the Adonis, a few blocks farther down Alexandrinen Strasse, no. 128—a little lounge for local Line Boys, truly seedy. Smoky room. Bare tables. Walls covered with cheap landscape paintings. A score of predatory eyes followed their arrival.

Line Boys—male prostitutes, heterosexual teens of the poorer classes—got their name from the lines they formed along walls in bars or back alleys. Since the Depression they seemed to lurk everywhere, almost uniformly dressed the way their customers most liked—as sailors. A rough-and-tumble lot, they gave the Berlin police their share of headaches. The swankier hotels often had to call out whole squads to chase them away.

Willi saw several now going around trying to sell packs of cocaine or black opium to the "aunties" who made up their clientele. One of these older gents, stoned, was banging away on an upright piano, while a gray-haired friend dreamily danced with a sailor. The piano player started singing:

Somewhere the sun is shining
So, honey, don't you cry!

Gunther seemed unable to take another step. Willi had to nudge him through the crowd.

"No, sir. Sorry, sir," a skinny waiter said. "Haven't seen Kai in a while, sir."

"Tell him Willi Kraus is looking for him."

"Yes, sir, Inspektor. Sir."

At Nollendorf Platz they entered a vast dance hall swept by colorful lights from a dozen revolving mirrored balls. Berlin of the republic was renowned for its open-mindedness, and men who liked men flocked here from around the globe. Nowhere was the freedom they sought more in abundance than at the Nollendorfer Palast. If Gunther had been shocked before, here he was stupefied.

The place was cavernous, filled wall to wall with a New Year's Day "tea dance" in full tempo. Countless hundreds of men swayed cheek to cheek to a dance orchestra playing "Love Is the Sweetest Thing." Tough types. Girlie types. Older couples in tuxedos and top hats. College kids with bow ties and big lapels.

"Mingle," Willi commanded.

"But, sir—"

"What?"

"I don't have to dance, do I?"

"Only if you're mad about the boy, Gunther."

Half an hour later though, not a sign of Kai.

Willi and Gunther went back outside. Evening was falling. A crescent moon had risen. Music drifted from the club.

"How about it, sir?" Gunther held out his arms.

"No jokes. We've got to find this kid."

At Cosy-Corner, blond men in their thirties wore schoolboy uniforms with little peaked hats as they leaned against the bar smoking. At the Magic Flute there was a floor show: Luziana, the Mysterious Wonder Woman—or Man, appearing with the Zusammen Bruder, a song-and-dance act of allegedly cojoined twins. The Mustache Lounge was filled with heavy drinkers sporting facial hair of extraordinary proportions, from elaborate sideburns to walrus whiskers.

But no one, absolutely no one, had seen Kai.

Finally it was getting late. Willi would have given up if he didn't keep seeing Paula in front of him, looking around for help.

One last place, he told himself.

Far down Friedrich Strasse, past the nightclubs and the cabarets, the greasy restaurants and sex bookshops, was a creepy leftover from the previous century, a grimy glass-roofed shopping arcade called the Passage, which even on the brightest days was daubed in gloom. Inside its peeling cast-iron colonnades, dozens of musty-smelling shops sold everything from paintings of the Virgin Mary to French ticklers. At night it became home to the saddest of all the city's kids on the make: the Doll Boys. These were Berlin's youngest hustlers, preteens, eleven, twelve, most of them scrambling to get something to eat or a place to rest their head at night. Their hangout was at the Anatomical Museum in the center of the Passage, a seedy exhibition hall of mannequins and real body parts illuminating every grotesque deformity known to man. Out front, the boys stood by the dozens, schoolboy hats and short trousers, dirty-faced and desperate, tussling over every man that came by.

"Any of you kids seen Kai of the Red Apaches?"

Their faces blanked simultaneously.

"Chief," Gunther whispered, "all this time we've spent looking for him . . . we could have been staking out Gustave's apartment. For all we knew he's home by now."

"Five marks to the kid who can bring me to Kai." Willi gave it one last try.

Half a dozen boys stepped forward.

It cost him thirty marks, but he got his answer.

And where was the chief of the Red Apaches?

La Traviata was letting out for intermission as Willi and Gunther screeched up to the grand old Opera House on Unter den Linden. Among the ladies and gentlemen pouring from the eighteenth-century building—one of Berlin's prize Schinkel masterpieces— Willi finally spotted the kid, all decked out in a shiny white tuxedo, smiling as he strolled down the main staircase with a rich-looking man. Willi quickly recognized him as the prince of Thuringia.

"Imagine this. Hello there." Willi pretended to have met accidentally. Shaking Kai's enormous hand, he leaned to his ear and added, "I must find Gustave."

"Give me a minute," the kid whispered back.

Willi and Gunther stood aside, awkwardly pretending to mix with the crowd of opera fans, fascinated by the sight of the chiseled eighteen-year-old at work on the wrinkled old prince. A minute later he was back.

"I convinced him to ditch the second act, thank God. I was dying of boredom anyway. He's taking me to this party; Gustave's supposedly there. Don't try to come in. There's a little park across the street. Keep in the shadows. I'll lure the son of a bitch over."

Willi's heart sank. "It won't work." He remembered the dozens of beautiful women Gustave liked to surround himself with.

"Inspektor"—Kai's eyes sparkled intuitively—"trust me. He's not the only one with hypnotic powers."

Willi and Gunther watched the kid slip a thick arm around the prince's waist and get him into a taxi.

They followed behind in the BMW.

The party turned out to be at the home of Heinrich Himmler, head of the SS. Willi's throat clenched as he counted half a dozen black-uniformed troops patrolling the perimeter. Through binoculars he made out an insignia on their caps he'd never seen before—a silver skull and crossbones. The death's head.

The big house was lit up like a bonfire, raucous laughter pouring from the windows, a dance band blaring, women shrieking. It made Willi's stomach turn. All these swine, living it up. And where was Paula? What were they doing to her?

At least they'd get Gustave, he consoled himself. The King of Mystics had sent his last sleepwalker on a voyage of no return. But what if he didn't cooperate?

"Gunther, take my key. Go to my apartment. Get my camera. It's in the front closet. And don't forget flashbulbs."

While Gunther was gone, the cold began to get to Willi. During the war he'd spent weeks out of doors. That was fifteen years ago already. He wasn't a kid anymore. His hands and feet were getting numb. More exposure. But think about Paula. Lord knew what she was enduring by now.

It was forty-five minutes before Gunther returned. Luckily he'd brought along a hot thermos of the broth from earlier. Willi was grateful, but even the delicious heat down his gullet didn't cheer him up. Surely Kai had overestimated his talents.

"Don't worry, Chief." Gunther seemed to read his mind. "One way or another Gustave'll be caught . . . in a web of his own making."

Inside they were singing Nazi songs at the top of their lungs.

Germany, awake from your nightmare
Rise up against the Jews!

The volume amplified as the front door opened.

In the light, an apparition: Kai in his white tuxedo . . . followed by a man in a shimmering black cape . . . Gustave! Willi and Gunther crouched in the shadows as the two crossed the street, Gustave, with his white gloves, carrying a walking stick, casually glancing about as if he were out for a breath of fresh air.

Always two-faced, Willi thought.

"You gotta admit the kid's good, heh?" Gunther whispered.

"I'll be damned," Willi said, watching them enter the park. "Got that camera ready?"

The rest was child's play.

Once in darkness the Great Gustave leaned against a tree and nonchalantly undid his tuxedo zipper. Gunther was about to step in but Willi held him back. Another second and Willi had the hypnotist exactly where he wanted him.

FLASH!

The King of Mystics turned to the light, his face a poster from a silent-screen melodrama. Eyes bulging. Mouth wide open.

As if he were about to be hit by a freight train.

Twenty

"You've got to be kidding. If you're not with the vice squad . . . there must be some— Wait a minute . . . I recognize you. Aren't you—"

"Kriminal Polizei." Willi flashed the badge. "You're under arrest for kidnapping."

"Impossible."

"We know all about it, *Freund*. From the Czechoslovakian track team to Melina von Auerlicht."

Willi nodded to Gunther, feeling the first real pleasure in days.

"Cuff him."

"But you're crazy . . . I don't know anything about any kidnappings."

They spirited him off to his swank apartment building on Kronprinz Strasse.

Upstairs, the French maid seemed instinctively to grasp what was happening and made a lunge for the telephone.

Willi cut her off. "No, no . . . *ma chérie.*"

The place appeared to have been decorated by the set designers of *The Cabinet of Dr. Caligari.* The walls and ceilings were painted black, emblazoned with phosphorescent symbols of the occult. Spotlights cast weird shadows over everything. Gustave's triangular office was studded with semiprecious stones and crystals, his desk, the size of the Reichs chancellor's, all glass.

Willi pushed him into the gold swivel chair behind it and pulled out a pistol.

"Herr Spanknoebel—if that's even your real name. Open your safe. And no funny business."

"Listen, Kraus. You've got me all wrong. I'm no criminal. I know how to use the powers of suggestion. I can put myself into a trance, see things others can't. But there aren't any tricks. No magic to it. I don't want to fool anyone. Least of all—"

"Open the safe." Willi cocked the pistol.

Gustave removed an oil portrait of himself from the wall, revealing a safe.

"My powers are a great gift, Inspektor. I use them to help people. I can use them to help you—"

Willi had to laugh.

So, the man who'd made untold millions from his clairvoyance, charmed Vienna and Berlin, given lessons to Hitler on crowd psychology, and sailed the Havel like a Babylonian king was now angling for a horse deal.

Willi pointed the pistol at Gustave's head. "Open the goddamn safe."

The documents inside proved fascinating, but did not have the names and addresses Willi needed. Hermann Göring, twenty thousand . . . Josef Goebbels, twenty-five . . . Rudolf Hess . . .

"*Gott im Himmel*—is there a Nazi in Germany who doesn't owe you a fortune?"

"Is it a crime now to lend one's friends money?"

"It depends, Spanknoebel."

"You've got it all wrong, Inspektor. They're gambling debts mainly. A few home-improvement loans. Göring needed to make a down payment on Karinhall. These National Socialists have had it tough the last few years."

Willi knew every second he wasted here was another Paula remained a prisoner.

"To the Alex with him. Let's see if a forestaste of life behind bars won't convince him it'd be wiser to cooperate."

"What about her?" Gunther pointed to the wide-eyed maid.

"She comes. No one's to know the Great Gustave has vanished."

"Some of those Nazis might be glad," Gunther noted. "With what they owe him."

All the way downtown Gustave kept insisting they had it all wrong. He started getting really agitated when they led him to the dark, empty cell deep in the dungeons of the Alex. "You're making a big mistake. Once they realize I'm missing, they'll come after you, Kraus. But I'll make you a deal—"

"You're forgetting the pictures I have, Gustave. Most unsavory."

"Are you kidding? Don't you think half of them—"

Willi slammed the cell door in his face.

"Kraus! God damn you . . . I'll get you for this!"

Willi looked at his watch. It was after midnight. He had to sleep. But he couldn't.

There was far too much to—

In the morning he awoke to find himself still at the Police Presidium, tucked in on the couch in his office, a blanket thrown over him. Gunther snoring on the floor.

Ruta was boiling a kettle on the little gas stove.

"Quite the New Year's bender you two had, huh? Good thing

you keep an extra suit around here," she grumbled, grinding the coffee beans. "Just look at those trousers, Herr Inspektor. The least you could have done is slept it off in your Skivvies."

Willi was glad he had an extra suit, too, although he could have used a shower.

Changing, he went directly to Gustave's cell, not waiting for coffee. No doubt a night in isolation had left the King of Mystics perturbed. Forlorn, Willi guessed as he spied through the cell door.

Now maybe he'd get somewhere with him.

Hearing the door, Gustave's eyes turned up with relief.

"Finally." He rose, reaching for his cape and walking stick. "I told you this was all a mistake." He smiled affably. "Who interceded for me? Göring? Hess? Not the Führer!"

"Keep your pants on, Gustave. None of them even knows you're missing."

A shadow crossed his face. "You're lying."

It was Willi's turn to smile. "Believe as you wish."

"Why are you doing this to me? What do you want, Kraus?"

"Tell me what happened to the girls. Cooperate and things will go easier for you."

"I don't know what you're talking about. What girls?"

"*You said it yourself, Willi,*" he recalled Paula saying. "*Gustave's just a pimp. What if you nab him and he doesn't talk?*"

Gustave's plain brown eyes filled with a look of innocence. Willi had to strain to keep from strangling him.

"*What if he really doesn't know?*" he remembered Fritz pointing out. "*Maybe he just sends victims to some prearranged locale.*"

"*He's still got to arrange it. Speak to someone.*"

"*Maybe they keep him in the dark.*"

"*But why?*"

"*Because,*" Paula had guessed. "*Maybe he's not really doing this voluntarily. Maybe . . . they've got something on him.*"

Willi thought again about Gustave's yacht. His publishing empire. The millions this guy was worth. Could he really have done what he did for more money? Could anyone be that greedy? Or might these Nazis in fact have something on him?

Willi had no patience to find out.

No time for a battle.

"Spanknoebel . . . one last chance to cooperate. If you're worried about your safety, I'm prepared to offer you protection."

Gustave looked at him as if bewildered.

All at once he broke out laughing.

"Offer me—" His laughter grew. "I know my fate better than anyone. It's written in the stars! Nothing you can do could alter it in the—"

Willi walked out, slamming the door again. All the way down the hall, he could hear Gustave screaming, "Get me out of here!" But if compromising photos and a night behind bars weren't enough to crack the master's resistance, it was time to shift gears.

Obviously Willi was dealing with a pro here. What he needed was another pro. He stormed upstairs to use the phone, but with a sudden shudder remembered the date: January 2. Kurt had said he was leaving on the second. Never mind the phone, Willi darted out to Dircksen Strasse with no coat. Where the hell had he parked his car?

His cousin lived in a fine old Wilhelmian building on Budepester Strasse, with winged dragons holding up the entrance. How well Willi remembered it as a kid, the long, winding flights of stairs that echoed like the Alps, the wonderful smells of cooking and laughter during the holidays. A strange echo reached his ears now as he rang the apartment bell. An anxious eye appeared through the peephole. Kurt's wife opened up and threw her arms around him, breaking into tears.

"Willi. For God's sakes I was afraid we'd miss you." Kathe's dark eyes were red with tension. "Come in. I can't offer you much. We leave for the station in a few hours. I called a dozen times so the kids could say good-bye, but Kurt told me the boys were in Paris and, well, you can't imagine what a week it's been."

Willi got a shock to see the big apartment. A few months ago he'd been here with Erich and Stefan to celebrate the Jewish New Year. The walls were covered with so many books and paintings. The floors snug with Persian rugs and Chinese jardinieres brimming with African violets. A baby grand gleamed in the corner. Now it was empty, as if all the belongings had been sucked into a giant vacuum cleaner.

The past swept away.

The future, too. Where would he take the boys next holidays?

His cousin and the three kids were seated about the floor on crates, breakfast plates balanced on their laps. Kurt jumped up in his shirtsleeves and suspenders.

"Well, look who's come to say good-bye."

Helmut, Stefan's age, started to bawl. "I don't want to go!"

Gregor, Erich's buddy, disappeared and returned with a giant model of the Fokker triplane the Red Baron had flown.

"Can you give this to Erich, Uncle Willi?" He held it aloft, trembling. "There's no one else I can think of who'll take proper care of it."

"Yes, of course, Gregor. Erich will be thrilled."

Willi's heart pulled in a dozen directions. He wanted to tell them not to go. That they were overreacting. That they were tearing up all their roots for nothing. The Nazis would never rule Germany. And yet . . . how glad he was his boys were in Paris.

"Kurt, could I speak to you a moment."

They stepped into one of the bedrooms. It took more than a moment, of course.

Kathe got impatient. "Is everything all right in there? Kurt . . . we haven't any time to waste."

"Hold on a minute, dear. It's important."

Behind their spectacles Kurt's eyes were wide with incredulity. "You know, Willi, as a psychiatrist I've heard my share of horror stories over the years . . . but I genuinely find this hard to believe. The entire fibula you say, transplanted in the opposite leg?"

"I'll show you the autopsy reports if you want."

"I want to help of course . . . but you heard Kathe. Our train leaves at two."

"You know I wouldn't ask if it wasn't a matter of life or death. God knows how many people they're holding out there. What they're doing to them."

"But what exactly can I do?"

"Hypnotize the son of a bitch. Get him to talk."

A smile drew across Kurt's lips. "There's nothing I'd love more than to get that charlatan under my spell."

"You'd have to do it against his will. He definitely won't cooperate."

"I could hypnotize Hitler against his will."

"Could you? Really? Then you'll do it?"

Kurt rubbed his glasses clean. Sighing, he put them back on.

Kathe clutched her scalp as if this were really the last straw.

"How could you leave at a moment like this? Everything in the balance? Our whole lives—"

"Listen, Kathe . . . some things are more important even than your own family. I've got to do this. Willi's promised to have me at the station by two. You're perfectly capable of getting the children there by taxi. Everything else is taken care of. Now . . . if for some reason I miss the train—"

"You wouldn't dare."

"If I do . . . I will catch a later one and meet up with you in Bremerhaven."

"Willi Kraus"—Kathe eyed him vengefully—"I swear I'll never forgive you."

When Kurt climbed into the BMW clutching his son's red model airplane, he turned to Willi with a grin. "You know,

Cousin—I'm forever in your debt. It may have come at an awkward moment, but this is a chance I've been waiting a lifetime for."

Yeah, well, it better work, Willi thought, tearing down the street.

Twenty-one

"*He's* your interrogator?" The Great Gustave sneered at the bald, bespectacled man in his cell. "Berlin police must be more desperate than I realized."

Willi forced a smile. "Why—not brutal-looking enough? Come now, Herr Spanknoebel. You don't suppose we intend to abuse you?"

Gustave shrank on the bed, clutching his cape.

Kurt leaned forward, eyeing him. "As long as we have to work together, you and I," he said in a kind yet emphatic way, "why don't we just relax? After all, this may take some time." He rose, patting Gustave's shoulder. "Don't you think it'd be a lot more sensible, more pleasant, if we both just . . . relaxed?"

"I don't want to relax. I want to get out of here."

"Naturally." Kurt took off his eyeglasses and cleaned them. "Who wants to stay in jail, Gustave? I may call you that, can't I?"

He put the glasses back on. "Of course, since there's no chance of your getting out before we get our information"—he put one foot on the bed frame, boxing Gustave in, leaning forward again and peering right into his eyes—"I'm quite sure you'll see the wisdom of accepting the inevitable. Look around. Where do you think you are? Deep inside the Police Presidium." Kurt's voice grew softer. "There's no escape. Not this time. This time you'll never be free again. Unless"—he was practically whispering now—"unless you accept the fact you're no longer in control. And surrender, Gustave. Surrender . . ."

Kurt leaned back ever so slightly, his voice the gentlest whisper. "No one wants to hurt you. Out there, maybe. But not here. We want you to feel safe, comfortable. In fact, let's get you out of this dark, smelly cell. Inspektor, may we go to your office?"

Kurt continued his patter all the way up on the elevator.

"The Inspektor's got such a comfortable couch. Really, one could easily fall asleep on it. So much more relaxing and comfortable than that terrible cell."

In the car ride over, Willi had worried a master hypnotist such as Gustave would not so easily succumb to having the tables turned on him.

Kurt disagreed. "All I have to do is soothe him, Willi. Soothe and lull him. He's a prisoner. Whatever brave front he puts on, deep down he's frightened as a boy. A hypnotist can use fear, like a dictator. Offer relief. Once he captures your attention, your *inner* attention, the induction begins. In a trance you're under his control, like it or not. It isn't magic. And it isn't science. It's an art. And I'm every bit as practiced in it as Gustave. Trust me."

They reached Willi's office.

"I'll just draw the curtains, if I might. That morning light is so bright. Herr Gustave, have a seat. Now what did I tell you about that couch? You could just fall right asleep on it, am I right? You might as well relax. Undo your tie. Take off your jacket. Go on, Gustave . . . relax. Just . . . relax."

Repetition, Kurt had explained, was what lulled the subconscious into a trance state, like lullabies with babies. Over and over, slowly but surely, the hypnotist placed suggestions into the subconscious. "You are getting sleepy . . . very very sleepy." Until gradually—"Lullaby . . . and good night"—the subconscious accepted them.

"The unconscious is primitive, Willi. Irrational. Intuitive. Which is why even raving psychotics can succeed. Look at Hitler. A master hypnotist. The man forgoes all logic and short-circuits directly to the unconscious. He doesn't make the least sense. Doesn't need to."

Willi recalled one of the Führer's recent radio addresses:

> The Germany of today is not the Germany of yesterday—just as little as the Germany of yesterday was the Germany of today. The German people of the present time is not the German people of the day before yesterday, but the German people of the two thousand years of German history which lie behind us.
>   *Sieg Heil! Sieg Heil! Sieg Heil!*

Once a trance was in place its effects were mechanical. A subject who surrendered would obey. Regardless of the faith he or she had in the hypnotist. Or whether or not he believed.

All the hypnotist had to do was induce the trance.

"What a night you must have had, alone in that terrible cell. I bet all you'd like to do now is forget the whole thing. Make it disappear . . . like an unpleasant dream. All the worries. All the thoughts you must have had. Just dissipate . . . with one long breath. Go on. Do it, Gustave. Take a deep breath. In and out. That's it. You're a lucky fellow. Think of all the people in Berlin shivering in the cold. Who aren't lucky enough to be cozy on a nice warm couch. Lucky enough to be able to relax as you are."

Gustave smiled, nodding slightly.

His eyelids fluttered—

Then his lips twisted into a sinister smirk. "You don't really suppose you can hypnotize me?" His brown eyes flared mockingly. "The Great Gustave. That's funny."

Kurt feigned ignorance. "Herr Gustave. That is the last thing I want—for you to fall asleep on me. I only want you to relax so we can have a conversation. Inspektor." Kurt looked at Willi. "Might I have a word with you please? Gustave, just . . . relax."

Kurt swore in the hallway. "I'm halfway there."

"You must be joking."

"Did you see the way his eyes were fluttering just before his resistance flared?"

"But he was only—"

"I need time. Sit with Ruta. Have a cup of coffee. What time is it?"

"Eleven."

"Give me an hour. One lousy hour. I'll get him, Willi. I swear I will."

As the clock ticked by though, Willi started going out of his mind.

Ruta was smoking cigarette after cigarette, flipping through *Berlin am Morgen*.

"*Lieber Gott*—look who's getting married. Garbo."

"Lucky her." He tossed about files, pretending to be searching for something.

"Sure it is. Why, you think she's pretty? Compared to Dietrich?"

He couldn't stop checking the clock. It was twelve thirty. To get to the Zoo Station in midday traffic would require at least thirty-five minutes. He pictured Kathe standing there with the kids. Forty-five to be safe. That gave them less than an hour.

"Come on, Kurt," he found himself chanting. "Come on—"

"And here's a good one." Ruta was blowing smoke rings. "A new movie about a giant ape that destroys New York. Something to take the grandkids to."

He practically leapt off his seat when the door flew open.

It was Gunther, back from Central Records, his eyes aflame, his Adam's apple jumping. "I got something, Chief!"

Willi didn't want to hear.

"Remember you told me to check if any complaints had been filed with local precincts about unusual smells along the Havel? Well . . . guess what. There were more than a dozen in 1932. And guess where they all came from?"

Willi shot the clock a glance.

It was nearly one already. What was taking so damn long? Was Gustave's willpower really that strong? Suppose he wouldn't go under? Suppose he faked it.

"Where, Gunther? Where did they come from? I give up."

"Oranienburg!" He handed Willi a file.

Inside was complaint after complaint filed to the Oranienburg police as well as several to the Prussian Ministry of Health on Konigsburger Strasse regarding a stench that engulfed portions of the riverfront when a southern wind blew. Even the mayor had filed one. On an imaginary map Willi followed the Havel south from the little town. There was the leather tannery of course. But it had gone bust the first year of the Depression. Still . . . someone might have got in there. And a mile or so farther, the brickworks. But what smell could come from that— unless it wasn't bricks they were making? Beyond that, all there was for miles . . . were those two little islands. But he needed proof. Confirmation.

He looked again at the clock.

A quarter past one. They had to leave. If Kurt hadn't got what they needed by now, it was just too—

The office door swung open. Kurt emerged with his coat and hat on.

"All right. Let's go. I'll tell you everything on the way."

"Gunther!" Willi erupted with tension.

Ruta looked as if he'd gone mad, without her even noticing.

"Yes, sir."

"Make sure our friend in there is comfortable," he whispered. "Behind bars."

"*Jawohl.*"

"And good work on those complaints."

Outside, a miserable cold had settled. A Berlin fog that seeped through the pores and went straight into the bones. Starting up the BMW, Willi calculated the fastest route. It was tortuous no matter what. Only two arteries connected Berlin-Center to its western districts—and both went through hair-raising bottle-necks. Unter den Linden would be impossible at this hour, he knew. The backup at Friedrich Strasse, all the way under Brandenburg Gate and into the Tiergarten, was too nerve-racking even for a lifelong Berliner. Constant parades. Demonstrations. Nazis. Communists. He opted for Muhlendamm instead, crossing the Spree easily enough at the Gertrauden Brucke only to be caught in that stickiest of webs . . . Potsdamer Platz.

As they neared it, vehicles of every description engulfed them.

"Gustave wasn't lying about the kidnappings," Kurt reiterated as they ground to a halt. "He hadn't a single memory connected with the Black Stag Inn."

Willi cast him an incredulous look.

The King of Mystics had finally surrendered—not because his willpower had weakened, but because he was hypersensitive to hypnosis, Kurt reported. And terrified of prison.

"How could he not have known he'd sent all those people? It's preposterous."

"Because he hypnotized himself, Willi, repeatedly—to forget everything he did in connection with the whole affair."

Willi shifted miserably in his seat.

"It's true—I had to clear his mind of all posthypnotic instructions for it to come back."

"And then . . . ?"

"And then he confessed there were thirty, perhaps forty women he'd sent to Spandau last year; he'd lost count."

"Good God."

"Plus a family of Hungarian dwarfs . . . special request."

Dwarfs? Why the— Willi closed his eyes. "What about Sachsenhausen?"

"Never heard of it."

"Scheisse!"

"All he knew was that after he found a girl they'd like, he'd phone the Black Stag to alert them. What happened after they arrived, he had no idea."

"For God's sake . . . what did he imagine happened to them?"

"He honestly believed, or at least allowed himself to, that they were being used as . . . sex slaves. That their 'sentence,' as he termed it, only lasted as long as their masters enjoyed them. Beyond that, he didn't want to know. He had no inkling none ever returned. That any had surfaced in the Havel. No concept of any medical experiments. Nothing beyond the Black Stag. Even there . . . only voices. Never a name."

Willi felt a dim nausea. From the upper window of a double-decker bus he noticed a young woman with green, longing eyes. For an instant he swore it was Paula. Only Paula was at Sachsenhausen. And he was back to square one again.

Vehicles bellowed as they elbowed into Potsdamer Platz. For fifty years this vortex of avenues had held the dubious distinction of being Europe's busiest intersection. Swarms of cars, buses, and taxis squeezed around endless lines of yellow streetcars rushing past each other at alarming speeds, suicidal pedestrians madly dashing through it all.

"What made Gustave do it then, Kurt?" Willi honked at a man who seemed determined to get run over. "If he found it so loathsome he had to hypnotize himself not to remember any of it?"

Waves of people poured from the Potsdamer train station. Across the street the showy Hotel Fürstenhof beckoned with *Jugendstil* towers. Electric advertisements flashed from a dozen directions: "Berlin Smokes Juno!" "Chlorodont—Used by Millions Daily!" Men in sandwich signs paraded the sidewalks. "Sale! Englehardt Men's Shoes." "Delectable! Grossmann's Delikat Essen."

"In a word, Willi, blackmail."

On the left the gilded portals of the stately old Palast Hotel seemed to offer a last vestige of the stability that had been imperial Berlin. In those days, Willi knew, people understood their lives, the world around them, through an iron sense of duty to their kaiser and his state. When all that toppled, everything became a frantic rush forward, a desperate search for some new center of gravity. A terrible fear the whole bottom would drop out.

"About a year ago, some guy named Heydrich uncovered a rather unpleasant fact about his past."

Willi became aware of mad honking behind him. A furious clanging of bells.

"Such as what, Kurt?"

A fire truck was trying to get through.

What could Heydrich have on the man that would strike such terror in him?

Willi managed to squeeze the BMW next to one of the old Schinkel gatehouses, its Greek Revival columns plastered with newspapers from a kiosk.

Commerce Bank Fails! Hitler Meets Industrialists in Cologne.

A clown on stilts was performing on the corner, surrounded by screaming children. A legless man rolled by on a little wooden cart, shaking a tin can. Two young women in silver fox kept laughing hysterically as they linked arms and tried to cross the street. A blinding advertisement overhead proclaimed, "Lux— Your Clothes Will Look Like New!"

"Gustave Spanknoebel's not from Vienna. And he's not Gustave Spanknoebel."

Life in Potsdamer Platz—the center of a nation spinning out

of control—was getting like a mad carousel ride, Willi thought. Everyone barely hanging on.

"His real name's Gershon Lapinsky. He's from a little village in Bohemia. Comes from a long line of what they call *Wunder* rebbes. Mystics. Healers. His father sold magic amulets inscribed with Cabala symbols. He's a Jew, Willi. A Jew. Hitler's clairvoyant!"

Ahead, Willi's eyes took in the stunning new office tower rising on the corner of Koniggratzer Strasse. Eight stories of horizontal glass walls curving parabolically with the traffic below. It was Erich Mendelsohn's most spectacular achievement yet, Columbus Haus. Mendelsohn, a Jew, was reshaping the heart of Berlin. Invigorating it with optimistic futurism. No wonder the Nazis hated it. Called it Bolshevik decadence. Goebbels declared that the day they seized power, they'd turn it into a center for reeducation, to teach men like Mendelsohn what it meant to be German.

"That's completely insane, Kurt. I don't understand. How could a Jewish kid become Hitler's clairvoyant?"

Willi's cousin yanked off his glasses and began polishing them frantically. "A lot of boys fantasize about it when they're twelve, but this one really ran off and joined a circus. Passed as a Christian ever since. Used every trick in the book to make himself a famous 'mystic': shills, word codes, elaborate hand signals. Confessed it all to me in tears. Years later, a big star already, he was introduced to Hitler's buddy Hess. Nazis are quite pathological about the occult, you know. Once Hess latched onto him, they all came. Hitler hailed him as a great seer. A German visionary. Can you imagine? And little Gershon was delusional enough to think he could pull it off. Until one day, naturally, this Heydrich fellow shows up from some Nazi investigative unit, SS or something, and says he's dug up all the dirt. If Gershon doesn't cooperate . . . that is, if he doesn't provide a steady flow of beautiful women free of charge, foreign-born only—he'll be one very sorry Lapinsky."

Past the towering Haus Vaterland, Jewish-owned, and the gargantuan three-block-long Wertheim's main department store, Jewish-owned, traffic began to ease a bit.

The Nazis proclaimed these establishments would someday belong to "Germans."

"If it's any consolation"—Kurt checked his watch anxiously—"The Great Gustave also foresees a violent end for Hitler. Naturally he never told the man. But he confessed to me that the Führer's astrological chart showed Jupiter in extreme opposition to Saturn, portending a stunning final defeat."

Willi looked at him.

Kurt smiled nervously. "Kathe's going to kill me if I miss this train."

He didn't.

Willi got him to the Zoo Station with ten minutes to spare.

They embraced on the sidewalk.

"Thank you for this, Kurt."

"Please. You can be sure I'm going to publish a dozen papers on it, at least. I'm just sorry you didn't find Sachsenhausen."

"Yes. Well, me, too. But . . . maybe I got a sniff."

"I'll write. Tell you all about Tel Aviv." Kurt pulled off his glasses, rubbing his reddening eyes, taking one last look around, a last deep breath of *Berliner Luft*.

"God, I'm going to miss this place."

"Get a good suntan for me." Willi's throat was burning. "And . . . apologize to Kathe."

"*Ach.* She won't even remember once we're out of here." Kurt rubbed a handkerchief across his face. "Take care of yourself, Cousin. And next year"—he shook a finger as he walked away—"in Jerusalem!"

Willi got back in his BMW. Making a U-turn on Hardenburger Strasse, he felt as empty as Kurt's apartment. Directly ahead loomed the unwieldy mass of the Kaiser Wilhelm Church, its multiple dark spires disappearing in the mist. As he waited for the light to change, he saw a red-haired woman staring at herself in a store window. The church was reflected in the window, too, and seemed to have sprouted twice as many spires, everything doubling on itself.

So Gustave was a Jew. And couldn't face what he'd done. He thought he could get the best of the devil. But the King of Mystics is as much a sleepwalker as the rest of us. . . .

The air seemed to shudder.

There was a snap of snare drums.

A crash of cymbals.

Willi's throat tightened. His ears filled with pounding leather on pavement. Not ten feet ahead, two close-knit files of storm troopers rounded the corner in rank after rank of brown uniforms, leather chest straps, bloodred armbands. People scrambled to get out of the way, but a slight, stooped man wasn't quick enough and got pushed aside. His hat toppled into the gutter. As he bent to pick it up, a storm trooper kicked him in the ass, and he fell along with his hat. *"Germany, awaken!"* the whole column started bleating.

Willi made a move to help the poor fellow, but as he opened the car door, he saw what had to be thirty men on bicycles racing down Hardenburger Strasse. All wore worker's caps and thrust their fists high in the Communist salute. The Red Brigade! Like a swarm of bees they fell upon the Nazis, pelting them with a venomous hail of bricks and bottles. Willi saw several Brownshirts topple, their steaming blood rinsing the sidewalk. Pedestrians screamed as they ducked into stores and under parked vehicles.

It became a scene from an expressionist movie. Bicycles flying. Store windows shattering. Mannequins standing there exposed in bras and girdles. Brass knuckles pounding. Truncheons flying. Whistles. Police. A water cannon opening. Nazis and Communists washed from their feet. People running. Holding heads. Red blood dripping.

A sudden opening in traffic.

Flooring it, Willi slipped down Kant Strasse just as the riot squads descended. He could still hear sirens and breaking glass several blocks away on the Ku-damm, where the well-dressed crowds were doing their damnedest to keep enjoying life.

Twenty-two

The big red clock on the Police Presidium read two forty-five as he stepped inside, his brain still echoing with the pounding of boots. The shattering of glass. That painful last look his cousin took of Berlin. Pressing the button for the elevator, he realized his hand was trembling. It was more than nerves. He felt shattered inside, as if someone had hit him with a truncheon. What had all his efforts achieved? Gustave—or should he say Gershon—was locked downstairs in a cell. But so what? The man could tell him nothing. He knew for certain the Black Stag Inn was a transfer point, but he could arrest everyone there and still not find Sachsenhausen.

Where was the goddamn elevator?

As if drawn by anger, the rickety old cage descended. Stepping into it, Willi told himself that he ought to go see Paula's mother. But as he pictured the old lady scrubbing on her knees, a cold dread spread through him. Bullets he could face. Barbed wire and minefields. A mother's wrath though? He closed the cage door and hit the button for six.

She'd have every right to try to strangle the life out of him. He should never have let Paula go. As the elevator yanked up, he had the most horrible image of her strapped to a gurney, being wheeled into an operating room, still looking for him, wondering how this could have happened.

Only once before, when Vicki died, had he felt as inadequate.

On the sixth floor he was hit by a harsh cigar smell. It brought to mind those complaints from Oranienburg. That stench, he reminded himself. The odor got stronger as he neared his office, irritating his throat when he opened the door. Ruta's eyes flashed at him. From his inner office he noticed clouds of smoke rolling out, as if it were on fire.

"The Kommissar," she stammered, "would like to have a word with you."

Horthstaler was occupying Willi's chair, feet up on the desk, a huge stogie plugged in his meaty lips. Okay. But why was pale-faced Junior Detektiv Thurmann, with his black, pencil-line mustache, sitting on his couch, grinning ever so smugly?

"At last." The Kommissar cast a gray gaze Willi's way. "You find time to return from driving your relatives around Berlin." He sat up with a grunt, the blood rushing from his beefy cheeks. "How very conscientious of you."

Why did Willi feel he'd just been blindfolded and pushed against a wall?

"I am not here on happy business." Horthstaler removed the cigar from his lips, pretending to study it. "So allow me to speak plainly. Your investigation of the Bulgarian princess has proven an unfortunate failure. Reichs President Hindenburg is most disappointed in you, Kraus."

Through a terrible plummeting feeling Willi had to fight an urge to laugh.

Reichs President Hindenburg could barely remember his own

name, much less that of a Kripo Inspektor. Willi recalled the article in *Der Stürmer.* And that Horthstaler now was a card-carrying Nazi. Obviously they were angling him for a swift boot in the ass. Their famous Jew Inspektor.

"You may be thankful I resisted the most extreme action in your regards." The Kommissar's gaze turned affectionate, as one might look at a pet. "You've been with us a long time, Willi. Had some spectacular successes."

Yes. Funny. A few months ago Horthstaler had used every opportunity to show off his close working relationship with the *Kinderfresser* catcher. The great star of the Berlin police.

"Your recent failures, however"—the gaze grew indifferent—"leave me no choice but to place you on administrative probation. Which gives you exactly ten days to find the Bulgarian princess—alive and well. In the meantime"—his fleshy lips tightened—"I am promoting Thurmann here as your deputy. In the event those ten days pass"—he flicked ash on Willi's floor—"and you have not succeeded"—he leaned forward, sticking the cigar back in his mouth and puffing until it flared—"Thurmann will step into your position. In preparation, you will grant him immediate access to all files in your office." Horthstaler sighed, smiling again at his faithful old bloodhound. "I suggest you take this situation seriously."

Again, the urge to laugh.

"Should your position be terminated, you know"—the boss hoisted himself from Willi's chair—"you forfeit not only any further possibility of civil service employment in this country." He took his cigar and crushed it out on the glass frame of Willi's Police Academy diploma. "But also the pension you've worked all these years to accumulate. So if I were you"—he patted Willi's shoulder—"I'd find that princess."

There seemed only one thing to be relieved about: they didn't appear to know about Gustave. The moment the Kommissar left though, the junior Detektiv was on him. "Inspektor, I am most anxious to see the files on the Bulgarian princess as well as the Mermaid case. Immediately."

This was it then. Little waxy-faced Thurmann with his oh-so-trim black mustache would inform his cohorts—and case closed.

"Here they are, Detekiv." Ruta enthusiastically handed him a large stack of files.

Willi felt a metaphorical knife plunge into his guts.

"I prepared everything for you in advance."

The knife slowly turned.

"How efficient, Frau Garber." Thurmann proudly smiled.

She gave Willi a glance. It took a second. But then he got it. She'd kept the most important files out. Given Thurmann only junk. Blessed woman!

As Thurmann disappeared, Willi felt like kissing her.

She didn't give him a chance. "Some messages while you were out, Herr Inspektor-Detektiv." She passed him two slips of paper, very businesslike. A small gleam in her eye though expressed it all. She'd do anything for him.

"Thank you." He quickly nodded. "Thank you."

The first message was from Fritz. He'd been released from the hospital and wanted Willi to contact him as soon as possible. The second was only a phone number.

"A most important-sounding lady." Ruta shrugged. "Didn't wish to give her name."

"I can't seem to keep them away." He managed a smile.

"You're a most admirable man, Herr Inspektor. Most admirable."

A small shock went through him when he dialed the number and heard a butler announce he'd reached the Meckel residence. It magnified several times when the widow of the late SA general got on.

"Herr Inspektor," she said, refraining from the least subtlety, "I've been waiting days to hear from you. Are you incompetent, or simply not interested in knowing who murdered my husband?"

Willi wondered. If he hadn't felt a fool before—

"On the contrary, Frau Meckel. It is of the utmost importance to me. If it pleases you, I shall come by immediately."

"Here? Are you insane? It must be done someplace in public. Extremely public."

On a tiny island in the River Spree—the very cradle of Berlin, where a medieval trading village had given birth to the city—there grew up in the 1800s a well-tended prodigy of the Age of Enlightenment. Museum Island was reared into one of the world's premier Temples of Art, an unparalleled ensemble of galleries . . . the Altes Museum, the National Gallery, the Neues Museum, the Kaiser-Friedrich Museum. And in 1930 a final gracing touch— the antiquities collection at the Pergamon. It was here, beneath the towering Gate of Ishtar, that Willi suggested Frau Meckel meet him.

Footsteps echoed off the marble floors. The enormous hall swirled with people, but Willi felt quite comfortable. Alone. A shiver of awe made him feel almost holy as he approached the ancient edifice, once the main portal to imperial Babylon. The ruins of this magnificent gate had been dug up from the plains of Mesopotamia and rebuilt here by German archaeologists, brick by brick. Now its crenellated battlements soared toward the museum ceiling nearly fifty feet tall, all of it sheathed in deep blue tiling, ornamented with intricate patterns and bas-reliefs, jaw-droppingly beautiful at two and a half thousand years old. Willi could practically see the sandal-wearing ancients parading beneath it. According to the description at its base, Nebuchadrezzar II, builder of the Hanging Gardens, dedicated the gate in 562 B.C. If Willi wasn't mistaken, this same Nebuchadrezzar had razed the Temple in Jerusalem and carried away the Jews.

Well, he thought with a tingle of pride, look who's still around.

"Herr Inspektor Kraus, I presume?"

In her green loden cape, feathered hat, black purse firmly strapped around the forearm, Helga Meckel appeared an archetypal German Frau. A stout, blond materialization of hard work and good sense. Practicality and self-restraint.

Yet a completely unbridled anguish overflowed from her eyes.

"The reconstructed gateway to a lost civilization." Her voice was sharp with irony. "A most appropriate setting you chose for our little meeting."

"Is it?" Her forthrightness came as no surprise after their phone conversation. "In what way is that, Frau Meckel?"

Facing him, her fair blue gaze fractured into a thousand bitter shards. "Because, Herr Inspektor, that is what these men will make someday of Germany. Ruins. Which will need excavating. Should anyone care to remember us."

Fumbling for a handkerchief she patted her forehead with it. "Forgive me. I've not been myself lately. If my attitude was improper earlier, it was only because it wasn't easy for me to contact you." She put the handkerchief away and snapped her handbag shut, offering him a weak smile. "None of this is easy for me."

"I understand."

"No . . . you don't." Her pale cheeks flamed. "I'm a good Nazi woman. Or I thought I was. But some injustices must be spoken out against."

She seemed suddenly not to be able to breathe.

"Frau Meckel," he urged, "then you must speak."

Her pale lips trembled. "My husband"—her stout chin rose—"was a genius, Inspektor. It was he who first theorized about the possibilities of transplanting and grafting human bones. After what happened in the Great War . . . the millions of amputees . . . he felt he had to do something. To give back, not take away. It was those young ones, the up-and-comers." She lowered her voice, darting her eyes around. "The ones with the SS."

"Forgive me, Frau Meckel . . . your husband was a member of the Institute for Racial Hygiene, was he not?"

"A founding member! But his concern was with the decline in the German birthrate and the sharp increase in mental illnesses. Hermann never spoke of the Jewish question or 'de-Aryanization,' as the ones who took over called it. Let me assure the Herr Inspektor"—her eyes widened painfully—"all decent Germans condemn this Jew-baiting business. *Es geht alles vorüber,* we tell ourselves. This, too, will pass. Hitler's bark is worse than his bite. We need him to keep the Communists out. But once he takes power, reason and logic will prevail."

Her lips began quivering, the tears rushing to her eyes again. "Now I don't think so." She dove back into her purse and hid her face in the handkerchief. "I don't think so at all."

She looked around, ashamed to let anyone see her.

Willi felt like taking the poor widow in his arms and soothing the grief he knew only too well. But he stood back, hands clasped behind him.

Summoning herself, she managed to continue, her whisper changing to something fearful. "They killed Hermann because he refused to go along with their crimes." Her eyes glazed over, cold and blue as the Babylonian tiles. "Oscar Schumann ordered it, I am certain. But only with the nod of Heydrich and Himmler."

"What crimes, Frau Meckel?"

She turned her eyes skyward as if pleading not to have to say it. "Certain . . ." She hiccuped. "Experiments."

Glancing about, her voice became frantic, a mothlike flutter. "The sterilizations started half a year ago, and then Schumann wanted to proceed with bone transplants. My husband was appalled. He terminated his association with the institute at once. They let him alone as long as he kept his mouth shut. After all, he was their mentor. But then this girl, this American managed to escape—" Her gaze flickered venomously. "And Schumann tried to pin it on Hermann. The only other one who could have performed such surgery. With Heydrich's help he set up the whole

Bulgarian princess affair—and made sure to put you on the case. You, the famous Jew Inspektor, lured to chase the red herring—my poor Hermann. But in the end the joke was supposed to be on you. The princess, you see . . . well, let me be blunt, Inspektor . . . she's one of them. Don't ask me how, but I've learned in no uncertain terms that this Bulgarian Mata Hari has for some time now been cozy at home back in the royal palace in Sofia!"

Now Willi felt like laughing. Horthstaler told him he had to find the princess. Alive and well. So there it was. A big fat setup.

Her brittle eyes glared at him. "You, Inspektor, not my husband, were supposed to be the sacrificial lamb." She clenched her teeth, rolling her eyes as if she might have spoken too loudly. "The whole affair was to have died with you! No one imagined you'd ever go to von Schleicher—and certainly not to Roehm. You're a man with, how do they call it in your language, *chutzpah*?"

"My language is German."

She seemed not to hear him. "Unfortunately for my husband, once word got back to the SS that Roehm was cooperating with you on an investigation, well . . ."

Willi was almost foolish enough to want to apologize. "Frau Meckel"—his voice grew adamant—"you must tell me at once: where is Sachsenhausen—this place they perform these ghastly experiments?"

Her eyes widened, as if he were mad. "Do you imagine I am privy to such information?" Her whisper edged toward hysteria. "I've never even heard that name. This entire matter has always been the strictest secret. And once it became *extralegal* as they call it, well . . . a word could cost a person his life!"

Willi glanced up at the mighty Ishtar Gate feeling, he supposed, as many a Babylonian must have at the sight of the advancing hordes of Persia.

"How can they be stopped?" he said as much to Frau Meckel as to whatever other forces for justice existed in the universe.

Her puffy, red eyes grew narrow and fierce. "It won't be easy." Her whisper blackened. "Unless you think you can take on the

SS. But there is one night they all come together. Everyone in the institute. Thurseblot. The Feast of Thor." She saw his face. "I know it sounds ridiculous to you, Inspektor, but you must remember, these men are truly . . . pagans."

A vision seemed to take shape before her. "There's an inn out in Spandau." One of her blond eyebrows rose. "Just across from the S-Bahn station." The thick corners of her lips twitched. "The night of January's full moon"—she turned to him, her whole face afire with bloodlust—"that's where you'll find them all."

Twenty-three

Willi's footsteps echoed as he left the museum—a proverbial man with the rug pulled out from under him. Night had fallen. A nasty chill seeped through his overcoat. He'd known for some time now he was being set up, but how badly he could not have imagined. Glancing up for a sign of the moon, he saw only darkness.

He'd never felt so alone.

On the footbridge over the Kupfergraben he was overwhelmed by the insane irony of it all. Ernst Roehm had saved his life, completely unwittingly. Himmler and Heydrich were too afraid to make an enemy of a man with half a million Brownshirts at his command. So they'd got rid of Meckel. But how long would that sanctuary last?

As he trudged the windy sidewalks of Georgen Strasse, only one certainty loomed: his career on the Berlin police force was done for. The mythic quest they'd sent him on—to rescue the missing princess—had been a fool's errand. Horthstaler painted the whole picture with his cigar. They wanted the Jew boy out. And they'd get him, too. One way or another.

Unless . . .

Unless he could bust Sachsenhausen. Then the case would be publicized all over Germany. People's minds change. Look at Frau Meckel. At least now, he lowered his hat against the wind, there's a chance of netting the whole depraved lot. Thurseblot. The very name sent a shudder through him. He'd have to find Sachsenhausen first, though. You can't get one and not the other. Signals would be sent. The disease would survive. The whole thing had to be cauterized simultaneously.

Only, he had no idea when the full moon was.

Across the street was a bookstore. An elderly man in a wool vest was just about to pull down the gate. He hurried to stop him. "Sir. Could I get in to check a calendar and find out when the next full moon occurs? It's terribly important."

The old fellow stiffened with disdain. "The way people depend on the stars and moon these days, you'd think there'd never been an Enlightenment."

Willi had no energy for a philosophical debate. "It's police work." He broke out his badge.

"Well then, the Age of Reason is most assuredly dead," the old fellow grumbled, "when the police are consulting the stars."

Perhaps he's right, Willi thought.

But whatever the age, a Kripo badge got things done in Germany, and he was soon enough able to ascertain the date.

Impossible. Not until the twenty-fourth? Three more weeks? He couldn't wait that long. Paula couldn't. And yet . . . what choice was there? Thurseblot was the only night they all came together. God in heaven.

Wrapping his scarf more tightly around him, he continued morbidly toward Friedrich Strasse. Dead ahead the lights of the train station seemed to summon him.

Paula's mother, he understood.

Poverty filled his nose when he reached the old tenement district. Vacant eyes stared from cracked windows. Dirty children lurked in the hallway. Paula's mother came to the door but could barely hold herself erect. Hair a mess. Eyes half-closed. The stink of cheap gin hung from her like her disheveled robe.

"Frau Hoffmeyer." His stomach burned with acid. How did you tell a mother her daughter was missing? That it was all your fault? "Inspektor-Detektiv Kraus here. I need to speak with you a moment . . . about Paula."

"Paula?" Her voice felt like ammonia hitting his face. So harsh. So caustic. "You're a little for that late, fella."

"Sorry?"

"They've already been here. I know all about it."

"Who's been here?"

Her eyes flared as if he were an absolute idiot. "You guys. Schupo. Security Police."

"I'm Kripo."

"So what? You gonna tell me a different story?" She shoved a hand into her robe pocket and pulled out a small ID card, waving it furiously at him. Paula's. But it couldn't be; she'd taken it with her that night. He'd seen her put it in her purse.

"You gonna tell me my daughter *ain't* been murdered?"

The breath completely left him.

"With her profession, and the kind of maniacs they got loose today . . . it didn't exactly come as a big surprise." She pretended to spit. "Dominatrix. I knew something would happen. But don't think it hurt none the less. To hear her skull'd been cracked in two." Her bloodshot eyes fixed on him. "At least she went instantly." The harsh voice broke halfway. "That's all I can be grateful for. Now, for Christ's sake, leave me alone!"

She slammed the door in his face.

He stood there as if his own skull had split. Gradually, through pounding pain, he began to piece it together. Paula must have kept up the charade of being Polish—until Sachsenhausen. Only . . . by then it was too late. She'd seen too much. They couldn't free her. A German mother, though, deserved notification . . . so they'd sent Schupo over with a story. Not a lie, entirely. They probably did crack her skull in two. The bastards.

He tried to hold himself together, but step by step as he headed downstairs, he could sense his inner springs detaching. By the time he reached the lobby his legs gave way. He slid down the wall. He crouched on the floor, emitting some animal kind of wail, holding his arms over his head as if being beaten. Pictures of Paula kept flashing in his brain. How clearly he could see her strutting Tauentzien Strasse in her men's tuxedo and silk shorts. That cancan she did, her white breasts bouncing. All zipped up in that tight pink gown, toasting 1933.

He crouched there sobbing, unable to stop, his shoulders wracked with spasms.

Was he any better than the Nazis who killed her? Why did he let her go? he asked himself. Because she was a morphine addict? Because she liked getting spanked? Did that make her a subhuman? Something to be . . . experimented with?

But then again, he had to remind himself—he hadn't exactly forced her. The whole idea was hers to begin with. She'd begged to go. Cursed him for denying her the one chance to do something meaningful with her life.

Whatever that meant.

She was a spectacular woman. Life just never gave her a chance. Who knew, the few weeks they'd had together might have been the best she'd ever had.

They hadn't been bad for him, either.

Eventually, no tears were left. Fishing out his handkerchief, he wiped his face and slowly lifted his head. Through his watery, exhausted eyes he noticed a crowd of children in the hallway staring at him transfixed, as if he were Charlie Chaplin or something.

The sky looked painted blue the next morning when he, his every muscle throbbing, and Gunther set out in an unmarked Opel for

Oranienburg. It was starting to get to him, this world they lived in. Impossible to believe Paula was no longer in it. That he'd been the one to let her go. How could he have been so stupid, so idiotically reckless? Poor Paula! Though shocked by the disciplinary action taken against Willi, Gunther managed to keep his chin up. "We'll find that Bulgarian princess yet," he kept saying. "You'll see. Ten days is a long time, Chief."

Willi didn't have the heart to tell him. By Thurseblot he'd be off the force. Out in the cold. With the rest of the unemployed.

But all would not be lost.

The chancellor of Germany was still on his side. And the armed forces.

"Just keep your eyes and ears open." Willi instinctively kept training the kid. "And your nose, Gunther. For that stench."

At least he didn't have to worry anymore about Paula. Miserable solace, but now that she was gone, he could take his time and do this properly. He'd rather have her back. But God only knew how many more souls were still out there waiting to be rescued. He was going to find them if it took his last breath.

Less than hour from the Police Presidium, Oranienburg was a fairy-tale village. All the buildings painted bright white with steep, red-shingled roofs. Horses clopping along cobblestones, hauling hay carts. Swans sunning on the riverfront. At City Hall the *Bürgermeister* pretended to be thrilled to see them, all the way from Berlin-Center. What had brought two Kripo Inspektors out here of all places, to their quiet town?

"Herr Bürgermeister, last July you filed a complaint with the Ministry of Health on Konigsburger Strasse."

The mayor knit his brows, making a big show of trying to recall. "*Ach,* yes." It seemed a revelation. "That fishy stink last summer. Well . . . *Gott sei Dank* that is all over with now. Some *Idioten* at the leather works spilled a barrel of tannic acid. Killed a whole school of carp. Can you imagine? A hundred marks we slapped on the slipshods. Plus the cost of cleaning up. They won't do that again."

Certainly not, Willi knew. That tannery had been closed since 1930. "There've been numerous complaints though," he added to the mayor. "Including several only last month. A foul, acrid odor along the river, like rotting meat."

"Well, along the river naturally there are always funny smells." The mayor smiled relentlessly. "It could have been a dozen things. Goodness knows we've our fair share of skunks out here."

Willi realized he was wasting his breath.

Between last July and now, obviously, someone had made it quite clear to the mayor that there *were* no foul odors in Oranienburg.

"Well, if there's no problem . . ." Willi put away his notebook.

"Of course not. No problem at all!"

"Then we've come out here for no reason, Gunther."

"Might I suggest"—the mayor brightly pointed out the window—"a tour of our baroque palace. A charming experience, I assure you."

"No doubt." Willi winked.

Outside, Gunther whistled with amazement. "Phonier than a glass eye."

Good, Gunther. Sharpen your senses. Always keep sharpening them.

Willi inhaled. The air was truly sweet. Country air that made one realize the foulness of what one breathed in town. Paula would have loved the place.

They skipped the palace and drove to six addresses where people had filed stench complaints. To a person, all agreed the offending odors had entirely disappeared. They questioned the barber. The florist. The dressmaker. Amazingly, Oranienburgers were unanimous in their conviction that nowhere on earth was the air any better than right here, along the gentle river Havel.

"Something sure stinks in this town," Gunther finally observed. "Everyone acts like a marionette."

"Then we've got to sniff around more. Find out who's pulling the strings, eh, Gunther?"

Climbing back into the little Opel, they headed south along the road parallel to the river. According to the map, about a kilometer and a half through the woods was the abandoned leather tannery. Sure enough, reaching the crest of a small hill, they spotted its towering smokestack. Willi hit the brakes.

There was no mistaking the heavy black smoke pouring from its top.

"Abandoned my ass," Gunther said.

Around the next bend the old tannery appeared about a hundred yards to their right, a long shedlike structure of unpainted wood just along the river. Willi pulled the car off the road. They loaded pistols. Climbing a nearby rise for an overview, they heard several bloodcurdling screams.

"Lord almighty," Gunther whimpered.

A small, worn-out meadow appeared below. At the far side of it, the ramshackle tannery, belching smoke. At the center of the field a dozen furiously shrieking children were on their knees in a rigid line, completely lost in a game of leapfrog.

Willi laughed.

The Great Depression had left thousands without homes. A few dozen evidently had taken refuge here. Outside the old building several ragged women battled winds to hang laundry on lines. Two men were unloading crates from a busted-up truck. This definitely wasn't Sachsenhausen.

Back in the car, another kilometer down the road they approached the Oranienburg Brickworks. Trucks stacked high with piles of red brick rumbled from the gate, turning past them down the road into town. A hot, gritty dust hung in the air. Nothing rotten.

According to the map, a kilometer farther was the turnoff to a bridge directly onto Asylum Island. Except that, beyond the brickworks, the paved road ended. A pitiful dirt trail led into the woods.

"Well, kid"—Willi shifted gears—"better hold on to your hat."

The Opel took each rut and bump as if its last. Several times

Gunther's head smacked into the roof. But on they drove, Willi's nerves getting tauter by the minute. He hated these goddamn gloomy forests. One never knew what was around the next bend. Thankfully they found the turnoff and saw the bridge straight ahead. But a barbed-wire barricade blocked their progress.

Out they got.

A large sign clearly proclaimed *Eintritt Streng Verboten!* It looked relatively new. A second sign beyond the wire showed a skull and crossbones. Next to it, an unmistakable warning: mines!

"It's a bluff." Gunther hadn't a shred of doubt. "Who'd plant mines an hour from Berlin? Where would they even get them?"

He wanted to cut the wire and drive straight through.

Perhaps he's right, Willi considered. Perhaps it was like people who put up Beware of Dog signs when all they had was a poodle. But one mine was all it took. And he wanted to see his boys again. Something awful.

"Better test it out, Gunther."

The kid gathered an armful of rocks and began throwing them over the barricade. Rock after rock landed harmlessly.

"You see? A big bluff! Come on, Chief. Let's cut."

A loud rustling silenced them. A warthog, of all things, ran from the bushes and scampered toward the bridge, snorting as if furious to have his slumber disturbed. Gunther and Willi burst out laughing.

Until the thing exploded.

Twenty-four

They hurried back down the rutted road toward Oranienburg. No wonder everyone's smile seemed glued on in this town, Willi thought. Whatever hidden hand was pulling the strings, it was damned determined. And well armed. As they reemerged from the woods, it was evident that the weather had worsened. The painted-blue sky had turned stone gray. A wind was gusting from the south.

"Gunther." He felt his neck hairs stand. "Take a deep breath."

"Jesus Christ." Gunther coughed.

There was no mistaking it. He'd smelled it a hundred times. On the Western Front. In the morgues at the Alex.

Putrefying flesh.

Not a soul in town would acknowledge it.

Gunther confronted a young mother pushing a baby carriage. "Can you tell me what that frightful odor is?"

"Sorry." She pointed at her nostrils. "Terrible cold. Can't smell a thing."

"Odor?" The postman looked baffled. "Not unless you mean from the *Italiener* over there." He motioned toward a restaurant. "Always uses too much garlic. No matter how many times we tell him: 'Vincenzo, this isn't Italy. We're Germans here.'"

"These people are out of their minds." Gunther finally held a handkerchief to his nose. "How can anyone ignore this?"

Willi agreed. They were out of their minds all right.

Scared out of them.

The fairy-tale village had turned gloomy. Darkened by clouds, the whitewashed buildings looked forbidding. The swans had left. For the first time Willi considered the possibility that whatever they were up against really *was* too big, too monstrous, to be stopped anymore. That the only thing left to do was run.

Across the street he noticed a middle-aged woman staring at them from a shop window. When she realized she'd been spotted, she instantly withdrew behind the curtains.

He nudged Gunther. "Let's try one last place."

It proved to be a used-furniture dealership, stacked to the ceiling with old desks, lamps, chairs, filing cabinets. The woman from the window busied herself with a feather duster, pretending not to notice them. Plain-faced with short gray hair, she had a nervous tic that shook her cheek as if with an electric shock.

"*Nachmittag,*" she finally said when she could no longer ignore them. "Might I be of service?"

Willi couldn't respond. Across the aisle his eyes had caught sight of what seemed a genuine miracle. Along the side of an old wooden desk, stenciled in big black letters, was unmistakably printed *Property Asylum Oranienburg.*

His whole body levitated toward it.

"Asylum Oranienburg." He did his best not to sound as if he were seeing a vision. "I was under the impression that shut down years ago."

The lady's tic grew violent. *"Ach so."* Her whole cheek convulsed. "Yes, of course it did. But, well . . . you see . . ." She started banging the customer bell.

"Are you insane, Lisel?" Her husband emerged from a back office. "You think I'm deaf or—" He transformed into a paragon of friendliness.

"Gentlemen . . . how do you do. If it's office furnishings you're looking for, you've come to the right place."

She reached a hand out. "But *Liebchen,* these men are—"

"Hundreds of items in dozens of styles." He brushed her aside. "That's our motto. Perhaps you've heard our radio ads: 'Greitz: hundreds of items in dozens of styles.'"

"I notice you have a desk here from the old Oranienburg Asylum."

"One? We've got *dozens* of desks from the asylum, dear fellow—desks and chairs and filing cabinets. We've even got old asylum clocks. And plenty more where they came from—"

The wife yanked his arm, shooting him a desperate, for-God's-sake-shut-up look.

"If you're interested in wholesale"—he swatted her away—"I assure you—you won't do any better."

"You've had this furniture since they closed the asylum, all those years ago?"

"Good heavens, of course not. I bought a big consignment only last year. They're renovating out there."

"Renovating? Who is?"

"Who?" The businessman's smile lost its urgency. "Well . . . whoever took control. Marvelous furniture, don't you think? Old but sturdy." He rapped the desk. "Like they don't make anymore."

"But who exactly took control? Who sold you the furniture?"

The smile dropped altogether. "I don't see as how that makes a difference."

"I'm just curious."

"Look, if you're not interested in making a purchase—"

"I didn't say that. I said I was curious to know who sold you the furniture."

Greitz rocked back and forth on his toes, shooting his wife a bitter blaming look for not warning him. "I do not discuss my sources, sir. It's bad business."

"Sometimes"—Willi broke out the Kripo badge—"it's good business."

The man drained of color.

His wife began crossing herself. With a terrible gasp, she broke out sobbing. "For God's sakes leave us alone! Do you have any idea what they'll do to us if—"

"Lisel—have you lost your mind?"

Willi fought fire with fire. "If you know what's good for you, you'll cooperate," he threatened. "Unless you want to see the inside of the Alex."

"Good for me?" Greitz's face trembled nearly as violently as his wife's. "If I know what's good for me, I'd chase you out of here with an iron bar!"

Willi could have arrested the fellow for that. But even on the battlefield he'd never seen two more terrified people. Obviously, whatever coercion they faced here at home was worse than anything he could dish out. He softened his tone.

"If you chase me out, Greitz, I'd only be back tomorrow with more Kripo men to arrest you. And if I arrest you, today, tomorrow, or next week, everyone in this town will know about it. And whoever you're so afraid of will know about it, too."

The woman's tic grew alarming. Willi began to fear she might slip into an epileptic fit. But he wasn't giving up.

"My partner and I have spoken to dozens of people today. No one need have any suspicion you said anything to us. In fact, if you feel better about it, you needn't say a word at all. Just . . . show me the bill of sale."

Willi left Oranienburg like a zeppelin in flight, the whole landscape suddenly laid bare before him. According to the bill of sale, in January 1932 the Greitz Used Furniture Emporium purchased 250 chairs, desks, and assorted other items from the old Oranienburg Asylum, under new management now by an agency that simply used its initials—IRH. And renamed Camp Sachsenhausen.

He'd found the cursed place.

All he had to do now was pull off a reconnaissance mission that worked.

He still needed to know how many people were out there, how many guards, how heavily they were armed. So that come Thurseblot . . . they could take the whole stinking thing down.

He remembered Fritz. That message yesterday.

"Gunther." He dropped the kid off in Tegel. "Take the S-Bahn over to the State Library. Don't stop even for lunch. Get me everything, absolutely everything, you can about that old asylum."

"Yes, boss." Gunther's blue eyes sparkled. "And, boss?"

"What?"

The sparkle got glassy. "Thanks. For everything."

He surprised Willi with a fierce hug before running off.

Fritz's big glass house in Grunewald glittered in the woods. The wounded warrior greeted him at the door, his shoulder completely healed he claimed—even though his arm was still in a sling. "For all that blood and gore, the damn thing was just a superficial wound. Come, come. Have a drink. That must have been the *tenth* time you saved my life, Willi."

Guzzling down a whiskey and soda, Willi filled him in on all that had occurred since that dire morn in the forest. The Great Gustave. His meeting with Frau Meckel. His probation. Paula.

Fritz's dueling scar blackened with rage. "Dear God. They stop at nothing, these ape-men. And to threaten you—"

"Never mind me."

"I'm calling von Schleicher." Fritz reached for the phone.

Willi held him back. "Fritz, what I need from you is help planning another reconnaissance raid. One that works this time."

Fritz's face filled with emotion. "You mean . . . you found Sachsenhausen?"

Willi couldn't help smiling.

An hour later, back at his desk in the Police Presidium, it didn't take long for his new "deputy" to show up.

"Well, well, Inspektor." Junior Detektiv Thurmann entered without knocking. "It seems you have friends in high office. The very highest. At least temporarily."

"I've no idea what you're referring to." Willi kept sorting through his mail.

"Don't you?"

Willi looked up long enough to catch the grin beneath Thurmann's pencil-line mustache.

"You may have won the battle, but you won't win the war, Kraus, I assure you. The day of reckoning is dawning. Heil Hitler!" An arm thrust up and he was gone.

Willi was stunned.

Obviously Fritz had phoned von Schleicher after all.

His probation must have been revoked.

But he wasn't sure whether to be more amazed at the chancellor of Germany's swift intervention on his behalf or that Thurmann, so confident in winning the "war," had addressed his superior with such outrageous impudence.

The next morning Gunther showed up with a real treasure trove. Not only books but detailed maps and floor plans explaining the whole layout of the Oranienburg Asylum.

"I made friends with one of the librarians." His jaw lengthened proudly. "What a cutie."

"A touch of Don Juan never hurt in a Detektiv."

"Whatever you do"—the jaw slackened—"don't tell Christina."

Willi spent all morning with the documents, finding himself quickly absorbed not only in the complex layout of the old facility, but the fascinating rationale behind its construction. Built in 1866 under the reign of Kaiser Wilhelm I, the Oranienburg Asylum for Lunatics and the Feebleminded had, he learned, been the first in Europe designed according to principles of one Dr. Thomas Kirkbride, an American proponent of environmental determinism. Rational buildings, the good doctor had firmly believed, made for rational people.

According to Kirkbride, an ideal asylum ought to be built in a beautiful setting, along the water or on the crest of a hill, housed in a single giant building of multiple wings dropping back to form shallow V-shapes, so that all the patients could enjoy tranquil views and fresh cross-breezes. A highly structured healthy environment, the doctor had been convinced, would restore a "natural balance of the senses" and create a sense of "family life." Diet, exercise, and work were essential to his therapy. He'd had his patients out tilling fields, milking cows, feeding pigs. A radical departure from the millennium-old belief that incarceration was the only solution for the insane, Dr. Kirkbride's philosophy had represented the most advanced thinking of his age—that the mentally ill could actually be treated.

For fifty years Oranienburg had been the foremost asylum in Germany, housing up to two thousand inmates at a time—until the Great War and Allied blockade, when it became unfeasible to maintain such a giant facility on so isolated an island. In 1916, Willi was actually sad to read, it was stripped of all usable metal and abandoned to the elements. Until, he thought, last year, when the Institute for Racial Hygiene moved in.

The phone rang, suspending him for a strange moment between asylum and office. Sometimes he wondered how much difference there was between the two. It was Fritz, insisting on lunch. He refused to take no for an answer. Willi sighed and agreed to meet him in half an hour at the Pschorr Haus. An odd choice, Willi thought, hanging up.

Looming over the Potsdamer Platz like a medieval castle, Pschorr was not just a beer hall but a beer *palace* according to its advertising, catering to Berliners as royalty—en masse. Its Great Hall seated nine hundred, replete with long tables, elaborate wood carvings, and shiny coats of armor. Nineteen kinds of sausages, sixteen sorts of dumplings, seven varieties of mustard—not to mention its world-famous pickled pork knuckles—at prices even a peasant could afford. It was the great drinking and gastronomic citadel of the petite bourgeoisie. Why Fritz, a champagne drinker for breakfast, lunch, and dinner, would want to meet him here, Willi could not imagine.

The place was as always packed for lunch, peppered with far too many Brownshirts for his taste. Wandering the aisles looking for Fritz, wondering what this was all about, he started getting good and—

He froze suddenly, as if hit in the gut.

Just ahead at a small table were not only Fritz but the other three men of his old reconnaissance unit: Geiger, Richter, Lutz.

Seeing him they rose in unison.

Willi had to fight back the burning in his eyes.

Geiger, the old medic, a pediatrician now in Dresden, snapped to attention. "Company K reporting for duty, sir!"

For years after the war they'd made it their business to have reunions. But as time went on, they became harder to arrange. Until 1928, Willi guessed it was, when they'd marked the tenth anniversary of the armistice. So many years . . . Yet what difference did time make to men like these five? The bonds they'd forged were unbreakable. The scars they bore so deep, so vivid still.

Geiger's ear, hideously cauliflowered by a shell fragment, was the butt of at least a dozen jokes dished up by Geiger himself, so his patients would laugh rather than recoil at it. Richter, the best wire cutter in the kaiser's army, had lost more than one chunk of skin to those barbed claws. A face like that he had now was a badge of honor in the army. Which is where he'd stayed all these years. Lutz, the old intelligence expert, able to distinguish French infantry units by the curses they used, had done well for himself as an accountant in one of the big Frankfurt banking houses—despite having left three fingers in France. Fritz, too, had suffered nightmares for years, still on occasion leaping up in the middle of the night drenched in sweat. Willi alone had come out barely scathed. Why, he had no idea. Perhaps, he sometimes thought, fate had saved him for dessert.

"Lutz here took the overnight from Frankfurt." Fritz beamed. "And Geiger arrived at the Potsdamer Station not twenty minutes ago."

"I don't understand—"

"Captain Kraus." Lutz saluted with his two-fingered hand. "We heard you had a mission."

Willi felt that awful burning in his eyes again.

Ringleader Hohenzollern submitted his report: "Richter's based at the Tegel Firing Range now, Willi."

"Quartermaster." Richter's chest puffed out.

"He says there are inflatable rafts up there with outboard motors. Not twenty minutes to Oranienburg. We can take them upriver, turn off the motors, and paddle into the channel, find out what those bastards have going on at the asylum."

Willi's throat was so constricted he could barely speak. "It's too dangerous. Lutz and Geiger—your families. And, Fritz—"

"Never mind." Fritz's scar reddened. "It's all arranged, Willi. Midnight tonight."

Twenty-five

How black the night was. How cold the air. Hope and fear tossed like waves in Willi's heart. He'd been through such storms of emotion before with these men—in the fields outside Passchendaele, along the banks of the Somme. But this time the stakes felt even higher. They weren't kids anymore. And not just the fate of the fatherland but the whole civilized world seemed balanced on their shoulders.

Unfortunately, an outsider could easily have mistaken the operation for a Keystone comedy. Five men in their thirties—one earless, one fingerless, one whose arm was in a sling, and one whose face was so mangled he resembled Frankenstein's monster—tiptoeing from a storehouse at the Tegel army base trying to nip two motorized rafts for the night. It'd been fifteen years since they'd worked as a team, crawling through enemy lines, up to the edges of gun and troop emplacements. Back then a twitch of an eyebrow said enough. Now, trying to reach the waterfront perhaps a hundred yards away, all their frantic gesturing couldn't keep them from knocking into each other and colliding with trees, practically puncturing the rafts. Richter, his monster-face stiff with anxiety, kept motioning to the nearby barracks, begging them to keep silent. His quartermaster duties included overseeing these patrol craft, but taking them without authorization would land him in the brig.

Toiling to uphold his end of a boat, Willi found himself increasingly irritated by the sensation that he'd been here before. Not once but many times. Until, like a howitzer shell, it hit him. Of course . . . the zeppelin field. This firing range was where the lighter-than-air ships used to take off and land. How in love with them he'd been as a boy. He used to cajole his parents all the time to take him here. That image of the LZ6—three city blocks long—floating into the cloudless sky like a giant white cigar was seared into his memory. Thousands had filled these fields that day in 1906 to witness its inaugural flight. And not only nine-year-old Willi, he was sure, but all of them firmly believed Count Zeppelin's marvel symbolized Germany itself—rising to take her place in the world. It would have been preposterous for them to imagine that less than a decade later the very same zeppelins would be dropping bombs on London. That anything that occurred after 1914 could ever have come true. Which it all did.

The trenches. The tanks. The poison gas.

For a moment, the cloud cover opened overhead. A single star shone down. At last the wide Havel River appeared before them. Willi's spirit inflated as they got the rafts in. Climbing aboard and turning on the motors, all the pent-up anxiety he'd been dragging around churned into determination. Across that darkness was Sachsenhausen. He knew exactly where it was this time.

Geiger, Richter, and Lutz set off in one boat, he and Fritz in the other. Icy spray hit their faces as they roared across the water. At least he was better prepared this time. Fleece-lined jacket, leather gloves. His stomach completely empty. All of them were dressed in black, their faces darkened to blend with the night. The old reconnaissance team on the move. But how choppy it was. Each time they hit a wave, Willi's bones rattled like dice. It wouldn't be long though, according to the maps, before they reached their turnoff.

When the little inlet finally loomed, his heart began to race. They cut the motors. Swift were the currents they had to paddle against to enter the channel. Having all but memorized the maps, he knew that around the next bend would be a thin spit of land, then the island with the potter's field. Farther upstream there'd be a dock where the ferries carrying the dead used to arrive. They could pull up there, hide the rafts, and set out by foot to the bridge that crossed to Asylum Island.

Everything was as it should be. The thin spit of land, and then straight ahead . . . the Island of the Dead. Completely overgrown now, a dull, flat panorama of weeds. No sign at all of the countless thousands interred there. Nearing the docks, however, a chill slithered up his spine. In the gray, frigid water, a skeleton—a half-sunk ferryboat stripped of everything from bell to wheel. Still visible across the bones of her hull, the name *River Styx*. What had once been the pier hadn't fared much better. Climbing onto it, they had to be careful not to fall through gaping holes. They dragged the rafts out of the water and camouflaged them in some bushes.

The waist-high grass rustled as it yielded beneath their feet. The air was thick with marshy odors. Every step, Willi knew, was over the final resting place of some impoverished soul. For half a century the indigent from across Berlin/Brandenburg had been buried in this muddy wasteland. What misfortunes each must have endured to wind up here, where for all eternity they lay unacknowledged like beasts instead of humans. Abruptly the high grass ended and they found themselves staring at something not marked on the maps. A slow-growing horror enveloped them. At their feet lay two parallel trenches, maybe six feet wide and at least fifty feet in length, covered with fresh black earth. There was no mistaking what they were. People were getting buried out here again on the Island of the Dead. A lot of them.

"Mein Gott," Gieger stammered. "What's going on at that asylum?"

Grim with silence, Willi took a long breath. The stiff wind blowing from the north carried only a dank scent of soil. No rotting flesh.

That stench plaguing Oranienburg wasn't from here.

It had to come from farther south . . . from the asylum side.

How grateful he was to find not a single SS man guarding the footbridge. No lights. No warning signs about mines. Only dark, heavy clouds and rustling leaves.

"Forward!" he whispered, not even embarrassed when his voice cracked with emotion. He was so relieved finally to have reached this place.

The cost had been too high.

He had the whole route, the whole mission, painstakingly mapped in his mind. To cover as much ground as possible, they'd circumambulate Asylum Island northeast to southwest, scouting the installations, the disposition of the prisoners, and the exact number of guards. He could only hope there weren't too many SS. In the worst case he imagined a full-scale battle erupting Thurseblot night between army troops and Nazis. God knew . . . it could spark a real civil war. Yet tonight as they crept along the island's northeast shore, not so much as a bird chirped. Just the gentle slapping of water against rocks.

When the compass fell due north, they reached the bridge to the mainland, the one planted with live mines. He steered the squad away from it and onto the approach to the old asylum, the dark silhouette of which was growing visible on the hilltop. The gravel road heading to it was flanked by rows of gnarled trees, beyond which opened vast lawns, riotous with weeds. These same lawns, Willi knew, had once upon a time been tended to by legions of patients. Now the sense of abandon, the emptiness, was overwhelming. Not a flicker of light traveled the darkness. Not a voice on the wind. As if the whole island were deserted. Which it wasn't.

Guided by their battery lights, a short hike uphill brought them to the granite gatehouse, its walls an idyll of chiseled lambs and saintly faces, a bold slogan engraved across the top: *Work Is Therapy.* The iron gates, long ago reduced to war matériel, had more recently been replaced with scrolls of barbed wire extending on either side into the darkness. An unmistakable perimeter fence. Willi was prepared. Under conditions considerably better than they'd been on the Western Front, Richter not only cut a fine passage through but reconnected the wire behind them. At all costs they couldn't let anyone know they'd been here.

Past the gatehouse the road continued to climb, curving around a grassy oval that had been a duck pond. Willi could see the remains of an Egyptian-style obelisk and the statue of a goddess strumming a harp, strangled up to her neck now in vines. Then in a sudden burst of theatricality the cloud curtain gave way, and a shimmering spotlight fell onto the old asylum itself. All of them froze, staring at it—a mile-long monastery for the mad. Straight on, the imposing administration building—a neo-Gothic castle with half a dozen spires lancing the sky. Right and left, the endless three-story redbrick wings receding at right angles to form their giant V. Turret after turret. Window after window— each with iron bars fixed in cement. If ever a building were haunted, Willi thought, this was it. Grimy curtains flapping in the wind. Whole sections of roofing collapsed. Bats flying in and out. But how clearly he could still see figures . . . peering from barred windows . . . walking the wards . . . tending the lawns. Not a speck of light. Not a trace of the living. But ghosts everywhere.

Sticking to the high grass, they kept a good fifty yards between themselves and the derelict monster, prudently circling it wing by wing, ward by ward, searching for signs of life. Kirkbride's model had called for a highly stratified organization of patients by age, gender, class, and diagnosis. The less disturbed were kept nearer the center, the more violent in the most distant wings. As they neared the last corner of the last wing, number 27, Willi felt about ready to check himself in with the most deranged. The building was empty. How could anyone perform medical procedures in a place like this anyway? It didn't make sense. Did he get this wrong?

He couldn't have. Could he?

An arm in a sling stopped him. Fritz motioned ahead. Just around the corner . . . an unmistakable glow.

Shrinking farther back, they crept through the high grass to the rear of the building. The light grew distinct. Willi could see it wasn't coming from inside the asylum but from several arc lamps affixed to an outside wall. They illuminated a guardhouse below. Inside were two men in black uniform. Focusing in with his binoculars, he made out silver skulls and crossbones on their caps. The section of building they guarded had definitely been renovated. New windows. A new roof. His throat parched when he saw sleek modern lettering across the main entrance: *Institute for Racial Hygiene — Camp Sachsenhausen.*

Fritz slapped his shoulder. "You're a genius, Willi! But how to get inside?"

He wasn't a genius. Just a hard worker. For hours he'd studied the asylum maps, and according to his calculations there ought to be a power-generating plant precisely to their west. He aimed the binoculars; it was there all right. Its tall smokestack not a hundred yards away. For half a century the brawny building had fed the entire facility with steam, delivering it by tunnel through huge copper pipes. The pipes had of course fallen in the war. But the tunnels still had to be there.

The rotting wood of the old plant door gave way with a good swift kick. A hundred bats flapped up, rushing to escape through holes in the roof. The place was cavernous. He'd seen pictures of the house-size generators and block-long fan belts that had once labored here day and night. The equipment was gone, but a few

minutes' search uncovered a dark, winding staircase to the basement. Here they found themselves confronted by half a dozen
man-size tunnels, each leading in a different direction.

The men looked at Willi.

Tunnel 15-27 was pitch-black, a cramped confines of brick
and cobwebs, barely breathable inside. Stiflingly hot. Crouching
through, they had only flashlights and rats to escort them. It
seemed to take forever. As claustrophobia was about to set in, a
passage to the right appeared, stamped 27. They crept through
and found themselves emerging onto a clean cement floor with
newly wallboarded walls. A shiny boiler giving off heat. They'd
reached the institute's basement.

He hadn't seen any lights from outside, so Willi doubted there
were people up there. The windows weren't barred. And there
were only two guards. It could just be laboratories, he figured.
Nobody'd be around at this hour. He'd take Geiger . . . with his
medical knowledge. The rest could stay here, nice and cozy with
the boiler.

"If we're not back in ten minutes," he ordered, "find us."

He and Geiger climbed the enclosed stairwell to the top.
The place was silent. Strangely peaceful. An icy breeze swirled
through the air. They could smell the river, just as Kirkbride had
planned. Willi didn't know what to expect on the far side of the
door marked *Three*, but what they found was crumbling plaster.
Rotting walls. No renovation at all. *Two* was the same. The Institute for Racial Hygiene was still just a ground-floor operation.

Pushing the door open to *One*, his mood brightened at the
sight of new floor tiling. Freshly painted walls. What pains it
had taken to find this place! He was about to step in but Geiger
yanked him back. "Willi . . ." He pointed. Their shoes were filthy
from the tunnel. There wasn't any way to clean them. What
choice did they have but to kick them off and explore the dark
hallway in their stocking feet.

They moved swiftly. Silently. Flashlights to the ground. The
freezing floor seeped into their soles. Willi kept one hand free,

ready to grab his pistol. But the hallway was blessedly empty. The first door they came to was clearly marked—*Operating Room*. As they slipped inside, their flashlights illuminated not one or two, but what had to have been a dozen operating tables. The whole place overflowed with medical equipment, cabinets of brand-new scalpels, drills, shiny sets of knives. In an astonished whisper Geiger stammered, "There's not a hospital in Germany with a setup like this."

The next door they came to was *Radiology*. Geiger had also never seen anything like it. X-ray after X-ray machine bizarrely arranged in sets, one facing the other. In between each, a weird wooden harness with long leather straps. It took some time before Willi realized these had to be for holding people.

"This can't be," Geiger rasped. "Simultaneous anterior and posterior radiation? But it's too much. It would burn a person. Kill them probably, horribly."

But then came the third door. The third room.

The sign simply read *Specimens*.

Inside were dozens of cabinets laden with small, liquid-filled jars. A closer look revealed that these jars contained floating objects. An even closer look revealed that these objects were organs.

Human organs.

Meticulously categorized and numbered.

OVARIES—32:
Serb—12. Russian—14. Czechoslovak—16.

TESTICLES—16:
Greek—8. Romanian—4. Spanish—4.

BRAINS—89:
Mentally Deficient—42. Delusional—34. Schizophrenic—13.

Willi braced himself against a filing cabinet. It was worse than anything he'd seen in the war. Far worse. He couldn't look at it. Turning away, his whole face broke into a cold sweat. His stomach cramped. He had to concentrate not to throw up. To keep calm, he cast his eyes to the floor and tried regulating his breathing. He was doing okay until he caught sight of an open drawer . . . the files inside . . .

—*The Effects of Radiation on Greek Reproductive Organs*
—*Unique Characteristics of Dwarf Testicles*

Severe tingling gripped his limbs. A distinct sensation he was having a dream. That this could not be real. That he was sleep-walking and ought to go back to bed. But reality reflected in Geiger's eyes.

They backed away, flying as if from a house of horrors.

Stumbling next door, they found themselves in some kind of clubroom for the doctors, wood paneled with large leather chairs, a gas stove, late-edition papers. They froze. Somebody was coming in through the outside door! Pressing themselves against the wall, they realized it was the guards.

"Why should I, when there are nice warm toilets in here?" one was saying.

They were in the lobby . . . outside the clubroom door. The toilets were across the hall.

"You know what those fat cats got yesterday? Fresh coffee. Let's sneak a pot. They won't notice. A few tablespoons."

Willi clasped the pistol, his eyes glued to the floor. His sock had a hole, his big toe sticking all the way out. No coffee, he prayed. Don't come in for coffee.

"You know what Huber got when they discovered he'd been helping himself to doctors' goodies, eh? Ten lashes. Not for me. Toilets, then back to the doghouse, that's what I say."

One whistled gaily while the other closed the bathroom door.

"Tomorrow." The whistling stopped. "Transport, ten a.m. Gonna be hell. The biggest batch yet."

Transport? Willi wondered, wiping sweat from his face.

The other yelled back from behind the door. "If they weren't so cheap, they'd get a few more men out here." He farted loudly. "A dozen only—to handle ninety-five?"

A dozen, Willi thought. Could that be all the guards they had?

"As long as we're the ones with the machine guns."

Ninety-five? Who were these people?

"Except half those screwballs from the asylum don't even know what a machine gun is."

The toilet flushed.

The guards went back to their "doghouse" without coffee.

Willi and Geiger were so desperate to escape they nearly forgot their shoes in the stairwell. Downstairs they drove the others ahead of them back into the tunnel. Hurrying through the dark, hot underground Willi shivered with horror. Each step another spasm of realization tore through him. That transit order Gunther had shown him weeks ago . . . for "Special Handling." Now he understood. Gustave's sleepwalkers were only just the icing on this cake. The foreign blood. But Sachsenhausen was being filled with German mental patients, kidnapped from local asylums. That's what "Special Handling" meant—slated for experimentation. For sterilization by radiation. For removal of testicles, ovaries, brains. Had there ever been such a scheme in human history?

Back outside he couldn't get enough oxygen. He kept coughing, gasping, wheezing for air. The others wanted to know what they'd seen, but neither he nor Geiger could speak. Were there words to describe what these doctors, these scientists, were doing up there?

Who were the lunatics in this asylum?

Lutz held up his two-fingered hand. "Listen!"

There was music on the frigid breeze, drunken singing.

A couple of hundred yards away, Willi knew, were a group of

cottages once used for staff housing. The SS must have fixed one up for their own. Down a gravel path, sure enough, they came upon five little bungalows in a semicircle. One had lights blazing from every window. A phonograph record was blasting inside.

Crouching in the high grass, through binoculars they could see men in there. Some were in the living room guzzling schnapps. Upstairs, one was dancing by himself, knocking things over. Another sat in the kitchen weeping tragically, as if the record were too sad to bear. Guard duty at Sachsenhausen certainly took its toll, Willi saw.

Then abruptly the record ended, and a moment of total silence followed. Which is when he heard it. Not from that house, but the one next door.

A distinct moaning.

It was dark, not a glimmer of light. Silent except for the strange whimpers. They seemed to be emanating from the basement. At first Willi thought it might be an injured animal, but as they crept nearer, there was little doubt. The sounds were from a human larynx. And not just one. The basement window was open, but solidly barred with iron mesh. Inside was pitch-black. They didn't dare shine a light through. Fritz motioned skyward, suggesting they wait for one of the periodic cloud breaks, so they backed off and sat there in the dark.

How many times had they waited like this? Willi wondered. For clouds to break. For troops to move. For an attack to commence. Fritz stuck a cigarette between his lips without lighting it. How familiar that taut, patient expression in his eyes. How extraordinary that they should find themselves once more in such an ominous pause between acts. Barely daring to breathe.

Then the cloud curtain drew apart. From high above, a billion distant galaxies cast a platinum sheen on the world.

Fritz and Willi peered through the wire mesh.

Silhouettes took shape in the basement below. Two of them. Upright.

Women. Very young. Very large breasted.

Completely naked.

Willi's throat burned when he realized they were bolted to the wall, their arms high above their heads, their bodies hanging limply. Their eyes rolled and they were moaning in tandem. In harmony almost. Across from them stood a bed, its rumpled sheets filthy with bloodstains. Shackles hung from its posts like in a medieval torture chamber. He yanked away, fending off another wave of nausea, trying to comprehend this.

The guards needed distraction. Sure. Their duties were odious. They'd plucked a few girls out for fun. Soldiers had done this since time immemorial. But keeping them chained to a wall, half-dead . . . why? Was their pleasure heightened by this . . . by suffering? To what degree of barbaric insanity had these men descended? In terms of sheer sadism, sheer calculated cruelty, nothing he'd seen in the Great War could compare to what was on this island.

The others took turns looking. Electric bolts of outrage shot between them. Willi had to restrain them from breaking in to free the poor creatures. It would jeopardize the mission. This had to be done right or the madness would only metastasize. God knew how many others were being tortured out here.

He forced them onward, sticking to the planned route. The trees disappeared and the landscape opened into great plains of weeds. Willi knew this part of the island had once been the agricultural zone. Almost all the food the inmates at Oranienburg consumed they'd cultivated themselves. He'd seen photos of the wheat fields and melon patches, the huge vegetable gardens. Sheep and cattle had grazed in these meadows. There'd been barns for horses and modern milking facilities. Where were they now? And where were the rest of the prisoners they had out here? An appalling thought occurred to him—not, God forbid, in those graves we saw earlier.

And that stench? He sure as hell hadn't imagined it. Whatever its source, it had to be in the direction they were heading. But every step brought them nearer to the end of the island. In another mile or so they'd be back at the footbridge to the Island of the Dead. The cloud cover at least seemed to have broken apart. The bright half moon now lit their way. Through the tangles of dead vines and high grasses they came upon the ruins of a chicken coop. A burned-out barn. The foundations of a greenhouse, sheets of broken glass still strewn around. Then like a blast from the depths of hell itself—it hit them. Worse than dead flesh. The most disgusting smell ever to reach their nostrils.

All of them staggered, coughing, gagging, clutching at their throats as if stricken with mustard gas. Willi felt he might actually pass out if not for a cross breeze off the channel. Every foot forward, the stench grew more revolting, until finally there was no doubt about its source. A series of long wooden sheds before them, now clearly visible in the moonlight.

For a second Willi had to mentally sort through all the old photos he'd examined until he realized what this place had been . . . the pig farm. Oranienburg had been famous for its cured hams and pork. They'd had a whole city of pigs out here. Hundreds and hundreds of them. Now, the ramshackle buildings were completely encircled with double rows of barbed wire. A sign above a locked gate read *Quarantine!* The odor was so bad that Lutz began puking.

Collapsing weakly onto the ground, gasping to take in air from the channel side, they waited while Richter cut the wire. When he was done, they summoned the last of their energy and crept inside. Through the cracked windows bright moonlight clearly illuminated the pig hut. Three tiers of plain plank bunks stretched its full length. Crammed into every square inch of these were human beings. There had to be a hundred of them, men to the left, women to the right, stacked against each other like cords of wood, all dressed in the same asylum smocks the Mermaid had been found in. Every head shaved. The longer Willi looked, the clearer it became they had all been . . . experimented on. Some had huge scars across their torsos, or hideous festering burns. Others had bizarre rashes in perfect geometric

Twenty-six

Three days later he was on a train to Paris.

He'd managed to sleep most of the way, but when his eyes opened, the memories rushed back. At some moments the last few days he'd been sure it was a hallucination, all the torments of that little island a bizarre dream from which he was about to awaken. Then he'd picture those jars of floating organs again, the half-dead girls chained to the wall, the reeking barracks crammed with prisoners—and he knew it was all too real.

The whole mission had gone like clockwork. They'd motored back across the Havel. Returned the boats. Richter had stayed. Geiger and Lutz boarded trains for home. But none of them would ever be the same. How could they, after what they'd witnessed? Those SS doctors were a hundred times more insane than the maddest schizophrenics. And yet . . . they were highly regarded specialists, top men in their fields. Someone was spend-

patches, as if they'd been intentionally infected. At the foot of each bunk was a clipboard. Geiger confirmed these were medical charts.

Most seemed asleep, or dead already. A few huddled around a wood-burning stove in the center aisle. Among them Willi noticed three skeletal women, one hanging on a pair of makeshift crutches, the others heaped on a lower bunk. All had Mermaid legs, like Gina Mancuso. Reversed! With a jolt of horror he recognized one. The great dark eyes filled with such pride and superiority before she was hypnotized on Gustave's yacht were now completely blank. The Greek countess, Melina von Auerlicht. A few bunks farther . . . two tiny ladies examining their breasts—the Hungarian dwarfs. But why were they on the men's side? In a flash he recalled those jars with the little floating things and the file marked *Unique Characteristics of Dwarf Testicles,* and clutching himself with grim comprehension, he let out a groan.

ing a fortune bankrolling their operation. After so many years with the police, all the horrors he'd seen of war . . . Willi didn't think he could be shocked anymore by the depths to which human beings could sink. But he was. He truly was.

Arriving at the Gare du Nord, he took a cab directly to Hedda's, desperate to see his boys' expressions when he showed up unexpectedly. *"Mon Dieu!"* the great-aunt exclaimed at the door. "Why didn't you let us know you were coming?" She kissed him noisly on each cheek, suffocating him in Chanel No. 5. Bracelets jangling, rings glittering, she led him into the parlor.

"But I'm afraid the children aren't here, Willi. They're off in town with their grandparents. Luncheon. Museums. And the Galeries Lafayette—to purchase lighter jackets. The ones they brought from Berlin were so heavy. We haven't those nasty winds blowing from Siberia as you do."

His mother-in-law's sister had married a Frenchman decades ago and lived in Paris ever since. Despite her ridiculously thick accent in French, she considered herself a real grande dame now and insisted Willi take an aperitif at once, "to revive yourself."

"You don't look well, *mon fils.*" She fiddled with her strings of pearls. "Not well at all. So pale. And those eyes. But people never look well when they arrive from Germany. A few days here and you'll be good as new. How long are you staying? We've plenty of beds."

"Just a few days. I needed to see the boys."

"Of course you did. But there's no cause for worry." She joined him for a tumbler of sherry. "Those darlings are having the time of their lives. Stefan told me the other day he could stay in Paris forever and ever. Such little angels. And so well behaved. Both of them."

"Thanks to Ava. Is she with them?"

"I'm afraid Ava's gone until Thursday." One of Hedda's tweezed eyebrows arched pointedly. "She's off on holiday, in Provence."

Willi's chest constricted. "By herself?"

A wry smile drew across the grande dame's lips. "No, of course not, my dear. She went with a marvelously charming young maiden. Marianne. Or something like that." Hedda's dark gaze narrowed. "Willi, you must take a nap, dear boy. You look positively enervated."

But the kind of fatigue weighing Willi down wasn't relieved by naps. He opted for a long walk instead. It'd been years since he'd strolled around Paris, and he was surprised at his keen delight seeing the ladies on the Champs-Élysées again strutting in their finery. Couples smooching on park benches. The animated conversations in cafés. Everything was so much less hectic, less tense, than in Berlin. So much prettier. He hiked across the river, wandering the narrow lanes of the Latin Quarter and into the Luxembourg Gardens. With its gleaming statuary and formal paths it seemed to him the epitome of civilization. Nature tamed. Earth's and man's. Slowly, imperceptibly, as Hedda predicted, he did begin to feel better. Happier to be a member of the human race.

Yet even in this oasis he couldn't stop thinking about Paula, what they'd done to her. What *he'd* done to her. Could he ever forgive himself? Only perhaps . . . if he wiped that Nazi torture camp off the face of the earth. It wasn't going to be easy. No less than his staunchest ally, von Schleicher, had been incredulous, hostile almost, to hear his report. "Such things simply cannot be!" He'd acted as if it were some sort of drunken fabrication. "Where is your proof? Your evidence, Inspektor!" Clenching his fists in his pockets now, Willi added another thing to prepare for Thurseblot night: a movie crew.

Hedda was also right about the weather, he acknowledged. It was warmer than in Berlin. The air somehow lighter, easier to breathe. He unbuttoned his coat and let his scarf dangle. One could almost forget things such as Nazis here. Strolling past the magnficent Fontaine des Médicis though, whom should he run into but his oldest school chum, Mathias Goldberg.

"Willi!" They embraced like brothers.

Goldberg's success as a "high-volt" artist had made him a minor celebrity in Berlin. Once upon a time Paris may have been the City of Light, but the torch had passed. Now, no place blazed like the capital of Germany. Its streets were afire with electric advertising, waving, flashing pageants of light that obliterated the night, and Mathias was one of its pioneers. In his most ingenious work he'd used four thousand bulbs over Breitscheidplatz to depict a dingy dress being cleaned: sparkling blue water, laundry powder dancing from bright green packets, a glistening yellow dress the result. How shocked he'd been to discover his name on the Nazi list of "decadent" cultural influences, a purveyor of Jewish merchandising.

"Thank God you made it out. Were the bastards after you, too, *Freund*?"

Willi realized he was being mistaken for an émigré. "No, no. I'm only here for—"

"There are so many others." Mathias grabbed Willi's sleeve. "You've got to see it to believe."

He dragged Willi over to the famous Dôme café, where a gang of real German émigrés sat hunched around tables in the back. There had to be thirty. Jewish mainly, but not all. Willi felt obliged to join for at least a few minutes. There were artists. Social Democrats. A Protestant pastor. Several had received real death threats: "Leave Germany or die!" Others couldn't bear another broken window or swastika on their doors. All had given up home and livelihoods, torn up roots, were adrift now in a foreign country. Lawyers without clients. Doctors without patients. Businessmen without a business.

"The European mind is capitulating." They spoke in such dark, haunting tones.

"The sediments of the human soul are rising to the surface."

"Human feeling counts for nothing anymore. Only brute power."

The longer he listened, the more Willi filled with the desperate urge to escape, not from Germany but from them. Miserable shivers wormed down his spine. Could this be a glimpse of his own future? Please, dear Lord, no. Thurseblot, he kept telling himself. It all comes down to the Feast of Thor.

"And such pleasure at suffering. Such outright sadism!"

A violent cough wracked his body and he leapt from the table, gasping for air. Excusing himself, he fled back into the Parisian sunshine, promising to get in touch with Mathias before he left, which he knew he never would.

Instead he spent three heavenly days with the boys. God, how he loved them!

"Your French is so improved." He couldn't help fussing over them. "And how you know your way around the metro."

Their grandparents had purchased not only wide-cut Parisian-style jackets for them but matching berets as well, and they looked like real little Frenchmen now. They dragged him up the funicular to Montmartre. Posed for photos on the terrace of Sacre Coeur. Made him pay tribute at the tomb of Napoléon. But all the while the fatigue that had plagued him since his foray to Asylum Island attacked in earnest. His joints and limbs, his muscles, felt as if someone were pumping cement into them. *Komm doch, Vati!* The boys grew impatient. "You're walking slower than grandma." His cough appeared to worsen by the hour.

The day before he was to go back to Berlin, he'd promised to take the boys wherever they wanted to go in Paris. The kids had no trouble deciding. Somewhere they'd read about a large tunnel complex running underneath the city streets . . . so off to Les Catacombes they went. Back from holiday, Ava gladly joined, though she made no bones about their choice of destination. *"Mein Gott.* Out of all the beautiful places in this city!" The entrance on the Place Denfert-Rochereau was a simple door you could walk right past, but the boys knew exactly where it was. After paying a fee they found themselves on a long stone staircase spiraling into an abyss. "Isn't this fantastic?" Erich cried, rushing ahead. At bottom, wet gravel crunched underfoot as they marched along a dark tunnel. Stefan's face ignited as he pointed out a sign indicating they were twenty-five meters beneath the street. When he grabbed Willi with one hand and Ava with the other, happily skipping between the two, Willi felt his chest constrict with a confusing sensation, which a moment later erupted into a deep, hacking cough.

"For God's sakes." Ava's face darkened.

"This air." He felt as if he were strangulating. "It's so damned dry."

Even though they could hear water dripping and see stalactites inching down from the ceiling, a gritty dust seemed to thicken the deeper they penetrated the tunnel. All this while, Willi'd been under the impression Les Catacombes had to do with the water system. Now as they entered a dimly lit chamber, a small exhibition hall enlightened him. Dating back to Roman times, these three hundred subterranean kilometers were originally limestone mines located far outside town. As the city expanded and real estate became scarce, the government reclaimed several centuries' worth of cemeteries by carting the remains down here. Thus had the old system of mines now directly underneath Paris been turned into a vast ossuary containing the remains of some 5 to 6 million former residents, which workers had reinterred with honorific artistry.

Please Proceed with Caution.

Five to 6 million?

Arrête! C'est ici l'empire de la mort, a sign above the next doorway warned.

"Stop! This is the empire of death."

"Come on, Dad. You're not scared, are you?"

Scared? Dad? How could Dad be scared? He opened the door. The dust grew so thick it felt palpable on his skin.

Down another long, dark hallway from which there seemed no escape, they came at last to a large chapel-like room constructed entirely, Willi realized, of bones. Human bones. Walls, ceilings, everything—bones. Thousands and thousands of them, all meticulously arranged. Tibias and femurs piled one atop the next, bordered by neat rows of skulls. Collarbones and hip bones formed into elaborate hearts and crosses. Ava grimaced and sighed with distress, but the boys could not have been more ghoulishly amused. Room after room, though, tunnel after tunnel, bone after bone, these displays began to wear on Willi until he saw skeletons rising up and dancing before his eyes. Around his head. Then everything began spinning around his head. His own skeleton refused to bear him a moment longer, and his legs just disappeared.

The next thing he knew a cool hand was on his forehead, gently stroking.

It required real effort to open his eyes.

"Ava—"

"Shhh. You're in the hospital, Willi. With double pneumonia."

A glimpse around confirmed it. How absurd. He'd never been sick a day in his life. But along with a rush of recollections came real fear.

"How long have I been here?"

"Shhhh."

"How long?"

"Five days, Willi."

Lord almighty. "What's the date?"

"Come on, you need to rest."

"The date, Ava. The date."

"The eighteenth of January. Now really, Willi—"

He heaved a sigh, straining to lift his torso. Thurseblot was the twenty-fourth.

"What do you think you're doing?"

"I've got to . . ."

The whole room suddenly turned to bones—and jars of floating testicles and brains.

"You've got to stay where you are." Ava's dark eyes flared. "You're running a high fever still. She squeezed his hand, her chestnut gaze mellowing with tenderness.

His head fell back but his blood boiled.

"Listen to me," he heard himself say, not sure who or what was speaking. "I don't want those boys going back to Germany. Do you understand? Not next week. Not next month. Never, Ava. None of you. Tell your father it's time to pull out. Register the kids in school here. Find an apartment. Do what you have to, only—"

"Stop." Her fingers fell on his lips. "We'll discuss this later. When you're well."

She leaned and kissed his forehead, arousing a tender sigh from in his chest.

But there was no later. Just before dawn he sneaked from the hospital and dragged himself over to the Gare du Nord, where he boarded the first train back to Berlin.

Twenty-seven

A wicked wind danced across the river Havel. January's full moon cast Spandau under a twilight spell. As the shadow of *The Third Eye* loomed across the Black Stag Inn, Willi gripped the iron bridge rail, his vision fixed on the dock below where the Great Gustave stood greeting guests, his black cape fluttering madly. It was Thurseblot—at long last. The air seemed alive with demons.

Townspeople were noisily clambering up the gangplank. Stifling one of the deep, hacking coughs that still wracked his body, Willi watched from the shadows. In the week since he'd fled the hospital, he'd all but willed himself back to health. Every time he thought of Sachsenhausen his fever had subsided. Now that the moment of truth was here, there was nothing to do but observe—like the Meistersinger of Wagner's opera, knowing that everything, all future happiness, rested on this contest he'd engineered.

How carefully he'd planned it, down to the finest detail. How many times he'd gone over it, making sure nothing could go wrong. But something always could, he knew. Like Paula. His throat clenched as he pictured her disappearing in that motorboat. All you could do was try to leave as little as possible to chance.

In the silver moonlight the Black Stag Inn with all its crossbeams and pointed gables looked like a fairy-tale illusion. Enjoying a pagan feast inside were six very real monsters. Devising a plan to capture them had given Willi a royal headache. Simultaneous raids in Spandau and Sachsenhausen were out of the question. He didn't have the resources. But one raid at a time was too risky. Too much chance someone could escape. One doctor. One guard. A quick call and everything would be ruined. So he'd had no choice but to employ some of the famous Jewish cunning the Nazis were always complaining about.

The idea had come to him in the hospital while he was lying there delirious. He thought he heard singing again—that song from the morning in the forest with Fritz. *Valderi, Valdera-ha-ha-ha-ha-ha.* And the strangest image took shape in his head. The man with a many-colored coat, skipping down the streets of Hamelin playing a fife, all the vermin dancing. *River Weser, deep and wide . . . A pleasanter spot you never spied.* Of course. That's what I have to do, he realized. *Lure* the rats out. Like the Pied Piper.

But how?

The answer had slowly dawned on him.

Downstairs in the Police Presidium . . .

As soon as he got back from Paris, he'd hurried there, but the Great Gustave was nowhere to be found. All the flourish, all the magic, that had been the King of Mystics had vanished. Left in the cell was a melancholy little man, Gershon Lapinksy. A man chastened not merely by the certainty that his days of wealth and fame were over, but a terrible knowledge that could no longer be blotted from his memory. During their hypnotic session Kurt had left Gustave fully cognizant of all he'd previously managed to black out . . . the face of every person he'd sent sleepwalking into oblivion.

"I've been trying for days to rehypnotize myself," he confessed. "But it doesn't work anymore. And you want to know why?" His eyes brimmed with bitter pride. "Because a hypnotist needs a willing subject, Inspektor. And I no longer am one."

When Willi told him about Sachsenhausen, his whole body seemed to collapse.

"Is that what happened to those girls?" Shaking fingers covered his eyes. "Oh, God. With the SS I knew it had to be bad. But that . . ." His head shrank between his shoulders. "Even a clairvoyant couldn't imagine." He burst into a fit of tears. "You know, Kraus," he sniffed, "I never was a lucky fellow. Even from the beginning." He dried his eyes with the handkerchief Willi handed him. "I was my mother's thirteenth child. Can you imagine? Thirteen. If only I'd left well enough alone and stayed at her side. But all the other twelve, you see, died . . . and I didn't want to be next. So I ran off and joined the circus."

He swore he'd do anything to bring the SS doctors to justice.

This time Willi didn't need a sixth sense to know the man meant it.

Now under the milky sheen of winter's full moon Gustave had returned to life. The Great Gustave, working his magic on the townsfolk, bowing, clicking, shaking hands, welcoming one and all. Every few seconds Willi noticed him cast an eye toward the Black Stag Inn, the swastika flag above its entrance flapping unremittingly. They both were waiting for that door to open. It was well and fine the locals had turned out, but if the good doctors from that institute didn't soon emerge, it was all for naught.

Why shouldn't they come? A feast in honor of Thor. An evening of music and sumptuous fare—courtesy of the Great Gustave aboard his famous yacht. Why look a gift horse in the mouth? They had nothing to be suspicious about. All the most prominent people in town had got invitations. Nothing could be more innocuous. Yet that door refused to budge.

But down on the gangway the rest of the guests kept pouring aboard, all dressed in their Sunday best, so colorful in their red-and-black armbands. How grateful they were, these hard-working folk, to be treated to such an evening. How completely oblivious to the nightmare upstream born of their insanity. Willi wanted to forgive them. Two decades of war, grief, hunger, revolution, and economic disaster, had made rich soil for extremism, he understood. But what he'd seen at that asylum was the result of their mad grandiose fantasies—this lunatic obsession with blood supremacy. Ruthless, calculated exploitation and murder. It was hard to forgive. Impossible to forget.

He looked at his watch. Eight p.m. exactly. These doctors weren't the types to come late. It was now or never.

I am the God Thor,
I am the War God.

He recalled the famous poem.

The blows of my hammer
Ring in the earthquake!

Meekness is weakness,
Strength is triumphant.

Longfellow must have known a few Nazis, Willi mused drily. Suddenly the inn door flung open. Furious laughter filled the night. Men in black uniform came stumbling out, carrying steins of beer, slapping each other on the back. Two. Three. Four. Willi counted as they climbed aboard. But not until the gangway pulled in did he feel a moment of relief. All six safe in the hold. The rats had taken the bait.

For the musical presentation Gustave had managed to pull from his hat the great Irmgard Wildebrunn-Schrenk herself, one of Europe's top sopranos. Heiner Windgassen, beloved tenor with the Bayreuth Festival, joined her, and with a surprise visit from the Potsdam Army Choir they offered up a stirring selection from *Götterdämmerung*: "Siegfried's Rhine Journey," "Brunhild's Immolation." The audience rocked the yacht with applause. "Only the best for my friends in Spandau!" The King of Mystics held out his arms as the performers took their bows. "In honor of our heritage. Our future. Our Führer. *Sieg Heil!*"

"*Sieg Heil!*"

The doors to the buffet were thrown open. Whole roast pigs and legs of lamb were spread among mountains of sauerkraut and potato. Beer and wine for all.

Willi watched from a dream hiding place—behind a two-way mirror overlooking the galley. Before him a panel of switches identified a score of hidden microphones, allowing him to tune in or out on practically any conversation on deck. This advanced spy system, seemingly set up just for him, was in fact all Gustave's—the means by which the King of Mystics had gathered tidbits for his "mind-reading" demonstrations.

"But where on earth have you been?" Willi turned up the mike with special interest on Gustave's conversation with several of the institute doctors. The speaker it turned out was none other than Oscar "Jew-damm" Schumann, the orthopedic genius. "We'd thought you'd been abducted by men from Mars or something."

There'd been endless speculation following Gustave's arrest. The Master was sick. The Master was dead. The Master was having plastic surgery. Finally, with the help of Fritz at Ullstein Press, pictures began appearing in the papers of the Master enjoying the solitude of a monastic retreat in the Carpathians.

"Just needed to recharge my spiritual batteries a bit," Gustave replied in a half whisper. "Say, Schumann . . . you and your buddies stick around after the rest of the crowd goes home, eh? I've some extra-special goodies you won't want to miss out on."

With sublime satisfaction Willi watched the surgeon throw an appreciative arm around the Great Gustave's shoulders.

A brass band was brought out. There were folk songs and riotous polkas. It was a night the people of Spandau would not soon forget—but a working night nonetheless. Precisely at eleven the band packed up. The townspeople bid tipsy farewells, thanking Gustave a million times. By midnight no one was left except the six doctors from the Institute for Racial Hygiene, eager to discover what Thurseblot goodies Gustave had in store.

From studying their dossiers Willi knew each by heart. Next to Schumann, with the long nose and bushy eyebrows, was Theodor Mollbaecker, a specialist in soft-tissue infection and leading proponent in the use of antibacterial sulfonamides. Wolfgang Heink, next to him, was the neurologist who specialized in lower-limb disorders. The fat one so drunk he could barely stand was Sigmund Wilderbrunn, Germany's leading practicioner of sterilization methods. That little one with the bad toupee was Horst Knapperbusch, endocrinologist and foremost theoretician on the effect of X-rays on genital glands. Last but not least, Mr. Bunny Teeth, Josef—whose last name Willi by now knew to be Mengele—an expert on racial differences in body structure, focused almost exclusively these days on the genetic traits of twins and dwarfs. He would have instantly clamped the cuffs on all six had Gustave not preferred a more delicate approach.

"You don't know what an honor it is for me to host such esteemed scientists." Gustave held out a welcoming hand. "Please, comrades . . . you must join me in my private suite. Come! I've been waiting all evening for this surprise." Willi watched the doctors follow like eager ducklings, full of fantasies no doubt of big-breasted fräuleins under magic spells. Ten minutes later Gustave buzzed him to come down. Entering the dimly lit suite, Willi felt his throat clench, viselike. All six doctors were lying as if dead on the floor—deep in a hypnotic trance.

The Third Eye's engines roared as they sailed upriver to Sachsenhausen. On the way Gustave commanded Oscar Schumann to get up, follow him, and use the radio transmitter he was handing him. "You are to summon every guard on Asylum Island to come at once to the pier. When we arrive, they will board this yacht and join our festitivies as my guests." Sure enough, when they pulled up, all twelve SS guards, skulls and crossbones glistening in the moonlight, were eagerly waiting. One by one as they pranced on board, soldiers of the Potsdam Army Choir—changed from tuxedos into uniforms—took each prisoner. Willi's eyes burned with tears.

He'd got every last rat.

The problem now was medical care for all those penned up at the pig farm. If the transport of ninety-five had in fact arrived that morning after their raid, there could be hundreds out there, he knew. All he could do was help them get to the Brandenburg Medical Center. How doctors down there would cope with the arrival of so many half-dead people was another matter.

The Thurseblot moon cast long shadows as he led twenty-five soldiers down the gangway. A still photographer and camera crew followed close behind. Across the waist-high fields of weeds they hurried toward the barracks. But with the strong southern wind blowing, the night air smelled too fresh, he noticed, too sweet. More surprising when they reached the pig farm, the gate was wide-open. The long, miserable huts inside were empty. Willi leaned against a door for support. How was it possible? Where could they have taken so many deathly ill people? It had only been two weeks. A hideous feeling coursed through his veins. Walking fast, then jogging, then running, he led the detatchment back across the channel onto the Island of the Dead. In a clearing sur- rounded by half-trampled grass, there was no mistaking three huge new trenches covered in fresh black earth.

Book Four

TWILIGHT OF THE GODS

Twenty-eight

Not one prisoner found alive. Their shaved heads and gaunt faces hovered accusingly before Willi's eyes. But for God's sake, he had to acknowledge, he hadn't done that badly. He'd beaten the bastards. Pulled the plug on the whole filthy operation. Arrested the whole sick pack of doctors. The guards. And most critically, got proof. Two dozen boxes of specimens. Two filing cabinets full of reports. Films. Photos. The hells of Sachsenhausen were all recorded history now. He only had to let the world know.

Sailing back across the Havel, he saw no reason to stop Gustave from rousing the malignant scientists from their hypnotic oblivion and confronting them with his fury. "You, Schumann." The Master's face trembled. "And you, Mengele." Gustave held up a jar with human brains. "So much to offer the world—how could you?"

But even in handcuffs these dogs refused to be humbled.

"Our work happens to be very much for the world." Schumann rolled his eyes as if bored. "Just not *your* world. In twelve months we learned more than most scientists do in lifetimes."

"So much suffering. So much death! What gives you the right to play God?"

Mengele bared his teeth. "You think you can stop us? We'll build bigger Sachsenhausens, you'll see. More efficient. All across Europe. The time is nearer than you think, Gustave. We Germans have been soft too long."

Docking at Spandau, Willi's chest swelled with pride as he sent the whole depraved lot packing by army truck over to Moabit Prison and its famously impregnable walls. May they never be unleashed on humankind again, he prayed. What to do with the evidence was a tougher choice. Half of him wanted to dump it on von Schleicher. "Here—show it to the world!" But practically, he knew, such a mass of material would merely overwhelm unless it was collated, summarized. The logical place to work on it was the Police Presidium, only he didn't dare. He would have taken it to his apartment had there been enough space. But he took it to Fritz's. How incongruous the mud-splattered military vehicles looked in front of his chic glass house. "What's this, an invasion?" Fritz said, laughing, when he saw them. But once he understood the contents, Fritz used his good arm to help lug it in.

For a day and a half the two of them sat on his white sofa, beneath the paintings by Klee and Modigliani, sorting through the hideous business. When they realized it was too much, they had Gunther come out to help. Even with all of them sifting and sorting though, they were still only able to piece together part of the picture. What a field day those mad scientists of Sachsenhausen had had.

In twelve months they'd forcibly sterilized hundreds of people. Vasectomy, castration, ovariotomy, tubal ligation, radiation— each was tested in comparison to the others. The result: X-ray radiation, the hoped-for "wave" of the future, had proven too slow, too costly, too painful, for use in any mass sterilization program. For males, surgical castration was the most effective method, cheap and quick. For females the results were still "under investigation." Several hundred more captives had been infected with everything from botulism to typhus, then given test medications. The result: the sulfonamide drugs, which Theodor Mollbaecker had invested so much hope in, did not prove of particular antibacterial value. Josef Mengele, Mr. Bunny Teeth, had conducted the most horrific experiments. Fixated on the role of genetics in heredity, he had anesthetized at least four sets of twins and five dwarfs, then dissected them while they were still alive, photographing and recording their organs. Oscar Schumann's work had produced the most substantive results. Of twenty-five leg and arm transplants conducted over two months, all but seven had been successful. In the future, bone transplantation, according to Schumann, would be routine.

From what they could calculate, at least 850 men, women, and even children had undergone medical experiments at Sachsenhausen. Not a single one survived. Each of their deaths had been recorded. "Succumbed to typhus." "Succumbed to radiation burns." An invoice found in a desk drawer indicated that two further transports of seventy asylum inmates each were expected the following week.

Fritz was all for plastering it across the front pages and calling it what it was: the greatest crime in German history. "In twenty-four hours we'll have the whole Nazi Party collapsing in disgrace," he insisted. " '850 Tortured and Killed!' " But Willi couldn't do that. As a precondition for using the Potsdam garrison von Schleicher had made Willi promise that all evidence of SS medical crimes would go directly to him.

Friday afternoon he and Fritz personally delivered a ten-page report and one full box of evidence to the Reichs Chancellery.

After perusing the pages and seeing the contents of several jars, von Schleicher turned green.

"It's utterly inconceivable. Beyond human imagination."

"Obviously not," Willi said.

"Take it all to von Hindenburg," Fritz demanded. "Get him to sign a presidental decree. Outlaw the Nazis!"

Von Schleicher had to prop himself on the desk. "I can't. Von Papen's so poisoned the Old Man against me I'm not allowed near the Presidential Palace just now. No, in that regard I am hand-cuffed."

Handcuffed? Willi's stomach dropped. Von Schleicher?

"Surely something of this magnitude—"

"Listen to me, both of you." The chancellor's face turned rigid as a death mask. "If there's one thing I've learned in this wretched office, it's that politics is timing. I want everything you have brought to me here. Do you understand? Leave nothing behind. When the moment is right, I assure you . . . the ax will fall."

"Who knows"—Fritz tried to summon some optimism as they exited the chancellery—"maybe the man actually knows what he's doing this time. Come on, I'll buy you dinner."

But Willi had lost his appetite.

Later that night Fritz was on the phone pestering Willi of all things about a woman.

"Remember, Willi . . . the one I said was perfect for you? Well, you won't believe it. I ran straight into her on the Ku-damm just now. She's coming tomorrow night as my guest to the Press Ball. You've got to come, too. Promise? You do have white tie and tails?"

Willi had about as much desire to go to the Press Ball as to the dentist, but the next evening he dutifully pulled on long for-mal socks and snapped them into calf garters. It was bitter out, he saw from the window as he stepped into his striped silk trou-sers. The wind was banging the electric streetcar wires madly together. Now that he'd overcome pneumonia, shut down Sachsenhausen, and got all the evidence to the Reichs Chancellery, what he really needed was a little sleep, he decided, slipping into the patent leather loafers with bows. He missed his boys. Paula, too. Grabbing the ridiculous shirt with the huge French cuffs from the closet, he cursed himself for having agreed to this.

The Press Ball was no ordinary fête but the absolute apex of Berlin's social season. At the banquet halls of the Zoological Gardens the champagne was overflowing. Cinchilla stoles and egret feathers tickled his nose as he squeezed past society ladies and movie queens, ministers of state, members of parliament. Anyone whose face Willi'd ever seen in the papers—including heads of the Ringverein, the city's notorious crime rings—was furiously drinking and gossiping.

Eventually he reached the tiers of reserved boxes where Fritz was to meet him with this superwoman. There was one box for the Mosse Press. Another for Bertelsmann. Numerous boxes for the foreign legations. Why was that large one in the middle empty, where the chancellor ought to be? Directly next to it was the Ullstein box, the five famous brothers all around one table with their jewelry-laden wives. Joining them were Erich Maria Remarque, author of *All Quiet on the Western Front,* and *très* elegant Vicki Baum, of *Grand Hotel* fame. Other tables were full of editors, columnists, photographers. Where was Fritz? Willi finally spotted him standing with a tall blonde, whose low-cut gown revealed a singularly muscular physique.

"A putsch to overthrow von Hindenburg?" Fritz's words were already slurring, his dueling scar bright scarlet. "Thassss too funny. I've known von Schleicher yearz dearie. Sly as a fox but trussss me . . . hasn't got the . . . why, Willi!" He threw an arm around him.

The tall blonde, Willi recognized at once, was Leni Riefenstahl—star of the popular Alpine-climbing films and notorious gal-about-town. She was who Fritz thought would be perfect for him?

"You know Leni, of course."

"To my shame I'm afraid I don't," Willi lied, shocked at his friend's absurd choice.

"But I know you." The muscular actress offered a vigorous handshake. "The great *Kinderfresser* catcher. The pictures in the papers did you an injustice." Her azure eyes examined him as if through various lenses. "Come to my studio sometime. Let me photograph you. I'll bring out your heroic qualities."

"Leni, I'd no idea you'd so many talents," Fritz proclaimed. "Photography now!"

"Just learning, Fritzi. But I've a pretty good eye."

She handed Willi a card. "Please," she insisted. "I'm experimenting with some fabulous new camera angles I'd love to try out on you."

I'll bet, Willi thought, stunned this could have been the woman Fritz had been prattling about for months. Willi was futher amazed when Riefenstahl blew a kiss and walked away. "You mean she isn't—"

"Her?" Fritz nearly fell over laughing. "Jesus, Willi. I'd just as soon fix you up with Goebbels. No, the woman I had in mind is—" His eyes widened, his dueling scar stretching with evident delight. "Well . . . she's coming right now."

Willi turned. He swore he recognized a pair of chestnut eyes approaching. A slender figure in a pale rose gown with a sweeping velvet train. That long, beautiful curve to the neck. Now he understood what Fritz meant when he'd said some cad wanted to pounce on her. "For Christ's sakes." Willi turned to him furiously.

"Don't be thickheaded, you fool. Just because she's your dead wife's sister—"

"This time you've really gone overboard, Fritz," Willi growled under his breath. But the swell of happiness as she neared was irrepressible. When she reached them, Willi managed to act surprised. "Ava, for goodness' sakes. What are you doing in Berlin?"

"I could ask the same of you." Her eyes darkened. Willi could see by the look she cast Fritz she was just as stunned by this setup as he. And still fuming over Willi's running away from the hospital in Paris. "Well, I'm glad to see you're feeling better anyway, Willi." She flung the train of her dress to one side.

Sensing this wasn't unfolding as intended, Fritz held up a finger as if to rectify the situation, when all at once the entire ballroom seemed to quiver with an electric shock. Some positively sensational news was jolting through the crowd. It took but an instant to hit them. Willi felt as if an anvil had smacked his head. "Have you heard? Von Schleicher and his entire cabinet are kaput! Forced to resign!"

But that couldn't be; he had to steady himself. Von Schleicher out? It was catastrophic. What about our evidence?

"Don't panic." Fritz's whole face darkened. "We'll go the the chancellery first thing in morning."

"Tomorrow's Sunday."

"Well then, Monday!"

Willi didn't think he could last that long. The music kept playing. The couples kept dancing. But this was really too much. He had no capacity left for pretense. The bottom was dropping out. Ava seemed to sense it, too. *After von Schleicher, who?* her eyes asked.

"Come on." Willi grabbed her by the waist. "Let's get out of here." They made a beeline for the coatroom. It was mobbed. Half the place were leaving. "What the hell are you doing in Berlin anyway?" he whispered tensely as they waited on line. "I told you not to come."

"Oh, you did now. So I'm taking orders from you?" Her eyes flared. "You also told us to sell the house and business."

"Shhh!"

He started up again when they got outside. "Your father should have come."

"He did." She clutched her collar against the wind. "And I came, too, so he wouldn't be alone. You've no right to critize me. I'm not the one who snuck out of a hospital with double—"

"I couldn't help it, Ava. There were things to do. Crucial things."

"Oh, yes. With you there are always things. Work's more important than life, isn't it? Never mind your health. Your family!"

Willi could barely hear her. All he could grasp was that von Schleicher was out and those boxes of evidence were in his office. The wind whipped wildly as a taxi pulled up. Ava climbed in, giving him an exasperated look. He longed suddenly to take her in his arms. Enfold her. Kiss her. But she slammed the door, leaving him there in the ice-cold night.

Twenty-nine

First thing Monday, Willi and Fritz met in front of the Reichs Chancellery. Police were all along Wilhelm Strasse, crowds already overflowing the sidewalks. Behind those walls everyone knew the fate of Germany was being decided by Hindenburg and a handful of high-hats. "What do you mean I can't get in?" Fritz said, astonished, to the guard at the gate. "Franjo. You've seen me here every week for years."

"I am sorry, Herr Fritz. It is not my decision. Your name is no longer on the press list."

"That's impossible. I write for the *Morning News*. The *Evening News*. The *Weekend Report*. I'm third cousin of the kaiser! Tell me at least if Chancellor von Schleicher is still in the building."

"No, he is not. Nor is the general chancellor any longer. He and all his belongings have been removed."

The word sent a sickening feeling through Willi.

They dashed by car over to Lichtenstein Allee, where Fritz knew von Schleicher had an apartment. The general's wife greeted them at the door. "But I'm afraid he isn't seeing anyone this morning." She held her head with grim dignity.

"It's all right, *Schätzchen*. Those two can come."

Sitting in a smoking jacket before the fireplace, his silver monocle perched in one eye, von Schleicher barely bothered looking at them. "That miserable von Papen." Flames danced from the monocle. "Couldn't be happy until he got revenge on me for having him sacked last November."

"Herr General . . . all those boxes of evidence we left with you."

"Hindenburg swore he'd never give in to Hitler. But Papen thinks he can tame the beast."

"The evidence," Willi pressed him. "What's become of it?"

"Do they really think they can come up with a stronger coalition than mine? Let them try! Fifty-eight days I got. Fifty-eight miserable days."

"Please, sir—all those boxes, all those pictures and files from Sachsenhausen?"

The ex-chancellor turned to them, pulling off the monocle. "It happened so fast." He looked a hundred years old. "In one hour I was out. Can you imagine, they made me pack myself. I hadn't a clue what to do with your boxes so I called Eckelmann."

"Eckelmann, the Socialist MP?"

"Socialist. So what if he is? I've known him thirty years. Elisabeth and I had a most congenial dinner with him at Aschinger the other night. Over cognac he explicitly said to me, "Kurt, if there's anything I can ever do . . ." So I called him. Naturally I didn't tell him what they contained, just that I had boxes full of vital material that needed protection. We arranged for everything to be taken by truck over to his office."

"His office . . . at the Reichstag?"

"Yes. They have mountains of things nobody cares about.

In the storerooms. Safe as a bank down there, I assure you."
Von Schleicher blinked several times. Slowly placing the monocle
back in his eye he returned his gaze to the fireplace.

Willi felt ill. They drove at once to the Reichstag, but the
whole building was cordoned off. They tried calling Eckelmann
at work, at home, but got no answer. There was nothing they
could do. Fritz kept muttering, "Why the hell was I removed
from the chancellery press list?" On the way to his office they
noticed little knots of people formed around the news kiosks.
Here and there cheers erupted. Fritz leaned out the window.
"What's going on?"

"We're saved!" a teenage girl cried out. "Hitler's in power!"

Fritz fell back in the car seat. "No wonder I'm off the press
list." He stared ahead. "We're done for then." He turned to Willi.
"Not just us. Europe."

Perhaps it's a mistake, Willi thought, like when he'd first
heard Vicki was dead. Why then were Jewish shops pulling
down their shutters? A hundred times Hitler had promised that
the day he took over, heads would roll. Who'd have thought the
idiots would ever hand things to him legally, without a drop of
blood?

People were grabbing up special banner-headlined editions.

"Maybe it's not as bad as it looks." Fritz practically seized
one from a street vendor. He seemed to be praying as he scanned
the front page. "Hugenberg . . . finance minister. Von Papen . . .
vice chancellor. Maybe they really can leash the dog."

"You always called von Papen a frivolous mutton-head."

By the time they reached Leipziger Strasse even black humor
faded. Bands of storm troops were roaming the sidewalks. "*Today
Germany—tomorrow the world!*" they were shouting, physically
harassing people going in and out of Wertheim's. There was a
loud smash. One of the big show-windows shattered. "Not as
bad as it looks." Willi steered around broken glass. "It's worse."

On Koch Strasse the Ullstein building already had the feel of
a castle under siege, employees rushing in for refuge. "I'll find

Eckelmann, one way or another," Fritz said as he climbed from the car. "As soon as I do, I'll let you know."

Willi drove straight out to Dahlem. In the bright winter light the Gottmans' vine-covered villa stood as serene as in a painting. "Willi!" Max embraced him as he entered. "The whole country's lost its mind. Hitler's coming on the radio any second. Hurry. We're listening to see if he doesn't moderate now that he's in office, as everyone predicts. You know, more statesmanlike, conciliatory."

Ava, sitting on the couch with an embroidered shawl around her shoulders, looked distinctly less happy to see Willi. "Hello," she said coldly, switching on the radio. "We certainly weren't expecting you."

"Your timing was extraordinary, Willi," Max blurted, beside himself with nervousness. Webs of veins popped from his temples. "You told me to pull out just in the nick of time. I managed to liquidate everything, house, furniture, the business—at a very reasonable price, all things considered. God only knows what Jewish property will go for tomorrow."

A gong sounded over the radio. "The new chancellor will address the nation." A moment's silence, then . . . a tense, hard voice.

"Germans! For fifteen years a corrupt republic has hung like a noose around our necks. Millions unemployed. Millions homeless. But now at last—I have grasped the reins of power!"

"Such arrogance," Max stammered.

"No longer will the international financiers and the international Bolsheviks and the international cabal of Jewish lice suck the blood of the German people. The day of reckoning is at hand. I am your Führer!"

Pulling the shawl more tightly around her, Ava turned to her father. "I think that shoots down your once-he's-in-office theory."

"My God, if anything he's more hysterical." The veins in Max's forehead pumped. "I wouldn't put it past those fiends to seal up the borders, trap us all like flies in a jar. I say we go. Better today than tomorrow."

Willi agreed to purchase tickets for the overnight train to Paris.

Before he left, Ava stopped him, her dark eyes imploring. "Later then?"

"Yes, of course." Willi squeezed her hand. There was suddenly so much he wanted to say to her. But no time.

At the Zoo Station the ticket queue ran down the block. He could feel the fear, the despair in the air, the disbelief that this had actually happened. The Nazis—in power! The tension was only worse later when he met Max and Ava on the platform. Mountains of luggage left barely enough room for all the people trying to say good-bye to all the people leaving. A crowd gathered to bid farewell to Kurt Weil and Lotte Lenya. Vicki Baum; Erich Mendelsohn, architect par excellence of the Weimar Republic; and the great Marlene Dietrich herself were already aboard. Willi waited until he'd got Max and Ava seated before he told them he wasn't going.

"I see." Ava blanched. "More crucial things, huh?" Willi lowered his head. If only he could make her understand. "What if they do close the border, Willi? What then?"

"I'm a decorated war hero, remember. I've slipped across no-man's-lands."

"You're not a kid anymore." Her dark eyes flashed. "You're a father for God's sake. Those boys need you."

"I need them," Willi sighed. "And you, too." He hugged her quickly, dashing from the train. He'd come too far to give up now. Call me an idiot, he thought minutes later climbing into the BMW. But there's no way I'm leaving without that evidence. Once the world sees what happened at Sachsenhausen, they'll chase Hitler from office. From civilization.

But approaching the Ku-damm from Hardenburger Strasse, a strange glow reflected off the buildings. Traffic came to a standstill. People were getting out of their cars. Willi turned off his motor. With every step toward the intersection his discomfort mounted. Crashing cymbals reached his ears. Smoke began to irritate his nostrils. At the corner he had to stand tippy-toe. His whole body went cold. As far as the eye could see, all the way down the great boulevard, an endless stream of Brownshirts were marching toward the city center in a vast torchlight parade. A conquering army. Flags unfurled. Drums pounding. All the neon advertisements of the Ku-damm couldn't hold a candle to this surging river of fire.

He barely shut his eyes that night. The only thing he could think of was getting those boxes out of the Reichstag. Fritz said his editor, Kreisler, had spoken to one of the Ullstein brothers. The company would risk publishing the story—if it proved verifiable. The boxes could even be stashed in an Ullstein warehouse. If only they could transport them.

First thing in the morning Willi and Fritz set out by streetcar in hopes of finding this Socialist MP at his home in Berlin-North. Fritz was in a buoyant mood, convinced that things were not as bad as they appeared. Numerous sources had bolstered his suspicion that a secret alliance between von Papen's Conservatives and Hugenberg's Nationalists would fence Hitler in, make him lose face, take the wind out of his sails, and, when the time was ripe, pull the plug on him. "Von Schleicher got fifty-eight days. I give Hitler forty-two. Six weeks. No more. You can bet your money on it. I already have—ten thousand marks!"

At Bulowplatz, though, it felt as if they stepped directly from the streetcar onto the set of a Fritz Lang horror movie. The large Communist Party headquarters across the square, draped in giant banners of Lenin's face, was completely surrounded by thousands of screaming Nazis. *"Reds, out! Reds, out!"* People inside were getting grabbed by their hair, thrown from the door, and forced to run a gauntlet of swinging truncheons, staggering away with bloody heads. There was a terrible crash. An upper-floor window shattered, and two Brownshirts dangled a screaming man six stories over the sidewalk. Willi's heart stopped.

They couldn't. They wouldn't. But like Romans in the Colosseum, the crowd roared, thumbing him down, and the victim fell with a hideous shriek, flapping his arms against fate.

Fritz and Willi practically ran down the block. At Eckelmann's no one answered the buzzer. The charwoman told them he'd gone underground, like all the Socialist MPs, the ones with brains anyhow. They stood there helplessly.

"Come on," Fritz said. "Let's take a cab back."

In the taxi he thoughtfully stroked his dueling scar. "I know it looks bad, but it's only temporary, you'll see. Once the Communists are smashed"—he turned to Willi—"all this madness will recede. I stake my life on it." When they reached Alexanderplatz though, he refused to let Willi leave until they'd hugged. "Take care, brother, huh?" Fritz had tears in his eyes. Willi's throat ached. There wasn't a more outspoken anti-Nazi in Germany than Fritz. They both were in the same boat now.

As Willi climbed from the cab, everything seemed the same. Crowds still poured in and out of Tietz. The long, yellow streetcars rushed by. But crossing Dircksen Strasse toward the Police Presidium, he saw a swastika already flying over Entrance Six. Over all the entrances.

"You shouldn't have come." Ruta stared when he walked in.

Willi wondered why he had. Pride? Stubbornness? Sheer stupidity?

"It's too awful even to describe," she whispered, mechanically turning her coffee mill. "They've purged the whole force . . . every officer who's not a Nazi, sacked. Inaugurated a whole new secret police. Oh, Willi . . . why did you come back?"

"Well, well. Look at what the wind blew in. I didn't think you'd have the gall."

It was Thurmann, his pencil-line mustache slanted in a smirk. "I predicted right, huh, Kraus? You won your little battle." A shiny new Inspektor-Detektiv badge hung on his chest. "But we won the war." His smirk lengthened into a sneer. "Now pack up and get out before I give you what you've got coming. And as for

you, Granny"—he glared at Ruta—"better watch your step. It's a
new day, in case you hadn't noticed. Now hurry with that coffee."

While Willi was packing, Gunther walked in, head hung low.
He was wearing a light gray uniform, his upper arm banded with
a swastika. "I'm *Geheime Staatspolizei* now." His voice trembled.
"Secret police. *Gestapo*, for short." Willi turned away. "Please
understand, boss: my life, my family, everything's here. I don't
speak other languages."

Willi went on packing. Could he honestly say he'd do any
differently in Gunther's shoes?

Gunther swallowed, his Adam's apple sliding all the way down
his long white throat. "I can't escape. But you're going to have to."

"I'm not going anywhere."

"You're going to have to." The kid's blue eyes bore into him
suddenly. "If you want to see your sons grow up." Willi stopped
packing. Gunther's cheeks flinched. "All Nazis in prison have
received pardons. A personal order from Hitler himself. The
Sachsenhausen doctors are already out. I'd be arrested if they
knew I was telling you but . . . your name is on . . . a death list!"
Gunther looked skyward, his voice cracking. "Oh, God, Chief,
how could they get away with this? There's no justice at all. You
taught me everything. Now what am I going to use it for?"

Willi spent the rest of the afternoon in the Café Rippa, pretending to read a newspaper. He absolutely couldn't think. He knew
he had to, but it was as if his mind had stalled out in midtraffic.
He drank coffee and sat there. Drank coffee and sat there. Not
until evening did a painful jolt jump-start his brain. His name on
a death list meant no more sleeping at home.

He drove by to pick up what he could. On Nuremberger Strasse
several women were in front of his building arguing. "Get your
hands off that!" "I had it first!" It was his dining room table, he
realized. Looking up, he saw his windows were open. All the
lights on. Storm troopers were tossing his books out, his photo-

graphs. The picture of his grandfather came crashing to the pavement. He backed away. Returning to his car, his body and mind cleaved in two. Half of him could simply not accept that this was happening. The other half drove off like mad.

The forest trees reached with menacing fingers as he raced along the dark, winding road to Fritz's. Here and there villas glistened in the night. He felt like screaming from the depths of his lungs, if that would help. But he turned with grim silence into Fritz's long driveway. At the crest of the hill the glass house was dark. He hit the brakes, his breath stopping. Two black sedans were parked in front. His fingers clutched the wheel. My God. Fritz was being pushed from the door by half a dozen storm troopers, his face white as a ghost, eyes blazing black with fear. He'd rescued Fritz many times. But those thugs had submachine guns. He could only pray they didn't spot him, too. He heard Fritz this morning. "It's only temporary, Willi, I stake my life on it." Just as Fritz was about to get shoved into a car, Willi's old war pal looked up and his eyes met Willi's. *Run, you goddamn fool,* they cried.

Willi let the car roll backward. "Hey, you!" A series of shots rang out. A loud bang scrapped the roof. He shifted like mad and hit the gas. More shots came as he shifted into second and sped into the darkness. Car doors slammed, a motor roared, screeching tires sped across gravel.

They were after him.

If he could just clear the forest, he could outrace the bastards, he knew. But the roads through Grunewald were so narrow and winding, pitch-black, completely unfamiliar to him. Through the rearview mirror he could see headlights, far enough behind that he'd still have a chance to shake them off, but keeping a steady pace. He made a hard right at the first street he came to, then a left. The headlights followed. Spotting a clearing he slammed on the brakes and skidded into a U-turn. Racing back, he caught a glimpse of the Nazis' angry faces. He cringed as they fired madly, managing to knock out one of his headlights. He'd gained half a block. They skidded into the same U-turn and resumed the chase. Down a deep slope and up a bend, he was at once blinded by oncoming lights. If that was the other Nazis, he was dead, he thought, swerving to the right as far as possible. When the car blew by, he could see again. Darkness, that is. Pitch-black. Guided by a single headlight, he hit the gas and sped ahead as fast as he dared.

This can't be happening, his mind kept repeating. He wasn't really being chased through Berlin by criminals who'd become the cops. Another rapid burst of gunfire sent him flying right out of his body, hovering above the forest. He could actually see the BMW racing from the black sedan. He, the Inspektor-Detektiv who'd tracked and hunted society's most vicious criminals, a hunted criminal himself now. How utterly childish he'd been to believe that justice was a man's due in life! From his bird's-eye view he watched himself losing his way in the gloom. He hated the forest. The more desperately he fought to free himself from it, the more confused, the more enervated, he became until hopelessness began darkening his vision, making him feel as if he were drowning.

A bright light pulled him back. On the roadside, an illuminated sign with a long arrow pointing like the arm of God itself: *Entrance—Avus Speedway.* Air filled his lungs again as he tore onto the empty highway. Smashing his foot into the gas as far as it would go, the BMW roared. Although he could see the black sedan following, now it only made him laugh. Once the little silver sports coupe leapt into racing mode—100-110-120—there was no keeping up.

Thirty

Back in the city he didn't know where to go. He was homeless in his hometown. Neon flickered on empty streets, Berlin eerily dead this second night of Nazi rule. Aimlessly he drove for hours, eventually recalling that card in his wallet, his throat so tense when he got to the villa on Tiergarten Strasse he could barely get a word out. "You said if I ever needed—"

"For heaven's sake." Sylvie hurried him in, her blue eyes flashing surprise and comprehension both. The news about Fritz hit her hard. "Oh, God, no. You don't think they'll—?"

"For years he called them gangsters, Sylvie. Swine, animals, vicious apes."

"Poor Fritz." She fell to the couch. "Such a big mouth." She stared blankly for a long time, then crumpled into Willi's arms, crying. "Thank God at least you're safe," she sighed finally, squeezing his arm. "No one'll think to look for you here. Stay as long as you want." *Forever*, her wounded voice seemed to say. "I'll fix some tea and run a nice hot bath for you. How's that sound?" He saw pity in her eyes, as if she was trying to compensate for her fellow Aryans stomping around out there. A bath was more than he could resist.

Submerged in hot water, his every muscle aching, he flinched when Sylvie entered without knocking, her blond hair loose around her neck. Wordlessly she knelt at the tub and started soaping his chest with a cloth. "I never realized what a strong man you are. Such broad shoulders."

"You were always too in love with Fritz." He smiled, sadly lifting her hand away.

"And you," she sighed, "were always too in love with Vicki." She twisted out the cloth and stood. "And now you're too in love with her sister." She saw him freeze. "There's no shame in it, Willi." She pulled her hair back. "Ava's the boys' mother now. If you two have found real feelings for one another, well, then"—she opened the door—"mazel tov."

Like a dead man he fell asleep on the couch. Until a loud buzzer nearly sent him from his skin.

"Relax." Sylvie emerged from her bedroom pulling on a night coat. "Storm troopers don't bother with doorbells."

It was Rudolf Kreisler, Fritz's editor, and his roly-poly wife, Millie, slouched under half a dozen suitcases. Willi had seen them the other night at the Press Ball. She'd been drunk as a goose, shamelessly tap-dancing with her shoes off. Now her goose looked good and cooked, her plump face colorless, her whole head sagging.

"We drove for hours to make sure no one was following." Kreisler mopped his dripping brow. "They arrested two Ullstein managers yesterday. The company's full of Nazi cells. They're taking over. The brothers will be out. We're fleeing for Prague in the afternoon but . . . well . . . they always come at night, you know."

"Forgive us," Millie rasped.

"Give me your coats." Sylvie held out her arms. "I told you I'd be here, and here I am."

More people arrived and departed Sylvie's house that first week of the new "Third Reich" than the Zoo Station. Students from the university. Teachers from the Bauhaus School. A celloist from the Philharmonic. Her hairdresser. Everyone was on the run. And everyone had whispers to pile on the growing trove of horror stories. Bloodcurdling tales of cellar dungeons. Torture. Bodies delivered to families in sealed caskets. Willi had no trouble believing a word of it. No trouble at all.

Like a man possessed, he had now become convinced he alone could save the nation. That the contents of those boxes in the storerooms of the Reichstag were the only elixir powerful enough to awaken Germany from her demonic sleepwalk. If Ullstein could no longer publish the story, someone else would. Somewhere. Somehow. He'd make sure of it. But the Reichstag remained under lock and key. The current parliament had been dissolved by Hitler the day he took office. The Nazis had grasped the reins of power but still had no legislative majority. Convinced he could finally "annihiliate" all opposition—*One people! One party! One Führer!*—Hitler had called for new elections the fifth of March. Willi had to get into the building before then. Getting in, he knew, of course, would be the easy part. Getting out again with all the heavy boxes was the challenge.

One of Sylvie's overnighters, an energetic young physicist bound for America, theorized that the Nazis knew very well they could never win free elections. A majority of Germans still opposed them. The labor unions would resist. All the guarantees of the constitution—freedom of the press, the right to assemble—remained legally binding. No, he was convinced, the Nazis needed some far more Machiavellian scheme for seizing total power, prior to March 5.

"Let's say a bullet was fired," he speculated over dinner.

"Any attempt on Hitler's life, even if it wasn't real—as long as it looked real—would be all the pretext necessary for declaring a national emergency. Nullifying the constitution, civil liberties. Banning the press. Outlawing opposition. Bam, bam, bam. A chain reaction resulting in a monstrous fusion of power."

Willi listened to Mr. Oppenheimer morbidly. If his theory proved correct, then it was all the more reason to do whatever necessary . . . before it really was too late.

For several days Willi stalked the Reichstag building. From varying angles among the statues and fountains in the Plaza of the Republic, he examined the massive steps and great carriage ramps leading to the front doors. From the Tiergarten he studied the neo-Renaissance façades and the towering glass dome allowing light to shine down on lawmakers. From Dorotheen Strasse he took in the rows of recessed windows and the spired towers rising from each of the four corners. It was a monumental structure. Bismarck had built it in the 1890s. Scheidemann had declared the republic from its balcony in 1918. Now Hitler was determined to make it a mausoleum.

From the freezing banks of the River Spree he scrutinized the soot-covered service entrances, who came, who went, how often, what times. Everything got scribbled in his notebook. The security precautions were vigilantly maintained, he saw. With the Reichstag out of session only Entrance Five was open, far on the building's north side. Visitors, staff, even members of parliament, were carefully inspected before entering. Punctual as a Swiss clock, evenings at seven a night watchman circulated, making sure every door, every window, was secure. The place was like a fortress. By the end of the third day though, he'd come up with a basic plan.

Evening was falling. An icy wind blew whitecaps on the river behind him. Along Sommer Strasse, the checkpoint to the Reichstag service entrances was cast in deep shadows. He was going to need a truck. Several regularly came and went, he'd observed. Every morning at eight, a yellow postal truck. Every morning at nine, a black garbage pickup. Mondays at ten a white linen supply, which returned again that night at nine. What he needed to find out was where those storerooms were exactly. A floor plan. Tomorrow first thing, the library, he made a mental note, allowing himself finally to flee the February wind.

Along the Spree Embankment barely a soul braved the cold. Relieved to find a bus near the Bismarck Memorial, he was staring out the window trying to warm his freezing hands when a kiosk came into view. Tacked under blazing spotlights, a dark, hypnotic gaze leaped from a dozen front pages. **Gustave, King of Mystics, Gunned Down in Tiergarten!** Willi's whole esophagus closed. He gave me that same corny publicity shot when we parted, he realized. Autographed it: *To Inspektor-Detektiv Kraus—a true German hero*. "When I'm dead, who knows," he'd said, "it might be worth something." From the look in his eyes it was plain Gustave knew he was a goner. This time he had seen the future.

The devil victorious.

The main reading room of the Prussian State Library had dizzying concentric circles of desks. By the time Willi arrived the next morning, twenty minutes after opening, the place was practically full. He checked out the Reichstag blueprints and took the only seat he could find, nervously guarding his notebook from neighbors while sketching the building's floor plans. Seeing no one so much as cast a glance his way, he found himself relaxing, thinking, this probably is the safest place in Berlin. He took a deep breath, his mind racing with possibilities as he finally finished around noon. The Reichstag storerooms, it turned out, were exactly opposite the linen supply.

Exiting the old brass doors, he was surprised to find it was snowing out, heavily. The famous rows of lime trees on Unter den Linden, the magnificent statue of Frederick the Great, everything was already draped in white. Only too late did he notice the crowd in front of the library gathered for a speech by the new information minister: reporters, newsreel cameraman, Nazi officials, a whole detachment of Brownshirts turning into snowmen as Josef Goebbels declared war on "cultural decadence."

"This great State Library," the little man cried, fighting to keep snow off his wide-brimmed fedora, "founded by our forefathers four hundred years ago, will be scoured top to bottom! All the lies, all the pornographic filth, all the degenerate Jewish propaganda, will be consigned to the flames!"

Flames? Willi wondered. What were they planning to do, burn the library? With a shudder he recalled the Great Gustave's prediction of a conflagration this February from which, like a phoenix, a great New Germany would arise. Could this be what he meant? Willi's contemplations came to a crashing halt when not ten feet away he spotted a large set of bunny teeth and two fiendish eyes fixed on him.

They *had* released him.

The lunatics really were running the asylum.

"Stop him!" Mengele's finger pointed. "That Jew stole my research!"

Work, Willi thought, leaping the only possible way he could—directly into westbound traffic. That's all the maniac cares about—his work. A piercing whistle blew. Funny. That's what Ava said about me. Darting around a bus and several autos, he made it to the center median, where the snowbound lindens tangled overhead. Daring to turn, he was mortified to see what had to be thirty Brownshirts after him. With a gulp of air he leaped in front of Frederick the Great into the eastbound lanes. Centimeters of snow already covered Unter den Linden, and halfway across his foot went flying, slamming him hard on his rear. Shocked, he looked up to see a truck bearing down, blowing its horn like mad. It jammed on its brakes, skidding to one side, stopping just meters away.

The driver rolled down the window. "Jackass!"

A whole chorus rang out from the far side. "Stop him! Thief!"

The man flung open the door. "Thief, huh?" He flew at Willi.

But the instant his foot touched the ground he lost his balance, and Willi took off.

In front of the Opera House a dozen whistles shrieked in a hellish choir. People stared through the curtain of snow trying to ascertain who the villain was. An old lady made a grab for his arm. A kid threw something at him. But slipping and sliding, he reached the Palace Bridge. The beautiful crossing looked like a gag photograph, all the marble deities draped in snowy togas. Half a dozen uniformed men were pushing industrial-size brooms to clear its sidewalks. When they realized he was on the run from Brownshirts, they stepped aside to let him pass. Across the Spree, he saw they'd closed ranks again, pretending not to realize they were hindering the Brownshirts' chase. Bless you, sanitation workers!

Propelled by sheer fear, he practically skated past the palace of the kaisers, remembering how when he was a kid, he used to watch the generals parading in and out of those grand entrances in their knee-high boots and plumed hemets. Now the great iron gates were locked and rusting. Cousins of the kaiser's were being pulled from their chic glass homes. The world had turned upside down—several times in his short life.

It was snowing harder by the minute, impossible to see. Every forward motion required total concentration, as if this were a minefield. The whistles were nearing again. The cries of "Stop him!" All they needed were torches and dogs, he thought, squinting at a moving patch of yellow ahead, and he'd be Frankenstein's monster.

A double-decker bus had pulled up to the corner. Thank God for public transport. He jumped aboard smiling lamely at the big conductor, trying not to pant too heavily as he fished for change. A delicious moment of relief came over him as the bell clanged and they lurched off. But a moment only. Through the heavy snow he realized the bus was traveling slower than the pedestrians. The chorus of "Stop thief!" grew. The conductor gave him one look and moved to block the door. Willi flung himself onto the spiral staircase. The upper deck was filled with snow. The conductor's heavy footsteps stormed behind. The guy would have to be twice his size, he thought, peering over the side. The pack of Brownshirts was almost upon them. "Papa!" He swore he heard his sons. If only he could be with them. The huge conductor was approaching, his nose steaming. A yellow streetcar rushed past eastbound. Just as a thick arm was about to grab him, Willi hurled himself over the rail.

"There!" he heard. "He got away!"

Landing with a thud flat on his back, he clung for dear life as the streetcar sped off, whipping around several corners onto Konigs Strasse. His whole face filled with snow. Too terrified to move, he just lay there squinting at the buildings flying by and the blinding flashes of electricity from the wires, praying to be invisible, not to fall, not to get electrocuted. Gradually he realized the screaming whistles were gone. Shaking off the snow, he lifted his head. People were too concentrated on navigating the blizzard to bother with him, he saw. As discreetly as possible he slid to the street, brushed his hat, and stomped along with everyone else past the red City Hall. My God. That was way too close. And he with plans of the Reichstag in his notebook.

Reaching Alexanderplatz, he felt relief to lose himself in the mass of snowy hats and shoulders in front of Tietz. His every bone was screaming, *You are too old for this, Willi. Time to act your age, like Ava said.* Conscious of an amplifying roar behind him, he turned, his whole neck hurting. Three motorized cycles with sidecars were thundering right down Konigs Strasse. His spine stiffened when he realized that it was Mengele in the first one, up on his feet scanning around. A stroke of ill fate brought his black eyes right to Willi's. The wide-gapped teeth appeared. "Stop! He's a thief!"

Of all the outrageous things to call me, Willi fumed.

He realized there was only one way to go: beneath the trademark glass globe and through the spinning doors of Tietz. How familiar the massive lobby with its chiming elevators and noisy throngs. How many times he'd entered here—as a child, clasping his mother's hand, as an adult, clasping his wife and children. And how many times he'd heard his father-in-law laud its legendary Jewish founder, Hermann Tietz. How everyone laughed in 1904 at his plans to build a retail paradise on run-down Alexanderplatz. " 'I don't need location,' " Max never tired of quoting. " 'I *make* location.' " And Hermann had. The most successful store in Germany. The most magnificent, inside and out. Great vaulted ceilings. Marbled colonnades. Upholstered sofas to rest tired feet, and polished mahogany to display the endless high-quality merchandise at cost-saving prices. Berlin, as the advertising put it, wouldn't be Berlin without Tietz.

Instantly, he saw it was White Week. Another of the store's marketing miracles—a giant February sale on linens—the whole atrium, five stories tall, transformed into a fairyland, chandeliers and balconies festooned in more white than the snowstorm outside. Lowering his face, he merged with the crowds. The rattling wooden escalators seemed straining to lift the hordes of hausfraus loaded with shopping bags. Looking around, he realized he was one of the few males in the place. His head shrank lower on his shoulders. Just as he nearly reached the camouflaging mayhem of the Mezzanine White Sale, his whole back cringed. "Stop that thief!" Mengele, flanked by two SS men, was heading toward the escalators.

Pushing between a pair of matrons, he felt his head knocked with a pocketbook. "In all my years shopping here!" His ear filled with a vengeful shriek. Passing Ladies' Lingerie on Two and Men's Outerwear on Three, similar resistance marred his progress. Punches. Kicks. His pursuers, though, clearly had no better luck against these shoppers, because by the time he'd reached Children's World on Four, he barely heard Mengele. Unfortunately, two uniformed store guards did hear him and picked up the chase. Sweat drenched Willi's back, his forehead, his neck.

He was starting to feel like a fox in a hedgerow. Tietz only had six floors.

As he bolted from the moving wooden steps into the crowded aisles of Fifth Floor Kitchen Wares, an ancient voice in him cried, *Hide!* Dive beneath the bins of silverware or those tables piled with iron skillets. Conceal yourself among the dish towels or the stacks of amazing new electric coffeepots. Anywhere, just . . . disappear! But something else in him revolted. Why should he? A furious anger steamed through him. What had he got to hide for? What had he done? There comes a point—he eyed the wall of glistening kitchen knives—when a man's got to take a stand. No? Grabbing the biggest blade he saw—a meter-long butcher cleaver—he instantly vowed that if he had to go, he'd take Mengele with him. Duck from the guards, wait for the bastard, and in one swift chop—off with his head. For Paula! For the 850! Sweating, he clenched the cleaver, picturing Mengele's blood spraying across the pyramid of wooden salad bowls, his head bouncing down the escalator. He deserved it. Didn't he? Didn't they all? What pleasure it would give him to see their filthy bodies twitching on the ground. Wouldn't it?

As the store guards appeared, though, rising toward him, he felt himself slowly backing up. If you manage to escape, his conscience asked, could you live with yourself, Willi? If you stooped that low, to cold-blooded murder? Doesn't even a wretch like Mengele deserve justice, like any criminal?

Dropping the cleaver, Willi flung himself back on the escalator, Mengele coming through loud and clear again: "Stop that thief!" The store guards were only a few people behind as he darted sideways into Home Furnishings, Floor Six. The end of the line. He and Vicki had bought their bedroom set here. He could still picture her sitting on the mattress, feeling around with her soft white hands. "I love it, Willi. We'll sleep so beautifully." His mother used to have her chairs restuffed here. "Good as new!" Where the hell were the fire stairs? The aisles were packed with big-hipped women refusing to budge a centimeter. "How dare you?" "Such manners!" The guards were gaining on him. "Tietz Security—let us through!" If he didn't do something, they'd be on him soon. From the floor he jumped onto a coffee table, and from there to a sofa, to an ottoman, to a queen-size bed and a love seat, cutting diagonally across the aisles. Salespeople tried to stop him. "Sir, that is strictly forbidden!" Shoppers shrieked. "He's drunk!" The store guards cursed, falling behind. But as he stumbed along a row of bedroom mirrors, mutliple reflections made amply clear Tietz Security hadn't given up, and that Mengele and his SS men were on the floor now, too.

He regretted dropping that cleaver. The fire exit, if there was one, was completely obscured by mountains of vanity tables, bookcases, night desks, reading lamps. How lax on the part of management. Someone could get killed! Turning a corner, he found himself lost in a terrain of Persian carpets, hundreds of them draped from display racks in delicate patterns and shimmering colors. If only he could find a magic one and fly away. But fate had other designs.

Directly ahead he spotted a giant figure in a Mexican poncho, gold earring hanging on a chiseled blond head. "Inspektor?" Kai stood by the register holding a receipt, a long Persian carpet rolled over his shoulder. In an instant he seemed to ascertain Willi's predicament because he let him pass, then stepped out and blocked the aisle. Gasping for breath, Willi turned and saw Kai lift the carpet on one arm and with all the determination of an early Teuton, hurl it spearlike through the air, knocking the first guard into those behind and sending them all, Mengele included, dropping like skewered pigeons. With a similar ferocity Kai grabbed Willi's arm and dragged him to the fire exit. "You owe me thirty-five marks," Kai cried as they flew down steps. "That rug was for my mother!"

Thirty-five, Willi thought.

Another bargain at Tietz.

Thirty-one

Thunder crashed across Berlin. Wild flashes of lightning ignited the narrow alleys behind Alexanderplatz. It felt as if the city were under artillery attack. Willi held out his hand to shield his face against the blazing wind. The blizzard, if possible, had only worsened. Blinding snow though was a small price to pay for the joy of freedom. Small pain compared to what the rest of me is feeling, he groaned inside.

"Getting old there, Inspektor?" Kai saw him limping as they made their escape along snowy Kieber Strasse, several blocks already from Tietz. What luck the kid knew every back staircase and broom closet in the store. It had taken twenty minutes but they'd lost the SOBs. It was one thirty now, he saw on his watch. He'd been running since he'd left the library at noon.

"You have no idea, Kai."

That jump to the streetcar would have been a cinch at Kai's

age. Now every cartilage in him felt crushed. Despite the pain though, he could barely keep from laughing. Mengele must have been shitting in his pants to know Willi escaped. One way or another—he felt the firm outlines of the notebook still in his breast pocket—he was going to get that precious "research" out of the Reichstag. Out of this goddamned country. And into every newspaper around the world.

Call him a thief.

"Kai . . ." He grabbed the kid's poncho, still trying to catch his breath. "I've got to ask you something . . . I have a job coming up. A really big one. I need someone I can trust."

"Does it have to do with why those Brownshirts were after you?"

"Yeah." Willi wiped snow from his face. "Everything."

"Then count me in, Inspektor."

The weather that February was brutal. Snowstorms. Ice storms. Bitter cold. Hiding by night at Sylvie's, Willi pushed himself hard each day, studying the floor plans of the Reichstag, working out his strategy. From the warmth of his BMW he followed the route of the white linen truck, observing how at ten each morning, at the southwest service entrance, two uniformed workers removed sacks of napkins and tablecloths used upstairs at the Reichstag restaurant, which remained busy even during the congressional recess. Leaving the south service gate on Sommer Strasse, the truck headed north, crossing the Louisen Strasse Bridge and continuing on to the Amalgamated Laundry Works on Invalieden Strasse, a twenty-minute drive depending on traffic. Another truck returned at night with the bundles of clean linen, crossing the Louisen Strasse Bridge between eight forty and eight fifty, also depending on traffic.

His third day out he noticed a small black Opel *Lieferwagen* several cars behind him and instinctively gripped his steering wheel. Could that be the same one he'd seen yesterday with the spare whitewalls on the running boards? He knew the model well enough: the Berlin police used it for unmarked vehicles. He'd driven one on a trip to Oranienburg not that long ago, with Gunther. Was someone trailing him? he suddenly wondered, wiping sweat from his forehead. He could easily outrace it if he had to, he knew. The Opel's maximum speed was only 85 kmh. But the last thing he needed was someone on his tail. Searching his rearview mirror again though, the little black car was nowhere to be seen. Just nerves, he decided. Paranoia. Of course, he recalled the morbid joke his cousin Kurt loved to tell: just because you're paranoid doesn't mean someone's not really following you.

Back at the Reichstag he took careful note that the south security gate was manned by two guards during the daylight hours, but only one at night. If he hijacked the night delivery and made it past this checkpoint, he calculated, by nine thirty he could conceivably have all the Sachsenhausen boxes loaded. By the time the people at Amalgamated Laundry began suspecting something had happened to their truck, he'd be halfway to Poland.

He was going drive straight through from the Reichstag an hour and a half north of Berlin to Schwedt, along the River Oder, among the easiest frontiers in Germany to cross, he'd discreetly learned. The guards there were only too happy to open a palm for the lucrative black-market trade. Once on the other side he'd continue five hours northeast to the Free City of Danzig, where he'd ship the boxes by freighter via Le Havre to Paris.

Well, not all. A few boxes he planned to drop off with Sylvie, just for insurance purposes. In case he got caught. "Someplace where no one can find them?" She wracked her brain. "I suppose I can take them to my mother's. You don't want to tell me what they are?"

"Personal things, Sylvie."

Her pretty lips frowned. "You are planning to go. Just like everyone else."

"Isn't that what you advised me? Weeks ago?"

"Yes. Of course it is." She lowered her eyes.

He squeezed her hand to cheer her up.

But his own mood shifts were marking time more regularly than a metronome.

Hope. Despair. Confidence. Dejection. A thousand possible mishaps occurred to him. What if there were extra guards that night? Or the truck broke down? Or there was another blizzard? It had to work. The whole country was depending on him. The whole world. But all he could do was all he could do, he reminded himself. He was only human. And yet . . . yet . . . when he thought of what was in those boxes, and Mengele out there loose again . . . he knew the whole world was really depending on him.

With the elections looming he arranged to meet Kai and finalize their plans in the safety of the ever-crowded Berlin Zoo. Stefan and Erich adored the place. He took them all the time. Or used to. Would again someday. Surely. As he entered from Budepester Strasse below the Chinese Elephant Gate, the most vivid memory suddenly hit him, reverberating gonglike through his brain, echoing back to another icy winter day when he was ten, walking beneath this gate with his father. Even then the carved elephants had stood for years, their long stone tusks dark with soot. "Obviously these fellows don't brush their tusks very well!" his father joked, squeezing his shoulder.

It was probably the last time he'd seen him.

Such a weak heart, even with all the clinics and medicines, and when Kraus Furriers was held up the next day, he'd literally keeled over. Willi took a deep breath. He hadn't thought of that in years. A cold breeze stirred from the seal tank. Could that be why he'd become a cop? To make up for his father's weakness? Avenge the bad guys he blamed for his death? One of the seals rose from the water, barking. Willi laughed, wiping away a tear. Why had that never occurred to him?

Why. The world's oldest question.

The Monkey House was jammed, the people inside making

more noise than the primates, pounding their chests and scratching their heads cleverly.

"The Reichstag?" Kai's chiseled face screwed up as they leaned against the rail by the chimp cage. "Why not choose someplace nice and easy, Inspektor, like Hitler's bedroom." He puffed on a Juno.

"I'm not doing this for sport, Kai. That's where the boxes are."

One of the chimps, reaching though the bars, indicated he would like a smoke.

"Breaking and entering federal property's treason you know." Kai stared at the delinquent monkey. Willi noticed the Wild Boy no longer wore his trademark gold earring, or his poncho. Just an old wool coat like everybody else, conformity obviously the latest word in fashion. "Even in the best of times that's a rotten rap, Inspektor. But now"—Kai crushed his cigarette out to the monkey's angry shrieks—"rumor has it they've dusted off the guillotines."

Heads would roll, Hitler had promised.

"I never said it'd be risk-free."

"May I ask how you plan to get from linen supply to the Members' Storeroom?"

"I told you, it's right across the hall."

"But what about the door? It's sure to be locked."

"Leave that to me, Kai."

You couldn't be a Detektiv without being able to think like a criminal. And act like one, when necessary. Well, it was necessary, Willi knew. They'd turned him into one. So he'd be one.

Five p.m. yesterday he'd waited in the freezing cold outside Entrance Six of the Police Presidium. "Inspektor." Ruta clutched her heart. "You scared me half to death." She tried not to show she was checking around to make sure no one was looking. "My God. How are you? You've no idea how badly I miss you."

"Could I buy you a schnapps?"

She took a deep breath, quickly looking over her shoulder again. "Yeah, sure. You bet."

More than once she'd let Willi know she'd be willing to do whatever was necessary to help him. Now he'd find out how serious she was. He took her to Lutter & Wegner, the city's historic *Weinstube,* founded in 1807. He could still taste the first sip of wine he'd had there when he was a kid. Rheinlander, extrasweet.

"The Master Set?" she gulped, downing her schnapps in a single swig.

By law, every lock in Berlin was subject to one of eleven master keys—a full set of which hung on a rack above Komissar Horthstaler's desk. It would mean staying late. Sneaking into his office. And under any circumstances making sure that set was returned the following morning. No doubt she, too, had heard rumors of guillotines.

"Could I have another schnapps?"

"Sure. The whole bottle if you want."

Ruta lowered her face, slowly shaking her head.

"Willi." Her eyes turned to him. For a second he could picture her in slinky oriental bloomers kicking her leg in rhythm with thirty other chorus girls at the Wintergarden. "Even without schnapps . . . you know I will."

Still kicking at forty-nine. He loved this lady.

But what about Kai? Was there a rebel left in him?

Fear worked differently on everyone.

One of the chimps was going ape, banging the wall.

"He wants his swing back." Kai smiled. "Won't fight for it though. Chimps never do. Unless"—his smiled faded—"unless they're absolutely certain of victory. Five or six against one."

"What are you saying? You want to back out, Kai?"

"I'm saying I don't believe in martyrdom." Kai lit another Juno, his sharp blue eyes glued to the cage. "A man's first responsibility is to himself. And then to his family. You can't help anyone if you're dead."

"There's a certain truth to that."

"Be serious, Inspcktor. If I remember right, you have two sons."

Way below the belt. Okay. Maybe this was risky. Willi gripped the iron rail. Maybe it was suicide. Maybe his sons would have to grow up without a father, as he had. But one thing was certain: he could never live with himself if he didn't do everything humanly possible to expose what had happened at Sachsenhausen.

Kai turned. The chimp who wanted a cigarette was happily picking bugs off his friend's head now, popping them into his mouth. "I don't want to back out, Inspektor. I just wanted to make sure you didn't."

Monday the twenty-seventh a bitter wind blew, bringing sharp little ice crystals stinging through the air. Willi treated Kai to a swank dinner at the Hotel Excelsior. Willi's last meal in Germany. At least . . . for a while. He kept picturing Helga Meckel beneath the Ishtar Gate. People's minds change. Times change. And tyrants far more powerful than Hitler had fallen to the sword of justice.

"What's the matter, Kai?" Willi said, digging into a stuffed quail with wine sauce. "You're awfully quiet tonight."

The kid pushed aside his plate of braised kidneys. "I went to the Nollendorfer Palast last night."

Willi pictured the New Year's Day crowds there: the tough types, the girlie types. The college kids with big bow ties. Gunther asking if he had to dance. Poor Gunther. How miserable he was going to be in the Gestapo.

"The whole club was boarded up. Hitler's face plastered all over."

And poor Kai. How miserable he was going to be in the Third Reich.

"You can take off with me, you know, if you like. Paris is a super city."

"I'm afraid I'm a little too German for Paris, Inspektor."

"How will you live then, in the New Germany? You've already dropped out of the SA. I don't suppose that leaves you in good standing."

The kid's sculpted face lit strangely. "Until this nightmare's over, we're retreating to the forest."

Willi frowned at him.

"It's true. Me and the boys have it all worked out. Found a place deep in the woods, where no one will know we exist."

"You aren't serious. But . . . what will you eat? How will you survive?"

"In thatched huts, like our ancestors did. Eat what we hunt: wild boar, rabbit. And when we can, plunder the townsfolk."

Kai had a seriously irrational look, Willi saw. An almost mad resignation, as if he knew well he was talking nonsense, but just didn't care. It was almost the same look Gustave had the last time Willi had seen him, as if he knew he was a goner. It frightened Willi. He excused himself. "I need to use the men's room, Kai."

In the mirror he studied the long Semitic features and shiny dark eyes proclaiming as loudly as any sign on Potsdamer Platz that here was no real German. Wherever else he went on this planet, that's all he'd ever be. German. But here, never.

As he returned from the men's room, his feet stopped short. Standing over their table was a paunchy figure in a brown SA uniform, his battle-scarred face looking none too pleased. Willi ducked into the shadows. Ernst Roehm. Why did he imagine the Excelsior'd be safe, he chided himself. Adolescent delusions of invulnerabilty, as Ava would say? Or had he just thought Nazis were too low-class to eat in a place like this? Probably doesn't pay his bill. Beneath Roehm's figure Kai looked pale, gesticulating as if trying to explain himself. No doubt the SA führer didn't appreciate his boys running off. But when Kai whispered something in his ear, it was Roehm who lost his pallor. His hand went up in a Hitler salute and he left. Willi returned to the table, proud of his kid.

"What'd you tell him, that you had syphilis or something?"

"Worse." Kai smirked. "That I work for Himmler now."

Huddled among the barren acacias along the Spree Embankment, nearly as frozen as the river below, they spotted the linen truck rambling over the bridge at 8:47. But where were Kai's boys? Without them the plan was botched. Improvise, pal, he commanded himself. Improvise. When the truck came to a halt for the traffic light, he straightened his back and walked to the driver's side. "Slide over." He aimed his pistol. No need to let them know it wasn't loaded. The uniformed laundrymen held up their hands. "What's this, a joke? You gonna steal a load of tablecloths?"

"Shut up. Do as I say and you won't get hurt."

They pulled the truck out of the streetlights and into the shadows. Willi made the laundrymen remove their uniforms, then Kai tied them up and gagged them with napkins from the back. "Good thing you're loaded with clean ones, heh buddy?"

If Kai's boys didn't show, what was he going to do with these two? Willi wondered. Stuff them in a laundry bag? But just as he was slipping into his dark blue laundryman's smock, he heard the clip-clip-clop of horses' hooves. A pair of Red Apaches pulled up in an old black hearse. Willi had them lift his captives into two pine coffins in the back and drape a tablecloth over each. "At the stroke of midnight you'll be freed," he promised. "Unharmed." And I'll be in Poland, he added silently. "Don't forget their taxi fare home." He gave the boys cash. As the hearse clomped off, he and Kai scrambled back into the truck. It was two minutes after nine. They were late.

The guard at the security gate looked confused. "What happened to Rudi and Heinz?"

Kai played his role to perfection, reciting his lines as if he were with the German National Theater. "You're aware, I'm sure," he whispered as darkly as any great Faust, "that they're both with the secret police now. I believe tonight they're out reeducating some of our Red brothers up in Berlin-North, if you understand me."

Willi saw the guard tense, clearly appalled but too afraid to show it, a vivid illustration of just how effective Nazi terror was. Even a hint. *"Ach so."* He offered an unhappy smile. When Kai shouted, "Heil Hitler!" the gate quickly lifted.

The huge gray Reichstag loomed dark and stoic, its glass dome reflecting the silver of the moon. All Willi's hopes, all his fears, seemed mirrored in that light. They swung around to the southwest corner and pulled up to Service Entrance Three. Ringing the bell they waited for the night watchman, who let them in without apparently caring they weren't the usual team. Wheeling two dollies piled high with laundry bags, they proceded down the long hall, passing a granite staircase to the first floor before reaching the linen supply. Willi opened the door with the key hooked to his uniform smock. When they got inside, he checked his watch. It was 9:05.

"Dump this stuff, Kai." Willi started pushing bags off the dolly. He still had to find the key that opened the storeroom, locate the boxes, and get them hidden in sacks before reloading them onto the truck. They couldn't arouse suspicion they were taking too much time in here. "What's that?" Willi froze.

"I didn't hear anything."

Willi had. Breaking glass. Upstairs.

They practically ran the empty dollies down a long aisle stacked with linens until they reached the rear corridor. Across the darkness they spotted a door. *Members' Storeroom.* Good. But holding the flashlight while Willi fumbled with the master keys, Kai trembled so violently the strobe-light effect seemed to speed up motion like an old-time movie. Get a grip of yourself, Willi wanted to shout. One of these has got to work. It's the law. Besides, we're okay. It's only 9:08. Except, what's that burning smell—is somebody cooking upstairs? Trying the fifth key, the bolt slid back. Amen. The moment he pushed the door, two fierce bangs rang overhead. Willi turned. No mistaking gunshots. In the glare of the flashlight he saw dark fingers of smoke creeping toward them.

"Wait here," he whispered, determined to find out what the hell was happening. Like an Olympic sprinter he tore down the hall, pausing at the granite stairs. It was completely dark. Clinging to the wall, he crept up, praying the night watchman didn't appear. Then halfway up, he stopped. Someone was running around up there. One, or many? He couldn't tell. All he heard were echoes. Frantic feet. Then nothing. The smell of smoke though was truly appalling. Reaching the top step, he froze, astonished. The carved wood ceilings ahead were glowing red. Down the hallway was crazy laughter. And dark shadows dancing across the plenary chamber walls. Was it one man—or many? He couldn't tell. But someone was setting the place ablaze. Arson!

"Stop!" he heard an all too familiar voice command from behind. His throat twisted. Disaster. His stomach clenched into a knot. "Hands in the air."

Obeying, he slowly turned, noticing a long, black Luger aimed at him, and the pasty face of Herbert Thurmann approaching up the steps.

"Well, well, well." His pencil-line mustache arched with real delight. "I knew you were up to no good, Kraus." As he neared, his smile lengthened with glee. "From the moment I spotted you outside the Police Presidium when you waylaid your secretary, I've been following you. Very careless of you not to notice."

The black Opel, Willi remembered.

"Losing your touch there, huh, Jew boy? You should have left Germany while you had the chance." Thurmann's whole pasty face glistened in triumph. What fun he was having. Like a cat oblivious of all but the joy of tormenting its catch. He paid not the least attention to the shadowy figure Willi noticed to their left, rushing around in the Reichstag restaurant. "Now the game is up for you." For all you subhumans, Thurmann seemed to be saying.

The arrogance, the sadistic thrill, made Willi's stomach sour.

What a sad turn. Not just for him, but for Ruta, who would surely be arrested, too, now. And for all those boxes downstairs. And his poor little Erich and Stefan, who would never see their father again.

All at once the restaurant burst into a swirling cauldron of flame, the arsonist's work accomplished. An enormous crash of glass and silverware grabbed Thurmann's attention. Willi seized the opportunity. Using his head, he rammed his nemesis square in the stomach, knocking him over and sending the Luger skidding across the polished floor. A sudden return blow to the solar plexus drained the air from his lungs, sending a black shroud over his eyes. Dimly he perceived Thurmann reaching backward for his pistol. This was it, he knew. The end. For one of them. And from deep within he summoned an energy he never knew existed.

Leaping on Thurmann, he grabbed the man's throat, pressing both thumbs against his esophagus. Thurmann's expression shifted from amusement to shock and then terror. With all his might he tore at the murderous thumbs, but Willi's fury had turned implacable. This is for Paula! he thought, filled with a black bile of revenge, glad to see Thurmann's pencil-line mustache contort in an agony of convulsions. And for Gina Mancuso and all those poor souls you tortured and killed at Sachsenhausen! Thurmann's face was swelling, turning blue, the eyes, so arrogant and sanctimonious moments ago, rolling backward into his head. Willi had killed a man only once before in close combat, during the war, when he'd plunged a bayonet into a French soldier's chest, sickening at the furious crunch of the rib cage. But this was different. This was justice.

This Nazi had to die.

And when the enemy hands trembled in a final rattle, his head falling motionless to one side, the eyes wide open, Willi was happy.

Rolling off him, he tried to catch his breath, until he realized it was smoke, not air, entering his lungs. The whole wall to his left had become a curtain of fire. Summoning himself, he staggered back down the steps, astonished to find Kai slumped on one side, the whole hallway a tunnel of black smoke. He had to get them out. But not without that evidence! Yanking the kid to his feet, he pushed him into the storeroom, insanely shining the flashlight around in search of those boxes. Von Schleicher had promised a mountain of things down here, probably his only accurate assurance, Willi mused, morbidly recalling the general's guarantee that "a year from now you won't even remember Hitler's name." His heart leaped. There they were! Just a dozen yards across the room, stacked in two neat piles.

Revived by fresh air, Kai helped yank the dolly through the door. But no sooner had they got it into the storeroom than the entire ceiling flashed like the underside of a gas oven. Willi turned to see a shower of sparks fill the linen room, whole shelves of table-cloths combusting. Parts of the storeroom were catching fire now, too. They had to leave. Delay meant death. But how could he let everything he'd fought so hard for—he began coughing—that Paula died for, all the horror stories in those boxes, go up in smoke? He started toward them. "Papa!" he heard both his sons crying, but ignored it. "Willi, please"—it was Ava. His throat was burning. Cinders singeing. He paid no attention, only to those boxes ahead.

"For God's sake, what are you doing?" He couldn't believe it. Vicki! He not only heard her but saw her walking toward him right through the flames. Her short permed hair glowing in the light. Her almond eyes glittering. "Those eight hundred and fifty people are dead, Willi. Your father's dead. I'm dead. Nothing you do can ever bring us back."

Is that all this is? he longed to ask her. His whole career, his whole life—just one big unconscious effort to bring back the dead? But she vanished. And in her place his cousin Kurt stood waving at him brightly. "Come to Tel Aviv." He was wearing a bathing suit. "The sunsets over the Mediterranean, Willi . . . magnificent. You'll never miss Berlin. The food a little maybe."

"Leave, Willi," Vicki commanded. "Go. For the boys. For the future."

The air was searing. Kai gasping for breath. The flames creeping nearer. His boxes of evidence were vanishing behind an impenetrable curtain of smoke. There wasn't another second. He pictured that man falling from Communist headquarters, flapping his arms against gravity. Some things you couldn't fight. Against hurricanes, against earthquakes, there was no justice. It was the most painful step he ever took. Tearing himself, as if leaving half his body, half his mind, half of God knew what else, he grabbed the boy and fled, leading him through a maze of hallways that were empty and black as his heart. Having memorized the floor plans, he at least knew the way out.

They tumbled onto Sommer Strasse, wheezing and covered in soot. It was pitch-dark. Freezing out. In the noise and chaos nobody noticed them. Fire trucks were screaming from every direction. Horrified spectators, holding their foreheads, pointing, faces flickering sickening red. The whole Reichstag was an inferno, long, fiendish tongues licking from the windows, the roof, the dome. But standing right next to them, a sinister-looking bunch in trench coats and fedoras seemed bizarrely heartened.

"At last," one spoke feverishly, his eyes burning as bright as the building. "The long-awaited hour has arrived. Your dark night is over, Germany. These flames call us—arise. Arise!"

"Police and auxiliary SA are already on the move, Führer."

"I want every Communist official shot . . . tonight. Communist deputies. Friends of the Communists. Social Democrats. Anyone who stands in our path."

"*Jawohl.*"

"Tomorrow we'll start on the rest."

Willi dragged Kai away, wanting to run, to fly and never look back. But the pull was too overpowering, and like Lot's wife he turned one last time, freezing into a column of bitterness. Iron girders supporting the Reichstag's glass dome twisted in a death agony, the whole beautiful emblem of freedom collapsing in a hellish roar. It was more than just a building burning, he understood better than anyone else. More than just the evidence from Sachsenhausen.

In those flames went the future of millions.

Thirty-two

In the darkness before dawn, driving west along the Tiergarten Strasse up to Breitsheidplatz, beneath the Kaiser Wilhelm Memorial Church—its bells tolling the bitter hour—he fled. Along the Ku-damm the great neon advertisements hung black on the streamlined-building façades. Only a few dog walkers were out. A yellow streetcar rattled past, the first of the day. The early edition of *Berlin am Morgen* was arriving at the kiosks. In another hour the mailmen would be on their rounds, he knew. Curtains pulled open in a million apartments, pillows and blankets plopped in windowsills. Gentlemen would be riding along the old imperial trails in the Tiergarten. Clerks and secretaries pouring into the U- and S-Bahn stations. Tietz would unlock its revolving doors. Ruta would grind her coffee beans, and police at the Presidium get down to business. All without him.

He was too numb to care.

Last night the walk back empty-handed from the Reichstag was the worst in his life. Worse than the capitulation march in 1918. Worse even, in different ways, than the stupefied crawl from the hospital when Vicki died. After giving Kai the master keys to get back to Ruta, he had to creep through the dark, dusty and grimy, still in his laundryman's smock, his eyes too pained, too overburdened, to take in what they saw. Trucks of SA Brownshirts racing down the streets. Lines of prisoners along the sidewalks, hands in the air, many still in nightclothes, some with signs hung around their necks: *I am a Communist pig.* At the headquarters of the Social Democratic Party, typewriters and desks flying from windows. Around the corner, in front of a wrecked flowershop, a man and a woman stripped to their underwear, holding bunches of gladiolas and forced to shout, "I am a Red traitor! These are for my grave!"

He could have prevented this. Saved the nation. The world.

But he'd failed.

Sylvie was waiting when he stumbled back after midnight. "You've got to leave, Willi. First thing in the morning. And consider yourself one of the lucky ones."

A few minutes later though, they learned that leaving had become more easily said than done. Germany's borders were sealed, according to the radio. No one allowed in or out without a special police visa, in keeping with the new "Decree for the Protection of the People and State," just enacted by our Führer.

"*Our* Führer they're calling him now, on the radio," she said, wringing her hands.

The Communist and Social Democratic parties were outlawed, their publications seized. Trade unions suspended. All newspapers under strict emergency regulation. Freedom of speech and assembly curtailed. Willi realized Mr. Oppenheimer's chain-reaction theory had proven exactly correct. An uncanny sensation made his neck hairs stand. So had the Great Gustave's prophecy . . . a conflagration burning through the House of Germany this February. Could it all have been planned months ago?

The Jews, too—the announcer's voice rose—would not go unpunished since they'd obviously benefited from this crime against the German people. That they were German people, too, or how they could have benefited from the Reichstag fire, wasn't mentioned. Only that on April 1 a nationwide boycott would be commenced against all Jewish business and professional services. Any German patronizing a Jewish store or Jewish doctor, Jewish lawyer, Jewish dentist, Jewish accountant, Jewish tailor, etc., would be considered a traitor to the fatherland. In addition, the Prussian State Library and the University of Berlin would be purged of all Jewish and other non-German-thinking writers that for a generation had been polluting young minds, including such profligate degenerates as Heinrich Heine, Albert Einstein, Sigmund Freud, Thomas Mann, Maksim Gorky, Victor Hugo, Émile Zola, Andre Gidé, André Malraux, H. G. Wells, Aldous Huxley, George Bernard Shaw, Ernest Hemingway, Sinclair Lewis, Helen Keller . . .

Sylvie turned off the radio. "I'm going to find some way to get you out of this nightmare." She grabbed her address book and started poring through it.

Willi lay on the couch, too depleted to move. He felt the way he had after Vicki's funeral. After his father's, during the ritual mourning week when they were sitting in the parlor, and gazing at all the objects he'd seen his whole life, he'd realized nothing looked familiar. That his whole world had slid out from under him, like a landslide.

He heard Sylvie finally hang up. "Okay, I found something."

Her lips were moving, but he could barely comprehend.

"My old school chum Trude lives on the Belgian border. I haven't seen her in ages, but she's trustworthy to the bone. Says she can get you across, but you'd have to come quickly. Things could tighten up fast."

Willi shut his eyes. For two thousand years his ancestors had been forced into exile, country to country, continent to continent, with only the clothes on their backs. Now it was his turn.

Why did he imagine this day could never come? Not in Germany. To him. An Inspektor-Detektiv. Bearer of the Iron Cross, First Class. Lucky he'd emptied his bank accounts. But what if it wasn't enough?

"How much does she want, Sylvie?"

"Want? I told you, Willi, she's a dear old friend. Besides, her husband's a fabulously successful businessman. She'll probably have a catered feast for you."

Something about it sounded too easy, he thought, driving quickly through the quiet streets of Wilmersdorf and into suburban Grunewald. Fritz's house grew clearly visible on the hilltop, its long, curvilinear glass walls glinting in the dawn. One last time he let his 320 loose along the Avus Speedway, pushing it to its full potential . . . 120 . . . 130 . . . 140 kmh, his heart pounding wildly. But slowing to leave Berlin via Potsdam, the gloom came back. No one was going to risk her life to sneak a total stranger across a closed frontier for nothing.

If he made it that far.

Clear across Germany though, Berlin to Hannover, Münster to Dortmund, down along the Rhine, no roadblocks, no searches. All that marred his progress were memories. Grasping the wheel with clenched fingers, locked jaw, mind adrift, he kept seeing images flickering across the white-cloud screens, making his eyes burn. His mother, pregnant with his baby sister, sitting by the window looking down at him playing in the street, blowing a kiss. Vicki waking up, stretching her long white neck and yawning. The boys trudging off to school, leather briefcases strapped to backs, the big one insisting on holding the little one's hand as they crossed the street. Even before he realized it, the sun was setting. And he had reached the little border town of Aachen.

Now would come the true test. How was this trustworthy-to-the-bone friend of Sylvie's going to get him across a sealed border? He pictured himself led through a dark, empty field alone, uneasy. Then held up for all he was worth.

Shot through the back of the neck.

But Sylvie's friend's house was on the border as promised.

Literally. Sitting on it.

"One step out that back door, Willi, and, voilà, you're home free. Take the bus to the train station and in less than two hours, Brussels."

Amazing. One step, and freedom.

Home, no. Statelessness. Rootlessness.

But life. Love. Family.

"Go freshen up and have some dinner first. You must be starved."

Sylvie was right about Trude's generosity, but obviously ignorant of her financial plight, he saw. Her house was well-enough furnished, but threadbare. The carpets worn. Her sweater elbows patched. Clearly her husband's "fabulous" business success had withered with the Great Depression, and Trude had been too proud to tell her old school chum. The meal was simple sausage and kraut. She refused to take a pfennig.

"Anything to help." She spooned him a second dish. "Those Nazis make me ashamed to be human." She looked at her watch. "You'd better go, love. There's a bus in a couple of minutes."

Opening the back door, she offered him a smile that seemed to say, *You're a lucky man, Willi. To have made it. When so many never will.* Willi smiled, too, knowing she was right. Then suddenly remembering something, he dug in his pocket and pulled out a silver key. "For your kindness." He winked. "The little BMW out front."

Handing it to her, he crossed the threshold. Night had fallen. It was freezing out. He felt completely naked, but never more awake, as he buttoned his collar and stepped into exile. Anyway, he thought, looking down the dark street, then up at the sky, better to be a wandering Jew—he saw stars through the blackness—

than a dead one. "I have set before you life and death, blessing and cursing." A quote from Deuteronomy rose to mind from somewhere in his boyhood. "Therefore choose life"—he walked on, chin held high—"that thou and thy seed might live."

Epilogue

OCTOBER 1945

Less than five months after the fall of Hitler's thousand-year Reich, Willi gave in to a terrible urge and returned. It had been twelve years, the darkest in human history. Fifty million dead. Twenty million Russians. Six million Jews. He'd read about the destruction of German cities, seen the pictures in the papers, but as he flew into Tempelhof, his first glimpse knocked the breath from him.

This was Berlin?

Block after block, street after street, of homes, businesses, schools, churches, all just hollowed shells. Mile after mile of desolate fields, here and there a chimney, a wall rising from the rubble. He recalled walking to work once during a transit strike, imagining the destruction another war might bring. But his imagination had failed him, utterly.

In his new home, from the fifth-floor balcony on Hayarkon

Street overlooking the beach, the turquoise Mediterranean practically lapped at his toes. Behind it sprawled the white city of
Tel Aviv, its broad, green boulevards bustling. Proud. Free. And
though goodness knew there was trouble aplenty in that hot,
little desert land, he had a good life. A good job as an inspector
with the municipal police. A three-bedroom apartment in a sleek
building designed by a protégé of Erich Mendelsohn's. A loving
wife and four beautiful children. But he needed to come back—
one last time. To see for himself. And to pay back some debts of
gratitude, if he could.

On the ride in from the airport he was even more shocked
than he'd been from the air. Long human chains of women, dirty
turbans tied around their heads, labored to clear mountains of
rubble, hand to hand, brick by brick—like insects trying to re-
pair their wrecked hives. Families in wall-less apartment buildings, like dollhouses, lived completely exposed to the street,
dirty blankets strung up for privacy. Gaunt, pale shoeless children played on charred tanks and antiaircraft batteries. His own
childhood, a dream by comparison. Scrawled in chalk on countless crumbled walls were notes: *Father, Anna and I are safe and
living at . . .*

It took two days, but through the post office he was able to
find the address of his former secretary. Her home in Berlin-East
a little shack amid the rubble, built of steel shutters and planks of
wood, a tiny vegetable patch eked along the side. She was shocked
when he appeared, too happy even to be ashamed, she said, crying in his arms.

"Oh, Willi, you were so lucky to get out when you did."

"Once you risked your life for me . . . now I want to help you,
Ruta."

He gave her enough money to move her whole family into the
Siemen's Housing Project, untouched by bombs and in the safety
of the American sector. She couldn't stop thanking him as he
pushed aside the torn blanket and stepped back into the sun.

Now of course he understood he had been lucky to have left

when he did. And to have fled France in '38, a year before it became too late. Perhaps, had he never seen those jars of floating brains, those barracks full of deformed prisoners, at Sachsenhausen, he'd never have been impelled to rip his family up a second time and smuggle them to an unknown land. He would have ended up like his boyhood chum Mathias Goldberg, the neon advertising genius, who, when war broke out in '39, got interned by the French for being a German, and again in 1940 by the conquering Germans, for being a Jew. Stamped with the yellow star in '42, he was "resettled east" with his wife and children, to that unspeakable realm presided over by the Angel of Death—Josef Mengele.

The mad doctor of Auschwitz.

Camp Sachsenhausen, as Mengele had promised, had indeed been rebuilt, a little farther north along the river Havel, bigger and better than before. Nearly one hundred thousand people perished there, while neighbors kept their eyes and mouths and noses shut.

From Ruta's he took a cab to Tiergarten Strasse to see if he could find Sylvie—but her little villa was gone. No chalk forwarding address. He went to the Adlon to see if he could find Hans, but the chief concierge had been lost in an air raid. The hotel smashed to dust.

As was the Kaiserhof. The Fürstenhof. The Palace. The Excelsior.

Ernst Roehm, and his whole SA leadership, had, of course, been wiped out in the infamous Night of the Long Knives back in '34, along with Kurt von Schleicher and his wife. Kai, Willi found out through some determined detective work, had been killed at Buchenwald with the rest of the Red Apaches. Gunther, the last week of the war, had been shot as a deserter.

Potsdamer Platz, once the wildly beating commercial heart of the city, was deceased, too, its arteries vacuous, its walls collapsed. The bare bones of Kempinski's Haus Vaterland, once the "Jolliest Place in Berlin," twirling and dancing with a pinwheel of neon, twelve restaurants, fifty cabaret acts, the famous Haus Vaterland Girls, a web of mangled girders staring over nothing: just a sign marking the dividing line between the British and Russian sectors.

In the government district, the Imperial Palace lay gutted. The dome blown off the cathedral. The Brandenburg Gate a cinder. Not a tree stood in the Tiergarten. Not a blade of grass. Here and there a singed kaiser still sat on horseback overlooking his capital. In the West End, Tauentzien Strasse, the cinemas along Brietscheidplatz, the Romanisches Café, the Kaiser Wilhelm Church, the whole grand Ku-damm, all burned-out hulks. At Alexanderplatz, Wertheim was obliterated. Tietz, three-quarters debris, its trademark glass globe hanging over the once magnificent atrium. Nothing was left of the Police Presidium. Only a few lone doorways leading nowhere. His eyes burned when he noticed on the lintel above one, *Entrance Six.*

The Reichstag, scene of the final battle between the Red Army and fanatic remnants of the SS, lay a shell-riddled corpse, decomposing. In its shadow, a black market thrived amid the few tree stumps still along the Spree Embankment. Where once he had stood and observed the comings and goings of a white linen truck, civilians with patched shoes and torn coats now hungrily hawked watches, silverware, valuable porcelain, for food and cigarettes from the occupying soldiers. Two young girls, hair neatly braided, ragged dresses washed clean, sat on the curb next to piles of old books they were selling for five pfennig each. As Willi strolled by, a dark set of hypnotic eyes leaped right off the cover of one, stopping him dead. My God, his throat clenched.

"Two for nine," the girls chirped.

Staring at the strange Kabuki expression he'd once seen work such magic on crowds, he handed them a mark and took the book.

The Ten Secrets of Life, by Gustave Spanknoebel, King of Mystics. Berlin, 1932. Clairvoyant Press. Gustave's own, he recalled. The very feel of it, the smell, the rustle of the old paper, seemed to peel away time, flipping color images before his eyes...Paula showing off her gorgeous legs in that tight pink gown. Gunther, suddenly turning from nowhere, hugging him. Fritz revving up his beautiful polished yacht. That little silver BMW. And Kai, gold earring glistening in the sun, surrounded by rushing streetcars, the swirling traffic, the crazy hustle of the Alex.

All vanished as old Berlin.

Little shivers pricked his spine as he turned the book over. The oddest sensation of lifting ever so slightly off the ground. In top hat and tails, wrapped in his long black cape, the Master loomed across the back cover demanding to know with those all-penetrating eyes, "Have you started living yet, dear friend? Or still just another sleepwalker?"

A Note on Historical Accuracy

The Sleepwalkers is fiction based on a great deal of fact. The details on the political machinations leading up to the Nazi seizure of power are accurate. The locales are real, except for the potter's field and lunatic asylum at Oranienburg, which are made up. Sachsenhausen concentration camp opened in 1936, not 1932. The Nazi medical experiments on living humans—the bone transplants, sterilizations, live dissections, and more—all occurred, but a decade after this story takes place. The SS doctors are fictional, except for Josef Mengele, the Mad Doctor of Auschwitz, who did not join the Nazis until the late 1930s. Much of the character of the Great Gustave is based on the real Erik Hanussen, who hid his Jewish identity and became Hitler's clairvoyant until he was gunned down, as depicted, shortly after the Nazi takeover. Ernst Roehm and Kurt von Schleicher are historical figures. Both met their fates in 1934, as the book states, during the bloody purge known as the Night of the Long Knives.